"Let us make a wager."

"What kind of wager?" she asked.

"If after three dancing lessons with me, you are still mortified and averse, I will never ask you to dance again...or attend a ball."

Audrey's face brightened. "That sounds like something to which I can agree."

"Then 'tis settled." He took her hand in his palm and bowed over it. Reid should have opted for a simple bow without a damned kiss. But now that he was committed, he had no choice but to close his eyes and savor pressing his lips to the back of her hand. He could feel Audrey's pulse thrumming as quickly as his heart hammered.

Had he just insisted on giving the lass dancing lessons? Dear God, he was daft...

ALSO BY AMY JARECKI

Lords of the Highlands series
The Highland Duke
The Highland Commander

THE HIGHLAND GUARDIAN

A Lords of the Highlands Novel

AMY JARECKI

FOREVER
New York Boston

Copyright © 2017 by Amy Jarecki
Excerpt from *The Highland Duke* copyright © 2017 by Amy Jarecki

Cover design by Elizabeth Turner
Cover illustration by Craig White
Cover copyright © 2017 by Hachette Book Group, Inc.

Forever
Hachette Book Group
1290 Avenue of the Americas, New York, NY 10104
forever-romance.com
twitter.com/foreverromance

First Edition: December 2017

Forever is an imprint of Grand Central Publishing. The Forever name and logo are trademarks of Hachette Book Group, Inc.

The publisher is not responsible for websites (or their content) that are not owned by the publisher.

The Hachette Speakers Bureau provides a wide range of authors for speaking events. To find out more, go to www.hachettespeakersbureau.com or call (866) 376-6591.

ISBN: 978-1-4555-9788-8 (mass market), 978-1-4555-9787-1 (ebook)

Printed in the United States of America

OPM

10 9 8 7 6 5 4 3 2 1

*To all those who enjoy reading
historical romance.*

*To the wonderful readers who lose
themselves in the pages of a book and
travel to a time without cell phones,
without automobiles, without running
water.*

*And to those who share a mutual love
of Scotland.*

I cherish each and every one of you.

Chapter One

*T*he gale blew through the English Channel like a savage rogue, making foam gush and spray from the sea's white-capped swells. Reid MacKenzie released a long breath. He'd navigated the treacherous crossing without incident. But his relief was short-lived. In his wake, a Royal Navy tall ship was gaining speed.

Nicholas Kennet lowered his spyglass. "They're following us, I've no doubt now."

"Stay the course," bellowed Reid. He wasn't only an earl, he was captain of his eighteen-oar, single-masted galley, and he'd dive to his death at the bottom of the sea before he allowed one of the queen's vessels to bully him into dropping anchor and submitting to an inspection. These were precarious times. A man must keep his opinions secret lest he be misunderstood. And in Queen

Anne's Britain, misunderstandings led to ruination—not only of one man's wealth, but to the annihilation of entire clans.

Reaching inside his cloak, Reid smoothed his fingers atop the leather-wrapped missive he carried in his doublet. A missive for those loyal to the cause to ensure the succession of James Stuart to the throne. "No cause for alarm. Many a nobleman has traveled to France to meet with His Highness."

Not a seafaring man, Mr. Kennet turned a ripe shade of green. He was a wealthy coal miner from northeast England and had proved his loyalty to the Jacobite ideals by helping to finance the expedition.

"The *Royal Buckingham* approaching portside, m'lord," said Dunn MacRae, chieftain of his clan and Reid's most trusted ally.

"Damnation." Reid pulled out his spyglass and trained it on the upper deck of the navy ship. The red-coated officers were watching them for certain.

"Shall we heave to?" asked Dunn.

"God, no. That would only make us appear guilty." He snapped his glass closed and regarded his crew. "Stay the course. Maintain present speed. Let the bastards sail past and find someone else to chase. We're nay pirates, and we've done nothing wrong."

"Then why are you not flying your pennant, my lord?" asked Kennet.

The corner of Reid's mouth twitched. "That galleon might outrun us in the open sea, but if we can keep her guessing until we reach the estuary of the River Tees, I'll have you sitting by home's hearth before the witching hour."

"Seaforth," said MacRae, his voice steady—too steady. "She's opened gunport one."

Reid didn't need his spyglass to make out the black cannon pushing through the open port like a deadly dragon. He swiped a hand across his mouth. "How near are we to the Tees?"

"Two leagues, Captain."

"Tack west. Aim for the shallows."

"Aye, Captain!" bellowed every man aboard the galley as the oarsmen increased their pace. Reid might be an earl when his feet were on land, but at sea, his clansmen called him captain.

"Surely they will not fire." A gust of wind blew Nicholas's hat and periwig to the timbers, and he scrambled over a bench to retrieve them.

Dunn pulled on the rudder while the boom swung across the hull, shifting the single sail. Ignoring the Englishman's question, Reid watched the galleon as it sailed alongside them. "They'll most likely launch a warning shot across our bow."

"Dear God. This is preposterous," said Nicholas, shoving his wig and hat low on his brow. "If I hadn't witnessed it myself, I never would have believed Her Majesty of such piracy."

The flicker of a torch flashed inside the gunport. "You'd best believe it, my friend." Reid turned with a scowl. "Bear down on your oars, lads!"

The barrel of the cannon flared with fire and smoke before the sound of the blast boomed through the air. Reid's skin crawled with the high-pitched whistle from the approaching cannonball. He ducked below the hull, praying the British ship had set her sights correctly for a warning shot.

With his next breath, the bow of his ship splintered into a thousand wooden shards. Water gushed into the hull, instantly soaking the men and pulling them into the frigid whitecaps.

"Swim for your lives!" Reid yelled as he climbed atop the rowing bench. Casting his cloak aside, he prepared to plunge into the icy swells of the North Sea.

"Help!" Nicholas shouted, his voice strained.

Taking a quick glance over his shoulder, Reid's blood turned cold. Dear God, a spike of wood at least a foot long protruded from Nicholas Kennet's chest.

"Jesu." Reid waded through the rushing water of his sinking ship and hefted his friend into his arms. "Hang on. Shore's in sight. I'll have you to safety in no time."

Strengthening his grip, the Earl of Seaforth clenched his teeth and leaped into the frigid sea. Air whooshed from his lungs, and the current dragged him downward, threatening to tug Nicholas from his grasp. Bearing down with a surge of power, Reid kicked fiercely, battling the undertow, his lungs screaming for blessed air.

If the briny deep claimed him this day, it would not be without a fight. Reid learned early on that even a man born of privilege must be fitter than his worst adversary. More cunning as well.

His head broke through with a desperate inhale filling his lungs. Arching his back, he shifted his grip under Nicholas's arms to ensure the man could breathe as well.

The freezing water sapped his strength, but he clenched his teeth and refused to stop. Swimming on his back with Nicholas secured against his chest, Reid propelled them toward the shore.

Behind, his ship was gone, sunk into the North Sea's merciless depths without a trace. The galleon had hove to as if the men on deck laughed at the poor Highland sops who fought to reach the shore before the sea swallowed them in her swells.

With his next breath, Reid looked to the coast as his teeth chattered uncontrollably. Hope infused his muscles with renewed power. But when the next thundering wave broke over their heads, the taunting sea gave Reid no choice but to clutch his arms around Nicholas and pray to God they'd bob to the surface before the air in his lungs expired.

Fighting with every fiber of his body, his head broke through the surf. He managed to gulp precious air before being pulled under once again. When they resurfaced, the next thunderous wave spat them out onto the beach like a pair of dead mackerel. Salt water blew through Reid's nose while he staggered to dry sand. Coughing and sputtering, he dragged Nicholas in his wake.

"Good God," Dunn hollered, running up beside him to lend a hand. Once clear of the surf, they rested Nicholas on his back.

Sucking in gasps of air, Reid dropped to his knees and placed his hand on his comrade's forehead. "We'll have ye set to rights in no time, mate."

Dunn caught his eye, thinned his lips, and gave a shake of his head.

The stake protruding from the man's chest was akin to a deathly blow from a bayonet.

"Please," muttered Nicholas, his voice weak. "Swear you will care for my daughter."

Reid's gut clenched. "Daughter?" *Shite.*

"She's alone—her mother gone."

"Are there any other heirs?"

"None."

"Christ." The last thing Reid needed was a ward.

Nicholas gasped and clutched Reid's cravat. "Swear it."

He had no choice but to give a stiff-lipped nod. "I give you my word. The lass will be cared for."

As if a great weight had been lifted from his chest, Nicholas Kennet released his last breath with an eerie sigh that faded into the rush of the waves.

"He's dead," said Dunn, now surrounded by men drenched and shivering.

Reid moved his hand to the man's nose and felt not a thing. Such a pity. And for naught. He glanced to the galleon, looming in the deep water. Through the shroud of early dusk, the wind again filled the sails as the naval ship resumed its course and got under way. "Is the crew accounted for?"

"Aye," said Graham MacKenzie, lieutenant and navigator. "Davy has a gash on his arm, but no other casualties."

"Thank God for that." Reid stood and looked to the town of Hartlepool. "Quickly. The tower of a church stands yonder. We'll take Kennet's body there for a proper burial."

The MacRae chieftain gave a somber nod. "Then you'd best find something to occupy his daughter. You're far too important to *the cause* to waste your time acting at guardian."

Reid ground his back molars. Dunn was right. He needed to think of some way to see to the heiress's maintenance without becoming involved. And fast.

* * *

The brass knocker on the Coxhoe House door hung from a lion's mouth. Reid had used it once before, but during that visit, he hadn't been introduced to Kennet's daughter. They'd been in too much of a hurry to sail across the channel for their meeting with the exiled king.

Exhausted and sore from sleeping in a copse of trees, he clenched his fist before knocking. With the missive from King James still secured in his doublet, the last thing he needed at the moment was to take on the role of guardian for a spoiled heiress. He had no doubt the lass had been cosseted—after all, she was the only child of a wealthy widower. Though her pampered world was about to shatter. He would break the news, make arrangements for her to be looked after, appoint a trustee to oversee her affairs, and that would have to suffice. Reid's role in uniting the clans to prepare for the succession was far too critical to *the cause*.

"Go on. Have it over with," said Dunn from behind as if speaking Reid's conscience.

Affixing a somber frown in place, he gave the knocker three good raps.

The door slowly opened with an interminable screech. The gaunt butler regarded them, eyes peering over a pair of round spectacles. "M'lord?" He drew his graying eyebrows together as he craned his neck and looked beyond the men. "This is a surprise."

"Good morrow, sir." Reid took in a deep breath. "I bring grave news."

The butler drew a hand over his heart as his face blanched. "Do not tell me Mr. Kennet…"

"He perished off the coast of Hartlepool. One of Her Majesty's galleons attempted to fire a cannonball over our bow."

"But the bastards missed and sank His Lordship's sea galley," finished Dunn.

"Dear God." The man stumbled backward and ushered them into the entry. "Forgive me, my lord. I am afraid this news comes as quite a shock."

"Understood." Reid grasped the man's shoulder with a firm hand. "Do you need a moment, Mister...?"

"Gerald, my lord," the man said, slowly drawing a hand down his face. After a deep breath, he regained his composure. "The pair of you look as if you could use a bit of respite, if you don't mind my saying so, my lord."

Reid glanced at his clothing. Matted by salt water, peppered with sand and dirt, he looked a fright. But nothing could be done about that now. "Aye, we could. After being forced to swim for our lives, we took Mr. Kennet's body to Saint Hilda's for burial, then slept in a copse of trees eight miles east."

Gerald glanced eastward, his eyes growing wide. "Do you believe it is safe to come here, my lord?"

Reid gave an annoyed nod. "I wouldn't be standing here if it weren't. They've nothing on us. The galleon even continued on her voyage. I think the warning shot was an attempt to make us heave to so they could board my galley and try to implicate me for some misdeed. To speak true, I have far more grounds upon which to seek damages than they have to accuse me of a traitorous plot." He didn't utter the word *Jacobite*—strange walls had a way of hearing things they shouldn't, especially in England.

"I reckon they kent it as well," said Dunn.

The butler nodded, his face drawn.

MacRae gave Reid a nudge.

He shot an annoyed leer at Dunn, a chieftain who not only paid him fealty but also acted as Seaforth's henchman. Dash it, Reid knew his task was not yet finished, not by half. "Forgive me, I ken you must be sorely smote by this news, however 'tis my duty to inform you that Nicholas Kennet's dying wish was for me to see to his daughter's maintenance."

"Aye," agreed Dunn. "The earl vowed a sacred oath."

"You, my lord?" Gerald scratched his chin, the furrow between his brows growing deeper. "I might have thought Mr. Kennet would have appointed someone a bit older."

Swiping the sand off his sleeve, Reid gave the man a scowl. Regardless of his age, the oath he'd sworn was an inconvenience, but duty was duty. "Och, if only the Earl Marischal of Scotland had been there, rather than me."

The butler cringed. "Yes, my lord." Gerald didn't need to say a word. The look on his face spoke volumes about his doubts, the pompous curmudgeon.

Reid guffawed and grabbed his lapels. Hell, he was one of the wealthiest, most hardy men in Scotland, and an elderly butler was frowning at the prospect of an earl's suitability for the role of guardian? Suitability wasn't remotely in question. "That's enough chitchat. Bring the wee lassie to me. I must notify her of this unfortunate turn of events forthwith."

"Straightaway, my lord." Gerald started off, but stopped before he reached the stairs. "Perhaps it would be best if she heard the news from me first. After all, I have known Miss Audrey since the day she came into the world."

Reid arched his eyebrows at Dunn. It certainly would

make his lot easier if he didn't have to tell a child she was now an orphan. "If you think that's best, then I shall allow it."

Bowing, the butler gestured to a pair of double doors. "Thank you, my lord. If you gentlemen would kindly make yourselves comfortable in the parlor, I shall have refreshment brought to you straightaway."

"Very well, but I should like to speak to Miss Audrey as soon as she is able to receive me." Since the butler had referred to the lass in the familiar, Reid figured it was best if he started doing so at once. After all, a guardian should be on a first-name basis with his ward.

Dismissing Gerald with a bow of his head, he led Dunn into the parlor. Decorated with Parisian plasterwork, the hearth posed the centerpiece, surrounded by an ornate relief depicting vine and leaves and painted porcelain plates. The gilded chairs' seats, arms, and backs were embroidered with countryside scenes. Reid chose the largest with a high back, near the fire. Dunn took a seat on the other side, crossing his ankles.

Weariness caught up with him as he brushed the sand off his doublet. He needed a meal, a bath, and a bed in that order.

"Have you given any thought as to what you'll do with the lass?"

Reid's gut twisted into a knot. He didn't have many options. He most certainly didn't need a child disrupting order at Brahan Castle—especially when he was away more often than not. "Boarding school, of course."

"Brilliant. I should have thought of that."

It wasn't brilliant, though it was where most heiresses went for finishing in this day and age.

The tension clamping Reid's shoulders had almost eased when a high-pitched scream resounded above stairs. The sound wasn't that of a young child, but one of a feral animal in deathly agony.

Dear God, what have I drawn myself into?

Chapter Two

*A*udrey flung herself across the bed and wailed into the pillow. In a heartbeat her entire life shattered.

Papa gone?

How could this have happened?

No, no, no. Not Papa. He was kind and giving, and the only person Audrey knew who understood her. Who understood what it was like to be deathly shy.

She'd only arrived home and had done nothing but plan the summer together with her father. There were outings and riding excursions and hunting quests yet to be enjoyed.

Never to be enjoyed.

"Noooooooooooooo!" she cried, her insides shredding with her grief.

He cannot be gone.

Completely unable to control her sobs, Audrey rocked back and forth, clutching the pillow. How could she carry on? She was now an orphan. There were no aunts, no uncles. Her grandparents had passed away years ago.

Her chamber door opened, but Audrey didn't care. She couldn't move, let alone look up to see who it was.

"Please, Miss Audrey." Mrs. Hobbs's voice sounded strained. "The Earl of Seaforth has been awaiting you in the parlor for over an hour."

Gasping and taking staccato breaths, she tried to calm herself enough to reply. "Can he not come back on the morrow? I am too distraught to receive guests." Audrey knew nothing of this man who'd brought the news of her father's death. What was a mere hour? For pity's sake Gerald had only just delivered the news and now she was expected to compose her person and meet a complete stranger? Mrs. Hobbs moved to the bedside. "I've brought you a tincture of chamomile to calm your nerves. You are the mistress of the Kennet estate now, miss. You mustn't keep the earl waiting."

I don't want to be a mistress at the age of nineteen. Audrey buried her face in the pillow.

The maid swirled a soothing palm over Audrey's shoulder. "I know, dear. But we all must see to our duty."

Taking a deep breath, Audrey willed herself to gain a modicum of control. She swiped her eyes and sat up, clutching the pillow to her abdomen. "I'd prefer to be left alone."

Mrs. Hobbs reached for the cup. "Have a sip of my tincture. It will help calm your nerves before you venture below stairs."

Nodding, Audrey accepted the cup and drank. At least the warm liquid soothed the burning in her throat.

"Have a brief chat with the earl, and then I'll draw you a warm bath."

"I don't want a bath. I want Papa back."

"I think we all do, miss. 'Tis a most unwelcome shock." Mrs. Hobbs sniffed and gave Audrey a kerchief.

With a sigh, Audrey cast the pillow aside, wiped her eyes, and sat a bit taller. Across the chamber, she caught her reflection in the full-length looking glass. She looked a fright with flyaways sticking out every which way, her eyes red and swollen like plums. Hiding her face in her hands, she shook her head. "I cannot possibly venture below stairs looking like this."

"Come." The maid took Audrey's hand and pulled her from the bed to the washstand. She poured a bit of water over her hands and shook them into the bowl. "I'll just pat your hair down and pinch your cheeks, and you'll be right to go."

"I would prefer to remain here and wallow in misery."

"But you must. Your father would have expected it."

The mention of Papa brought on a wave of melancholy that Audrey stifled by clapping a hand over her mouth. "You are right. I admit. The sooner I get this over with, the better."

* * *

Unaccustomed to being made to wait for anyone or anything, Reid paced in front of the hearth. An hour ago, he'd sent Dunn and the men out to ensure they hadn't been followed. Though he was confident the naval threat had passed, Reid never left anything to chance. With a bit of effort, in as little as a fortnight, he could ensure the estate's affairs were in order and send the lassie to the nearest boarding school. He'd have to see her on holidays and whatnot, but by then he'd have a chance to arrange for a governess and whatever staff the young gel needed.

When he finally heard footsteps coming down the stairs, he faced the entry with his most somber expression, ruing the task before him. Even in all the time he'd been waiting, he still hadn't come up with any gentle words to deliver the worst news this little girl—no doubt cossetted all her life—had ever heard.

With a bowed head and folded hands, the lass stepped into the parlor.

"Lord Reid MacKenzie, Earl of Seaforth, allow me to introduce Miss Audrey Kennet," said the butler before taking his leave.

Reid blinked in utter astonishment. Then he gulped. This was no wee lass. A woman fully grown stood before him, staring at her clasped fingers. "Ah..." Remembering his station, he bowed. "Miss Kennet. Please allow me to offer my most heartfelt condolences."

Her gaze flickered up and met his with a pair of very red and swollen eyes. Flinching as if mortified to be in his presence, Miss Audrey quickly looked to her hands again as if those slender fingers provided her salvation. The lass's nose was redder than her eyes, and her blonde tresses appeared as if she'd just lost a fight with a wildcat. But the thing that twisted Reid's gut into a knot was that he'd completely underestimated the enormity of the promise he'd made to this lassie's father. Wee Miss Audrey could be no less than sixteen years of age, and quite possibly older.

He gestured to a chair, waited for her to take a seat, then sat opposite.

"Can you tell me what happened, m'lord?" she asked tremulously, almost in a whisper.

"We were returning from France..." He explained it all, including the fact he believed the navy ship had only intended to fire a warning shot across the galley's bow. All the while, Miss Kennet kept her eyes averted and listened quietly while she twisted a kerchief between her fists. "Your father's last request was for me to become your guardian and—"

"Guardian?" she said, her voice shooting up. A blush spread across her entire face, but she continued to keep her gaze lowered, twisting her kerchief as if she could wring it to death.

He adjusted his scratchy, sea-salt-encrusted cravat. "I assure you. I am of sound means and quite capable."

Her lips disappeared into a thin line, but she didn't look up. "I fear I am too old to have a guardian, my lord," she whispered.

He regarded the lass with a more critical eye. "What, pray tell, is your age?"

"If you must know, my nineteenth saint's day came a fortnight past." She raised her chin.

Merciful Father, it was a good thing Reid was sitting. He'd taken a solemn oath to be the guardian for a woman past her majority? What in God's name was he supposed to do with a woman fully grown?

"Indeed, 'guardian' isn't the right word in this instance," Reid spoke aloud. "Mayhap my role is more one of benefactor in this instance. I did give your father my word I would see to your care." His mind raced to come up with a solution. "Have you attended finishing school?"

"Of course." She rolled her eyes aloft—very dark blue eyes. "I graduated only last month from Talcott Ladies' Finishing School."

Given she was nineteen years of age, his question had

been rather absurd. Nonetheless, the sooner he was relieved of this burden, the better. "What about marriage prospects? As an heiress, I'd imagine you've been to court?"

She twisted the kerchief so tight, her knuckles were white. "Court is mortifying."

"Have any gentlemen come to call...ah...recently?"

"I've only been home for a few sennights, and most of that time, Papa has been away."

Good Lord, what was Reid to do with an heiress past her majority who had no marriage prospects? "What about male relatives? I ken you have no brothers, but do you have any cousins, or an uncle, perchance?"

This time her shoulders drooped with the shake of her head. She sniffed, looking like she was about to burst into tears. If there was one thing Reid could not endure, it was sitting idle while a female cried. He'd already felt helpless enough.

"Not to worry," he said in his most soothing voice, resisting the urge to hop to his feet and do something daft like draw her into an embrace. "'Tis why I'm here. We'll set everything to rights in no time." *God willing.*

"I beg your pardon, but everything will *not* be set to rights." Though soft-spoken, the lass appeared to have a stubborn streak. She even stiffened her spine. "I've just lost my father. Not only that, there are a host of miners who will be looking to you for direction. Are you familiar with mining, my lord?" As soon as the words left her lips, she drew the kerchief to her mouth and demurely glanced aside.

A tic twitched in his jaw. Was she toying with him? Was she shy or was the kerchief-twisting a ploy to solicit his sympathy? That she had cunning was for certain. Mining? Reid was a land baron, a cattleman, but this was no time to appear inept. "I assure you, I ken a great deal about anything concerning trade in Great Britain. I am an earl in control of vast estates in Scotland."

"Forgive my impertinence. I am distraught." She let out a long sigh and rested her forehead in her palm. "I want to attend my father's grave."

"I shall accompany you there myself when 'tis safe."

"A mere carriage ride to Hartlepool is not safe?"

"My men are scouting the byways to ensure there's no retaliation planned by the government troops."

"Government troops?" Her eyes grew wide. "Was Papa involved in something *illegal*?"

"Of course not." Reid pursed his lips and glanced away. He'd been in this lassie's presence for all of ten minutes and he was about to strangle her. It was not her place to question him about his business prowess, nor was it her place to imply that Reid had acted outside the law.

He took a deep breath. "Your father and I were but working to see to Britain's future."

He stood and addressed her with a stiff bow. "I shall endeavor to put things in order and protect your interests as heiress. Presently, however, I am in sore need of a bath."

"Very well," she whispered, practically twisting her kerchief in two.

"Until the evening meal, miss." He turned and paraded out of the parlor in search of the butler. Perhaps Reid would be able to face this whole mess with more vigor once he'd washed away the salt and sand chafing his skin.

* * *

After Reid MacKenzie marched out of the parlor, Audrey wanted to collapse into a heap. Instead, she sighed and covered her face with her soggy kerchief. Not only was her entire life in complete upheaval, Papa had appointed the Earl of Seaforth to see to her maintenance? The overbearing Scotsman hardly appeared a day older than she.

I do not need a benefactor. I need my father.

And Seaforth was unbelievably uncouth. He'd arrived at Coxhoe House in such a disheveled state that, if he hadn't been announced, Audrey would have thought him a beggar. Scraggly hair, unshaven, and filthy. Worse, he had the most disconcerting glint to his intense green eyes. The entire time she'd been in his presence, she was worried he'd draw that mammoth sword from his hip and cut her to the quick.

When seated, it bothered him not at all to have his knees bare, popping from beneath that immodest kilt. Must he wear a kilt? True, he was Scottish. No doubt from the Highlands, reputed for producing dangerous and barbaric savages.

How could she trust this man? Though an earl, what on earth had he been doing with her father in France of all places? Papa hadn't told her he was going to France. Such a voyage was perilous. Britain was at war with France. Papa hadn't lied, but he'd skirted the truth by telling her he had business dealings on the Continent. Naturally, she'd assumed it had something to do with coal. Her father's mines produced more coal than any other operation in Britain, and she was well aware of the Kennets' substantial fortune.

She dropped her hands to her lap and stared straight into the fire. Something was amiss. Her father had been killed by his own countrymen? The earl had his men scouring the land to ensure it was safe to travel to Saint Hilda's Church, only ten miles away?

What on earth is going on? And why had Papa not entrusted me with his plans?

Never in her life had Audrey been off the Kennet estate without an escort, but presently she needed answers. Whom could she trust? Certainly not the behemoth who just went above stairs to bathe.

No, she could trust no one.

She must take matters into her own hands swiftly or else the mine and her very life could be ruined. And that meant bucking up her courage and going to Hartlepool alone. Two hours ago such a thought would have mortified her down to her toes. But now she had no choice but to dare to be bold. Resolutely clenching her fists, Audrey headed for her chamber to don a riding habit.

Chapter Three

*J*effrey, the stable hand, led Audrey's trotter down the aisle, saddled and ready to ride. "I don't blame you for wanting to take a turn around the grounds, miss. The news was a shock to us all."

She took charge of the bridle and ran her fingers through Allegro's mane. "I still cannot believe it." Her stomach roiled with the tempest inside her. She couldn't speak her mind to Jeffrey, but riding to Hartlepool would help her think. Cantering Allegro with the wind at her face always helped Audrey gather her thoughts. Presently her mind was in such a muddle, she didn't know what was right and what was wrong, what was true or false. All she knew was she must make haste away from Coxhoe House with all its memories of her father. She couldn't think there.

Audrey led the horse to the mounting block.

"When do you reckon you'll return, miss?" Jeffrey held the bridle while Audrey looped her knee over the upper pommel and slid into her sidesaddle.

"Not certain." She pursed her lips. She wasn't about to tell anyone where she planned to go, lest they try to stop her.

The stable hand patted Allegro's shoulder. "All right then. I'll keep an eye out for you."

"Thank you." Taking up the reins, Audrey cued her gelding for a trot, steering him straight to the drive. She had no time to waste. As often as she'd made the journey to the shore with her father, she could travel to Hartlepool blindfolded if need be, especially when riding her faithful Allegro.

The Earl of Seaforth thought Coxhoe unsafe because of government troops? How ludicrous. The dragoons who patrolled County Durham were there to enforce law and order, not circumvent it.

Invigorated by the crisp wind at her face, she urged the gelding into a gallop. Something thundered in from her left. Her heart flew to her throat. Had the earl been right? Outlaws lurked not but a mile from her home? Without looking back, she slapped her crop on Allegro's rump. "Faster!"

Out of the corner of her eye, riders moved in on her flank. A dark-haired man wearing a kilt bore down on her. A grimace contorted his rugged features while he reached for her reins.

Allegro whinnied and reared. Leaning forward, Audrey grappled for his mane, for anything to steady her seat. Upward, the horse rose, making an ungodly noise as the barbaric Scots surrounded her.

Crying out, Audrey sailed through the air. She threw back her hand to break her fall. Hot pain shot up through her elbow and clear up to her shoulder as she landed with a jarring thud.

The Highlander who'd reached for her reins hopped down from his mount and sauntered toward her, his hairy, bare knees flexing from beneath his kilt. "Are you hurt, lassie?" This man's brogue was even more pronounced than the earl's.

Audrey clutched her fists beneath her chin. "Stay back, or I-I'll scream." Truly, there wasn't a bone in her body that didn't hurt, but she couldn't afford to show fear to these savages.

The man stopped and thrust his fists into his hips. "Then what are you doing trespassing on Kennet lands?"

"I am Miss Kennet, you scoundrel." Regardless of her aching backside, she stood without the barbarian's assistance and shuffled away. Obviously this man was too thickheaded to offer a hand.

"Och." The man dropped his hands to his sides. "You are the heiress?"

"Who else would be riding like the devil to visit her father's grave?"

The man scratched his head. "I thought Nicholas Kennet's daughter was a wee bairn."

"Evidently so did the Earl of Seaforth." Gracious, her hands were shaking like saplings in the wind. Could these men not carry on with their business and leave her be? And what was it about these Scots? They brought out the absolute worst in her. She'd never been so outspoken in her life.

Flicking his wrist, the Highlander gestured to the others. "Forgive us for frightening you, miss, but 'tis not safe to be out riding alone, not when there are redcoats combing the countryside."

"And why would government dragoons pose a threat? They're here to protect law-abiding citizens."

"In the perfect world, aye. But your father was just murdered by a cannonball blasted from Her Majesty's Royal Navy—friends of those dragoons you think so highly of." The man dragged his fingers through his thick brown hair. "The name's Dunn MacRae, and I'm proud to call the Earl of Seaforth my friend. Come along now and we'll take you back to the manse afore you're set upon by a mob of real outlaws."

You mean to say that you and your lot of scraggly brutes are not outlaws? The more she considered it, the more doubtful she grew. Audrey clutched her fingers in front of her rib cage to stop her trembling and squared her shoulders. She'd realized at the manse it was up to her to take matters into her own hands. Shy or not, she must make a stand. "Sir. I am not following you anywhere. Either you escort me to Saint Hilda's Church, or…or…" *Blast it.* One of the accursed Highlanders was holding Allegro's reins, and he didn't look like he was about to give them back. "Or I will walk if I must."

The MacRae man stepped toward her. "Nay. His Lordship must give his approval first."

"I need no guardian's approval. As you can see, I'm a grown woman. For all I know, you and the earl have fabricated this entire story. If you really want to see to my protection, leave me be." Audrey's entire body shuddered, but she fought her fear by raising her chin just as she'd seen her father do many a time. "At present, you are making me feel quite vulnerable."

Scowling, Mr. MacRae motioned for the Highlander to move forward with her horse. "You wouldn't want me to show you exactly how vulnerable you are, now would you, lass?"

* * *

No sooner had Reid toweled off than the door to his chamber burst open. "Jesus Saint Christopher Christ." Dunn barged in, swearing like a heathen.

"Do you not knock before shoving into an earl's chamber?" Reaching for his plaid, Reid tucked it around his hips.

The MacRae chieftain looked like he could plunge his dagger into someone's heart. "Holy hellfire, the wee lassie Nicholas asked you to tend is a fiery-tongued vixen sent by Satan himself."

Reid almost smiled. Dunn was about as refined with the lassies as a deerhound. "Och, so you met Miss Audrey, did you?"

"I thought you were going to speak to the lass, ease her mind, help her understand we're working for *the cause* and how sensitive matters can be."

"I don't recall saying all that."

"Aye, but you were."

Reid scrubbed his hair with the drying cloth. "Tell me what happened."

"I thought she was a thief or worse."

"Wee Miss Kennet?" Now he'd heard everything.

"Aye, well, she was riding for the gate like a bloody thief. When we stopped her, she carried on as if we were a mob of rogues preventing her from burying her da." Dunn thrust his finger at Reid's chest. "She doesn't believe you are an earl. I didn't even bother telling her I'm the chieftain of Clan MacRae, not that such information would impress her in the slightest. Christ, she's as feisty as a badger."

"I thought she was demure and shy." Reid grinned. It

wasn't often MacRae was this rattled. "You've been confounded by my wee ward, now have you?"

Dunn scowled. "I thought she was supposed to be a child of six, not sixteen."

"She's nineteen."

The big ox threw up his hands. "That makes it even worse."

"I ken." Reid pulled a clean shirt over his head, though it was too tight in the chest. He'd borrowed one of Nicholas's shirts and had his kilt and doublet brushed clean by Mrs. Hobbs.

"Things were bad enough when we thought you'd be looking after a child, but what are you to do with a *woman*?"

Reid swallowed against the thickening in his throat. The same question had plagued him since meeting the lass in the parlor. "I aim to write Baron Barnard at Raby Castle. As lord lieutenant of County Durham, his baroness will no doubt ken the appropriate suitors nearby. Mark me, I shall secure a betrothal for the lassie within the month."

"God save the man who takes an oath to spend eternity with that sharp-tongued hellcat."

"Truly, Dunn? I found Miss Audrey quite pensive, just as one would expect of an English rose."

"A Sassenach thorn is more apt."

"You're overreacting." Reid threw the hairy grouch a drying cloth. "There's still some warmth left in the bath. I suggest you wash afore you let the wee thorn fester under your skin."

Dunn dropped the cloth onto the chair and loosened his belt. "You'd best take her to Saint Hilda's to see her da on the morrow, else I reckon she'll arm the servants and start her own bloody war of independence."

"I plan to." Reid pulled his plaid over his shoulder and secured it with a brooch, all the while chuckling to himself. The lass wasn't as difficult as Dunn made out. In no time, he'd have her married off and out of his hair, then they'd both head to the Highlands and forget they'd ever met her.

"Ye ken she's madder than a swarm of bees..." Dunn continued on to explain how she'd been thrown from her horse and threatened to walk to Hartlepool. She'd only agreed to return to the manse after he'd made her think he would throw her over his shoulder and smack her behind.

The more Dunn talked, the hotter Reid grew. "Dash it, could you not be gentler with her? She's only just lost her father."

"Next time I'll send a lad for you so you can be on the receiving end of her barbed tongue." Dunn slid into the bathwater. "How long do you reckon we'll be in this abominable place?"

"Not certain, but we cannot tarry. We need to summon a gathering at Brahan Castle by the end of summer. If the queen passes her bloody Occasional Conformity Act, we'll all be sunk." Reid shrugged into his doublet. "You didn't say. Did you see any redcoat activity?"

"A retinue of dragoons rode into Coxhoe this afternoon."

"Looking for us?"

Dunn wrung out a cloth over the top of his head. "Seems likely, though I didn't intercept them and hold an inquisition."

"Why not?" Reid chuckled. "That might have been fun."

In fact, Reid had thought about doing exactly that. The navy had just destroyed his ship without provocation. He should be making a royal case out of such an abomination, and he planned to as soon as he settled things with the Kennet estate.

Without another word, he made his way to the dining hall. Audrey was already sitting at the long table, which was set for a feast and festooned with candelabras and a soup tureen. The lass didn't look his way, but sat erect, her hair fashionably pinned up with curls framing her face. She wore a blue taffeta gown suitable for the evening meal. At least her finishing school lessons proved useful. Finding her a husband ought to be uncomplicated.

"Good evening, Miss Audrey." He slid into the chair at the head of the table.

"Were you aware your men chased me across Coxhoe lands and startled my horse so that I was thrown?" She stared at her soup tureen as if speaking to it instead of him.

A servant poured him a glass of wine. "I just received word." Reid gave her a once-over. "Were you injured?"

"I've a bruised elbow." She shifted her seat, glancing downward. "And elsewhere."

"Apologies for that. It seems you quite befuddled the chieftain of Clan MacRae." Though she didn't take the bait, he regarded her profile. Pleasant, her nose wasn't too large, her chin not too long. Even the red blotches on her face had disappeared into smooth, porcelain skin. A twinge of heat coiled low in his belly. "Do you oft venture out on your own?"

"No." She shook her head. "But I've never lost my father...a-and to such suspicious circumstances."

He took a sip of wine. "I understand you must be out of sorts, but—"

"I am devastated," she whispered, finally meeting his gaze.

Reid gulped the sip down while that wee coil of heat shot through his chest. Holy Christ, the piercing stab of her stare cut straight through his heart. The lass expressed more feeling with one look than a preacher could throughout an entire Sunday sermon. She was angry and hurt, and more than anything, distrust filled those brooding blues.

Reid licked his lips. "I know you are mourning."

Pursing her lips, she shifted her eyes to the folded hands in her lap.

"I sense more than my words are troubling you."

"I'm fine."

If he was going to be her guardian, she needed to be forthright with him. *I'm fine* was not an acceptable reply. "No, you are angry. I can feel the anger billowing around you."

She glanced up, but only for an instant. "How on earth could you know what I am feeling, my lord? I have just become an orphan."

He understood far more than she realized. "As a matter of fact, I became an orphan at the age of eighteen and was made a ward of the queen until I reached one and twenty."

She looked away as Gerald filled her bowl with a ladle of soup. "How am I to believe a word you say?"

He pulled his seal from his sporran and tossed it on the table. "Only one of these exists—the seal of the Earl of Seaforth, given to me by Queen Anne herself." *Though I would have preferred if it had come from James.*

With a huff, she picked up the seal and examined it. "So, you are a *Scottish* earl." She slid it back toward him while her shoulders squared and her chin rose. "I never heard a good word about Scots during my years at Talcott Ladies' Finishing School."

He ran a deprecating gaze from her head down to her bowl. Two could play her game. "Were there any Scots in attendance? Any Scottish instructors?"

"No." Her shoulders dropped a bit.

"I thought not."

"Why is that?"

"Because then you would have had an opportunity to judge for yourself rather than rely on the opinion of ignorant and inexperienced schoolgirls."

Groaning, his ward rolled her enormous blue eyes, then fixated on her lap again. "Nonetheless," she said softly. "I cannot allow you to run away with the profits from my father's mines."

"Did I say I was looking for profit?"

"Aren't all men? Especially Highlanders?"

Reid was beginning to understand Dunn's frustration. Dear God, the lass could be incorrigible. "I see Talcotts didn't do much to teach you about honor...or respect for nobility." He flicked a bit of lint from his lapel. He was a guardian, not a bloody teacher. "I gave your father my word that I would see to your maintenance. And that I will do. There are a great many affairs requiring my attention, and the sooner I can set things to rights here, the sooner I can resume my own dealings. On the morrow I will take you to your father's grave and then make an appointment with your da's solicitor so he can administrate the estate on your behalf." He bit his tongue, deciding it was best to wait to tell her about marrying her off until a suitor was found.

"I would like to visit the solicitor with you."

He frowned. "I doubt the conversation would be of interest."

"You are quite mistaken, my lord. When the conversation

includes my father's estate and my affairs, I must be very interested, concerned, and invested. I refuse to sit idle whilst men whisper and plot my future in secret."

He blinked. "Well then, by all means, you are welcome to attend."

"My lord," said Gerald as he stepped into the dining hall. "Captain Richard Wilcox from Baron Barnard's Forty-Second Dragoons has come to call. Shall I ask him to wait?"

Chapter Four

*A*fter the earl excused himself and went to the library to meet with Captain Wilcox, Audrey set her spoon beside her bowl, dashed into the kitchen, and raced up the servants' stairs. As a young girl, she'd often played in the narrow corridors hidden from the family's view. Alongside the library there was a shelf with a stained-glass window where Gerald replenished her father's brandy. More than once, she'd overheard conversations while hiding in that very spot.

"It is odd to receive visitors after six. I assume your news is grave, sir," said the earl, his voice resounding through the glass and sounding full of importance.

"I was advised of the death of Mr. Kennet by the vicar at Saint Hilda's, my lord. The death of such a prominent member of County Durham comes as a great shock."

"Agreed. Mr. Kennet's passing is a most untimely and unfortunate state of affairs."

"But I am surprised to see you here. What is the nature of your relationship with the Kennets?"

"The man was a business partner. With his last breath he asked me to see to the maintenance of his daughter."

"Business partner?" the captain asked, distrust filling his voice. Audrey didn't blame him. She didn't trust the earl either. "Then you are aware his estate employs a great many local laborers in the mines."

"I am aware, and that further exemplifies the need for a learned man to set Kennet's affairs in order."

"The Lord Barnard will be following your endeavors with great interest. Ah...is there a will?"

"I'm meeting with Mr. Kennet's solicitor on the morrow to ask the same question." The earl hesitated for a moment. "In fact, I intend to write to Lord Barnard upon my first opportunity."

Audrey knit her brows. *What business would Seaforth have to do with the baron?*

"I'm sure His Lordship would be pleased to hear from you."

The earl cleared his throat. "If there's nothing else, I should like to return to my meal."

"Ah...there is one more question I must ask."

"You'd best make it fast."

"Why were you sailing from France?"

Audrey leaned forward, knocking a glass off the shelf. Stifling a squeal, she caught it in midair. *Whew.* Her heart pounded so loudly, she feared Seaforth would hear it, too.

"Cologne," said the earl.

"I beg your pardon?"

"Have you not heard of it? Eau de Cologne is all the rage with the ladies in Britain. It's from the region of Cologne, Germany, and very popular in Paris. And because of the overzealous captain on the *Royal Buckingham*, I lost an entire shipment valued at a thousand pounds, and let me say, I am very unhappy about it. I am personally on good terms with the lord high admiral, and to be certain, he will be hearing from me with a formal complaint. Why with two wars, the Royal Navy goes after a small Scottish sea galley, I cannot surmise, but you have my word, justice will prevail."

For pity's sake, now Audrey was even more confused. Papa entertaining a perfume venture? That didn't sound like him at all.

Chapter Five

*R*eid rolled to his back and stared at the purple bed-curtains. Nicholas certainly spared no expense when he outfitted his wife's chamber, rest her soul. Purple dye came only from Tyrian snails, and it took twenty thousand of them to make an ounce of dye. The cost to outfit an entire bedchamber from coverlet, to canopy, to curtains was nothing short of a display of great wealth. Reid had taken the lady of the manor's chamber because it was in the west wing near the lord's chamber and as far away as possible from Miss Kennet's rooms.

From the light streaming through the shutters, he could tell it was morning, but that did nothing to allay the throbbing in his head. Worse, someone saw fit to play a harpsichord directly below his bed. Only a lass as maddening as Audrey would wake at dawn and attack the ivories like she was herding a mob of deer.

Regardless that he could sleep until noon, he had naught but to rise and face the day. Last eve he'd penned missives well into the wee hours. One to the lord high admiral to make good his case for a new sea galley to be paid for by the crown, one to the Lord of Barnard to find Miss Audrey a husband, one to the vicar of Saint Hilda's that included a note from Reid's own coffers to pay for Nicholas's burial, and dozens to the Highland Defenders, trusted Jacobite clan chieftains throughout Scotland, explaining in code that the hunt of the king stag had failed and new sights must be set for *the cause*.

Reid had summoned the Defenders to his lands for a gathering three months hence. In his estimation, that should provide plenty of time to put the Kennet estates in order, secure a betrothal for Audrey, and make his way home to set his own affairs to rights.

He placed his bare feet on the cold hardwood floor and stretched. Dash it, if Audrey awoke every morning and practiced scales ad infinitum as she was presently doing, he would be all but mad by the time he was ready to part ways.

After dressing and grooming, he followed the music until arriving in the drawing room. Audrey had exchanged her scales and arpeggios for a ballad—a far more soothing tune than the repetitious plunking of notes. As a matter of fact, she was quite good. A certain emotion flowed from her fingertips to the keys, bringing an expressive quality to the melody.

Reid stood in the archway and listened. Moreover, he watched. Miss Audrey, sitting with her back to him, sheet music spread across the stand as her fingers danced over the keys. She wore her tresses much like she had last eve during the meal, with the length pulled up into a chignon at the back and ringlets in the front. The curls bounced with her movement. The lass had a long, slender neck, tapering to demure shoulders. *Delicate* was the first word that came to mind, followed by *lovely*, *precious*, and *accomplished*. Something in his chest stretched, though he ignored the sensation.

Today she wore a black frock, tight around the bodice, and from what Reid could see of it, fanned out into billowing skirts. He wasn't overly fond of black, but since they would be visiting Nicholas's graveside this day, the color was appropriate.

The ballad ended with a minor chord, one that filled his chest with a hollow void—hollow because of the intense sadness imparted through the lassie's fingers and because the tune had ended. How he would have enjoyed watching her unawares for a wee bit longer.

She inclined her ear toward him, as if she sensed his presence.

"Very nice," he said. "You are quite accomplished."

"'Tis a way to pass the time when you are the only child to a widower."

Reid expected to hear the sadness in her voice, but the regret surprised him. "Did you ever entertain your father's guests?"

"On occasion, when I wasn't away at Talcotts." She turned. "I've ordered the coach to meet us in the courtyard at half past eight."

Reid glanced to the mantel clock. "Well then. 'Tis a good thing your practice woke me, else I'd still be abed."

"Do you oft sleep late, my lord?"

"Only when I've been up until the wee hours setting quill to missives." He gestured toward the door to the tune of his growling stomach. "Shall we?"

* * *

Once in the courtyard, Audrey placed her fingers in the earl's outstretched palm and allowed him to assist her into the coach. Her fingers tingled as soon as she touched his hand. With a gasp, she met his gaze. The corner of his mouth ticked up while crinkles formed at the corners of his penetrating eyes—fathomless green eyes encircled by a dark ring around his irises. Those eyes were disconcerting to say the least, hawkish and cunning. What was it about this man that made her feel so out of sorts? He'd offered her a hand, the simple gesture as confounding as being among an entire hall of courtiers. Often she'd been aided into the coach by her father or by Gerald, and never once had she been so discombobulated.

Though she preferred to sit riding forward, she purposely took the seat with her back to the team, because a man like Reid MacKenzie would definitely sit opposite. In no way did Audrey want to sit shoulder to shoulder with the earl. But when he took the opposing seat, she almost regretted her choice all the more. Now she'd have to endure the hour-long coach ride to Hartlepool staring at the man's face. Oddly attractive with chiseled features, he didn't seem to smile much. His fierceness mightn't be as frightening if he smiled more often. Truly, with that sharp-eyed stare, he could fluster even the most courageous of maids.

And Audrey wasn't courageous in the slightest. In fact her behavior since the arrival of the Highlanders had shocked her down to her toes. She set the roses she'd picked that morning beside her and folded her hands. Staring at her fingers, she turned them over three or four times, wishing she'd brought some knitting, or anything to keep them busy.

"Are you nervous?" he asked.

Yes, and I'd rather be anywhere than inside this coach with a man as disconcerting as you. "No." She snapped open her fan and cooled her cheeks.

"Aside from playing the harpsichord, what do you enjoy? What fills the days of a bonny heiress?" He smiled politely, as if he cared how she filled her days. And as she'd predicted, his smile made him appear amenable.

Audrey wanted to appreciate his friendliness, but now was not the time. "I paint fans."

"Fans?"

She placed her fan in her lap and spread it open for him to see. This one had a circle of dancing nymphs— one of her favorite paintings. "I paint these for a merchant in London. He takes as many as I can send him."

"I am impressed." Seaforth plucked the fan from her fingers and examined it, holding it to the light shining in from the window. "Look at the detail. You are quite talented, I'll say."

"Thank you. Papa always said my hobbies kept me out of trouble."

"Did he now?" He folded the fan and gave it back. "Your father was a smart man."

She glanced down to her fingers and bit her bottom lip. "Tell me, my lord. How did you meet Papa?"

"We were introduced by a mutual acquaintance in London."

"Oh? Whom, may I ask?"

"The Duke of Gordon. Do you know him?"

"I cannot say I do." She drummed her fingers against her lips "Gordon? Does he not hail from the north of Scotland? And tell me, what does he have to do with French perfume?"

"When did...?" The earl frowned, drawing his eyebrows together and looking rather dangerous—and rather like he saw straight through her ruse.

Audrey smiled inwardly. Papa had, on occasion, taken her to the mine, and they'd discussed some of his business dealings. But surely, after the years of conversation, she must have picked up some of his acumen.

And, there was no time like a dreary coach ride to test her theory. "I'd like to try a sample of the new fragrance from Cologne."

"I would have been able to give you a bottle if I'd salvaged anything from my boat afore it sank." He arched his eyebrows. "Your father told you about the Cologne venture, did he?"

"Mm-hmm," she said, staring out the window at the rolling hills of pastoral land rather than hold his gaze.

"I'm certain he did."

Nothing made a lick of sense. If she wanted answers, she would have to seek them out for herself. As far as she was concerned the earl spoke in riddles. And by the way he was now studying her from across the coach, she was quite sure he suspected her of listening in on his conversation with the captain.

Nonetheless, Audrey didn't care if Seaforth thought she was listening or not. She aimed to find out why her father was traveling with an earl from the north of Scotland, and why they were in France together.

She didn't believe the Cologne ruse for a moment. Papa was a coal man with little time to dabble in anything else. Especially ladies' perfume.

Something was afoot, and if the Earl of Seaforth found himself on the wrong end of these affairs—if he in any way was implicated in her father's death—she would make him pay.

* * *

When the coach turned into Saint Hilda's, a cold chill spread across Audrey's skin. She looked out the window to see a grave with recently turned dirt, shaded by weeping willows. Her throat turned dry as a tear slipped from her eye. She pulled a kerchief from her sleeve and drew it to her face. "Merciful Father."

The earl reached out as if he might touch her knee, but swiftly snatched his hand away. "Would you prefer to wait a bit?"

She shook her head.

As Seaforth accompanied her through the wrought iron gate leading to the graveyard, they were met by the vicar. His black robes billowed as he approached, wringing his hands. "My heavens, Your Lordship, I didn't expect to see you returned so soon."

Seaforth stopped and bowed. "Good day, Father Brown. Might I introduce Miss Audrey Kennet. She has been ever so distraught since I delivered the news of her father's untimely death. 'Twas very important for the lass to pay her respects."

The vicar regarded her with a concerned frown. "Oh, my dear, you must be out of sorts by the shock of it all."

"Indeed I am." She looked to the new grave. "You gave him a proper burial?"

"Surely, we saw to everything. The earl's instructions were to spare no expense."

She looked to Seaforth. "You paid the bill?"

"He did." Father Brown grasped Audrey's elbow and led her along the path. "Walk with me."

She glanced over her shoulder. Seaforth didn't follow,

thank heavens. "And you are certain the man you buried was Nicholas Kennet?"

"Quite certain, miss. Your father was a benefactor of Saint Hilda's, did you not know?"

"I did not." It seemed there were a great many things she didn't know about Papa. And to think, at one time she believed there were no secrets between them.

"Many miners attend this church. Your father always took care of them. He was a warmhearted man, loved by many. I do hope you intend to keep the mine open?"

Honestly, in the past day Audrey hadn't thought about anything but her own grief. Considering all the many things left untended by Papa's passing made her head swim. "I intend to," she replied, making a mental note to discuss the mine's operation with the solicitor.

They stopped at the grave and she stooped to place the roses on top. "Have you ordered the headstone?"

"Indeed. A large granite stone befitting of your father's importance to the community—ordered by Lord Seaforth, of course."

She nodded. "And the inscription?"

"The year of birth and death, his name, and the words 'loving father' as requested by His Lordship."

She pursed her lips. She wanted to detest Seaforth ever so much, but she couldn't fault him for doing the right thing by Papa. If only she could be certain the earl wasn't the reason for her father's untimely death.

Death.

The mere word made her want to crumble into a heap and sob. Dash it, for the first time that day, she couldn't hold in her tears. Seeing Papa's grave was like learning of his death all over again.

Father Brown stood beside her in silence for a time,

and after her tears abated and they prayed together, he led her toward the church. "Would it ease your pain to spend some time alone in the chapel?"

"Please." She sniffed.

After she was seated in a pew and left alone in the small chapel, Audrey sat quietly with her hands folded. A hollow bubble expanded in her chest as her melancholy set in. In the distance, a muffled Gregorian chant of male voices brought a certain peace to the chapel with its stone walls. A cross hung over an altar, festooned with green linen and two candles, one on either end.

There she sat, alone in this world with no one to love.

She leaned forward and lowered the kneeling rail. Folding her hands in prayer, she stared at the cross with thoughts of her father and the times they'd shared. Perhaps they had grown apart in the four years she'd spent away at Talcotts. She hadn't wanted to go to boarding school at first, but Papa had convinced her it was for the best. She'd learn refinement and how to be a lady—things Mother could have taught her had she lived.

But Mama died of smallpox when Audrey was but four years of age. She barely remembered her mother. And now all she had left of Papa were memories. At least Audrey's parents were together now. Her father had never remarried—a testament to the love he bore for his wife.

Audrey prayed for a long time, asking for redemption for Papa's soul. She prayed for strength to continue on and honor her father's memory, not to bend to the earl's will, but to discover the truth for herself. She prayed to be blessed with Papa's shrewd acumen, for he would have wanted her to take an active role in his affairs. Finally, she asked for forgiveness for being unduly outspoken.

Heaven knew why she'd been so brazen toward the earl. She should be mortified with herself, but for some reason she wasn't.

She didn't know how long she'd been kneeling when a monk entered from the side door with two candles tucked under his arm. He wore a brown hood pulled over his head and went about his business changing the candles on the altar.

Audrey slid back into the pew and sat quietly. Perhaps she should go find the earl before he came looking for her. She dabbed her eyes as the monk strode down the aisle, but rather than continue on his way, he stopped beside her. "I am sorry to hear of your loss, miss."

The man's voice had a gruff tone, not at all serene like she would expect. It resonated with a nasally twang. Turning her face up to him, a gasp slipped through her lips. Shocking grey eyes peered from beneath a straight line of eyebrows. The monk had a thin moustache, and the beard on his chin was unkempt. But more unsettling was the track of his mouth. His upper lip disappeared into his lower, and the corners turned up as if in a sneer, almost as if he was judging her.

Drawing a hand to her chest, Audrey snapped her gaze away. "Thank you for your concern."

He inhaled sharply like he intended to comment further, but after an uncomfortable pause, the peculiar monk continued on his way.

* * *

Before slipping out the postern gate, the monk looked over his shoulder to ensure he hadn't been seen. Then he hastened into the shadows of the trees and continued to the dank alleyways where he knew how to blend in and move without notice.

He didn't expect Miss Kennet to recognize him. After all, they'd never been introduced, and until now, his station had been far beneath hers. She'd been born into wealth, had lived a life of privilege. And he? He'd led a life in the gutter.

But not for much longer. The monk had a few secrets of his own and, now that Miss Kennet's father was out of the way, he would seize his fortune.

Nonetheless, this business with the earl was an unexpected turn of events. While her father was in France, the monk had set his plans in motion, acted on a number of dirty secrets he'd collected in the past year. If he'd learned anything in the gutter, it was that everyone had something they wanted to hide, and once he discovered what it was, it was easy to convince them to turn to his way of thinking.

Fortunately, he possessed a tidbit of dirt on the Earl of Seaforth. He'd rather not take on a man as powerful as Reid MacKenzie, but if the behemoth didn't return to Scotland soon, the monk would have no choice but to play his card.

Thank God, he'd intercepted a letter from the earl to the lord high admiral. If that document had reached London, the monk's every effort would have been foiled.

Chapter Six

*A*fter they returned from Saint Hilda's, the earl excused himself to do whatever it was earls did with their men. He said something about sparring, which only made Audrey roll her eyes for the hundredth time. Doubtless, Seaforth would need to be skilled with all manner of weapons if he was constantly at odds with Her Majesty's Royal Dragoons.

Nonetheless, Audrey seized the opportunity to slip into the library where her father kept his books of accounts. She closed the door behind her, tiptoed to the desk, and removed the key from the secret chamber at the back of the top drawer. Ever since Audrey was a little girl, Papa had written in his journal at the end of each day. He'd always kept it locked away in the strongbox behind the portrait of his brother that hung to the side of his writing desk. She'd never been allowed to read the journal, but now she firmly believed it was her duty to do so.

In the past two days she'd learned her father had commenced on a perfume venture in France, enemy territory, no less; had befriended a number of Scottish nobles; and sided with the Tory Party. Did she even know the man?

As Audrey reached for the corner of the portrait, she paused. She'd never paid much attention to the painting of her uncle Josiah. He'd been a year younger than Papa and died a single man—when Audrey was a young child. Her father had rarely spoken of him, except to say that Josiah imbibed too much brandy and had an affinity for the ladies on the waterfront. It was only after reading about the woman at the well in Bible class at Talcotts that she guessed the profession of the waterfront ladies.

Curious, she leaned nearer the portrait, taking in the stare of her uncle from beneath a line of dour eyebrows as if accusing her of some misdeed. Mayhap she was causing herself undue trepidation because she felt like a thief sneaking into the library and reading the forbidden journal.

But I am the heiress and I have a right to be here. Besides, 'tis the only place I might be able to find answers.

Steeling her resolve, she pulled open the picture, used the key, and peered into the strongbox. The journal sat upright against one wall. Near it were papers. Letters, deeds, and notes of payment, and heaven knew what else. She removed the journal, then replaced things as she'd found them, especially the portrait of Uncle Josiah.

Since His Lordship had been using the library to set the estate's affairs in order, Audrey most certainly didn't want Seaforth to suspect her of meddling, and moreover, she didn't want him to know about the strongbox. Not until he proved his trust beyond a shadow of a doubt, and not until Audrey learned what her father had been up to.

Once she made her way to her chamber, she sat in the

window embrasure and opened the journal on her lap and set to reading:

20th April, 1708: The Earl of Seaforth arrived yesterday but didn't tarry. Advised his sea galley will be sailing for Calais on the morrow. I have no choice but to accompany him. The plea for James to embrace the Protestant faith hath never been so crucial. The line to the succession must be defined, lest the entire country be forced into civil war upon the queen's death.

Audrey continued to read about the daily operations of the mines and a few snippets regarding the manor that she'd been aware of, until her finger stopped:

15th April, 1708: My beloved daughter arrived home from Talcotts today. Lord, how I've missed my English rose. She has grown into a fine woman and looks so like her mother. I will enjoy her company this summer. But alas, the time has come for her to marry.

Audrey's jaw dropped. If marriage was so vastly imminent, why hadn't Papa mentioned it? The mere thought tied her stomach in knots. Had Papa started the process of finding a suitor? Were any of the letters in his strongbox about her? Perhaps she should have been more thorough when she was in the library.

Then another entry caught her eye.

1st March, 1708: Returned from London, where I met with Lords Seaforth, Gordon, Tullibardine and

*many others in the Tory Party. We are all in agree-
ment that it is our duty to defend the succession. The
sooner the better, in my opinion. The taxes imposed
by Her Highness to support her wars on two continents are bleeding my coffers dry. Had the queen
received any education in the governance of a kingdom, things might be quite different. But we were
forced to suffer the reign of her sister and now
Anne. James must succeed to the throne, lest we
all suffer the consequences of foreign rule and, no
doubt, taxation that will send miners out of business.*

On and on Audrey read about her father's political
beliefs and problems of running the mine until she sat
back and stared out the window. Papa had never discussed
his political leanings with her, but with all she'd read,
things began to fall in place. Though she never would
have guessed, her father had been a *Jacobite*, a man who
supported the descendants of James II and their claim
to the throne, even though they followed the Catholic
faith. At Talcotts the ladies were never permitted to utter
such a word, nor were any of the ladies allowed to attend
Catholic mass.

But her father's concerns had nothing to do with religion. He wanted fairer taxation. He disapproved of Britain's involvement in the wars. Those two things alone
made a great deal of sense to Audrey. And it was high
time she started paying more attention to the administra-
tion of the mine and the estate...especially if she was to
avoid being forced into an undesirable marriage.

Goodness, why hadn't Papa mentioned marriage to me?

At least he hadn't named any suitors in his writings.

It also eased her mind considerably to know that Lord Seaforth was not an imposter. That he had joined with her father to pursue changes Papa believed in.

But why the ruse with the fragrance from Cologne?

She smoothed her fingers over the leather-bound journal.

Oh dear, possibly the same reason they were fired upon by the Royal Navy. They would have needed some kind of ruse if anyone suspected they were actually meeting with Prince James.

She hid the journal under a cushion and headed for her paints. She needed to think, and there was no better way to do it than with a brush in her hand.

One thing was for certain. Their Cologne scheme hadn't fooled someone out there. Had someone tipped the officers off? Was Britain in the midst of three wars rather than two?

Heavens, there was far more to Papa than Audrey had ever imagined.

* * *

A few days had passed when the solicitor came to call. As he'd promised, Reid sent Gerald to collect Miss Audrey for the meeting, and they gathered in the library. The young lady opted to take the settee facing the hearth, and she sat with her hands folded in her lap. Reid and Mr. Watford took opposing chairs cornering the settee. Reid felt this a much less formal arrangement than sitting at the table in the drawing room, which he hoped put Audrey at ease.

Reid first went through all the formalities of explaining what happened and the reason for his involvement in the estate. "There is a gathering I must attend in Scotland at the end of summer, and I'd like to see a trust established to benefit Miss Kennet before I take my leave."

"Apologies, my lord." The man's periwig jostled as he shook his head. "But it will take a fair bit longer than that. Mr. Kennet left no directives, and the estate must go into abeyance whilst we search for a male heir."

Miss Audrey opened her mouth with a wee snort.

"Abeyance?" Reid sank his fingers into the cushions of the armrests. "Can that not be avoided? Clearly, Miss Kennet's maintenance was of utmost concern to her father."

"It is highly irregular to have a woman inherit, especially an estate as large as Mr. Kennet's." The man shook his head again. "An investigation must be done. 'Tis the law."

Miss Audrey held up her finger. "But—"

"Since I am here," Reid interrupted, "and able to look after things until a trust can be arranged, I wouldn't think it would be necessary to keep Miss Kennet's inheritance from her." Mr. Watford made clear he sided with the common view that women were incapable of managing their own affairs. Anything Audrey said to the contrary would only make the man dig in his heels.

The solicitor drummed his bony fingers against his lips. "I do not know…"

Reid leaned forward. "Have any male heirs approached you with a claim on the estate?"

"No, not as yet."

"Then it is settled. The estate will *not* go into abeyance during the time in which it takes you to set the legalities to rights." Reid looked to Audrey. It was time to bring her over to his way of thinking. "My thoughts were to hold the estate in trust for you until a husband can be found."

"Husband?" Her voice shot up as if she'd never considered the possibility of a betrothal.

"Yes, miss," agreed Mr. Watford. "It would simplify things considerably if you were to marry."

Audrey's fists tightened in her lap as her lips disappeared into a straight line. Evidently, the idea of future wedded bliss did not sit well with the lass.

Fortunately, the solicitor continued with the agenda, and produced a few slips of parchment from his satchel. "Mr. Kennet did entrust me with an accounting of household effects, which I will need you to review and confirm all is still in the possession of the estate." He handed the papers to Reid.

He leafed through them. "I believe Miss Kennet is best suited to such a task."

Though she didn't smile, her face brightened as she accepted the list from Reid with blue-paint-splattered fingers—the reason she had been clenching her fists so tightly. "Thank you for realizing my mind is full of more than just bird feathers."

Mr. Watford crossed his legs and ignored the lass. "Have you been to the mine?"

Reid shook his head. "I must do that on my very next opportunity."

"Mr. Poole will be anxious to meet with you, I'm sure," said Audrey. "He and all the miners will want to know if we intend to keep operations going."

The solicitor frowned and knit his brows. "Perhaps Miss Kennet would prefer to retire while we speak about business?"

She sat straighter, clenching her fists again, but this

time her knuckles grew white. "Most certainly not," she said, fixating on her hands.

Reid chuckled. "I'll wager the lass kens more about mining coal than the two of us put together."

The solicitor blinked dumbly from beneath his pompous wig. "I beg your pardon, my lord, but it is a well-known fact that women are slaves to their sex. A woman can no sooner run a mine than she can lift a fifty-pound boulder and throw it."

Reid opened his mouth to issue a retort, but Audrey beat him to the punch. "I beg your pardon, Mr. Watford." She looked up, revealing a pair of beautiful, astute blue eyes. "But I did not realize it took brutish strength to calculate a list of sums or to make a decision about prices, or markets in which to sell. As a matter of fact, my father, who founded the Coxhoe Mine, said a good business owner needed to be shrewd, well-spoken, and have an eye for profit." She held up that blue-splattered finger and shook it while her face turned scarlet. "Yet he uttered not one word about tossing fifty-pound boulders."

The solicitor's eyes bugged. He looked to Reid as if the lass had just proved his point about being featherbrained.

But Reid refused to play the man's game. It might be fortunate if Audrey knew about the business. She'd be able to coach her future husband as he takes up the reins. "See, Watford? The lassie obviously has benefited from her father's tutelage."

The man shifted in his seat with a grumble. "With talk like that, I ought to put the estate into abeyance forthwith. 'Tis the right thing to do, after all."

"Och, things always have a way of sorting themselves out. Trust me." Reid agreed with the solicitor on one thing, anyway. The sooner a suitor was found for Miss Audrey, the better.

They both looked at him as if they were each about to question trusting a Scot, but they held their tongues, thank God. Especially Miss Kennet. If she'd spoken out against him after he'd stood up for her, he would have been more than a wee bit disappointed. Her gaze lingered for a moment. When he grinned at her, she quickly looked to her hands, again folded in her lap, again hiding the paint splotches. Truly, there was far more to the lass than Reid had initially thought.

The meeting went on for about an hour before Mr. Watford made his excuses and Reid walked him to the door. "As I said, the best thing for Miss Kennet will be for her to marry. The sooner, the better."

Reid clapped the man on the shoulder. "I've already started the wheels in motion—sent a letter to Lord Barnard to request the baroness's assistance."

"What about you, my lord? You're single, are you not?"

"Me?" Reid batted his hand through the air. "I'm not ready to settle down. Besides, I'm far too busy. A wife would never see me at home." He intended to avoid matrimony like the plague. He'd been quite adept at holding the subject at bay thus far, though he'd have to face his father's promise eventually.

The solicitor snorted. "That mightn't be such a bad thing."

He motioned for Gerald to open the door and show the solicitor out. "I'll have the lass betrothed by the end of the month, mark me."

Of course, he should have known he'd rue those words. Miss Audrey met him at the top of the stairs with her arms crossed. She even looked him in the eye. "What is this grand plan you have to hastily marry me to some stranger so that you can continue on with your demanding agenda?" She snapped her hand over her mouth like she'd uttered a curse—which she practically had.

Reid brushed past her and headed for the library. "Och, what did you expect once you'd graduated from finishing school? Were you planning a tour of Christendom? Sail to the Americas and pray not to contract scurvy and die on the crossing?"

She followed on his heels. "I expected to spend the summer strolling the gardens with my father."

He marched through the library door and stopped. Good God, he felt like an arse every time he thought about Nicholas Kennet's death. If only he'd been smarter. If only his damned pride hadn't stood in the way, he could have told the lads to heave to. The poor man might still be alive. Reid closed the door and faced her. "I am sorry. And you have had so little time to mourn."

"You cannot possibly know what it's like to be in my position. I have no prospects, and I refuse to latch on to the first available suitor who passes by because I am desperate to marry." She turned away and hid her face in her palms. "I-I would be mortified to meet some...some...*man*!"

Damnation, why did she have to discount the whole idea of marriage before she even had a chance to meet a parcel of eligible men in the north of England? And what was this sudden fear of men? She'd certainly proved her mettle to Reid.

He plopped down into the seat in front of the hearth. "No one is going to force you into doing anything."

"It didn't sound that way to me. I heard you, *my lord*."

She spat his courtesy as if it were a curse. "You said you would see me betrothed by the end of the month."

"I was appeasing the solicitor. He was already on the verge of putting the estate into abeyance. All your father worked for would become the property of the kingdom until either you marry, or a male relative is found. You would be forced to request funds for everything you want to do. If you need a new gown—ask Mr. Watford, and then he would in turn have to submit letters explaining exactly why you need the new gown, or a horse, or a new wheel for your coach, or a new set of paints for your bloody fans."

"Stop." She threw up her hands, making the pieces of parchment with the inventory list scatter to the ground.

Reid dropped to his knees and reached for a page just as Audrey did the same. His fingers brushed hers. Such a minuscule touch, but his heart thumped. Holy saints, the accursed thing even fluttered.

Then a wee gasp slipped through her lips.

Not a gasp of fear but a bone-melting, feminine gasp. Audrey expressed more in that one wee sound than she'd done all afternoon. Reid could read far too much into that whisper. Attraction, being the first. Self-awareness, being another.

His gaze snapped to her mouth. Full lips curved in a rosy bow. They weren't pursed, but slightly parted as if she wanted to smile but couldn't allow it. Her high-boned cheeks blossomed with an adorable blush. And when Reid met her gaze, her eyes grew dark.

The first time he'd seen Audrey, her blue eyes had been swollen and red, her nose, too. But now there was no trace of a weeping, wilting English gel. She was a fully grown woman in her prime. A woman fresh out of finishing school who'd just lost her father and who was desperately trying to maintain control over the course of her life.

Reid gulped, his gaze again dropping to her lips. Had the lass ever been kissed? With lips as plush as Audrey's, she certainly should be kissed, and often. When her teeth grazed over her bottom lip, he blinked, suddenly realizing he'd been staring.

"Ah..." Words refused to come to his tongue. He glanced to the parchment he still clasped and released. "You'd best have a look at that soon so we can advise Mr. Watford of any discrepancies."

Her face grew even redder with her nod. "Yes, of course." She collected the other bits of parchment and drew them against her stomach as if they could provide protection.

"My lord." Gerald stepped into the library. "A letter has arrived from Baron Barnard."

Chapter Seven

The following morning Gerald informed Audrey that she'd been summoned to the library by His Lordship. She had paced in her chamber wringing her hands before she started down the corridor. There was no doubt in her mind the earl wanted to speak to her about whatever was contained in Lord Barnard's missive.

Marriage.

The word was like the death knell ringing from the church tower. Her throat thickened and she perspired as if the sun were shining straight on her face. Never in her life had she been so completely mortified. She couldn't meet a man—a potential suitor. What would she do? What would she say? As soon as a man took one look at her, he'd know she was a clumsy wallflower. He'd run for his horse and gallop away like he was fleeing a swarm of angry bees.

The marriageable girls at Talcotts were all flirty. They giggled and chatted like finches. Audrey often didn't speak, and when she did, she was chided for being too abrupt and opinionated. Men preferred women who could laugh at nothing and embroider for hours on end.

Dear Lord, what am I to do?

Glancing at the mantel clock, Audrey realized she'd been pacing for over a quarter hour. If she didn't leave now, the earl would no doubt come to her door, which would be highly improper. No. She'd best face the music, then figure a way to dance around it.

Audrey dashed through the passageway and down the stairs, and as she reached for the latch, the library door opened.

"Whooooooa!" she cried, stumbling forward, straight into the hard chest of Reid MacKenzie himself.

He wrapped his big arms around her, pulling her flush against him. Audrey's hands slipped to his trim waist to steady herself. It was as if time slowed for a moment— as everything became crystal clear. All at once she was keenly aware of his masculine scent, his solid form beneath his doublet, feeling so different from her own curvy shape. The rush of his warm breath swept across her hair.

For a brief moment she wondered what it would be like to kiss his lips.

But with her next inhale, he grasped her shoulders and stood back. "Are you well, Miss Audrey?"

Her mouth gaped as her gaze met his, but she couldn't manage a word. She simply nodded.

"Forgive me. When I heard you approach, I thought I'd open the door and welcome you." He gestured to the couch. "Please, have a seat."

Her fingers started to tremble. Here it came.

Doom.

After they both sat and she took a deep breath, she

found her voice. "Is this about the baron's correspondence?"

"Indeed it is." Reid smiled as if it were Christmas morn.

Audrey wrung her hands. *Maybe the news is a celebration for him, but not for me.*

"Baron and Baroness Barnard have invited us to a ball a fortnight hence."

Her mouth ran dry. "A-a ball, did you say?" Of all the things that were more mortifying that meeting a potential suitor, it was meeting a host of potential suitors and then being expected to dance with them.

"I did." His smile was replaced by a frown and a pinch between his brows. "I thought you would be delighted."

"No, my lord."

"Och, but why not? All lassies enjoy kicking up their heels."

Afraid she was about to fall ill, Audrey shoved herself to her feet. "All lassies aside from this one." Clapping a hand over her mouth she made a dash for the door.

"Wait!" Seaforth rose and grasped her wrist. "You will explain yourself. How on earth am I to find you a husband if you do not attend Lord Barnard's ball?"

"Do you not understand? I cannot dance."

"Preposterous."

"If you think it so, then ask the headmistress at Talcott Ladies' Finishing School. I received top marks as a non-dancing wallflower." Audrey wrenched her wrist free and dashed for the solace of her bedchamber.

* * *

Regardless of Audrey's reluctance to attend the ball, a

day later Mr. Hatfield, the tailor, and his assistant must have spread thirty bolts of cloth across Audrey's bed. She stood in front of the looking glass while the man held up taffetas and damasks in every imaginable hue.

There was something wrong with every color, and now the green Mr. Hatfield held to her face had to be the absolute worst. Audrey frowned at her reflection. "It makes me look as pale as a dishrag."

"I agree, green isn't your color, dear," said Mrs. Hobbs, who was supervising the whole debacle. "Why not go for the champagne pink, it is ever so fashionable."

"Indeed, the pink suited you, miss." Mr. Hatfield gestured to his pigeon-toed assistant to fetch the pink for what seemed like the tenth time.

Audrey again regarded her image in the mirror. She often wore pink. The color had always suited her. "The red." Lord only knew why those two words spewed from her mouth, but as soon as she'd uttered them, her mind was irrevocably made up.

Mrs. Hobbs's jaw dropped. "The red taffeta? Why, that would be scandalous."

"Though we could make it work," added the tailor, clearly grasping at an opportunity to finally come to a decision.

Audrey shot the housemaid a pointed stare. "If I am to be paraded around the ballroom like a piece of raw mutton, I may as well look the part."

The tailor took the bolt of red taffeta from his assistant. "Oh no, I wouldn't allow that to happen—"

"Miss Audrey, what on earth has come over you?" said Mrs. Hobbs. "Red is no color for a demure lady such as yourself. And His Lordship gave me strict orders that you must look like the belle of the ball."

Audrey moved her fists to her hips and regarded the only ally in her bedchamber. "Will you be able to make me look enchanting in red, Mr. Hatfield?"

"I will make a gown so stunning, not a soul will be able to take their eyes off you."

"This absolutely will not do," Mrs. Hobbs declared. "Good heavens, if you show up at Raby Castle wearing a scarlet gown, you could very well end up ravished."

Though Audrey didn't care for the idea of anyone touching her, let alone ravishing her, she stood her ground. "Isn't that what Seaforth wants? Marry me off to some rogue so he can return to his life in the wilds of Scotland and forget he ever set eyes on me?"

"I think a stomacher with pearl beading in a paisley pattern would do," mumbled Mr. Hatfield.

"My dear girl," said Mrs. Hobbs, completely ignoring the tailor. "What did you think would happen now you've returned from Talcotts? Even if your father had lived, he would have needed to arrange your betrothal."

"Yes, but not in such haste." Audrey waved her hand at the tailor. "A beaded stomacher sounds ideal."

The man's face brightened as he moved closer with a flourish of his hands. "And the same beading for the neckline, leading to cap sleeves." He held up a sleeve of ivory linen and lace that he'd shown her an hour ago. "And beneath the caps, virago sleeves festooned with ivory ribbon."

"Red ribbon, please." Audrey grinned.

"Indeed, I think red would be lovely as well."

Mrs. Hobbs drew her hand to her forehead. "Oh my heavens. His Lordship tasked me with planning your gown, and you're intending to show up looking like a bloodred rose."

"She will be stunning," said Mr. Hatfield, his remark met with a sharp snort from the housemaid.

Audrey reached for the red taffeta and rubbed the cloth between her fingers. "I agree with the tailor. Besides, why on earth are you acting like the Earl of Seaforth is lord of this manor? When he returns to Scotland, there will be naught but me."

The woman's finger shot up. "And your husband."

Audrey bit her tongue. She was not about to agree to a swift marriage. The solicitor and Reid MacKenzie could take their scheming and stuff it in their enamel-coated snuffboxes. She didn't need a husband. The estate was thriving—even without the coin she brought in with her fan painting. Why could she not run things?

Because I am a woman?

Well, if that's what they believe, 'tis time I showed them differently.

After hours of being pinned, poked, and prodded for a gown that had to be finished in a fortnight, Audrey headed for the stables. The afternoon was fine for a change, and she needed to fill her lungs with fresh air, and moreover seek silence from Mrs. Hobbs's grumbling.

It took no time for Jeffrey to saddle Allegro, and Audrey's heart swelled when the stable hand led the high-stepping trotter down the aisle. Oh, how she loved her old gelding. She smoothed her hand down his blaze. "I've missed you in the past sennight."

The horse snorted as if telling her he missed her, too. Allegro had been a gift from her father for her tenth birthday. At the time he'd been a spirited six-year-old pony. He might be a tad long in the tooth now, but they'd grown up together and she loved him. Being an only child and living in the country could be lonely, and often Allegro

was on the receiving end of whatever worries happened to
be on her mind. Together they'd enjoyed years of riding
lessons and walks through the estate. Now at the age of
fifteen, he had a bit of gray intermixed with the sorrel on
his muzzle. But this fellow still had plenty of spirit left.

A cool breeze fanned her face, and the frustration of
the day was whisked away and replaced with Allegro's
smooth gait. Audrey breathed deeply and pointed the
gelding toward the far paddocks. There she could ride for
miles and stay on the Kennet estates.

So many warring thoughts filled her mind, the most
confounding being Lord Reid MacKenzie, the Earl of
Seaforth. True, her father had trusted the man. And he
seemed to be acting honorably, at least on some accounts.
He'd paid for Papa's burial and he'd agreed to stay on at
Coxhoe House until she was settled. At least that's how it
seemed, though he was in such a hurry to return to Scotland. How could the solicitor's affairs be sewn up within
a month or two? Would the earl be forced to return again
after he took his leave?

*He most likely is trying to do everything in his power
to see there is no need for him to return.*

And, of course, that led to his ridiculous notion that the
solution to all her problems was to marry with haste. The
mere thought soured her stomach. Obviously he didn't
realize she was the shyest person who'd ever graduated
from Talcotts. There was no way on earth Audrey could
meet someone—a man of all people—and charm him in
a fortnight or less. She needed first to find a good match
with whom she was compatible, and then she intended to
be courted for a very long time, followed by a lengthy
engagement. The whole concept of marriage was mortifying, and Audrey wasn't like Miss Prudence at Talcotts,

who had known whom she was to marry since the age of two and had been looking forward to her wedding day. For pity's sake, it was always a relief to spirit away from Prudence for the summer recess so Audrey didn't have to listen to the girl carry on about her Lord Wexford.

And then there had to be the convenience of Baron Barnard's ball. Why couldn't His Lordship have scheduled his ball for last month? Then it would be over. But no. The accursed Reid MacKenzie sends a single missive and receives a swift reply that the baron and baroness just happen to be having a ball at Raby Castle in a fortnight and they would be honored to have Lord Seaforth and Miss Kennet attend as their esteemed guests.

Esteemed? Clumsy is more apt.

I told His Lordship I abhor balls and he completely ignored me. He's insufferable!

How much more did she need to disclose of her utter ineptitude? Dancing lessons at Talcotts had been a disaster. The dance instructor told her she'd fare better if she found a settee and sat against the wall. If the dance dictated she turn right, she invariably turned left and smacked into the poor girl beside her. She'd earned more bruises from falling in dance class than on the back of Allegro. Truly. Worse, once the dance master discovered she could play the harpsichord, he suggested she join the orchestra and stay as far away from the dance floor as possible.

And he'd been right.

Papa had taken her to a royal ball in London two years past. Queen Anne had been in attendance, no less. Throughout the duration of the debacle, Audrey had been mortified. She'd tripped over her own feet and stumbled across the aisle straight into lord someone-or-another, whose name she'd conveniently forgotten. Mortified, she ran to the drawing room and plopped into a chair, where she remained until it was time to go home.

Audrey cued Allegro for a canter.

And now I'll be attending a grand ball at Raby Castle dressed like an overripe tomato.

She had to laugh at the irony. Regardless of how she was dressed, she would embarrass herself the first time some gallant gentleman asked her to dance. At least now, the Earl of Seaforth could share in a bit of discomfort escorting a vixen in red on his elbow. Gracious, Audrey had never done anything so scandalous in her life.

Perhaps Father's passing had certainly brought out her disagreeable side. Perhaps the red gown was her way of showing she was in no way, shape, or form ready to marry anyone.

She tapped her riding cane on Allegro's barrel. "Come, lad. Let us jump the hedge."

The privet had grown a few inches since last summer, though they'd cleared it with ease then. Leaning forward in the saddle, Audrey gathered the reins and steadied her bottom leg tight to the lower pommel. How wonderful it felt to have the wind at her face with the heightened anticipation of an approaching jump. Her heart soared as Allegro's front hooves tucked up while he flew over the hedge. It was a perfect setup and a perfect launch. If only someone were there to see. At least she wasn't clumsy when riding.

Allegro landed on the other side with a sudden jolt. Audrey clenched her legs tightly, reaching down to his withers for a bit of mane to stop herself from falling. Allegro faltered. Concerned, she pulled him to a stop. "Are you well, old chap?" She leaned over to look at his pasterns, but could see absolutely nothing for the volume of her skirts. "How about testing with a few steps?"

But when the horse tried to walk, he faltered again. She glanced back over her shoulder. The stable was already miles away. She'd been so consumed by her own thoughts, she hadn't worried about how far they'd gone.

"Curses, there's naught else to do but to walk." And she'd need to walk around the hedge, too.

After she dismounted, Allegro nudged her with his nose. She gave him a pat and examined his legs. Nothing seemed swollen. "Where are you sore?" She led him forward a few steps.

The horse definitely favored his right front. Smoothing her hand down his left leg, she tapped his fetlock and encouraged him to raise his hoof.

"Oh dear, Allegro, you've torn your frog, and 'tis bruised as well. I imagine that doesn't feel good in the slightest." She dropped his hoof and straightened, moving her hands to her hips. "There's nothing to mend such an injury except Father Time, and one of Jeffrey's poultices."

Allegro groaned. Yes, he knew it, too. And it was going to be a long walk back to the stables.

"Audrey?"

Though she recognized the voice, she nearly jumped out of her skin. "My lord," she said, her voice almost shrieking. She cleared her throat to calm herself. "Whatever are you doing out here?"

He reined his mount to a stop beside her, his dark eyebrows drawing together. "I was about to ask you the same. Are you all right, lass?"

"I'm fine." She gestured to her horse. "Allegro has torn his frog."

"Then 'tis a good thing I ventured past." He dismounted and swept his gaze from head to toe. Once again, he regarded her with a hawk-eyed stare that bordered on dangerous. Must he always look so menacing, glaring from beneath his thick tawny locks? It didn't help matters that he towered over her like a muscle-bound warrior. Truly, there was no need for an earl to be so powerful, was there? "Do you always venture this far from the manse alone?" he asked.

"At times." In fact, she rarely ever rode this far by herself. Papa always used to accompany her on long rides.

"Well, I'd prefer it if you would take one of my guards in the future—or the stable hand. It is never a good idea to ride without an escort."

She glanced over her shoulder, then feigned a guffaw. "But you are alone."

"Aye, though I am a man." He gestured to the dirk on one side of his sporran and pistol on the other. "And a well-armed man at that."

She heaved a sigh. "I suppose that makes all the difference."

"It does. What if someone, an outlaw, set upon you? How would you fend off an attack?"

"I would gallop back to Coxhoe House faster than you can blink." And next time she ventured out, she'd bring a musket.

"On a lame horse?"

She looked to the sky and groaned. Must guardians be so unbearably insufferable? "I wasn't expecting my horse to go lame, my lord."

He offered his hand. "Come now, we can ride back together. We'll lead your horse along slowly. The best place for him is in his stall."

Agreeing, she allowed him to give her a leg up. In

truth, it was a relief the earl ventured past when he did. Until he slid into the saddle behind her. Suddenly, Audrey couldn't breathe. Brawny arms reached around her and he took up the reins. His fingers were long and rugged with small scars, as if he'd met with many nicks in all the sparring he did. His scent washed over her as if they were riding through a paddock of sultry spice.

"I meant what I said back there." Lord Seaforth's voice rumbled through her insides like a lazy roll of thunder. Good heavens, it even sounded deeper. "You mustn't ride unescorted."

Audrey wanted to oppose him, but her actions had been a bit impulsive. Had Papa been there, she wouldn't have taken such a risk. Since the earl had arrived, she'd surprised herself by being quite bold. Bolder than ever before. She ought to be mortified with herself, but honestly, her tad of brazenness made her feel empowered.

"Agreed?" he pushed.

"Yes." The word came out breathless as she closed her eyes and leaned into his wall of a chest. By the saints, what woman wouldn't agree with such a man when he had his arms around her waist, power radiating off his chest like he was lord high protector of all of Britain. She allowed herself a moment to ponder what it would be like to marry someone like Reid MacKenzie—someone who would protect her, stand up for her. No, it hadn't slipped her notice that he'd placed some confidence in her abilities when the solicitor visited. Heavens, if it weren't for the earl, her lands would be in abeyance at the moment.

He took in a deep breath, which made his chest press into her back a bit more. And then when he let it out, warm air slipped past her ear. Audrey watched his fingers work the reins, holding them in an easy grip as if he'd been riding all his life.

Most likely, he has been.

She released a long breath at the thought and relaxed against him. She'd never admit it, but she rather enjoyed the way he made her feel. Her skin tingled as she rode safely protected between his brawny arms.

In truth, Audrey ought not to be enjoying herself so much. She knew very little of the earl, aside from the fact that he was a Jacobite and lived somewhere in Scotland…and he'd been orphaned as a teen. She hadn't seen his man MacRae for days, either. What other business did the earl have that necessitated the urgency for him to return to the north?

She grazed her teeth over her bottom lip and glanced up to his face—handsome as the devil. "Where has the MacRae chieftain gone off to?"

"Dunn has taken missives to my colleagues in the north."

"About your visit with James?"

The man chuckled—a laugh that rumbled all the way through Audrey's insides and made her heart hammer. "Your father told you about that, did he?"

"In a roundabout way, yes." Papa's business was now her business. "He said the taxes levied from the wars were bleeding him dry."

"Him and near everyone else."

"Ah…how did your meeting go with the prince?"

"Nowhere near as favorably as I would have hoped."

She tsked her tongue. "I would think James would be anxious to come home—to claim his rightful line to the throne."

"'Tis quite dangerous to speak of such things."

"But you set out on a perilous mission—and with my father. Why should I not discuss them with you?"

"Because it is far safer to remain ignorant."

"So why did the Jacobites prevail upon you and my father to appeal to the prince?"

"We volunteered. Though 'tis not wise to utter the word 'Jacobite.' Not ever. Not even out here in the paddock."

"But you uttered it."

"Many times. But only in the right company. Otherwise we call our quest *the cause*."

"So tell me, my lord, do men fear you?"

"Some do." His voice grew deeper. "If they're wise."

"Goodness, you do sound quite dangerous."

"Believe me, lass. I *am* dangerous."

Chapter Eight

*G*od's teeth, Reid meant every word of his warning to Audrey not to ride out alone. A weaker man than he would have raised her skirts and slid into her right there on the back of the horse. Use a bit of that rocking motion to bury himself deep inside the lass.

He might have tried it, if he hadn't taken an oath to protect Nicholas Kennet's daughter. But now he could only grind his back molars while the horse ambled toward the stables as Miss Audrey's thigh rubbed into his cock with every step. He enjoyed the sensation and hated it all at once. Jesu, merely the lavender fragrance of the silken tresses teasing his nose was enough to send him undone. Wisps had escaped her chignon and lightly brushed his cheeks.

With his next inhale, he nearly moaned aloud. Next time he came upon Miss Audrey with a lame horse, he'd opt to walk. What was he thinking, mounting behind his bonny, fully grown female ward? His bloody mind had run amok because this business with Prince James had kept him from bedding a woman for months.

Damn it all, must those breasts tempt him like no tomorrow? Miss Audrey could pass for a princess with her long, slender neck, supporting a lovely, heart-shaped face with eyes that could seduce any man's soul.

He released a breath that skimmed down the arc of that ivory neck. Gooseflesh instantly pebbled on her skin as she drew in a subtle gasp.

Reid grinned when she didn't turn his way. The lass had strength of character he hadn't seen in many other women. Aye, since the age of sixteen, he'd grown accustomed to turning the female head. In fact, of all the women he'd fancied over the years, not one would have ignored such a flirtatious gesture. Though Audrey kept her gaze turned toward the path ahead.

Thank heavens the lass had no idea of the effect she had on him. He was her guardian, for Christ's sake. He had no right to ogle the lass, and that definitely included fixating on her breasts. She was in mourning…and undertaking foolish actions like riding without an escort. Reid knew Nicholas Kennet well enough to realize the man would not have approved of his daughter riding off alone. She was taking liberties. But why? To prove her independence?

Audrey shifted and turned toward him. Dear God, she was bonny, and when her gaze met his, an improper stirring swirled low in his loins. "How did you happen past me at that very moment?"

Ah, yes, the reason he was in this predicament in the first place. "I was returning from a visit to the mine. Met with Mr. Poole."

"Oh." A hint of disappointment resounded in her voice. "I would have liked to meet with him as well."

"'Tis a good idea, though I wanted to have a word first—let him know you are in charge with my backing— you ken, ensure there's no attempt at swindling."

She bit her lip and nodded, the sun making her eyes sparkle. "Thank you—especially for believing in me."

His heart fluttered, the damned thing. "We'll need to sit down and go over the books of accounts. I'll say your father established a thriving and healthy business. And Mr. Poole is eager to continue."

"Papa was very proud."

"The overseer, however, told me the men haven't had a pay increase in two years."

"Oh?"

"Indeed, Mr. Poole said it would raise their spirits a great deal if we would give them another shilling per week."

She blinked, a furrow forming between her delicate eyebrows—a bit darker than the burnt honey of her tresses. "But the miners are already taking home ten shillings."

"True, though the going rate for coal miners' pay is ten to fifteen shillings per sennight. Your men are at the low end. According to Mr. Poole, if they wanted to, they could move to Yorkshire and earn at least an additional two shillings."

"And you've verified the profits can absorb this?"

He arched his brow. Most women would have deferred to his better judgment, but Audrey asked a very logical question. "Indeed I did. In fact, the profits are quite bountiful. You could double the pay increase without feeling undue hardship to the estate's income."

"Though such a raise would be unheard of. You're already suggesting upping their wages by ten percent—twenty would leave little room for increases in the future."

Reid was doubly impressed with her figures. Though a simple calculation, how many heiresses understood fractions and statistics? But it mightn't be wise to show over-awe. "My sentiments as well."

Audrey had a great deal to learn in a very short time, and moreover, he needed her to fall in love with a suitor at the damned ball. If she believed herself to be too competent and smart, she just might make his job more difficult if not impossible.

Chapter Nine

The eve of the ball at Raby Castle came all too soon. Ida, the chambermaid appointed to help Audrey dress, stood back and admired her handiwork. "You will be the most beautiful woman at the ball, miss. I am certain of it."

The best thing about living twenty miles from Staindrop and being an esteemed guest meant that Miss Kennet and the Earl of Seaforth arrived early and were given lavish accommodations and servants to help them prepare for the grand ball. Besides, the earl outranked the baron, and was treated accordingly.

Audrey stood in the midst of a chamber trimmed with rose silk. The furnishings and wainscoting were hewn of mahogany wood that contrasted with the white marble hearth. However, when she gazed at her reflection in the looking glass, she was nowhere as convinced about her appearance as Ida. The scarlet gown was a work of art—something she might see worn by a countess in a portrait. It most certainly wasn't anything a demure, shy wallflower like Audrey Kennet would ever allow herself to be seen wearing. She tugged up the bodice in an attempt to cover her exposed bosoms, but the mounds of flesh only swelled higher, making panic shoot through her veins. Dear heavens, if the neckline were any lower, she'd be able to see the tips of her breasts.

Help. This gown is absolutely the worst idea I've ever had in my life.

"Is there something amiss?" Ida stepped beside her. "Did I lace you in too tightly? Are the sleeves secure enough?"

Audrey frowned. Everything was perfect, from the billowing taffeta to the ornate stomacher in white pearled beads, swirling in a paisley pattern. The sleeves were her favorite part of the gown, lacy, cinched with red ribbon in three puffs descending down her arm. Mr. Hatfield had truly outdone himself.

"Please, I can fix anything," said the chambermaid.

Audrey took in a deep breath—or she tried. Indeed, she'd been laced too tightly to allow for deep breathing— but past experience always proved that the laces would ease as the night wore on. "Your work has been splendid." Audrey again cringed at her reflection. "I'm just afraid red doesn't suit me after all."

"I must disagree with you there, miss. That red makes you look ravishing."

She flipped open the ivory lace fan she'd painted with red roses for this occasion and cooled her face. "That is what I'm afraid of."

The chambermaid sighed, grinning as if she harbored not an iota of trepidation. "It must be splendid to attend a real ball. To wear a gown like that. Why, I'd reckon your frock would cost an entire year's wages."

Audrey shifted her attention from her overexposed cleavage to Ida. "'Tis odd, is it not? I'd like it ever so much if I never had to don another ball gown again."

"'Twould be a folly, miss. For you look ever so lovely. Every man will want to have a dance with you this eve."

Audrey gulped. "Unfortunately, I'm not much for dancing, either."

"An heiress who does not dance? I've never heard of such a thing. Did you not have lessons?"

She gave the maid a humored look. "I did, and the dance master told me I'd be better off in the orchestra."

"What an awful thing to say."

Snapping her fan closed, Audrey shook it toward the mirror. "It was truthful. I'm clumsy."

"Well, mayhap so many guests will arrive, your duties in the welcoming party will keep you engaged."

Audrey again regarded her bosoms. Then she critically spied her reflection as she curtsied, managing to keep her nipples hidden.

I'd best keep my back ramrod straight else I could be on display for the entire hall.

"Miss Audrey?" The Earl of Seaforth's voice rumbled through the timbers while a rap came at the door. "Are you nearly ready? The baron has requested our presence in the receiving line."

Ida patted Audrey's hand. "You'll have a grand time, I am certain of it." She hastened across the room and opened the door, dipping into a deep curtsy—one befitting an earl, and a courtesy Audrey hadn't observed since the Highlander first darkened the halls of Coxhoe House.

She clasped her fan between her hands and tried to swallow against the thickening in her throat.

Reid MacKenzie stood in the doorway like he was king

of Scotland. The man didn't wear a periwig. He didn't need such an embellishment. No one would ever want to cover up such thick, tawny waves. Though he oft wore his hair tied back with a ribbon, this eve it framed his face, hanging well below his shoulders. The style accented the striking masculinity of his features. Bold dark eyebrows slanted over intense eyes, piercing like a bird of prey. He wore a fine tartan woven with dark blue and hunter green, crisscrossed with red and white. From beneath the hem of his green velvet doublet, the plaid draped around his back and over his shoulder, secured with an enormous brooch. With an aura of power in his commanding presence, he stepped into the chamber, his eyes growing darker—like the coal in her father's mine.

"Och," he said, his mouth parted, his gaze sliding down to the exposed flesh above her bodice.

Never in all her days had any man stared at her with such raw fervor in his eyes. Was he angry that she'd worn red? Audrey's heart sank. Mrs. Hobbs had been right.

The neckline is far too revealing. I knew it.

A fire spread through her cheeks. The evening hadn't begun and it was already a disaster. "Perhaps I should don my day dress, my lord?"

"Huh?" he uttered with non-earl-like composure—though he looked more like an earl this evening than he ever had at Coxhoe House.

She snapped open her fan and jammed it atop her cleavage. "Forgive me, but I didn't try on my gown before we arrived. I fear it is too *revealing.*"

"I think 'tis stunning," said Ida in her colloquial, north-ern England brogue.

Seaforth's Adam's apple bobbed as he shifted his gaze to the maid. "That's one way of putting it." White teeth skimmed his bottom lip. "Though I would have used the word 'exquisite.' 'Dazzling,' perchance."

Audrey wanted to slip into the garderobe and lock herself inside. "'Tis not too audacious?" she asked.

The corner of the earl's mouth turned up while his eyes grew darker. "'Tis a ball, lass. Though Mrs. Hobbs should have warned me. I'll be forced to keep one hand on the hilt of my dirk throughout the night." He offered his elbow, his gaze slipping to her cleavage. "Shall we?"

With a long exhale, she joined him as together they made their way to the gallery. "Are the pair of you conspiring against me now? What did you mean, Mrs. Hobbs should have warned you?"

He gave her a sideways glance while his tongue slipped out the corner of his mouth. A rather devilish expression to say the least. "Och, 'tis simply I'm surprised with your selection of color and design. No man within viewing distance will be able to keep his eyes off you."

If she weren't laced so tightly, her shoulders would have slumped. "To my dismay."

"Come now, doesn't every lass want to find a husband?"

"I suppose most do."

He pulled a small flask from his sporran. "My mother oft said there was nothing like a tot of whisky to steel her nerves." He held it out to her. "Just a wee tot, now."

She thrust up her palm. "Absolutely not. The nuns at Talcotts said drink leads to man's ruination and must never pass a lady's lips. "

"Are you insinuating that my mother, the Countess of Seaforth, was not a lady?"

"I—"

He chuckled. "I think your finishing school may have been a bit starchy with some of their guidance. Speaking out against Scots, telling a lass she shouldn't dance, and now bemoaning the medicinal value of fine whisky? I'm not suggesting you chug the flask, but I swear on my mother's grave the countess firmly believed a wee nip emboldens ones nerves."

Audrey looked to the flask. Mayhap she needed something to ease the jitters flitting about her insides. "If your mother recommended it, perhaps a tiny sip would be permissible."

"Only if you believe the nuns at your finishing school won't discover your misbehavior and race up here to give you a good rap on your knuckles."

Audrey had to smile at the thought. In fact, it made her want to take a healthy swig as she'd seen Papa do from time to time. But decorum won out and she took a small drink. The liquid burned a stream of fire all the way down her throat. She coughed and patted her chest while her eyes burned. "Heavens."

"There's a good lass." Reid took the flask and tilted it up. Wiping his mouth with the back of his hand, he grinned. "Nothing better than pure Highland spirit."

"It burns."

"Only with the first sip." He returned the whisky to his sporran. "How do you feel?"

She squared her shoulders. Honestly, she was slightly light-headed. "I'm fine. No different."

"Hmm... if you'd like more..."

"No, thank you."

He offered his elbow. "Shall we continue?"

"If we must, my lord. And throughout the eve you can find me holding up the most obscure wall in the hall."

"Och, you're carrying on as if your lessons at Talcotts had been a total waste of effort."

"Some girls are not as graceful as others. I, indeed, am quite adept at stumbling." They ambled along the passageway toward a winding stairwell. "Do you think the orchestra might need a harpsichordist?"

"Nay." He gestured for her to enter first. "You'll be fine. It would be my honor to dance your first set. If that would help to calm your trepidation."

"It wouldn't at all." She took up her skirts and strode past him. "That's what my father said right before I collided with Lady Saxonhurst at Whitehall."

"You bumped into Saxonhurst?" Seaforth chuckled. "I would have given a crown just to have seen the look on that scheming woman's face."

"You know the lady?"

"Not a soul hath been to court without the displeasure of her acquaintance."

"Did she act against you?"

"Not me, but her false accusations nearly sent Lady Magdalen Keith to the gallows."

Audrey pursed her lips, trying to place the name while the back of her neck burned. The earl hadn't mentioned any women in their discussions. Was he courting someone? "Is this lady a friend of yours?"

"Aye, she married the Marquis of Tullibardine not but six months past."

Audrey had no idea why, but this news served to put her at ease—until she stepped from the stairwell into the enormous hall. Though she'd passed through earlier when they'd been ushered to their rooms, servants had been scaling ladders to dust sconces, and the chandeliers had been lowered for cleaning and candle replacement. Now, everything looked like a fairy tale. Brilliance glowed with gilded opulence from the stormy scene painted on the ceiling to the wall reliefs depicting vases overflowing with golden flowers and fruit. Up top on the gallery, the orchestra was seated and tuning their instruments.

Oh, how Audrey would prefer to be among the musicians—a very scandalous thought, indeed. In truth, ladies didn't join orchestras. They gave recitals to small, private parties.

Fortunately, padded chairs lined the walls. She spied one in the far corner that would suit. If only she could attach a sign to it that read "Reserved for the Clumsiest Tomato in the Hall."

They joined Lady and Lord Barnard in the entry hall. The couple looked every bit the part of regal country nobles, he in a suit of ivory silk and Her Ladyship wearing a gown to match.

When introduced, Audrey dipped in a curtsy. "Thank you ever so much for inviting us. Everything is opulent."

"Does your chamber meet with your approval?" asked the baroness, her gaze coolly raking down Audrey's gown.

"Lovely, thank you. And Miss Ida saw to my every need."

"Splendid." Her ladyship turned her attention to Seaforth. "She is as delightful as your missive suggested."

It took every ounce of resistance Audrey could muster not to flip open her fan and hide her face behind it. Merely the mention of correspondence regarding Audrey's lack of prospects set her blood to boiling. She hated to be on display, and in such a public spectacle. But since the Earl of Seaforth was the highest-ranking peer in attendance, his presence was required in the receiving line, and because of his acquaintance with Audrey, hers as well.

Almost as soon as they took their places, guests began to arrive.

The master of ceremonies boomed forth the introductions before the couples and single men would proceed down the line with smiling faces as they spewed greetings that sounded about as sincere as the yowl of a tomcat.

Every person who passed Audrey complimented her gown, though she doubted any of the men actually were looking at the fine craftsmanship of her stomacher and sleeves. Not one of them met her gaze, either, which did very little to put her at ease. If she was expected to find a courtier who would sweep her off her feet this eve, he certainly hadn't made an appearance by the time the dancing began.

Seaforth, however, appeared undaunted.

As he promised, he escorted her to the dance floor.

"We could sit out the first set," Audrey suggested. "Give the guests a chance to settle in."

"I think not." He shifted his gaze downward and inclined his lips toward her ear. "You really ought to try to have some fun. I can feel the unease radiating off you like an aura of foreboding. Rather than an exquisite rose, you are acting like a nervous hen."

She gave him a sideways glance. Nothing like having her guardian tell her she came across as anxious as she felt. In the past hour, she'd done nothing but try to look pleasant and accommodating, regardless of the fact she wanted to run to the stables and hide in a horse stall.

"Oh, thank you for such words of encouragement," she said. "It makes me feel so much better." She took the deepest breath she could and lifted her chin. "Genteel, graceful, unassuming."

"I beg your pardon?"

"I'm reciting Talcotts motto. Every maiden must endeavor to be genteel, graceful, and unassuming, especially when in public."

He pulled her into position for a minuet, but squeezed her hands before he released his grip. "The graceful part is all well and good, but you are the brightest rose in all of England. Do. Not. Ever. Let yourself doubt it."

She blinked, wicked thoughts playing on the tip of her tongue.

The wilting rose? Dying rose? Seaforth hasn't seen me dance.

Perspiration beaded her brow as the orchestra played the introduction. Her stomach rolled over.

Reid offered his hand, leading to the first step. Her fingers trembled as she took it. Rather than allow her to simply place her palm atop his, he gripped her hand in his powerful fingers. Inhaling, Audrey stepped with him and executed the serpentine pattern flawlessly. Encouraged, she followed the earl's lead and continued with the dance she'd practiced hundreds of times during her years at Talcotts.

Oddly, Seaforth had a knack for easing her trepidation.

By the end of the dance, she'd only stumbled twice, and she prayed no one noticed. Fortunately, her feet were completely hidden by the volume of red skirts.

The only problem?

As soon as the music ended, a gentleman tapped her shoulder. "May I have the honor of the next set, Miss Kennet?"

She shot a panicked look to Seaforth, but he provided not a lick of help. The rotter grinned and bowed. "It has been my pleasure, miss." Of course he was all too happy to leave her alone with a smelly middle-aged man wear-

ing a gold silk waistcoat and breeches that appeared to be
two sizes too small.

And there came the end of Audrey's newfound grace.
As soon as Seaforth left her alone, her clumsiness miraculously returned.

The evening proceeded in a jumble of missteps and unpleasant dancing partners, most of whom had used far too
much eau de toilette for Audrey's taste. She stumbled her
way through dance after dance, enduring the licentious
gazes from men twice her age. The few younger suitors
who danced with her could not hold a candle to the earl—
they were either too thin or had gargantuan noses, or were
balding. One was even shorter than Audrey, and they all
stank.

She shot a forlorn look to the dais to Seaforth, but he
was too engrossed in conversation with Lord Barnard to
notice. Doubtless, he'd completely forgotten about her,
leaving her to the wolves. Praying for a reprieve, she
started for the corner chair she'd pegged on her arrival,
when someone cleared his throat behind her. "I beg your
pardon, miss, but would you do me the honor of the next
dance?"

Audrey tried not to cringe as she turned around. If only
it were polite for her to refuse. But if she'd learned anything at Talcotts, it was that ladies must always graciously
accept invitations to dance...unless there was a matron
on hand who could make appropriate apologies. Worse,
this man looked the most disagreeable of them all. His
face was pinched in the most unpleasant stare, and his
gray eyes were taunting beneath a straight line of eyebrows. He wore a thin mustache and goatee. His mouth
twitched in a sneer, almost as if he were willing her to
err in some way. With no wig, he tied his thinning brown

locks back with a ribbon. He bowed politely, however. "I am at your service, Miss Kennet."

She took a step back and narrowed her eyes. "Have we met, sir?" She couldn't recall his being introduced earlier that eve, but something about him was familiar all the same.

He sniffed, leering like he harbored a secret. "Perhaps you will recall during the contredanse." He gestured to the floor and smiled.

The musical introduction had begun and everyone turned to stare. With no other choice, she gave a single nod and allowed the strange man to lead her to the line. Beneath her fingers, his hand felt like the skin of an eel. Racking her mind, she tried to remember. Had he been one of Papa's colleagues? Had he worked at the mine? His suit of clothes showed wear—clearly this man wasn't wealthy. Regardless, she needed to fulfill her promise and see the dance through to the end.

Fortunately, there was a great deal of interchanging with other partners during a contredanse, and Audrey was spared the man's penetrating glare for the most part.

When the dance ended, the conductor announced a brief recess. Relieved, Audrey curtsied. "Thank you, sir."

He gave a hasty bow, then stepped in and grasped her elbow. "Come. I need a moment."

"This is highly improper," she hissed as he pulled her toward the inner courtyard door, his fingers boring into her elbow like iron tongs. She absolutely could not exit the gallery with someone she didn't know, let alone trust.

Just before they reached the doors, Audrey managed to yank her elbow free. "You, sir, are uncouth and insolent, and I shall thank you for remembering your manners and keeping your hands from my person."

Turning, she started to hasten away, but he grabbed her arm yet again and pulled her into an alcove, out of sight of the others. "I only need a moment." He cackled wickedly. "Do you not know my face?"

A brown hood came to mind. One framing gaunt features. "The monk?"

He snorted. "You would remember only that. I have known you all my life. I have watched you from afar—on those shoreline walks you used to take with your father—at the summer fetes when you were eating honeyed crisps."

Audrey's heart raced. She tried to tug away, but his grip only became stronger. "Let me go!"

"I've always wanted what you have. It should be mine. You should be mine."

Audrey glanced over her shoulder. Where was her hulking guardian when she needed him?

As the man pulled her against his revolting body, he twisted her arm up her spine until she could hardly bear the pain. "If you speak out against me, your earl will meet a gruesome end. If you refuse me, I will shut you out with nothing, just as your father did to my mother."

She winced at the pain of her arm on the verge of being dislodged. "Who are you?"

"Never mind that." His unpleasant breath steamed across her face. "You *will* be hearing from me, and you *will* bend to my bidding. Make no bones about it. I am a man of my word. If you utter a single hint of our encounter to the Earl of Seaforth, he will meet an unfortunate end just like your father."

Ice pulsed through Audrey's veins. "You are responsible for the death of my father?"

"I informed the captain of the *Royal Buckingham* of

your father's treachery and alliance with Seaforth." A sickly grin spread across the man's lips as he released her with a shove. "Only Nicholas Kennet was responsible for the accident that claimed his life. And only *you* can keep more men from dying." He headed for the door.

Audrey straightened and clenched her fists in front of her chest. "I demand to know your name, sir!"

Pushing through the door, he glanced over his shoulder. "Wagner Tupps. When next we meet I'll expect you to remember it."

Chapter Ten

*R*eid continued to shift his gaze across the gallery while Lord Barnard droned on about every political issue affecting the kingdom. Unfortunately, the man spoke like a Whig puppet. Reid's opinions on every matter were quite different from the baron's, though voicing such would only create discord with his host. Presently, he needed all the help he could garner, and that meant enduring long-winded and one-sided dialogue about Britain's state of affairs.

This untimely and inconvenient role of guardian had him on edge. How the devil was he supposed to remain impartial while Audrey Kennet paraded around the dance floor with every slavering, bombastic Englishman within fifty miles of Raby Castle? God's bones, he'd come close to spitting out all his teeth when he first saw the lass wearing that red gown.

Why couldn't she be wearing pink or blue or white? He'd trusted Mrs. Hobbs to select something appropriate, not a frock that screamed, *Here I am, come and plunder me.* Christ, Reid was but a man. He wasn't a marble statue without blood thrumming through his veins. And, by God, that gown made things thrum in more places than his veins.

The next time Reid scanned the dance floor for Audrey, some spindly-whiskered ferret was practically drooling on the lass. The earl cracked his thumb knuckles while images of all the ways he could make the weasel beg for mercy riddled his mind. There wasn't a single man in the entire hall good enough for Miss Audrey, and the man who presently pointed his toes in the contredanse had to be the worst candidate for a husband he'd seen yet.

So help me, if that bastard lays one single inappropriate finger on Miss Audrey, I'll wring his scrawny neck.

"Why is it I sense you are on edge?" asked the baron.

Reid shifted his gaze back to his host. "Pardon?"

"You're wound tighter than the coil of chain holding up my portcullis."

Groaning, Reid feigned a smile. "'Tis not easy being the guardian of an heiress."

"I should say not, though a girl as lovely as Miss Kennet should have no difficulty finding a suitable match— and a wealthy one at that."

Reid clenched his fists. If one more person said anything about marrying Audrey to the highest bidder, he'd bury his fist in the braggart's snout.

"She has turned every suitor's head, just as you'd hoped," said Lady Barnard from her perch. "You simply must give me the name of her tailor."

Reid regarded Her Ladyship and splayed his fingers. Perhaps he was growing a bit overzealous. Besides, it would be very unpopular if he buried his fist in Her

Ladyship's nose. He almost laughed at himself until he realized the music had ended. Fully expecting to see Audrey walking toward them, his heart nearly stopped when she was nowhere to be seen. Nor was the vulture she'd been dancing with.

Standing, he dipped into a hasty bow. "If you'll please excuse me, I have a matter to attend." Putting on an air of calm reserve, Reid made his way along the gallery wall, looking into every nook along the way, while praying Audrey hadn't been so dimwitted as to take a stroll outside with a man who looked about as trustworthy as a snake.

Before he made it to the French doors, a bit of shiny red caught his eye. He crossed the floor and found her in an ingress, hiding her face in her hands, standing alone, thank God.

He strode toward her with purpose, making damned sure he looked like a concerned guardian. "What the devil happened?"

She peeked at him through splayed fingers. "Ah..."

"Is all well?" He stepped nearer, and a bit of light flashed on the moisture beneath her eyes. His gut roiled. *I'll choke the life out of that damned weasel.* "Have you been crying?"

"No," she squeaked.

"Has someone said something inappropriate to you?"

Shaking her head, she again hid her face in her palms. "I-I cannot speak of it."

Glancing over his shoulder to confirm no one was gawking, he quickly opened the door and led her into a small octagon-shaped chamber where china plates were on display behind glass. An oil-burning sconce on the wall had been lit, and there was enough light to see. Stopping in the center of the room, he grasped her shoulders.

"Please, tell me why you're crying, because if anyone has dared to touch you or hurt your feelings, I'd like nothing better than to call him out for a duel of swords."

She took in a deep breath as if suppressing her emotions. "'Tis nothing. I am simply ready to retire."

Oh no, Reid wasn't about to let this pass and give their excuses, especially not when they were the guests of honor. "It would be rude to our hosts to make our apologies this early in the evening."

"Please do not make me go out there again. 'Tis far too…too mortifying."

"Whatever has come over you? You are the bonniest lass of all. Every courtier for miles has been lining up to dance with you." And not a one had been suitable. In fact, Reid would relish a good row with one of the Sassenach fops.

With a groan, Audrey turned her back. "Everyone but you. You only danced with me because you felt it was your duty."

Reid's stomach flipped backward, then forward again. He reached out his hand, but stopped it in midair. If only he could run his fingers along the soft, exposed curve from the neck to her shoulder. If only he could step into her and brush his lips over her succulent skin. But he clenched his teeth until his jaw twitched. Och aye, he'd noticed how bonny Audrey was, he'd noticed it all too well. He wasn't even supposed to be in England at the moment. But there he stood, trying to make good on a promise to a dying man—a man whose blood stained Reid's fingers.

Searching for the right words and coming up with nothing, he finally whispered, "Pardon?"

Her breath stuttered with her next inhale. "Call me a

featherbrained wren, but I've compared every man at the ball to you, my lord, and not a one measures up." She whipped around. "How dare you do that to me?"

Something inside his heart snapped and soared while Reid fought against his urge to smile. No matter that he was unable to court the lass himself, it always stroked a man's ego to have a lassie admit her attraction—though she had a confounding way of going about it. "I..."

With a wail, she flung her arms around him, most likely as she would have done if her father were standing there instead of Reid. "I've been trying to be strong. I've been trying suffocate the grief in my heart, but this whole sham is *killing* me. It's too soon. I've lost my father and now everyone's trying to force me into a hasty marriage, and I'm just not ready."

"There, there, lass." Against his better judgment, he smoothed his hands up and down her spine. Dear Lord, she was trembling, but now everything made more sense. In truth, Reid might have taken up arms if someone had forced him into marriage right after his father had died. He could be an unfeeling buffoon. Audrey buried her face in his chest.

Closing his eyes, he embraced her, ruing the day his father had made that damned pact with his uncle—a pact he needed to evade without ruining alliances between Clan MacKenzie factions. Reid's goal was to unite the Highland clans and foster loyalty, not to destruct centuries of kinship. His damned hands were tied. Worse, the longer he remained in England, the more Miss Audrey's wiles baffled his heart.

I cannot put my desires before those of the cause. And for the love of God, a Sassenach lass would wither at Brahan Castle whilst my da rolls in his bloody grave.

Nonetheless, he didn't want the lass to suffer on his account. She already was suffering enough. Surely there must be some other way to keep her estate out of abeyance. He lightly kissed her temple, breathing in the heady scent of lavender as it laced its way around his heart. "Everything will be all right, lass. I vow to you, I shall not force you into an unhappy marriage."

"But—but—but I cannot bear to think of losing you, too."

"I'll not be going anywhere, not until you're settled and happy. I promise." He bit his tongue. Something told him he'd better bite back his lustful MacKenzie urges and grow comfortable at Coxhoe House. His role as guardian had just grown more complicated.

Chapter Eleven

A sennight after returning to the manse, Reid sat in "his" chair in the library and read a letter from Lady Barnard, babbling about how successful the ball had been and providing a list of six potential suitors who had expressed interest in courting Miss Audrey. She gave a detailed dossier on each man, singing their praises. With every description, the ache in his head grew worse.

They all seem like gutless fops to me.

He crumpled the parchment between his hands and groaned. He had already spent far too much time in England. *The cause* needed him, and there he sat, playing guardian and matchmaker for an heiress. If only he could pass this task off onto someone else.

Gerald stepped into the library and cleared his throat. "Mr. Watford to see you, my lord."

Reid smoothed out the letter, folded it, and slid it into his doublet. "Perhaps he has some favorable news."

"I take it the missive from Lady Barnard did not meet

with your approval?" The butler was fishing. Everyone in the household was fishing, wondering whom Miss Audrey would wed, and whether they'd be employed in the future.

Reid didn't blame him. "If only there was an honorable and stalwart man among the lot of suitors, I might be a bit more content." He flicked his fingers. "Show the solicitor in."

After the requisite greetings, Mr. Watford took a seat and propped a satchel on his lap. "I had to visit straightaway. A male heir has come forward."

Reid hid the churning of his gut beneath a frown. "An heir, you say? Who?"

Watford pulled a slip of parchment from his bag and placed it in Reid's hands. "Mr. Wagner Tupps. He's the son of Josiah Kennet, Nicholas's brother."

Reid glanced back to the portrait of the said sibling. He only knew who it was because of the brass nameplate attached to the bottom of the frame. Why didn't Audrey mention she had a cousin? "Tupps?" He narrowed his gaze. "Why is the surname different?"

Watford sniffed and crossed his legs. "It appears the young man is of illegitimate birth."

"A bastard cannot inherit over Miss Kennet."

"I know his circumstances are a bit peculiar, but Mr. Tupps has filed a claim with the court, and I can cite at least one other example of where the magistrate ruled in favor of an illegitimate male over an unwed legitimate daughter."

"And you have verified his parentage with his record of birth?"

The solicitor gestured to the paper in Reid's hands. "Indeed I have, my lord, as the document clearly states."

Reid skimmed the scrawling penmanship. It appeared Mr. Tupps was born on the fifth of June 1678 to a Miss Felicia Tupps, occupation, gentleman's companion. The boy's father was listed as Josiah Kennet.

Reid's mouth grew dry. "This is a load of hogwash. The man's mother was a whore. How in God's name could a fortune-hunting tinker lodge a claim for an estate the size of the Kennet's and be taken seriously?"

"Have you found a suitor for Miss Audrey?"

Reid tugged at the itchy cravat strangling his neck. "I am very close. As a matter of fact, I have a list of potential suitors from Lady Barnard in my possession."

"It is my duty to inform you that Mr. Tupps has consented to marry Miss Kennet forthwith to ensure her circumstances remain unaffected."

"Och, how convenient for a conniving, backbiting bastard."

"I suggest you give his suit some serious consideration. After all, he is an arguable candidate as the male heir for whom we have been searching. If you ask me, things couldn't be better. And the last time we spoke, you were anxious to return to Scotland. With this news, I would think you could wash your hands of your responsibility and head home within a fortnight."

Reid sprang to his feet and thrust his finger toward the door. "You, sir, are speaking as if I have no concern for the welfare of my ward. Leave her in the hands of an unproven wastrel? That is your solution? What in God's name am I paying you for?"

* * *

Anger shot through his veins like steam blowing through

a kettle as Reid marched straight to Audrey's wing, tracking the scent of lavender like a bloodhound until he burst through a door at the end of the hall. "Miss A—" His mouth hung open as his gaze homed in on the most perfect pair of wee breasts he'd ever seen in his life.

"Eep!" she squealed, while she crossed her arms, hiding such exquisite beauty and sliding lower into the wooden tub.

"My Lord Seaforth." Mrs. Hobbs stepped between them with her hands on her hips. "I must ask you to leave immediately."

Leave? He didn't care if the lass was standing naked in the midst of an icy loch. He was Audrey's goddamned guardian for Christ's sake. He would ignore the inopportune stirring of his loins. His loins had absolutely nothing to do with his anger, and he would not pay them another mind. He turned his back. "I'm afraid that is not possible. Please grant us some privacy. What I have to say to Miss Kennet must be uttered in utmost secrecy."

"But—"

"I shall keep my back averted. Now please leave us." Reid swiped his fingers over his eyes while Mrs. Hobbs scurried out the door. Bloody hell, how was he supposed to erase the image of Audrey's breasts from his mind? Perfectly round and rosy-tipped and pointing straight at him when he'd boldly burst through the door. How was he to know she'd be bathing in the middle of the day?

When the latch clicked, Reid turned his head to speak over his shoulder. "Did you ken you have a cousin?"

"I beg your pardon?" Water trickled. "I have no cousin. And what was so all important that you could not wait even a single minute for me to don a robe? I must say, your presence in my bedchamber is highly scandalous and disconcerting."

A tick twitched in Reid's jaw. "His name is Wagner Tupps." Audrey gasped with such vehemence, Reid couldn't help but face her. "Do you know him?" he demanded.

Her eyes grew as round as silver crowns. "N-n-no. I did not know he was my cousin."

"Well, it appears he is. Your uncle Josiah had an illegitimate son who has lodged a claim on your estate and asked for your hand in marriage."

Curling into the fists under her chin she looked terrified. "Oh, help."

Bloody hell, the lass kens more than she's letting on.

"What is it, Audrey? What do you know of this Mr. Tupps?"

"N-n-nothing. I just…I just…I just cannot."

Reid slammed his fist into his palm. There he stood, towering over his ward while she tried to hide, curled into a wooden tub, and he was madder than a mob of swarming bees. "By God, I shall send out my own spies to ferret the bastard out of his hellhole, and then I shall show him exactly what happens to fortune hunters who bury their shovels in my paddock."

"No, no, no. You mustn't confront him yourself. You could be hurt."

He sauntered toward her, his mind running wild. Christ, it didn't help matters that she was dripping wet, completely naked, and looking more ravishing than she'd been in her damned red gown. If only he could tug her arms away from her breasts and pull her up to his aching body. Jesus Christ, the bed was only paces away…and she was so goddamned wet.

"Please...I am bathing, my lord..." She sank deeper into the tub while her eyes grew round as a doe's.

His tongue slipped to the corner of his mouth while he tried to focus his mind. He was missing something, but could not yet see it. All he could see was a woman he wanted, but could never have because she was his blasted ward...and he was...

Damnation.

Before he left, he needed one more peek. Just one more glance at perfection.

Gulping, he slowly strode toward the wooden tub and allowed his gaze to sweep downward. Though she kept her arms taut across her breasts, their softness swelled above. And lower, a tiny waist flared into sumptuous hips—hips made mesmerizing by the water.

Reid grew weak at the knees while he glanced to the bed.

Dear God, I'm too damned close.

She curled forward, giving him a glimpse of the silken skin on her back. "I-I beg you not to put yourself in harm's way, my lord."

He shook his head as her softly spoken words smashed through his improper thoughts. "Do not concern yourself with me. I am very certain I have dealt with far more devious scoundrels than Wagner Tupps." Before he did something he'd regret, he turned on his heel and pushed out the door.

Chapter Twelve

*D*ry and dressed in a yellow day gown, Audrey frantically paced the floor. Her fingers trembled like saplings in a storm, and she clasped them across her stomach while she tried to think. Good heavens, she could have died when the Earl of Seaforth marched straight into her chamber with that tempestuous look on his face. And without knocking!

For a moment, Audrey feared he might ravish her. And after listening to the news he'd imparted, she almost wished he had. Then she'd be a ruined woman and all this talk about marrying that evil-eyed villain would be moot. She might be tossed out of her home, but she could support herself with her fan painting.

Couldn't I?

Audrey shuddered and looked up to the ornate ceiling relief above. Aside from Talcotts, she'd never lived anywhere else. But a dingy one-room hovel had to be preferable to a life with Wagner Tupps.

Why hadn't Papa ever spoken of him?

During their brief encounter, he'd admitted to inform-
ing on her father. He'd admitted to being the catalyst that
had led to Papa's death...and then he'd threatened the
earl. If she dared speak out against Mr. Tupps, who knew
what he would do next?

Audrey shuddered.

What a complete, unequivocal mess!

If she had told Reid—er—Seaforth about the man's
threats at the ball, she would have put the earl's life in
peril. His Lordship even said he'd challenge the man to a
duel for upsetting her. She could never, ever ask him to
risk his life to bring honor to hers. And Mr. Tupps had
been very clear: The earl would meet a gruesome end.
Moreover, Tupps admitted to having a hand in Papa's
death. The foreboding pulsing through Audrey's blood
warned that Mr. Tupps was evil. She must not pique the
man. To that end, the earl had already done enough for
her. How could she send him into Satan's den? And he'd
acted ever so angry. She must prevent him from confronting the vulgar brute. A blackguard as evil as Mr.
Tupps would be devious for certain. And if anything happened to Reid because of her actions, she would never
forgive herself.

She squeezed her arms around her midriff, trying to
still the sickly bile churning in her stomach.

How can I stop this?

Audrey dashed to the window embrasure and removed
her father's journal from beneath the cushion. Scanning
the pages as fast as her eyes would allow, she desperately
tried to find an entry mentioning Wagner Tupps or Uncle
Josiah. Her pointer finger shook as she traced it down
each page, and when she reached Papa's last entry about

traveling with the Earl of Seaforth, she leafed to the front and read the date of inception—17 March 1709.

With an enormous sigh, she looked to the door.

I must go back to Papa's strongbox.

She nearly jumped out of her skin when someone knocked.

"A missive for you, Miss Audrey," Gerald called through the timbers.

"Come in." She met the butler halfway as he delivered the letter on a silver platter. "Who is it from?"

"Doesn't say."

That was unusual. "Is the Earl of Seaforth in the library?"

"No, miss. He's gone to scout the grounds with his men."

Audrey plucked the letter from the tray and examined the seal. It was blank as well. "Thank you."

A letter from one of her friends would definitely bear a seal. Those accursed fingers started shaking again as she ran them under the glob of hardened red wax.

Dear Miss Kennet,

By now Mr. Watford should have paid a visit to your bumbling guardian, and I imagine my desires have been presented to you. To be perfectly clear, I am the only heir to the Kennet estate. I intend to make you my wife and you will carry out my bidding. If you defy my generous offer, I will not only expose the Earl of Seaforth for being a Jacobite involved in a traitorous plot, but I will smear the good name of your father with the same testament. You will be ruined in the eyes of society just as my mother was.

You will be cast out into the mire of the poverty-stricken, and I will show you no mercy, exactly as Nicholas Kennet showed my father.

That said, I trust you realize that we were born to be wed. Together we will build a strong and thriving family and make the Kennet coal mine more successful than ever before.

Your ardent suitor,
Wagner Tupps

Audrey closed the missive while a tear slid down her face. As she stowed the letter in the bureau drawer, her throat thickened until she could scarcely breathe. What had she done to deserve such wickedness? And he truly thought they had a chance to build a happy and content family?

Over my dead body.

* * *

Reid removed his riding gloves and tossed them on the entry table as he ascended the stairs to Coxhoe House's first floor as if he'd lived there for years. He groaned. He'd already been there a month, and it didn't appear as though he'd be heading home to Scotland anytime soon. This development with the interloping nephew had just added layers of complexity to his problems.

And after finding Audrey in the bath, and being too bull-brained to politely excuse himself while she dressed, he'd insisted on confronting her and questioning her about her cousin. What he hadn't counted on was the lass being completely and utterly confounding and impossible to forget. And far bonnier than he'd ever imagined.

With his every step, his loins had stirred to life. By the time he'd left her chamber, Reid's cods were tighter than a boxer's fist. He needed to head home to Brahan Castle and resume his life. Bloody hell, even the passageways at Coxhoe House smelled of lavender and Audrey. He'd needed a brisk ride with his men to cool the fire thrumming through his blood. The only problem was, as soon as he entered the house, that damned lavender scent turned him into a lusty fool. He needed a woman, and there was no place nearby to find a suitable one.

He opened the door to the library and stopped short. God's bones, no wonder the passageway smelled of freshly milled lavender soap. Audrey snapped her head up from her reading, looking like she'd been caught pinching a plum tart cooling in the kitchen window. She stood and wiped her hands on her skirts.

Reid knit his brows and strode forward, taking in the piles of parchment and journal she had strewn across the table. Aside from that, the picture of Josiah Kennet was open...hinged, like a cupboard. Behind it, a strongbox door also hung ajar. "What is this?"

"Da's journal and parcel of old letters."

"You kent he had a hidden strongbox and you did not tell me about it?"

Her shoulders dropped forward as she shook her head. "Please forgive me. I-I didn't trust you at first. And then with the ball and the gown and everything else, it slipped my mind until a few hours ago."

He scrubbed his knuckles through his hair. He'd been sifting through bookshelves and crannies for a damned month. He moved behind her and looked over her shoulder. "Have you found anything mentioning Mr. Tupps?"

She threw up her hands. "Nothing. Just some grumblings about being forced to pay Uncle Josiah's debts. There's an entry on the day of Uncle's funeral, but never a word about a nephew, illegitimate or not." She shoved the journal away. "Papa's entries only go back as far as 1690, two years before I was born."

"He was quite prolific." Reid leafed through the journal nearest and found his name. "Holy hellfire, he's even written things about *the cause*. If these fell into the wrong hands, someone might misunderstand what we're trying to do."

"Would they think Papa a traitor?"

"Jacobites have been thusly accused, though we are only trying to protect the succession." He clamped his mouth shut, but then decided things had progressed too far for silence. Audrey already knew more than she ought. "Presently we're trying to prevent the Occasional Conformity Act and push for the abolition of religion dictating the suitability of a king's right to rule."

She nodded. "I know. Papa wrote in detail about the queen's insane fear of popery." She pulled back the volume she'd pushed away and opened it to a page she'd marked with a slip of paper. "This is an entry where Papa speaks of Uncle Josiah's abhorrent behavior." A tear slipped from her eye. "He was vile—a libertine and a fop."

Reid placed his hand on her shoulder. "You have nothing to concern yourself with, lass. I will not let that slug claim you for his bride. I shall go to the ends of the earth to prove him a liar if I must."

"No!" She twisted from under his palm and pounded her fist on the desk, her hands shaking. "You must not. Do you not see you must leave immediately? He will do you harm."

Reid chuckled. "I've only met one man who could match me, and that was afore I reached my prime."

She backed away, her eyes filled with fear. "But there are methods other than force to hurt a man like you. Please, do not take on Mr. Tupps. I fear it will come to a grave end if you do."

Dear Lord, her lips quivered. This whole affair had the poor lass at her wits' end, and she seemed more worried about him than about herself. How could that be? Tupps was trying to force her into an unwanted marriage. Reid needed to protect Audrey, needed to ensure gold diggers didn't try to take advantage of her. His heart swelling, Reid pulled the lass into his arms and ran his hands along her back. Christ, she seemed so delicate. "Leave this ugly business to me. I'll find a way to discredit him."

She tensed. "You must not. I have a very bad feeling about him."

"'Tis my duty to see to your protection." He cupped her face between his palms. "Do you trust me?"

"Yes," she replied airily, whispered through kissable, pert lips that could only have been hewn by an angel's hand.

They both stood breathless, gazing into each other's eyes. Reid's heart hammered as if he'd run a footrace. Heaven help him, he wanted this lass. Wanted her so badly, he couldn't think straight when she was near, couldn't rationalize between his duty to protect her and his unequivocal desire to do so.

As if pulled by forces outside his body, he inclined his head downward.

Audrey's gaze slipped to his mouth. He needed to kiss her, at least once, and this time neither heaven nor hell would stop him.

As if sensing his thoughts, Audrey pursed her delicate lips. He slid his hands to her shoulders, dipped his head, and plied those delicious lips with the gentlest kiss he'd ever given in his life. She softened to him and, a growl rumbling in his throat, he slid his arms around her again to feel her body mold to his. Heaven help him, her pert breasts against his chest practically begged to be released from the cage of her stays.

He teased her lips with his tongue until she blessed him by parting ever so slightly and allowing a taste.

With every new sensation, Reid's desire grew. Fighting to maintain a tempo befitting Audrey's inexperience, he coaxed her mouth wider until he entwined his tongue with hers. Her eyelids fluttered closed with her sultry sigh, a sigh that shot straight to the tip of his cock with a spark of pure pleasure. For all that was holy, her mere utterance could bring him to his knees.

Sliding his hands to her buttocks, he sank his fingers into pure heaven while he held his desire against her. Lithe fingers tickled their way around his waist while the lass grew bolder and matched his kisses stroke for stroke, fanning the flames that had begun as mere cinders.

It was all he could do to keep from rocking and grinding his cock into her. Instead, he traced the curve of Audrey's neck with his mouth. A wee whimper came with a course of shudders. "W-w-what are you doing?"

"I'm kissing you, lass." His voice grew husky as his lips met her collarbone. He inhaled and watched her breasts rise and fall above her bodice. Ever so lightly, he brushed his fingers along the velvety flesh of her shoulder.

Bending his head further, he nearly fell forward when Audrey sucked in a sharp gasp and jumped back.

Stunned, he stared. She did, too.

"You must never, ever do that again."

Before he could utter a word, she whipped past him and fled out the door.

Dear God, I must be the greatest cad who ever walked Christendom.

Chapter Thirteen

*U*nable to sleep, Audrey rose early and headed for the stables. Though she'd promised not to venture out alone, she could keep to the riding arena and put Allegro through his paces. She needed to think, and her mind no longer worked shut up in her chamber. She'd painted all night. As testament to her efforts, her fingers sported every color of the rainbow, but she didn't care. And playing the harpsichord was out of the question. The earl slept in the east wing, right above the drawing room. He'd hear her for certain.

If he came in while she was playing, she might die. In fact, she rued having to set eyes on him again. Holy Moses, what had come over her in the library? One moment she was doing her best not to tell him about Mr. Tupps's threats, and the next she was swooning in Reid's arms.

Reid. She loved the name, loved uttering it in the early hours when she'd come awake and no one was near to hear. Oh, holy help, she indeed had swooned—and in his vigorous embrace. And moreover, she'd allowed him to kiss her.

Who knew kissing could be so entirely mind consuming?

His body had felt so hard and wonderful pressed against hers. So many emotions bubbled through her insides, she might go raving mad if the intensity of her feelings did not ebb. How did he make her feel that way? What sort of power did the Highlander wield over her?

When he placed his hands on her with his lips plying her mouth, together with trailing succulent kisses down her neck, had made her so light-headed, she would have collapsed had his brawny arms not been wrapped around her.

Then she'd had no choice but to stop him. If he fell in love with her, Mr. Tupps would ruin him. He'd made threats. He'd indicated he'd had a hand in her father's death. Oh, heavens, she couldn't let that man ruin, and possibly kill, another person she cared for.

Walking across the lawn to the stable, Audrey rubbed the outsides of her arms, reliving Reid's bone-melting embrace. If only she could ask him to put his hands on her again. If only she could kiss him forever.

But no.

She marched the distance to the stable doors.

She was right to push him away. Aside from the danger, the earl had made it clear he wanted to marry her off. She could not entertain spending another moment in Reid's arms. He'd told her he was dangerous, and now she knew exactly what he'd meant.

He is a lady charmer.

"You're up early, Miss Audrey," said Jeffrey, peeking his head out a stall. "Shall I saddle Allegro for you?"

Now that his frog had healed, the trotter was as good as new. "Yes, please."

"And shall I ride with you? The earl said you're not to venture out alone."

"No thank you." She glanced over her shoulder as a sudden chill slithered down her spine. "I shall put him through his paces in the arena today. That will have to suffice."

Jeffrey agreed and had her mount saddled in no time, thank heavens. Riding Allegro with a cool breeze on her face was always invigorating, even if she was restricted to the arena. There were two jumps and poles spaced to perform a serpentine pattern they hadn't attempted yet this summer.

As she rode, the connection between horse and rider took over. She focused on leading Allegro through the patterns, on lead changes, on preparing for jumps, taking him through smooth gait changes from walk to trot to canter. Oh yes, a couple of hours in the saddle was exactly what she needed. She didn't think about marriage, or blackmail, or Highland earls. Audrey became one with her horse, just like she'd been as a young girl.

By the time she rode back into the stable, at least the tension between her shoulder blades had eased. "Jeffrey," she called, dismounting on her own.

When there was no answer, she began loosening the saddle's girth strap.

Something moved out of the corner of her eye.

Her heartbeat spiked as she glanced back. "Jeffrey?"

"No," came a reedy voice from inside the tack room. Wagner Tupps stepped into the light and lowered his hood. "Considering all that has transpired, I thought it best if we talked. Had a secret meeting, if you will."

Every muscle in Audrey's body tensed as she retightened the girth and glanced back to the mounting block. The horse skittered sideways.

"Are you thinking of fleeing?" The blackguard dashed toward her.

Audrey started to run. "H—!" Before the word *help* escaped her lips, he clamped one hand over her mouth and trapped her with his other. "Shut up. Fleeing is no way to greet your intended."

She gulped against her churning stomach and wrenched her mouth from beneath his vile palm. "You are not my intended," she seethed.

"I beg to differ. Did you read my letter?"

"Please. This is madness. I can pay you. How much do you need in order to be on your way?"

He threw back his head with a cackling laugh. "So the heiress thinks all that matters to a scoundrel is coin?"

"Is that not what you desire?"

He sniffed. "I will gain far·more if I own the entire Kennet estate. With you in my bed, I will be the cock of Coxhoe, and I will crow to my good fortune."

Audrey struggled to free herself. "You, sir, are mad."

"Hmm. You could call it that. I'd rather call it angry. You see, I was born to the wrong brother. But I learned to pull myself out of the gutter by taking advantage of the dupes who surround me." He laughed again, a hideous sneering titter. "After all, isn't that why God put wealthy fools on this earth?"

"Help!" In a panic, Audrey twisted her shoulders and tried to spin from his grasp, but he was faster, gripping tighter, and again he covered her mouth.

"Shut your gob, wench," he growled in her ear. "I have a document tucked away. 'Tis written in your father's hand, and it will bury Seaforth."

Audrey shook her head and garbled "no" against his dirty palm.

"Oh, yes. This is too good to pass over. Unless you proclaim your undying love for me, I will take this news to Captain Fry, the warden of Durham Gaol, and to every magistrate between here and London. Within a sennight Seaforth will be arrested for treason. He'll be taken to Whitehall, where they executed King Charles. Indeed, he will meet the headman's ax." Wagner sniggered. "I wonder if the blade will be dull or sharp. I wonder if the big, kilt-wearing earl will beg for mercy. Will he wither and weep in front of the crowd?"

Thrashing her body side to side, Audrey screamed into the filthy palm.

Wagner squeezed his hand tighter and jammed her face-first against the wall. "Swear you will marry me."

Her mind raced. If she refused him, she would be sending a good man to his grave, a man she cared very much about. Frantic to be free, she rapidly nodded.

"Do you promise not to shout again?"

She gave another nod.

Tupps's hand eased, but he pressed his fingers to one side of her jaw and his thumb to the other. "I will pay a visit to Mr. Watford in three days, and he had best have received the news that you have accepted my proposal of marriage."

Audrey gulped. Life with this monster would be unbearable. But what other choice did she have?

Chapter Fourteen

*J*effrey entered through the stable's forward doors, carrying two pails of water. He'd missed it all. "How was your ride, miss?"

Audrey clasped her hands in front of her stomach to quell her jitters. Tupps had exited by the rear, leaving her alone. "Quite invigorating, thank you." Her voice was emotionless. "Please see to it Allegro receives a double issue of oats this eve." She patted her gelding on the rump, savoring the touch of something warm and unassuming beneath her fingertips. "He's earned it."

After setting the pails down, the stable hand grasped the horse's bridle. "You spoil him."

"He spoils me." She gave Allegro one last pat. "I have a pressing matter to attend. Please excuse me."

Holding her chin high, she made her way back to her bedchamber, praying that no one could sense the tempest brewing inside her. Only after she closed the door did Audrey allow herself to crumple. She pulled the kerchief from her sleeve and hid her face.

What on earth am I going to do?

Running away would solve nothing. Not only would Mr. Tupps betray the earl, Reid would go after her for certain. If she suddenly disappeared, the earl would see it as his failure to protect her. And if she'd learned anything about the Earl of Seaforth in the past month, it was the man could be fiercely tenacious.

She brushed away her tears and paced. This was no time to melt into a puddle. Pushing the heels of her hands to her temples, Audrey focused.

Two things are for certain. First of all, in no way can I betray the Earl of Seaforth. My father trusted him, supported him, embarked on a perilous undertaking with him.

She shuddered and paced some more.

Secondly, I cannot imagine a life as the wife of someone as vile as Wagner Tupps.

The more she paced, the more she realized that both problems contradicted each other to the point of stalemate. If she relented to Mr. Tupps's demands, she might gain some time. But how long would she be able to keep him at bay? If she convinced Seaforth of her undying love, he might leave for Scotland, and once he was gone, could she then sail for the Americas or somewhere she would never be found?

If only she could find a way to stall. After all, she'd always wanted a long engagement. Perhaps she could make clear her wishes to Mr. Watford. Once things had been set in motion, the earl could wash his hands of his responsibility for her. His purpose would be fulfilled. And he'd made it clear he did not intend to remain in Coxhoe overlong.

But Audrey must use utmost care when she confessed news of the betrothal. If she so much as hinted at Mr. Tupps's blackmail, Reid would go after the man and risk the consequences.

Whatever I tell him, I must be believable.

She stood in front of the mirror and cleared her throat. "I had a visit from Mr. Tupps today..." Biting her knuckle, she shook her head. If she mentioned the blackguard had come to Coxhoe, Reid would discover Tupps hadn't been properly announced.

She again addressed the mirror, shoulders back. "I have received a lovely missive from Mr. Tupps and have decided to accept his suit of marriage." Everyone knew she'd received a missive, and lo and behold it had been from Tupps. She cleared her throat. "And furthermore—"

Audrey practically jumped out of her skin when Mrs. Hobbs burst through the door with her arms full of linens. "How is your painting going today, miss?"

Audrey glanced to the bureau drawer. "I spent the morning riding Allegro."

"Ah, yes. 'Tis a splendid day for it." She set the washing on the foot of the bed. "You look a bit pale. Are you coming down with a fever?"

"Of course not. I'm perfectly fine." Before the maid could ask another question, Audrey slipped out the door and hastened to the library.

Unfortunately, she found the chamber empty with the scowling painting of Uncle Josiah glaring at her as if all this had come about because of her actions. For pity's sake, of all the times for the earl to step out, it had to be now when her confidence was at its peak. Oh no, she wasn't about to wait for him to return. If she did, she might lose her nerve.

After pattering down the grand staircase, she found Gerald polishing the china plates in the parlor. He advised her the earl was in the courtyard sparring with his men, and suggested she wait until they finished because she could very well end up injured with all those mammoth Highland swords swinging about.

Audrey dismissed his warning with a roll of her eyes. How on earth was she to wait pacing in her bedchamber while Mrs. Hobbs changed the linens? She straightened her spine and marched out the door.

Her stomach instantly turned into a cloud of flitting butterflies.

Perhaps Gerald's advice had been wise.

The day was overly warm, and every single kilted Highlander had opted to remove his shirt. Their muscular torsos gleamed with perspiration as they faced off, lunging and swinging their swords.

Clangs rang across the courtyard as, completely mesmerized, Audrey watched the sparring pair in the center. Reid MacKenzie focused on his partner like a man intent on murder. His teeth bared, his gaze unfaltering as he defended strike after strike.

With his every motion, the muscles in his torso rippled. His movement blurred while he wielded his sword with big arcs in a tireless dance. He spun outward, away from a hack. As he came around, he thrust his blade upward, his massive arms straining with sculpted sinew. A booming clang rang to the heavens while Reid's opponent lost control and his sword sailed through the air, landing five feet in front of Audrey's toes. She scooted backward with a gasp.

"Miss Kennet?" Using a more formal address in front of his men, Reid strode toward her, his every muscle flexing. "Are you all right, lass?" he asked as if he was completely dressed and not looking like an Adonis from a page in her Greek mythology book.

Her gaze shot to the others, who were all watching, blast them. "I-I am well."

He bent down for his sparring partner's sword, then addressed her, his glistening chest heaving while he held an enormous weapon in each hand. "Was there something you needed?"

She licked her lips and dropped her gaze to the muscles rippling in his abdomen.

Just out with it, you ninny.

"I have received a missive…I mean a *lovely* missive from Mr. Tupps and realize he is quite right. I will accept his proposal of marriage."

The earl's jaw dropped. Unmistakable hurt, alarm, and disappointment filled his eyes. "You cannot be serious."

"I am." Audrey couldn't look him in the face. Spinning around, she dashed through the door and made haste for the sanctity of her bedchamber. After a good cry, she'd spend the rest of the day painting. Yes, painting ought to make the stabbing pain in her heart go away.

* * *

Reid stared at the door to Coxhoe House while it closed in his face.

What the devil just happened?

Ply a woman with the most stunning kiss I've ever imparted in my life and she turns around and announces she's decided to marry a backstabbing milksop?

Just like that? No deliberating?

Miss Audrey didn't seem like the type to make sudden

rash decisions. Even if she had received "a lovely missive" from the bastard.

Christ. Reid pushed the hair away from his eyes with his forearm. He'd been a damned fool kissing her. He'd lost his head.

But how could she just cast him aside as though his kiss had meant nothing?

Of course, he hadn't proposed marriage. Even if he were in a position to make such an offer, such a proposal took time, took a great deal of forethought. One didn't just dive into wedlock as if it were a business transaction—unless entering a marriage contract between noble families for the prosperity of one's estate.

Which Reid understood far too well.

But there was no use burdening himself with something he could do nothing about. He could only hope his uncle would see sense and call off the agreement pledged by Reid's father. If Reid had his way, he'd live the life of a bachelor forever.

"Does that mean we'll be heading home soon, m'lord?" asked Graham from behind.

Reid handed the guardsman his sword. "Perhaps, though I wouldn't count on it."

"Isn't this what you wanted? To marry her off?"

"Aye." Reid's stomach clenched with his leer. Indeed, he'd planned to marry her off all along, though to a gentleman or a respected businessman like her father. "But I smell a rat."

Sheathing his sword, he marched up the portico and pushed inside the house. Miss Audrey couldn't just blurt out such a declaration and leave him standing there like an ox.

He took long strides and he skipped two stairs at a

time until he reached the second landing. Turning west, he hastened down the lavender-scented passageway while rage thrummed through his veins. "Miss Audrey?" He pounded on her door.

"Go away. I have made my decision, and there's nothing more to say about it."

"I will not leave until you show me Mr. Tupps's missive."

Footsteps pattered until she flung her door open. Then her eyes nearly popped out of her head while she gasped, her gaze shifting to his bare chest.

Reid glanced down. Perhaps it would have been mannerly if he'd donned his shirt, but this couldn't wait. Without apologizing, he barged inside. "Where is it?"

"I beg your pardon, but such a letter is private. A lady doesn't just allow gentlemen to read her confidential correspondence."

"I beg to differ. I am your guardian. That means I need to give my seal of approval to this match, and presently, I think you are acting quite hastily."

Audrey turned her back and put her hand to her cheek, blocking her eyes from him. "I have no intention of proceeding hastily, except you must notify Mr. Watford straightaway."

Reid threw out his arms. "Please, just allow yourself a sennight to consider."

"No. A sennight simply will not do." She looked at him, then snapped her hands over her eyes. "If you would please don your shirt, we might be able to discuss this civilly."

"We are having a civil discussion," he boomed, jamming his fists into his hips and planting his feet. "And I do not agree that you are making a well-informed decision. I insist that you give it some time, find out more about this man's intentions."

"I have made my bloody decision!" She shoved him in the shoulders. Good Lord, she'd gone red in the face. "Since you insist on standing there like an overbearing, shirtless oaf, I must inform you that I do intend to sign a contract of betrothal. And because Mr. Tupps's *confidential* and *private* letter contained an overtone of urgency, I believe it pertinent to inform you that I intend for this to be a very long engagement. In no way will I agree to be unduly rushed and paraded to the altar."

"Unduly?" Reid dropped his hands. She wanted to rush into a betrothal, but then draw out the engagement? She made no sense whatsoever. Did she not realize that she would be signing her writ of misery?

"Exactly." Spun tighter than a fiddle string, she brushed past him and sat at her painting table. "If there is nothing else, I have an order for ten fans that must be dispatched by the end of the week."

For a moment, Reid didn't move. He didn't like this sudden turn of events one bit. Last eve, she was rifling through her father's papers looking for something about Wagner Tupps, and now she was ready to declare her undying love?

What changed?

She picked up a paintbrush and swirled it in a glass of water. "Was there anything else you needed, my lord?"

Dear God, she could be maddening. "Not a thing," he clipped as he turned on his heel, and strode away.

Chapter Fifteen

*R*eid hoped to God that Dunn had enough wherewithal to bring back a cask of whisky when he returned. He poured another dram of brandy and turned the cup between his fingers. He hated English brandy, but it was the only thing in Nicholas Kennet's liquor cabinet strong enough to cool his ire.

Sitting in the library, he reclined in the chair by the hearth and stared at the flickering flames. He hadn't even bothered to light a candle.

He should meet with Mr. Watford in the morning, sign the goddamned papers, and head for the border. Why should he care if Miss Audrey wanted to throw her life away?

Christ, Wagner Tupps might even be a respectable man.

Reid's gut churned. He'd never overlooked his gut instincts, and he just couldn't allow himself to do so now.

He took a long draw on the brandy and wiped his mouth with the back of his hand. He'd go meet Watford in his rooms on the morrow and do some digging. He owed the lass at least that before he stepped aside and allowed her to ruin her life.

After tossing back the remainder of the brandy, Reid poured another. Dash it, he felt like shite.

Rejected by a timid English rose? And for a bloody bastard?

He slid down in his seat and crossed his ankles, focusing on the hypnotic flames. Bloody hell, he'd had no business kissing the lass anyway. Not with a clan alliance hanging in the balance. He had a duty to Clan MacKenzie first. This had been ingrained in him all his life. Christ, he might never marry. He'd avoided it thus far, and he didn't intend to be driven to it by his ward. Hell, she was English. And there was no bloody way he would ever live in England. Aside from the importance of uniting the Highland clans to stand behind James Stuart, Reid had his own enterprises to look after— cattle, sheep, wool, and oats. He was a busy man, a wealthy landowner, not to mention an earl and a member of the House of Lords.

So why am I acting like a goddamned fool?

He'd asked himself that question a hundred times and still hadn't come up with a satisfactory answer.

Had his kiss meant nothing to her? Like it or not, it had meant something to him. He just couldn't figure out what. True, he'd kissed his share of maids—English and Scots alike. And truth be told, he'd always preferred hearty Highland women over stiff, snobbish English women. Perhaps he just needed to go home.

But, devil's spit, was Miss Audrey so fickle his kiss

had frightened her? And he'd tried to be so goddamned gentle.

How could I have misread her so?

With a groan, he took another sip of the fiery spirit and stared at the flickering flames... until the door opened.

"My lord? May I enter?"

Reid leaned forward and regarded Mrs. Hobbs standing in the doorway and holding a candle. He wasn't in the mood to listen to complaints from one of the housekeeping staff. He frowned and scratched his chin.

"Please, it concerns..." She glanced over her shoulder, then cupped her hand to her mouth. "Miss Audrey."

With the next tick of the mantel clock, his heart jolted. He hopped to his feet, blinking away his bloody gloom. "By all means, please come in."

She carefully closed the door so it made no sound, then addressed him after setting the candle on a table. "When I was putting away Miss Audrey's washing, I found a letter."

His ears piqued. "I take it, a confidential correspondence?"

She nodded.

"From Mr. Tupps?"

With a big sigh, Mrs. Hobbs looked to the ceiling. "Heaven forgive me for snooping, but I love that girl and would never wish to see anything bad happen to her."

"I understand." Reid gestured to a chair. "Would you care to sit and have a tot of brandy?"

"Me, my lord?"

"Why not? 'Tis late. Surely a wee sip of spirit will help you sleep."

Sighing, the matron moved to the couch. "You are a generous man. I could tell that when you arrived. You haven't tried to take advantage of Miss Audrey—we've all been watching—and you have only acted responsibly."

Reid collected a second tumbler and poured for the maid, keeping his face passive while his chest tightened. Thank God the entire household hadn't heard about his brazen kiss, otherwise Mrs. Hobbs mightn't have come forward. "I owe a great deal to Miss Audrey's father."

"And I can tell you want to see to her happiness."

"I do." Sensing where this was leading, he resumed his seat and picked up his glass. "Tell me, what is the nature of the missive you found?"

The maid sipped the brandy, her fingers trembling a bit. "As you guessed, it was from Mr. Tupps, and though he signed it, 'your ardent suitor,' it was shocking."

Always trust gut instincts.

A tick twitched in Reid's jaw. "That is grave news."

"I thought a great deal about it, and I firmly believe it is my duty as a servant of the Kennet family to divulge the details." She patted her chest. "Mr. Tupps claims he is the only heir...but if Miss Audrey didn't marry him, he would implicate the late Mr. Kennet and you, my lord, as Jacobite traitors, and such implication would ruin Miss Audrey as well."

Reid shifted his gaze to the candle and sought to tamp down the flames that had ignited in his chest. But nothing would cool his ire now. "Did he say how he would go about implicating me and Audrey's da?"

"No, my lord." She cringed. "I do not oft have the opportunity to read, but I learned how. My parents served Nicholas Kennet's father, and I was allowed to take lessons with Mr. Josiah for a few years."

Glancing over his shoulder, Reid regarded the portrait of Wagner Tupps's sire. "What was he like?"

Mrs. Hobbs took another wee sip of her brandy and coughed. "As a boy, he was lazy and resentful of his elder brother, but he was quite flirtatious as well."

"Sounds like he maintained those qualities into adulthood." Reid drummed his fingers. "Tell me, was Nicholas's da a coal miner?"

"No. He was a physician. Mr. Kennet founded the mine himself."

Reid should have asked about that when he'd first arrived, but for some reason, the question hadn't seemed important at the time. "Does Miss Audrey have any idea you've seen her missive?"

"No, my lord. I put it back just as I'd found it." She covered her mouth with her finger. "Please forgive me. I know I shouldn't have been nosy."

Standing, Reid offered his hand. "Rest assured you did the right thing. I will protect your confidence, and I will most certainly deal with this scoundrel. An attempt to blackmail Miss Audrey is an attempt to blackmail me."

"Thank you. You have no idea how much it puts my heart at ease to hear you say so."

After Reid ushered Mrs. Hobbs out of the library, he strode to the writing desk and dipped a quill in the inkwell. He pressed hard to steady the anger shooting through the tips of his fingers. Too right, his gut instincts had pinned the bastard. And to think Miss Audrey was willing to throw her life away to protect his reputation and her father's?

This will be the last time Tupps takes advantage of an innocent maid.

Reid used bold strokes to explain his dealings in

Calais, something he should have done as soon as his galley was sunk by the bumbling Royal Navy.

A mere vagrant thought he could ruin the Earl of Seaforth? He'd call this blackmailer's hand and unleash his ire. Reid would denounce the maggot's claim on the Kennet estate once and for all.

Chapter Sixteen

*A*udrey sat up fully awake, roused by the sound of horse hooves pummeling the cobblestones in the courtyard— not a common sound in the country in the middle of the night. Without lighting a candle, she dashed to the window to find Reid and his men cantering down the drive and heading for the gates.

She snapped her gaze to the mantel clock. Three in the morning.

What possibly could be so urgent it cannot wait until dawn?

Determined to find out, she hastened to tie her stays in the front and stepped into her riding habit. After securing her tresses at her nape, Audrey shoved her tricorn riding hat on her head and quickly made for the stables.

The oil lamp secured to the stone wall was still alight. Down the alleyway, the stable hand shoved a stall latch closed.

"Jeffrey, do you never sleep?"

He jolted. "Miss Audrey? What are you doing up at this hour?"

"I believe I asked you the same question."

The lad shrugged and walked toward her, rubbing his eyes. "I was asleep until the earl's man roused me."

"Why on earth did they ride off at three in the morning?" Sensing Jeffrey might try to cover up the truth, she shook her finger. "And do not lie to me. Even I know 'tis too early to set out on a hunt."

He shrugged. "Why would they tell me what they're up to? The only thing I heard was they needed to find some swindler's domicile from the solicitor. The earl was crackin' angry, I'll say."

Audrey gasped. How could he have found out? She grasped Jeffrey by the lapels. "What else?"

Wrapping his fingers around her wrists, he twisted them just enough to make her release him. "I don't know. I had cobwebs in my brain." He scratched his head. "But the earl did say he wanted every missive delivered to this house to be presented to him no matter to whom it was addressed. Why would he do that? What the blazes is happening?"

"Nothing good, I'll say that right now." Audrey thrust her finger toward Allegro's stall. "Make haste. We must stop them before the earl does something that can never be undone."

* * *

The village of Coxhoe was dark without a single candle burning in a window when Reid pounded on the door to Mr. Watford's town house.

"What is the meaning—?" The butler didn't finish his question as Reid pushed inside.

"Tell your employer he is needed for an urgent meeting with the Earl of Seaforth. I expect to meet him in the parlor within two minutes, or I'll have no recourse but to start kicking in doors."

"Yes, my lord. Straightaway, my lord."

The man must have taken him seriously, because it was but a minute when Mr. Watford appeared in his dressing gown belted around his waist. "My lord. Why the devil are you calling in the middle of the night?"

Reid cracked his thumbs. "Where is he?"

"I beg your pardon?"

"The festering pustule who is blackmailing my ward? Where the hell is he?"

The man's face blanched. "Are you referring to Wagner Tupps?"

"Who else is trying to sink his talons into the Kennet estate?"

"I must protect the privacy of my client."

Reid moved closer, making the solicitor's neck crane. "I thought I was your bloody client."

"Ah, you are. You b-b-both are." A sheen of sweat sprang out across Watford's brow.

Something is amiss.

"Wait a moment." Reid took a step back, looking the man from head to toe and crossing his arms. "What does Tupps have on you?"

"I have no idea to what you are referring, my lord."

"Nay?" Reid snapped his fingers at his men, who stepped away from the wall with their hands gripping their dirks. "Either you tell me where I can find this backstabbing varlet, or my men will rifle through your documents until I find what I'm looking for."

The solicitor looked terrified. "Please, do not tell him who gave you this information."

"Jesus Christ, the bastard has you by the cods."

"In a word, yes." He glanced up the stairs. "My wife mustn't know I've been blackmailed."

Reid didn't give a lick about the man's plea for discretion. "Well, he's crossed the wrong man this time."

Watford clutched his hands over his belly. "Do you promise I shall not be implicated?"

"Bloody hell, it is not you I am after." He flicked a hand at his men, telling them to back away.

"Christ," Watford whispered with a backward glance over his shoulder as if the walls could hear his every word. "Tupps mustn't know, either—"

"Of course, dammit. Where do I find the bastard?"

"He lives at the back of Madam Chester's on the waterfront in Hartlepool."

Reid started for the door. "That would be right. He wallows in the mire with a gaggle of whores."

* * *

By the time Reid reached the shore, the sun shone like a blinding disk on the horizon of the North Sea. A month ago, he'd washed up on this same shore and had said good-bye to a friend. Ever since, his life had been in turmoil. What seemed a simple task had turned into a shambles.

But now it is time to set things to rights.

Madam Chester's was a ramshackle alehouse, wooden

with two stories. The floor at the top catering to the wiles of lonely sailors, no doubt.

Putrid trash lined the side alley, and rats scampered for hiding places as Reid strode to the rear. Wagner Tupps was a scoundrel of the worst sort. If a man like that lived on MacKenzie lands, Reid would deal with him the Highland way. Tupps would be hung from the great oak outside Brahan Castle. Reid had only hanged one man by the gnarled branch—a man who had committed rape and murder. For the most part, his kin lived by a code of honor, though that couldn't be said for the MacLeod pirates to the west.

Just as Watford had said, there was a room with a separate door at the back.

I should have known the son of a bitch wallowed in a pigsty.

He motioned for his men to stay put. Then, drawing his dirk, he turned the latch on the rickety door and slipped inside. The eerie glow of dawn shone through the cracked windowpane.

Inside, the chamber stank of stale beer and piss. Good God, the man was contemptible. Across the floor, a snore pealed through the air. Wagner slept on a narrow bed, and he was alone.

Reid silently moved to the bedside, where he could gaze upon the devil. Riding from Coxhoe, he'd had hours to think about how he'd confront this bastard. If he ran his dirk across the varlet's throat, he might be brought up on charges for murder. In England, such a contrived charge might actually hold. But there was no law against calling a man out.

"You'd best wake and face your reckoning, ye heap of worthless lard."

Shaking his head with a snort, Tupps opened his eyes. He moved like an eel, but Reid was faster, pinning the man to the mattress and pressing his dirk to his throat. "Blackmail is a crime."

"So is treason," Tupps spewed, the stench of pickled ale on his breath.

"But having a conversation with an exiled prince is not."

The man's eyes shifted to a sword leaning against the wall near the headboard. "How did you find me?"

"That's not important." Reid leaned harder on the man's chest until his breathing became labored. "I could slit your throat now, but that would be too easy. I hereby challenge you to a duel. You have five minutes to pull on your breeches, secure your sword, and meet me in the street. My men are posted outside. If you try to run, they will cut you down. If you are not outside in five minutes, they will drag you from this very hovel."

Wagner wheezed under Reid's weight.

The earl pressed down harder. "Do you understand?"

Sickly fear oozed off the man as he gave a single nod—subtle enough to avoid cutting his own throat on the razor-sharp dirk at his neck.

With one last shove to ensure the bastard knew he meant business, Reid straightened and took a step back. "Five minutes," he growled as he backed toward the door.

Roaring, Tupps sprang from the mattress wielding a knife.

Stepping aside, Reid caught the scoundrel's wrist and snapped it downward. The dagger dropped to the ground while he twisted the cur's arm up his back. Wrenching it to the point of breaking, he pressed his lips to Wagner's ear. "You'd best make a showing with a bit more flair, else you'll not last long, ye maggot."

He gnashed his teeth and pushed Tupps to the timbers, then stormed out the door.

Christ, the man had no idea how to fight. Even if he did, he would meet his end this day.

Chapter Seventeen

*T*he sun glowing low on the horizon made it difficult to see as Audrey and Jeffrey rode east into Hartlepool. She'd ridden Allegro so hard, the old horse was about to drop. But bless him, he'd kept up. They'd lost precious time while Mr. Watford had tried to talk them into returning to Coxhoe House. When finally she'd persuaded the solicitor to tell her where the earl was headed, the eastern sky had already taken on a hue of cobalt with the promise of dawn.

Now she gripped the reins in her fists while her thundering heart beat even faster as they approached the shore. A crowd had gathered outside the alehouse.

"Look." Jeffrey pointed to the center of the street. "'Tis the earl."

As soon as Audrey saw Reid standing like a Highland king, sword drawn and ready for battle, she whipped her riding cane against Allegro's hip. "My lord!" she shouted above the crowd.

The earl's face snapped around, while anger flashed through his eyes. "Audrey? Stay back!"

Allegro's rear end dipped low as she pulled the reins and skidded to a sudden stop. Audrey leaned forward and shortened her grasp for better control while the crowd grew thicker. "Let me pass."

Out of the corner of her eye, a flicker of movement made the hair on her arms stand on end. Her instincts took over, making her urge the horse forward.

A hand came from out of nowhere and grabbed Allegro's bridle.

Audrey tugged the reins away to steer the horse aside.

"Stop that man!" Reid bellowed while the crowd suddenly spread.

The hand holding the bridle didn't release.

Audrey lashed out with her cane, twisting her body and coming face-to-face with Wagner Tupps. Baring his yellow teeth, he launched himself behind her. "'Tis ever so nice of my betrothed to come to my rescue," he growled, reaching for her reins.

Audrey thrashed the leathers, trying to make the horse rear. "I am not betrothed to you yet," she seethed.

"You will be." Wagner overpowered her hands and kicked his heels, forcing Allegro to run for the beach.

Frantically trying to free herself from the madman's grip, her gaze darted over her shoulder. "Jeffrey!"

But it wasn't the stable hand barreling toward her. Audrey recognized the bay stallion Reid had been riding since his arrival. The horse was far younger and thrice as fast as her old gelding. Sand kicked up behind them as she stretched back her hand. "Help!"

Holding tight to the reins, Wagner squeezed his arms around her. "You're mine."

"I'm not," she growled as the earl closed the distance. His horse grunted with loud snorts as he galloped to Allegro's left, the same side as her legs. Twisting sideways, Audrey struggled to release her knee from the upper pommel.

"Give me your hand," Reid shouted, reaching out.

"Never!" Wagner pulled a dagger from his sleeve and sliced it at the earl's forearm.

"Argh," he bellowed, his horse losing pace.

"No," Audrey cried, stretching her arms out to no avail.

But Allegro was no match for the stallion. Within paces, Reid again rode in beside them...closer this time. Before Tupps made another strike, the earl threw a punch, hitting the blackguard in the temple. As Wagner recoiled, Reid snatched Audrey by the waist. With her next blink, she landed square on Seaforth's lap while he wrapped his powerful arms around her.

"I have you, love." His growl was so low, she wasn't certain she'd heard right, but she was safe, cradled in Reid's strong embrace as he turned his horse and headed for the onslaught of Highlanders now galloping down the beach toward them.

"Run him down and show no mercy!" Reid roared as he pulled the stallion to a halt.

"Aye, Captain!" Graham shouted as the men galloped past.

Audrey clutched her fists under her chin, trying to catch her breath. "I-I-I was s-s-so afraid."

He cradled her head to his chest with a massive hand, so gentle and soothing, it felt nothing like the viselike grip that had snatched her away from doom. "Are you all right, lass?"

"Yes. But he has Allegro!"

"My men will bring him back, not to worry. They ken how much the old fella means to you."

Seeing blood staining his sleeve, she gasped. "But you're hurt."

"Bah. 'Tis but a scratch." He chuckled with a hint of worry making his voice deeper. Closing his eyes, he pressed his lips to her temple. "Och, I never want to see that vermin place his hands on you again."

She shuddered. "He's vile."

"Think not of that man. I have you now." He kissed her ever so tenderly. "Och, why did you not tell me about the missive?"

"I wanted to protect you." Her stomach squeezed as heat spread through her cheeks.

"I'm nay the one who needs protecting, lass."

Audrey thought back—the linens. "Mrs. Hobbs?"

"Aye, but she did the right thing in telling me."

Audrey wasn't convinced. "But Mr. Tupps said he would ruin you—and me." She'd give the housemaid a firm talking-to upon their return.

"I'm a Scot, and a Highlander to boot. I'm not that easy to ruin. You forget, I'm also one of Her Majesty's favorites."

Audrey had to make him understand. "Nonetheless, please do not challenge that man. He admitted to having a hand in Papa's death—he leaked information to the captain of the *Royal Buckingham* to lead them to become suspicious of your activities in France, and worse, he has proof you spoke to James."

"The bastard," Reid growled with ire oozing from his throat. After a deep breath, he shook his head. "There's no law against meeting with the prince."

"But what of the queen's fear of popery? Does she not fear her half brother because she has taken a vow to defend the Protestant faith and prevent Catholics from ascending to the throne?"

"She does. But she also has no living heirs." Reid slowed the horse to a walk, and ambled along the shore. "Let us not worry about politics or illegitimate cousins. The day is too fine not to enjoy it."

Audrey relaxed and rested her head on his chest. She didn't want to think about Mr. Tupps's threats. She wanted to savor this moment alone in Reid's arms. With him, she could overcome any adversity. If only he wanted to marry her, then she wouldn't have to wed some fobbing noble she knew nothing about.

Again, he skimmed his lips over her temple. "I nearly died when I saw that scoundrel racing away with you and Allegro."

"Honestly, I did as well. That man is horrid."

"He is and I never want to hear another word about his baseless claim on you and the Kennet lands."

Warmth spread through her chest as she nuzzled against the protection of his chest. "Thank you."

"Och, you're fine to me." He inclined her face up to his with the crook of his finger. "I want to kiss you, lass."

Though she'd tied her stays loosely, her head still swooned and her shoulder melted into his sturdy chest. His eyes grew dark as their gazes met, and his lips met hers with an easy brush. Though scandalous enough right there in the outdoors on the shore, Audrey wanted more. Her eyes fluttered open with her sigh. "I feel safe with you, my lord."

"I'm glad of it. And 'tis high time you started calling

me Reid." He encouraged her to again rest her head on his protective chest as he drove the horse back up toward the alehouse and met Jeffrey.

"Where to now, my lord?" the stable hand asked, his face somewhat pale.

"We'll meet my men back at the manse. This part of the waterfront is no place for Miss Audrey." He glanced down at her with an arch to his brow. "And I reckon you didn't sleep overmuch."

"No more than you." On a sigh, she smiled and slipped her hand around his waist—to hold on, of course. And to sink her fingers into him, to be near him, to breathe in the spiciness of his scent.

Oh, how she wished the Earl of Seaforth wanted her.

True, he'd kissed her again, but this time, his kiss had been fleeting, reserved, though not delivered with any less emotion. If only Jeffrey weren't there, Audrey might work up the nerve to ask Reid why he'd kissed her and if he'd melted a little as she had done. Alas, she didn't even dare steal another kiss.

Such a brazen public display could never be. She might die of embarrassment. Never in her life had she been shameless, and now was no time to start.

She heaved a heavy sigh while a twinge of melancholy made her fatigue catch up with her. How many times did she need to remind herself that the Earl of Seaforth had no intention of staying?

Might there be a way she could change his mind?

* * *

Once they arrived at the manse, Audrey met Reid in the parlor with her medicine bundle. "I'll have that wound of yours set to rights in no time. At Talcotts each student prepared a basket of remedies."

He chuckled at the obvious pleasure she took in her accomplishment. "Let me guess, yours received top marks."

She sat beside him on the settee, placing the basket on the table in front of them. "Yes, but how did you know?"

"Just a hunch. I've noticed anything you undertake is done with precision."

"Anything worth doing is worth doing well." She pointed. "Now roll up your sleeve, my lord."

He complied. "Using 'm'lord' all of a sudden?"

She gave a nod as she took his arm and examined it studiously. "'Tisn't too deep."

"I said it was but a scratch."

She took a bit of cloth and moistened it with a bottle of avens oil. "Nonetheless, it needs to be tended, lest it fester."

"Och aye, m'lady."

She snorted. Reid could tell she was smiling, though she didn't look up. Gently, she wiped away the blood that had congealed around the cut, hovering over his arm as if his injury were grave. He sat back, enjoying the attention, grateful that she wasn't a blubbering mess after her ordeal. She had a stalwart backbone that he wouldn't have guessed in a spoiled heiress. And why was it the lass surprised him at every turn?

She stopped dabbing for a moment and examined her handiwork. "Have you ever thought of marriage?" she asked as if speaking about the weather.

Reid could have spat out his teeth. Straightening, he cleared his throat. "M-me?" His voice shot up like an adolescent lad.

She glanced over her shoulder. "I do not see anyone else in the room."

Reid swiped his free hand over his mouth. "Thought of it, I suppose. But I'm not the marrying type."

"No?" She resumed her wiping, though her strokes grew choppy and coarse. "I think an earl would have a responsibility to marry—to produce heirs..."

"Aye, but I'm only three and twenty," he argued.

"I'm nineteen and you expect me to marry forthwith." She scrubbed the cloth over the cut like she was cleaning a spot off a silver plate.

He grimaced. "Your circumstances are different."

"I fail to understand why."

He knit his brows, and affected his most stern scowl. How could he expect Audrey to have any idea the extent of an earl's responsibilities? "I have a duty to the House of Lords, to my clan, my lands, my crofters, not to mention *the cause*. And I'm rarely ever home to boot." He bit his tongue. He wasn't about to mention exactly how important clan unity was to *the cause* and how carefully he must tread. There were forces to the north that must be drawn together with an alliance, and bringing a Sassenach into the fray might tip the balance from Reid's favor.

"Mm-hmm." She dropped the cloth in her basket and slapped a bit of salve over the top of his cut, none too gently.

"Ow."

"Did that hurt?"

He pulled his arm away and shoved down his sleeve. What the bloody hell did she mean by *mm-hmm*? She didn't understand a damned thing.

Chapter Eighteen

*A*fter encouraging Audrey to rest, Seaforth headed for his chamber and collapsed on the bed. When Wagner Tupps had abducted the lass and headed for God knew where, Reid's blood had set to boiling. Thank heavens Audrey rode that old nag, or else the blackmailing swine might have eluded him.

Throughout the entire return ride to Coxhoe, Reid had kept a firm grasp around her. In such a short time Audrey had come to mean so much to him, it made his head spin. The thought of another man touching her made him want to hit something. She had no idea how every sound had set him on edge. Even the calls of the birds had made his skin twitch. He needed Dunn to return with the rest of his army, and fast. He was beginning to hate England, not that he'd ever relished being there, but they'd be far safer at Brahan Castle, where his lands were surrounded by hundreds of loyal clansmen.

Audrey would like it there, he decided out of the blue. Highland folk might be a wee bit suspicious of a Sassenach lass at first, but no one could fault her for anything. It wouldn't take long and they'd love her. She'd charm them with her music or her painting or...or...her smile.

Och aye, how Reid enjoyed watching her smile. Especially when she wasn't worried about how she might look. Unfortunately, Miss Audrey hadn't had many reasons to smile as of late, aside when she'd confounded him with that damned red ball gown.

Rather than sleep, Reid spent the next few hours staring at the canopy above the bed, thinking about Audrey and not solving a thing. He could have used a good nap, but no. His mind had to go on racing, mulling over everything that had happened since setting sail from Calais what seemed like a year ago.

He was still wide awake when his men returned, and Graham rapped on his door.

Beckoning him inside, Reid was almost relieved for the interruption, until he heard the news.

"The bastard gave us the slip."

Reid regarded his lieutenant while a furrow formed between his eyebrows. "What the devil? The milksop was riding a gelding older than Ben Nevis and you say you lost him?"

"Aye, well, we recovered Miss Audrey's horse, but Tupps turned down a wee causeway. We thought we had him cornered, but when we made chase to the rear of a building, he'd disappeared."

"What say you? No one simply vanishes."

"I ken." Graham stretched his hands out to his sides. "We hunted around, turned over every stick of wood, pounded on doors. Tupps either had an accomplice or he's a bloody sorcerer."

"A man who lives in a shite hole like the one I found him in is nothing but a swindler."

"I agree with you there, my lord."

Reid scratched the stubble that had grown on his face since the prior morning's shave. "We must strengthen the guard—patrols on the hour. And I do not want Miss Audrey stepping outside this house without an escort. As a matter of fact, I will not allow her outdoors unless she is with me."

Graham shook his head. "I don't think she'll like that one bit."

"Aye, she will not, but Nicholas Kennet asked me to do one thing, and that was to see to the care of his daughter. On my oath I will protect the lass until Wagner Tupps is behind bars, or better yet, led to the gallows."

* * *

A fortnight had passed, and Dunn still hadn't returned when Reid set his correspondence aside and listened to the sounds of the harpsichord resonate through the library. During his stay, he'd caught himself more than once closing his eyes and allowing Audrey's music to take his problems and make them float away. This occasion was no different. The lass had a way of expressing deep emotion through her music.

Had she been a man, she would have been a candidate for an organist at a cathedral. Her talent seemed to be wasted on the drawing room below stairs where few listened aside from the passing servant.

Today she'd selected a slower, melancholy tune. And why wouldn't Audrey be feeling a bit low? Since their return from Hartlepool, Reid had been busy undertaking every precaution he could think of to safeguard the manse and lands. Presently, the guard was out on patrol and he had a bit of idle time for a change.

After wandering down to the drawing room, he leaned his shoulder against the wall and crossed his ankles. Her fingers flying over the keys, Audrey hadn't noticed his arrival. She sat on the bench with her back erect, her hair pulled up in a chignon with curls framing her face as she oft wore it. Her delicate neck reminded him of a beautiful and graceful swan swimming on a loch while rich, wistful notes flowed like the cascading of a waterfall.

Audrey's gown scooped low, allowing him to watch the fine muscles just below her nape work while her fingers commanded the keys. At once, her back stiffened while she struck a chord and then another. The resonance of the harmony filled Reid's chest as if he could feel the sadness she imparted through her music. She struck four more chords before her head dropped forward and the chamber fell silent.

Transferring his weight to both feet, Reid stood very still for a moment while the sound of his own breath rushed in his ears. As if she could hear his next inhale, she turned. "I thought I'd heard you come down."

"Whilst you were playing?" He moseyed forward. "I wouldn't think you could hear over your bonny music."

"Do you play?" she asked, gesturing to the bench beside her.

"Nay." He took the seat and pushed his finger on a key. With a tad of resistance, it twanged the note like a harpist might do. Leaning forward he lifted the lid, peeking over innumerous strings. "How does this thing work?"

She pointed. "Pressing a key makes the jack rise, and the attached quill plucks the string."

When Reid looked in, she played a note. "Fascinating." He plunked a few more keys. "It isn't all that difficult to make a noise."

"No, but it takes a lot of practice to combine the notes into something that sounds..."

"Beautiful," he finished, his voice but a whisper.

A lovely shade of rose filled her cheeks, and she averted her gaze to the keyboard. "You have artistic fingers, my lord."

Reid frowned, following her line of sight. The skin on the back of his hands was riddled with thin, white scars, a testament to any man who wielded a sword. "To be honest, they're warrior's hands."

"I don't know." She grasped his left in her palm and examined it. "Your fingers are large, but they're quite long." She stroked her pointer finger from his wrist clear to the middle nail. "I believe your hands are both artistic as well as warrior-like."

Reid's mouth ran dry. Did she have any clue how erotic her light touch felt? He leaned closer. "Do that again."

This time her touch was more deliberate and slower.

Gooseflesh tingled all the way up his arm to the back of his neck. Dash it, if he didn't find a diversion soon, he'd have his arms wrapped around his ward, begging for another wee kiss. Forcing himself to glance away, he regarded a puppet theater against the far wall. "That's yours, I presume?"

"Yes. Papa gave it to me for my seventh birthday."

"I imagine you're quite practiced with the marionettes as you are with everything else?"

"I enjoy working with them, but I prefer to paint their faces." She blushed again. "The puppets are about as skilled at dancing as I am."

He stood and tugged her up. "As I recall, you aren't half as bad at dancing as you think you are."

"Perhaps the red gown emboldened me, distorting your opinion." She tapped her fingers to her lips, silencing a giggle. "Any well-executed dance steps were the fault of the dress."

"And I do not believe that for a moment."

She led him behind the theater, where marionettes hung from hooks on the wall. Bending down, Reid examined each one—children, a chimney sweep, elegant ladies young and old, a boxer and a tinker, and a dapper gentleman complete with periwig. "These are extraordinary. Such detail."

Audrey's face beamed. "They kept me occupied. Being an only child was tedious at times."

It had been for Reid as well. "What happened to your mother?"

"Succumbed to smallpox when I was four years of age."

"'Tis an awful malady. It takes far too many before their time."

"It does."

Reid returned his attention to the puppets while an awkward silence filled the air. If only he could make her happy. Talking about death and scoundrels like Wagner Tupps, and trying to find the lass a husband, brought on far too much worry—and now Watford had advised he'd gone ahead and recommended abeyance to the magistrate, the coward. Ah, well, Reid could deal with Watford in time. The estate was Audrey's, and he'd attest to the fact in any court of law in the kingdom.

Reid toyed with the chimney sweep's strings. "Which is your favorite?"

Audrey grinned with a low chuckle and reached for a puppet dressed in a voluminous, low-cut red gown, with many beauty spots, as well as a pile of coiffure atop her head that would put any courtier to shame. "Undeniably Lady Fanny, the Duchess of Ne'er-Do-Well." Cradling the puppet in her hand, she gazed upon it with amusement.

"And why is that?"

"Because the duchess is everything I am not." Audrey grasped the wooden operating cross and let the marionette drop, then waggled Lady Fanny's shoulders. "She hasn't a shy bone in her body. Indeed, the duchess says exactly what she thinks about everything. She's haughty and aloof and would never allow anyone to embarrass or insult her."

Reid enjoyed the lassie's animation when she described the puppet's character. He suspected that deep down Audrey was more like the marionette than she realized. "Indeed, the Duchess of Ne'er-Do-Well sounds a wee bit like my ma."

"Oh please. There is no one in Britain as pompous as this audacious lady."

Reid pulled the tinker puppet from the hook. "Very well, then show me."

"Why did you choose the tinker and not His Lordship? The Duke of Ne'er-Do-Well is every bit as pompous."

"Two pompous nobles?" Reid snorted while he made the tinker dance a floppy jig. "Such a combination would be as dull as attending a royal ball."

"All right." Audrey dropped Lady Fanny onto the puppet stage. "How does our story begin?"

"Perhaps the Duchess of Ne'er-Do-Well is having a miserable day?"

With a nod, Audrey made the puppet frump to the tiny settee and draw her hand to her forehead. "I do believe it has not stopped raining for an entire fortnight."

Reid let the tinker topple down to the stage. "Och, m'lady, it might be rainin' but ye canna allow a bit o' unpleasant weather to sink your spirits."

The marionette duchess sat erect. "Who are you to enter my abode and tell me what I can and cannot do?"

"I'm nothing but a tinker, a traveling minstrel who brings joy to the hearts of all who listen." Though Reid spoke with a Highland brogue just like any self-respecting Scot, he poured it on like a native Gaelic speaker would do.

"A minstrel?" Audrey made the puppet's arms loop in a circle. "You should be sent to the stocks for addressing me with such familiarity."

"Dear lady, why are ye being discourteous to me? I have not been overly familiar. I have not referred to ye as 'Fanny the Frump.'"

"Gasp!" The duchess stood. "How did you possibly know that is what they called me in the queen's court when I was but a child?"

"I ken a great many things, m'lady." The tinker sauntered toward the duchess. "I'll make ye a wager—one surely to raise your spirits."

"Alas, nothing can raise my spirits this day."

"Aye? But I beg to differ. I wager if I sing, your heart will be mine."

"No, no, no. I'm afraid that could never happen. A duchess isn't allowed to give her heart to anyone she pleases."

"Och, but ye havena heard me sing as of yet."

Sighing, the marionette resumed her place on the settee. "Then serenade me, sir, and I shall see to it you are fed in the kitchens before you go on your way."

"Ahem." Reid overexaggerated a clearing of his throat, then launched into a Highland ditty he'd always loved, substituting a few words to fit their story:

The fair prince sailed o'er the high sea
Searching for the lass who was meant to be
His intended bride fer all to see.
He called in every port from Edinburgh to Inverness
He donned his boots and hiked the slopes o' Ben
    Nevis
But his efforts left him dejected and loveless.
As he made his way back to the birlinn
His shoulders drooped along wi' his chin
When a lass stepped in his path with a bonny grin.
In the blink o' an e'e his heart was hers
An' once they were wed, they lived happily for
    years
This, my duchess, is the story o' our tears.

Reid quickly exchanged the tinker puppet for the one with the periwig. "Do you not see, lass? I am Prince Ne'er-Do-Well, come to make ye my bonny bride."

"Oh heavens, I may swoon!"

Boldly, the prince wrapped his floppy arms around the duchess. "I shall catch ye in me brawny arms. And I shall love ye forever!"

"My savior!"

With an infectious laugh, Audrey pulled her marionette up and hung it on the peg. "That was fun."

Reid followed suit. "It was."

Again, Audrey turned as red as her scarlet gown had been. "You have a beautiful bass voice. Have you had singing lessons?"

"I did—commanded by Her Highness, Queen Anne."

"The queen? Whyever would she command you to take singing lessons?"

"She assumed my care after my father's death. I spent three years at court as her ward. She insisted I pick something musical to study along with mathematics, history, Latin, French, and military strategy. I chose singing."

"Well, it suits you. You should sing more often." She smiled warmly.

Reid pulled one of her ringlets and watched it snap back into place. "Mayhap I should."

Audrey's tongue slipped to the corner of her mouth, her gaze drifting sideways.

He felt awkward, too. His fingers itched to touch more than just her hair, so he crossed his arms and leaned against the wall instead. "What else do you like to do aside from playing the harpsichord, painting fans, and dallying with marionettes?"

"I like riding, and long strolls in the wood."

"You do?"

"Yes, and outdoor meals."

"Och, 'tis a fine time of year for an outing."

"It is. And Papa used to take me hunting in the autumn."

"Hunting? Bows or muskets?"

"Muskets, of course. Papa trained me well."

"I think 'tis good for a lass to be skilled with a weapon. The Baronet of Sleat's missus is a markswoman not to be surpassed."

"Honestly?" Audrey shook her head. "Well, don't tell that to any of the instructors at Talcott Ladies' Finishing School. They allowed archery as a sport, but frowned upon noisy muskets."

"Would you like to do a bit of shooting?"

"Me?"

Reid glanced over his shoulder. "I do believe we've been alone together for quite some time. Aye, of course you. On the morrow." He held up a finger. "And dancing."

"Oh, no. Not dancing."

"Yes, dancing. I want you utterly confident at the next ball I escort you to."

She waved her palms in front of her face. "Please, no more balls and no more dancing."

"I'll tell you what. Let us make a wager."

"Like the one our marionettes just made?"

"Somewhat. If after three dancing lessons with me, you are still mortified and averse, I will never ask you to dance again...or attend a ball."

Her face brightened. "That sounds like something to which I can agree."

"Then 'tis settled." He took her hand in his palm and bowed over it. Assaulted by lavender and lace, Reid should have opted for a simple bow without a damned kiss. But now he was committed, he had no choice but to close his eyes and savor pressing his lips to the back of her hand. Beneath his lips, Audrey's pulse thrummed as quickly as his heart hammered.

Had he just insisted on giving the lass dancing lessons? Dear God, he was daft.

Chapter Nineteen

Of course, it had to rain the following day. Audrey would have much preferred a shooting contest over dancing. But at least Seaforth had given her a way out. After three lessons, he'd realize she was completely lacking in dancing talent and would relent. Thank heavens she'd never be forced to attend another ball.

She awaited the earl in the long assembly hall with its wooden floor, built by the family from whom Papa had purchased the manse. Audrey had rarely ventured inside the room. It was stark and lonely, because Papa didn't care for dancing and balls, either. Though a shell, crystal chandeliers hung from the ceiling and the walls were painted light blue. The ivory reliefs of dancing nymphs, framed by wreaths of ivy, left no question as to what the hall had been designed for.

Mrs. Hobbs had helped Audrey dress the part, and she wore a frosty blue gown with a matching fan, her slippers snug so as not to fall off and trip her. She had enough trouble managing to avoid tripping without her slippers making her twist an ankle or worse.

After taking three turns around the chamber, Audrey about decided the earl had forgotten their appointment, when the big double doors opened.

Reid grinned, moving through the doorway with broad shoulders, looking like a king. He, too, had dressed the part, his hair a wild mane cascading in waves to his shoulders. Atop his shirt he wore a navy velvet doublet and a lace cravat. As usual, he opted for a kilt in dark plaid rather than breeches. The muscles in his legs flexed as he stepped inside, his sporran swinging to and fro, though he wore no dirk in his belt as he usually did. "I see you found the assembly hall," he said, arching an eyebrow.

She laughed and gestured to the empty space. "I do believe Gerald had to send in a cleaning crew to polish the floor."

"A shame for such a magnificent chamber to have been ignored." He slid one foot forward and bowed. "Shall we start with an English country dance?"

Country dances were Audrey's favorite because they involved a great deal of standing and clapping. "Very well, but what shall we use for music? Perhaps I should ask Gerald to wheel the harpsichord in?"

"Nice try, lassie." With a wry grin, he waggled his tawny eyebrows. "But since you didn't cover your ears when I was singing yesterday, I thought I'd hum."

Audrey chewed the inside of her cheek. His song had made her skin tingle. She'd nearly whimpered when it was over. And now he was planning to hum while she stumbled through a series of dances?

Holy help.

But hum Reid did while they both sprang into motion

for the country dance, standing across from each other as if they were queuing in imaginary men's and women's lines. Another good thing about country dances was there wasn't much touching and far more promenading. Audrey curtsied and he bowed at the end of the first set.

When Reid straightened, he examined her from head to toe. "You executed the steps quite adequately."

Adequate was about the best compliment she'd hear. "Good enough to earn a passing grade at Talcotts at least."

"My guess is you are a far better dancer than you give yourself credit." He thrust out his hands. "Next we shall execute a minuet."

Audrey took a step away, drawing her fists under her chin. "Oh, no. Surely we should do at least five more country dances before we try something as challenging as a minuet."

"But why? As I recall, we danced a minuet at Lord Barnard's ball."

"Under duress and in a red gown."

"I doubt your attire had anything to do with your feet."

"Ah, but in that dress I could be someone other than Miss Audrey Kennet, wallflower, painter, and harpsichordist."

His eyes narrowed as he drummed his fingers against his lips. "Very well. Imagine yourself to be the Duchess of Ne'er-Do-Well. I would imagine a prideful woman such as the duchess would flourish when in the public eye. Even if she didn't flawlessly execute every step, she would hold her head high and act like the queen of England."

Audrey cringed. "Miss Mortified Wallflower suits me better. Did you see that puppet hanging behind the others?"

"I did. And that wee marionette looks nothing like you, Miss Audrey." When Reid spoke her name, his voice dropped even deeper than usual. He drew it out as if she were the only woman in the room—well, since she was in fact alone in the assembly hall with him, he most likely had nothing else to focus upon. But still, his tone made her stomach flutter as if a hundred butterflies had sprung from their cocoons.

Licking his lips, he stepped closer. "Let's try something."

She resisted her urge to back away. In fact, she squared her shoulders. "What would that be, my lord?"

"Close your eyes and stand very still."

"What are you planning to do?"

"You'll see. Now close your eyes."

Letting out a sigh, she complied. No dance master had ever asked her to perform a minuet with her eyes closed. They knew she'd fall on her face, no doubt. The earl stepped so near, she could feel the warmth of his breath on her face. She could feel the masculine heat radiating off his body and with it, the scent of a vat of simmering cloves. "I want you to imagine yourself in a field of daisies." His deep brogue rumbled. "You are not wearing a red gown, but one of gold, like the sun, gold like the precious metal that gleams when burnished."

Audrey took in a long breath, sensing the golden sun radiating on her face.

"Birds are singing around you, their song filled with happiness," he continued in that same deep bass. "You feel bubbles rolling inside like sea-foam on the shore."

She licked her lips and smiled while her insides tickled.

He lightly touched her neck and caressed his finger

down one side and up the other. "Can you feel the bubbles?" His fingers slipped to the back of her head, making her tingle all over.

"I do."

"Good." His fingers continued to caress. "The willow warbler is singing so beautifully, his music makes you want to laugh and spin. Can you imagine laughing and spinning beneath the warmth of the radiant sun, lass?"

Her entire body surged with glorious warmth. "Yes," she whispered breathlessly.

"Do not open your eyes," he growled, his lips very near her ear, so much so, he barely had to whisper.

In the next instant, he lifted her by the waist. Air swept beneath her slippers as together they twirled across the floor. Reid's deep laughter filled the room. "Let go, lassie. Dance amongst the daisies."

Audrey threw back her head and allowed laughter to peal from her throat. "I'm flying!"

"You're dancing. You ken the tempo; you've played it hundreds of times on the harpsichord. One, two, three, four, five, six," he repeated while he executed the dance and scandalously held her in his arms. "Say it with me, lass."

Keeping her eyes closed, she imagined the minuet in her mind's eye. "One, two, three, four, five, six . . ."

Before she knew what had happened, her slippers lightly touched the floor as Reid's cadence continued, so light and refreshing, she couldn't help but follow along with him. One, two, three, four, five, six, they executed the pattern over and over like they'd been drawn together for the soul purpose of dancing a minuet. Reid's leg brushed hers. Their palms lightly touched. Audrey opened her eyes. His gaze remained fixed, staring into her soul as he counted the rhythm, slowing ever so gradually. Unable to think of anything but the beautiful green eyes captivating her, consuming her, Audrey had no choice but to dance and dance.

Until their feet stopped moving.

She stood breathless, enchanted.

One corner of his mouth ticked up in a grin while he cupped her cheek with his palm. "That was the most flawless minuet I've ever danced, lass."

"Was it?" she managed to say while her heart hammered.

A lock of hair slipped over his eye, making him look devilishly handsome. She sensed him moving closer.

Am I floating?

Her insides fluttered with anticipation while his lips moved closer, looking as delicious as the filling for a cherry tart. Reid's long lashes fluttered closed. As soon as their lips met, dizzying euphoria swept over her. But their kiss didn't start with a soft brushing, a hint of teasing. This was a body-crushing, bone-melting, and provocative kiss. Fire thrummed through Audrey's blood while passionate heat spilled through her soul.

Slipping her hands around Reid's waist, she dug her fingers into the thick bands of muscle undulating across his back. Allowing herself to cast aside all trepidation, she followed his lead, swirling her tongue and clinging to him as if he were a buoy in an ardent storm.

Every inch of her flesh craved more. More kissing. More touching. To have him hold her tighter. He kneaded his fingers down her spine until he grasped her buttocks and pulled her flush with his hips. Heaven help her. But something deep inside her still craved more. More hands. More rubbing. More closeness.

More hard, masculine flesh.

Lowering his head, Reid's clean-shaven chin slid down her neck, fluttering kisses all the way. He moved a hand to her waist and slowly up her side until his knuckles lightly caressed the top of her breast.

Gasping, Audrey's knees gave out as his tongue swirled over the sensitive skin where his hand had just been. Her hips thrust forward while another unbelievable wave of euphoria swept over her. How could a girl withstand so many sensations at once? When she felt his hardness against her abdomen, Audrey had no misgivings.

The part that frightened her most?

She wasn't frightened.

She wanted him to rub against her. She wanted his mouth on the tops of her breasts and his fingers kneading her through the heavy damask of her gown.

Audrey didn't open her eyes until something hard hit the back of her head.

Chapter Twenty

*F*or the love of everything holy, fierce desire clamped Reid by the balls and sent his mind into a maelstrom of lust. Jesus Christ, the tiny sighs and moans whispering from Audrey's throat were enough to bring any man to his knees. Reid had bedded his share of women, but none so lithe and incredibly virile as the lass in his arms.

Och, how her laughter had set his heart to soaring. If only they could have twirled across the floor eternally so that he could listen to her laugh. Such unabashed and happy emotion had ensnared him, had captured his heart and taken over his mind. He should never have gathered her in his arms. And by the time he realized his folly it was too late.

She'd caught him. And he wasn't free to be caught.

And then he'd lowered his gaze to her lips. Sweet, moist, red lips that begged to be kissed, that pleaded and beckoned his head to lower. Heaven help the burst of fire spreading through his loins. In two ticks of the clock his hands grew a mind of their own while he kissed her. Showed her exactly what he wanted and how much he wanted it. His fingers kneaded, discovering every inch of her long, slender back until he finally found soft, feminine buttocks.

God, save me.

Not one logical thought filled his head while he backed her to the wall. He needed more. More kissing. More touching. More Audrey.

She flinched and gasped when her head rapped the wall.

Reid did, too.

For a moment their gazes locked. Staring. A hunger so fierce swirled low in his gut. Her tongue slipped over her bottom lip as she looked away while color flooded her cheeks.

Reid's throat thickened. What in God's name was he doing? There he stood wanting the lass as if she were an alehouse tart. Audrey wasn't a woman to be used. She was a jewel, a princess. The lass was a delicate flower, a woman on the precipice of adulthood who knew nothing of men and their goddamned wiles.

For the love of life, he would kill any man who attempted to take advantage of her as he was doing now with one hand groping her arse and the other cradling the most delicious breast he'd ever had the pleasure of cupping in his palm.

He blinked, sliding his fingers to her neck.

He wouldn't ruin her and he couldn't marry her.

Can I?

No bloody way. I cannot ignore clan loyalty. I need my uncle's fealty, and creating a rift at this juncture could be a setback for the cause.

Nor could he forget his duty. There was the succession of the kingdom to plan. His meeting with Prince James had been a complete and utter failure. Worse, Reid had no more time to dally in Coxhoe and hunt for suitors. Especially when Wagner Tupps was at large. That man could surface at any time.

Forcing away all amorous thoughts, he released his hands and cleared his throat. "Forgive me."

"Wha—?" She stopped herself from asking as bewilderment filled her tempest-blue eyes. Then the color in Audrey's cheeks deepened as she tapped her lips with her fingers, shuttering those eyes with a downcast glance. "I believe I have some fans to paint, my lord," she said, the tension in her jaw reflecting her humiliation.

Ah, hell, what should he say? Christ, why couldn't he control himself whenever they were alone together? It was supposed to be a dancing lesson, not a mauling.

Audrey dashed for the door.

Reid caught her arm. "Wait."

She didn't turn to face him. "We mustn't be alone together again. I cannot trust myself."

Jesus Christ, that was an understatement.

"Nay," he growled. "'Tis me you cannot trust." He loosened his grip slightly as he stepped nearer. "I've been waiting for MacRae to return with word from the northern clans, but I now realize 'tis time to head for the safety of Brahan Castle."

She inclined her ear his way. "You're leaving?"

"As are you, lass. You cannot remain at Coxhoe House whilst Mr. Tupps is at large." When he released her arm, she faced him.

"You mean to say you're taking me to the wilds of Scotland?"

He chuckled at the surprise forming on her swollen lips. "Wilds?"

"I-I…" Bewilderment filled her eyes. "Me? Travel all the way to the Highlands?"

"Aye. We'll leave on the morrow."

"So soon? But…" Audrey's once rapturous expression now pulled taut with fear. "I've heard they do not care for English girls in Scotland."

"Not true," he replied, though he knew what she meant. Highlanders were suspicious of Sassenachs—outsiders. "You're under my care, and nary a man will question it. I should have spirited you away home as soon as I'd heard that Tupps eluded my men. From Brahan Castle, I can raise an army of three thousand with the snap of my fingers. No one will harm you there."

"But on the morrow?"

He flicked his fingers toward the door. "Go. Find Mrs. Hobbs and set to packing."

As soon as he arrived home he'd take up his quill and write to the potential suitors from the Barnard Ball. He was finished with England and Watford's ridiculous missives. Christ, Reid could fight the abeyance from Scotland. He'd take Miss Kennet's papers to his solicitor in Dingwall and settle her affairs from there. Bloody hell, he should have made this decision a month ago.

* * *

Standing on the stoop of her beloved home, Audrey crossed her arms and tapped her foot. "I cannot possibly leave my harpsichord behind."

"Where do you suggest we stow it?" Reid asked, thrusting his hand toward the trunks already stacked two high on the wagon hitched to a pair of enormous oxen. "How on earth can a woman pack an entire household in a day? I travel with a bedroll and a satchel with a change of clothes, and if you haven't noticed, we cannot fit a mere pocket watch on the wagon, let alone a harpsichord."

She wanted to cry. How dare he first pretend their kissing had meant absolutely nothing, and then pull her away from everything she held dear. Squaring her shoulders, she stamped her foot. Her request might be a tad excessive, but that didn't mean it should be cast aside with an overbearing remark—at least five pocket watches could squeeze into the nooks and crannies she could see. "Pardon me, my lord, but a lady doesn't set out for the far north without any idea as to when she will return without taking along her possessions."

"Aye, we have a chest full of fans and paints and five filled with garments for every occasion imaginable, and that only left us a wee bit of room for food, canvas for tents, and cookware for our journey."

"Tents?"

"Aye, there are no inns when crossing over the peaks, lass."

"We're crossing mountains?"

"That's why they call them the Highlands." He gave her shoulder a clap like he would another man, not a woman he'd held in his arms and showered with kisses one day prior. "Not to worry, we'll be following drovers' trails through the glens. They're well traveled."

"Aye," said Graham as he tied a rope to secure the load. "If ye ken where you're going."

All the men chuckled.

Audrey gulped. She'd heard about elusive Highland tactics. The English dragoons hated chasing their quarry in the Scottish mountains. Rumors were Highlanders disappeared into the mist like ghosts, never to be found again. The mountains were wild and rugged and...

Scary.

Audrey folded her arms tightly across her rib cage. "Is there, perchance, a place near Brahan Castle where I might be able to practice a harpsichord?"

Reid scratched his chin and looked skyward. "Hmm—"

"There's an organ at the Dingwall Kirk," said Graham.

The big Highlander gave her a grin. And why did her pitiful heart have to flutter? She was angry with him. Seaforth was taking her away from the home she loved. When would she return?

"Aye," he agreed. "I'm sure the vicar will be amenable to allowing you to play when there's no one else about."

"I didn't realize I'd appraised so poorly, my lord." Heavens, had everything he'd said been a ruse to soften her up so she would be amenable to his kisses?

Blast him.

"Nay. I meant what I said. You are quite practiced." His eyes darkened. "How many female church organists have you encountered, Miss Kennet?" Now he was being impudent. She'd referred to him as "my lord" twice, and he was making a point, showing he'd noticed.

To her dismay, she knew all too well what he meant. The only women in the church were nuns. Indeed, women like Audrey were supposed to marry.

Full stop.

Marriage was an heiress's goal in life. Other pursuits like earning a living from painting fans were frivolous endeavors. Moreover, playing an organ in a church when there were people present was taboo. She knew it. She was a graduate of Talcott Ladies' Finishing School. She knew Papa was planning to find her a husband this season. And now Reid MacKenzie planned to finish the task from Brahan Castle—an archaic fortress, no doubt. He wanted to be rid of her because she suspected she had the same effect on him that he had on her. Every time they were in close proximity and alone, her heart raced and her insides jumped with all sorts of inexplicable emotions.

Was she in love with him?

How could she even ask herself such a question?

They scarcely knew each other.

They were from two different worlds.

And he continually repeated that he was a busy man, too busy and too young to think about marriage, though he was four years her senior.

"Redcoats!"

With that one shouted word, Audrey's life spiraled into mayhem.

Chapter Twenty-One

*R*eid's gaze darted to the horses and back to the army of mounted dragoons approaching from the drive. If it weren't for Audrey, he might try to run, but playing the odds bore too much risk someone might end up shot in the back—especially the lass riding the old gelding.

Graham pulled the ramrod from his musket and charged the barrel with powder.

Slicing his hand through the air, Reid stopped him. "We're outnumbered."

The Highlander lowered his weapon and rolled his gaze to the sky. "Christ."

Audrey stepped nearer, so close her aura of fear was palpable. He placed a reassuring palm on her elbow. "You needn't worry. There's no law against traveling north, and that's exactly what we're doing."

"I disagree," the lass whispered with a shift of her eyes. "Mr. Tupps is riding alongside the captain."

Reid narrowed his gaze, looking closer at the approaching regiment. "Ballocks."

"What do you think they're planning?" she asked.

"With an army of fifty or so men?" He glanced her way. "Nothing good."

"What are we going to do?"

"I reckon anything they fancy. No use making a run for it with fifty muskets trained on my heart—even if they're lousy shots, one will likely hit its target." He urged her behind him and looked to Graham. "If I'm taken, stick to the plan. Miss Audrey is no longer safe in Coxhoe, not with slithering Tupps lurking in the grass."

The Highlander nodded as horse hooves clopped into the cobbled courtyard. The retinue stayed in formation, riding directly to the porch.

"That's him, Captain Fry." Wagner pointed a spindly finger at Reid. "The double-crossing Earl of Seaforth."

Feet planted wide, Reid ignored the weasel and jammed his fists onto his hips while staring at the red-coated captain. "Come to call with an entire regiment, sir? Seems a bit excessive."

Captain Fry sat his mount with an air of disdain. He had pinched features and a pockmarked face—most likely a third son, or a titled man with no coin. Regardless, by his expression alone, he carried a chip on his shoulder the size of the Stone of Scone.

After reining his horse to a stop, he motioned and a dozen dragoons dismounted while the rest drew their muskets, cocking them and raising the wooden butts to their shoulders. Once they had Reid surrounded, Fry cleared his throat. "Reid MacKenzie, Earl of Seaforth, you are hereby charged with treason."

The six dragoons marched toward the steps, swords

drawn, but for one. Graham and the MacKenzie men blocked their path.

Reid folded his arms, not yet ready to tell his men to stand down. "What evidence do you have for such alleged treachery? The word of a guttersnipe over that of an earl?"

"I've seen proof. Correspondence to you from the late Mr. Kennet was intercepted by this esteemed gentleman and is in safekeeping."

"Aye? What deviousness is this with signatures and stamps verified? I say your man is a gold digger of the worst sort and he aims to take you to the gutter with him."

Fry moved his mount closer. "I do not want to turn this into a bloodbath, my lord, but if you do not tell your men to step aside, I will have no recourse but to order mine to cut you down without mercy."

Reid regarded the mounted musketeers. Every one of them had his gun pointed at his heart. *No use dying this day.* "Stand down, men. When the queen hears of this I will ensure she strips you of your rank, Captain." Reid caught Graham's eye. "Send word to Dunn."

"You, sir, are the felon," bleated Tupps. "Not only did this man commit treason, he broke into my home and wrongfully assaulted a citizen in good standing."

Reid could have fired black powder through his eyeballs while the wretched louts slapped a pair of iron manacles around his wrists. "Good standing? I very much doubt you ken what that means."

Audrey rushed down the steps. "Where are you taking him?"

Captain Fry smirked down at her, stroking his fingers through the tines of a whip tucked in his belt. "He'll be my guest at Durham Gaol until and *if* we receive word from Her Majesty." He rubbed a bit of the braided leather between his fingertips. "I aim to make him feel quite at home."

"No!" She drew her hands together and pressed praying fingers to her lips. "That place is hideous. It should be condemned. My father petitioned for it to be torn down years ago."

Wagner dismounted and sauntered to the lass. "Your father was a traitor."

A flash of ire darted through her gaze, but she didn't back down. "My father built an empire."

Good lass.

Tupps threw back his head and cackled. "An empire I'm poised to inherit—along with your hand."

Christ, Reid should have run a blade across the bastard's throat when he'd had the chance. He bared his teeth and yanked his wrists against the manacle chains. "There's no way in hell you'll inherit a farthing, and if you lay one finger on the lass, I'll hunt you down and ensure you suffer a long and painful death."

"See, Captain? This murderous traitor is full of threats." Wagner shifted his eel-eyed glare to Reid. "While I'm bedding this fine morsel, you will be sent to the Tower. You'll stand trial and hang in London for all your highborn friends to see."

"I beg to differ," Reid growled, then he looked to Audrey and lowered his voice. "Remember what I said."

"My, my, he even talks like he thinks he's a king, though his lands will soon be forfeit." Wagner draped his arm around Audrey's shoulders. Shoulders too pristine, too pure, too perfect for Reid to touch, and now he seethed while a wallowing pig touched her and smiled like a lecherous cur. "Ready your wedding dress, Miss Kennet. As soon as Watford procures the papers to transfer the deeds to my name, I'll be dragging you straight to the church."

Audrey tugged away from Tupps and moved between Graham and Davy. The MacKenzie guardsmen surrounded the lass.

"Enough talk." Captain Fry beckoned with his fingers. "The evidence against Seaforth is incriminating. The man is guilty and I aim to see him pay."

As the dragoons led Reid to his horse, he watched the varlet out the corner of his eye. Tupps turned, his sneer gloating. In one move, Seaforth looped his arms over the maggot's head, wrapped the chain around his neck, and clamped him in a stranglehold. "If you place one finger on my ward, I'll sever your cods." Tupps's face turned scarlet. Reid clenched his arms, tightening his grip. "That's a promise."

"Release him!" the captain commanded, pulling a flintlock pistol from his holster while a dragoon struck Reid in the back with a club.

He arched his spine with the sharp pain, but that only made him squeeze the manacle chain tighter.

Reid watched Tupps gasp and struggle for air. Just before the man lost consciousness, he eased his grip slightly and pressed his lips to Tupps's ear, whispering so only his quarry could hear, "The next time we meet I'll not be so lenient. And mark me. We *will* meet. Soon. Without a contingent of dragoons in your wake. Aye, think of me when your head hits the pillow each night 'cause I aim to be your worst nightmare."

With a grunt, the dragoon recoiled for another strike,

but before he followed through, Reid shoved the varlet to the ground, ducking away from the swinging club.

* * *

Watching the man who claimed to be her cousin retreat with the dragoons and the earl, Audrey still couldn't believe what had just transpired.

"We cannot possibly leave for the Highlands now." She whipped around and faced Graham. "What will become of His Lordship?"

A MacKenzie guard shoved his sword in its scabbard. "I don't feel right about leaving, either."

Graham glanced away, his lips disappearing into a thin line. "You heard him. He ordered us to continue. Miss Kennet isn't safe."

"I'll be damned," said Jeffrey, pointing beyond the stable. "Isn't that the MacRae chieftain?"

All heads turned toward the copse of trees lining the northern property line. Sure enough. Dunn MacRae led a regiment of twenty rugged-looking, kilt-wearing Highlanders cantering straight for the manse.

"His timing is a wee bit off," Graham said, shifting his fists to his hips, looking like a smaller version of the earl.

Audrey clasped her hands, saying a quick prayer. "Thank heavens."

When Dunn reined his horse to a stop, everyone spoke at once. They shouted about the dragoons dragging the earl away and accusing him of treason. If they'd only left one day prior, they would have avoided the whole confrontation, but Reid had been hell-bent on waiting for Dunn, and what the hell had taken him so long.

"One at a bloody time!" The Highlander looked over the men and glared at Audrey as if this was her fault. "Where are they taking him?"

"Durham Gaol," said Graham.

"Jesus Saint Christopher Christ, do not tell me he's fallen into the hands of Captain Bainbridge Fry? That man has a reputation as gruesome as the poor souls who rot in Durham's bowels."

"Lord, no!" Audrey pushed through the men and grabbed Dunn's horse's bridle. White foam leached from the garron's neck as his nostrils flared with labored snorts. "Mr. MacRae, you must go after His Lordship immediately."

"Not without a plan, and a damned good one." Dunn looked at her like she'd grown two heads, then he dismounted and shoved Graham in the shoulder. "Why did you not stop the backbiters, damn it all?"

Graham puffed out his chest and stood his ground. "Too many muskets locked, loaded, and trained on Seaforth's heart, else I would have taken half a dozen myself."

"It doesn't matter what happened," Audrey said. "What matters is what we're to do next."

This time as Dunn eyed her, she straightened her spine and mirrored Graham's stance, thrusting her fists into her hips for added effect. Behaving the wallflower would do nothing to save the earl. The situation was grave, and Audrey had naught to do but bear down and assert herself. Mr. MacRae might be a chieftain, but he paid fealty to the MacKenzie clan and something needed to be done. Now, not after he held a clan meeting.

"Seaforth told us to take the lassie to Brahan," Graham

said, going on to explain the whole mess with Wagner Tupps.

"Jesus Christ." Dunn removed his bonnet and scratched his mop of dark tresses. "I told him not to grow too involved with the lassie's affairs."

Audrey stamped her foot. "For pity's sake, you men are standing around like you're discussing politics in the parlor. We must take action."

"Aye, and that's what I aim to do, lassie." Dunn flicked his hand toward the door. "Go back inside and tend to whatever it is English heiresses tend to."

Crossing her arms, Audrey didn't budge.

"We need an army," said Graham.

Dunn narrowed his dark gaze and smirked. "Nay, nay. Not on this side of the border. I aim to aid in Seaforth's peaceable escape." Audrey opened her mouth to speak, but he thrust his finger in front of her face. "And I reckon I'll need your help, Sassenach."

Her heartbeat spiked. "Anything."

"Remember what I said about Tupps." Graham moved closer. "Miss Audrey isn't safe here."

Dunn snickered. "You mean to tell me you're afraid of a sniveling Englishman?"

The MacKenzie guardsman threw out his palms. "A lying, cheating, devious—"

"I am not leaving before His Lordship is freed," Audrey said, standing her ground.

"Enough!" Dunn sliced his hand through the air. "She's right. We're not going anywhere without Seaforth. Leave the rat to me and Clan MacRae." He peered at Audrey with a sharp-eyed stare. "Can you sew, lass?"

This Highlander was nearly as uncouth as Mr. Tupps. Even his scowl appeared sinister. But if Seaforth trusted him, then she had no choice but to do so as well. She nodded. "Yes. I am an accomplished seamstress."

"'Tis fortunate." He winked and grinned like a devil. "You'll need to stitch your fingers to the bone, 'cause I have a plan."

Chapter Twenty-Two

*D*uring the long ride to Durham, Reid kept his gaze forward, but he could count every redcoat dragoon out of the corners of his eyes. If only Dunn had returned, he mightn't be in this mess. And if he'd received a response to the missive he'd dispatched to London, he would have avoided it altogether for certain. Fighting wasn't the answer, either. Now was no time to start a rising. Too many things needed to be orchestrated. Besides, marching into battle was never the first option.

But all the while, Reid thought. He thought about Audrey and devised a hundred ways to murder Wagner Tupps, but most of all, he thought of what led him into this mess.

The directive from Prince James that Dunn took into the Highlands was to bring the clans together and train for war—words he'd never uttered on British soil, words he'd never written with his quill. It was damnable enough to carry such a missive, which he'd done fully aware of the risks it bore. Though his actions had not been treasonous.

The Jacobites would continue to behave peaceably until the death of the queen. Only then would they unite and defend James's ascension to the throne—preferably without bloodshed, and preferably without legislation in place to prevent a Catholic from becoming king. Not only did they need to build their forces, but those loyalists sitting in Parliament had a responsibility to abolish the Act of Settlement and prevent the ratification of the Occasional Conformity Act.

Damnation, he'd been so close to arriving at a solution to the succession without the threat of bloodshed. And now, rotting in the bowels of a notorious prison was to become his lot? Why hadn't the queen sent a reply? He'd been forthright in his letter to her. With her husband dead and no surviving children, surely Her Highness would appreciate Reid's efforts to convince her half brother to accept Protestantism.

A tick in his jaw twitched when the spires of Durham came into view. And as they rode into the city, people stopped and stared. They put their heads together, men hiding behind hands and women behind their fans. None too discreetly they gossiped about Reid's bare knees and his tartan, no doubt casting judgment on the barbaric Scot who sat the saddle. Soon they'd all be chattering with excitement once they discovered Captain Fry had brought in a Highland earl accused of treason.

That ought to keep the vultures entertained for a fortnight or more.

After passing the town hall, the retinue turned right and proceeded under a dark, stone archway. The sound of shod horses resounded among the city's walls, becoming deafening in the dank tunnel. On the other side, the archaic gaol's bailey stood thirty feet high, made of sandstone and streaked with black from years of withstanding coal-burning fires. Above, sentries watched from atop the wall, armed with muskets and wearing tall grenadier hats.

Blackened iron gates with teeth honed to cold spears screeched open like a welcome to hell.

Once inside the outer courtyard, the horses stopped. Six dragoons pulled Reid from his mount and urged him under another dank archway, jabbing him with the sharp points of their bayonets. The same six men bared their teeth and coaxed him beneath a portcullis with deadly iron spikes.

Once in the courtyard, Captain Fry hastened ahead and pointed to a lone wooden post with an iron ring nailed high up the shaft, waiting to anchor its next victim's wrists.

Reid's gut twisted, but with his following blink, he memorized the faces of the six dragoons who'd coaxed him from his mount with the point of their bayonets. He would not forget the faces of oppression. Nor would he forgive.

Grinding his teeth, Reid fought against the men while they tried to force his manacled wrists up to the iron ring. Until Captain Fry pressed the barrel of a flintlock pistol to his temple. "I'd like nothing better than to end this right here, mate."

Ice shot through Reid's blood as he blinked and saw an image of Audrey. His men were good, but Tupps would stop at nothing to get what he wanted. Without Reid to intervene, the lass would fall into the bastard's hands.

My men must protect her. But where the bloody hell is Dunn?

Willfully, he raised his wrists to the ring. "You are making a grave mistake, raising your hand against me. I'll have you know I am one of Queen Anne's most beloved."

"You won't be once she sees the missive from Kennet."

"That I visited her brother in France? Many a noble has made the crossing. Tell me, who would you see on the throne when our great queen is gone?"

The captain hit him in the shoulder with the base of his pistol, but not before he hesitated. "You speak with the smooth tongue of a traitor."

Reid sneered and ignored the throbbing pain. "You, sir, cannot tell me you are acting solely on the word of a known liar. A known swindler. A man who prides himself on collecting tidbits of scandal on unsuspecting subjects for his own gain."

"I speak the truth!" Wagner marched into Reid's line of sight and smirked. "You met with James in France. I saw the missive Nicholas Kennet dispatched to you with my own eyes."

Reid groaned. There had been many missives and not a one constituted treason.

Captain Fry shoved the weasel in the shoulder. "Visit the factor's rooms for payment. This is government business now."

Reid tested his wrists against the chains, his fingers already growing numb from hanging above his head. "I am an emissary of the queen." He eyed the captain, commanding his attention. "I suggest you wait to receive word from Her Highness before you flog a peer of the realm."

The corners of the man's mouth turned up as he pulled the cat-o'-nine-tails from his belt and combed his fingers through the braided thongs. "I've received enough proof.

Behind these walls, titles count for naught. When you are a guest of Durham Gaol, you are mine."

"Truly? Do you ken I was fostered by the queen herself?" Reid matched the captain's smirk with one of his own. "Even from this shite hole I can see to it you are shipped to the Americas in chains."

Fear flashed through the captain's eyes so fast, if Reid had blinked he would have missed it. With a spike of his heart, he inclined his chin over his arm, leaning his face in spitting distance of the red-coated maggot. "What's your story, Fry? Why are you stuck in this miserable outpost? What is it? Are you the fifth son of a baronet—the lowliest of peers?"

The man's jaw twitched. His eyes darkened.

"Ah, 'tis worse, is it not?" Reid goaded. "You're a bastard."

The man struck with lightning-fast reflexes. Nine tarred leather strips, knotted to lacerate the skin, sliced across Reid's cheek. Ignoring the sting, he laughed out loud.

"You are guilty of treason, and I will have your confession by the day's end." The captain's heels clicked the cobbles while he marched out of view. "Cut off his coat."

Blood seeped down Reid's cheek while a dragoon used a dagger to cleave through layers of fabric, exposing his flesh to the cool breeze. Bile churned in his gut as he closed his eyes and steeled his mind to the pain that would come. "You're wasting your time."

"You visited the Pretender in France. Admit to it!"

Leering, Reid glanced over his shoulder. "I visited him, aye. And Her Highness, Queen Anne, kens my purpose."

"Lie!"

The whip's tines hissed through the air, ripping through his skin like knives. Every muscle clenched with the toe-curling strike.

"You are a Jacobite traitor!" bellowed Fry.

"No," Reid growled through clenched teeth, his nerves throbbing with the sting.

Another strike ripped through the flesh on his back, making his knees buckle as a feral wail pealed from his throat.

"Admit you're trying to overthrow the queen."

"Never!" Reid growled. He blinked through the sweat dripping into his eyes. But regardless of his will, frayed and exposed flesh too easily succumbed to grating pain. His arms strained against the iron manacles chained above his head while tremors weakened his legs. Holding on to a thread of sanity, his mind focused on one thing— Audrey. His ward needed him. He must survive for her.

Reid clamped his teeth until they nearly shattered and took his lashings, counting each vicious strike as he fought to retain his wits. Hot blood seeped into the waistband of his kilt as his back stung like he'd been crisscrossed and carved by a madman's blunt knife.

Once his legs gave way, Reid's head lolled, his arms straining, about to tear from their sockets. Bitter bile scorched his throat while he leaned into the pole for support. With his next blink he saw Audrey smiling. Audrey laughing.

The captain blocked the cooling wind when he sauntered up and shoved Reid's hair from his face. "See, MacKenzie? It doesn't matter if you're an earl or a thief, all men bleed the same." He slapped Reid's back, sending a fresh bout of searing pain across his raw and bloodied flesh.

A savage bellow ripped from his throat as the court-yard spun around him.

"'Tis a pity you cannot see the beautiful artwork on your back." Fry snorted with scorn. "You see, I am an artist of sorts. I carve patterns that will never fade. Patterns that will live in your memory for the rest of your days—which I suspect will not be long."

"You're mad." The words came out dry and bitter.

The captain leaned forward. "What, what? Are you ready to confess, Jacobite?"

Reid's head shook as he forced himself to raise his chin and level his gaze with Satan. "I will meet you in hell."

Behind, someone cackled in a grating laugh.

Mercifully, that was the last sound Reid heard as his mind slipped into the blackness of oblivion.

Chapter Twenty-Three

*C*rouched behind the woodshed, Wagner watched the manse. He'd hidden there many times over the years, observing the activity that passed in silhouette across the windows after dark. Night was his friend. He could move anywhere without drawing attention to himself. People revealed their closest secrets in the dark. And it was under night's cloak that he could be a ghost.

This was the first time he'd visited Coxhoe House since Seaforth's abduction five days ago. Now that the Earl of Seaforth was out of the picture, there was little to stop him. Wagner had stayed away on purpose. Nicholas Kennet's daughter needed to reestablish her priorities, needed to foster a bit of fear in her heart. It would be far easier to turn her to his side without that beast of a Scot playing guardian. And now that Seaforth was in the clutches of Bainbridge Fry, the man was doomed.

Fry had proved an ally more than once. The officer was almost as power hungry as Wagner. And through the years it came to pass that they had much in common. They both suffered illegitimate birth, though Fry was the son of the bishop of Durham—formerly a Catholic who had turned to Protestantism with the times.

But the bishop of Durham ran everything in his jurisdiction, including the gaol. Fry had received an education at the expense of the church, though he was never permitted to live under his father's roof. Now that Fry had become a man, the bishop had seen to it his son was promoted to captain and made the prison warden. An apt post for a man who loved control. A tyrant who gained power from the pain and torture of others.

Wagner both respected and feared Captain Fry. As long as he could feed the man with dirty secrets, their relationship would continue. But he wasn't daft enough to grow too close. Wagner might enjoy watching the ruination of others, but he lacked Fry's thirst for blood. The man wore a countenance of steel, yet every time Wagner met with him he sensed the captain on the verge of becoming unhinged.

But nothing about Captain Fry's madness mattered at the moment. The officer had Seaforth locked behind the gates of an impenetrable prison—a gaol with the worst repute for sending her guests to Hades. And if the earl managed to survive her atrocious conditions, it was only a matter of time before Queen Anne ordered his execution. Fry promised to dispatch a report to London when he gained a confession that would bury the earl once and for all.

True, the missive Wagner had intercepted from Kennet's messenger wasn't incriminating enough to stand on its own. Kennet had written that he believed the visit to Prince James was the only way to convince His Highness to convert to Protestantism. It was close to treason, but not an all-out admission. Nonetheless, Fry was confident he'd be able to gain a confession from Seaforth in short order.

Wagner rubbed his hands.

That is one beheading I cannot miss.

He watched the light flicker in a window in the west wing of Coxhoe House. He'd seen Audrey's feminine form pass behind the curtains of that window so many times, there was no doubt it was her chamber. Her lair. Excitement pulsed through his veins as he ached to run his fingers through her golden tresses.

Tonight he'd have her for himself. Another hour and she would be his.

* * *

In the past it had usually been easy to slip into Nicholas Kennet's manse. The cook had rarely latched the kitchen window, and no one ever checked. Kennet had a number of servants, but no army. Once Seaforth had moved in, it became more of a challenge—not impossible, but Wagner needed to be stealthier. And now guards patrolled the perimeter of the manse. Wagner waited until the patrol passed the kitchen and turned the corner before he made his move. Wasting no time, he ran to the window and heaved it up, but the damned thing had been latched. He chuckled to himself as he drew his knife.

This blade hasn't failed me yet.

He levered it between the upper and lower pane and pushed the lock open. In moments he was inside.

He checked his pocket watch by the glow from the hearth. Half past twelve. He tiptoed to the door and stood very still, holding his breath. Not a voice or footfall echoed from the passageway beyond.

Thrice before Wagner had slipped inside and wandered these halls. The last time had been when Kennet was away with Seaforth. That time, Wagner made his way to Audrey's chamber and stood outside her door. He'd pressed his ear to the timbers and listened to her slumber. He'd inhaled her scent and bathed in it…until a loud creak had startled him from his quest. He'd been so anxious to see to the ruination of his uncle, a man who refused to recognize his nephew. Wagner's plans might have been foiled by Seaforth for a time, but no longer.

Wagner slithered up the servants' stairs and into the west wing passageway until he arrived at her door. He closed his eyes and reveled in the rush, the thundering of his heart, the lust swirling in his loins.

His fingers trembled with anticipation as he lowered them to the knob and turned. A slight click sounded.

He froze and held his breath, waiting for her to wake. Perhaps the beauty would call to him. Closing his eyes, he willed it to be so, but after a moment's hesitation he slowly opened the door and crept inside.

The fire in the hearth cast an amber glow throughout the chamber, just how Wagner liked it. Across the floor, she curled beneath the bedclothes, the heavy coverlet piled high as she slumbered. He smiled to himself. Audrey was a burrower. He liked that, too.

He locked the door behind him. "Audrey," he whispered, hoping to rouse her enough to avoid startling the lovely. Things would be so much easier if she were willing.

She didn't stir, though her breathing grew heavier.

Pulling a cloth from the purse he wore at his hip, Wagner crept forward. He didn't want to gag the girl, but he couldn't take the chance on her sounding an alarm. He stood at the edge of the bed for a moment, preparing to strike. His movement must be flawless. Tingles of anticipation fired across his skin.

"Audrey," he said softly, drawing the bedclothes away.

Blue steel flashed.

Wagner's heart flew to his throat. This wasn't Audrey.

A hulk of a man took aim.

The flintlock fired with an earsplitting boom.

Something seared the side of his head. His ears rang as he stumbled backward.

The brute sprang off the bed. "You flea-bitten bastard, I'll run ye through!"

Bare feet thudded on the floorboards. A dirk hissed from its scabbard.

His heart nearly exploded as Wagner sprinted for the window. In one motion, he slammed a chair through the pane while taking a flying leap. Crashing into the ground, his knees buckled, but he used the momentum to roll away. Another shot fired as he ran into the darkness, cursing under his breath.

Hot rage churned in his gut.

No one double-crossed Wagner Tupps.

Now he had no choice but to make Audrey pay. She'd forced this upon herself.

* * *

Audrey's eyes flashed open at the sound of musket fire. Even from the east wing she could hear Mr. MacRae shouting curses followed by the sound of breaking glass. Springing from the bed, she raced into the corridor.

Mrs. Hobbs was already there, candle in her trembling hand. The matron gulped, her eyes filled with fear. "It appears the chieftain was right."

Audrey nodded, clutching her fists to her chest. "I'm glad I didn't argue when he insisted I sleep in Papa's chamber and he in mine."

Below stairs, it sounded like an army was mustering. Men shouted and footsteps raced.

Audrey dashed to the bedside and retrieved the musket she'd kept loaded and stowed beneath the bed since Reid's capture. She beckoned to the housemaid. "Come."

Mrs. Hobbs grasped her elbow. "I think we'd best remain where we are."

"Are you jesting?" Audrey surged forward. "How are we to know what really happened?"

When they arrived in the foyer, they found Dunn MacRae shouting orders. "He ran north, the coward. Seaforth's men will guard the lass. No one sleeps until we're certain he's gone."

"What will we do if we catch him?" asked a MacRae Highlander.

"Kill him." When a floorboard creaked beneath Audrey's slipper, Mr. MacRae spun on his heel. He regarded her from head to toe as if she were a crazed wildcat. "Miss Audrey, you must go back above stairs."

She didn't budge, pointing the muzzle of her musket downward in case it misfired. "Was it Tupps?"

"Aye, the bas—the lout." Dunn took her by the shoulder and urged her to turn back to the stairs. "You'd best return to bed. The excitement is over."

"But how am I to sleep? Surely there must be something I can do rather than waiting for Mr. Tupps to abscond with me."

"He's nay going to lay a finger on you, lassie. Now, how many of those red coats have you and the housemaid completed?"

They had been working tirelessly for the past five days while Reid continued to suffer in Durham. "All six finished this eve, sir."

"And the breeches?"

"Starting on them next."

"Then I bid you set your fingers to sewing."

She gave a nod, clicking closed the cock on her musket and wishing she could ride with the men. Her fingers and wrists ached from hours of stitching. In the past five days she'd only stopped to take her meals and to sleep. But they were nearly done. And breeches were so much easier to sew than the coats with their gold buttons and yards of piping.

Chapter Twenty-Four

*E*very inhale stretched Reid's skin, making the welts on his back sear with agonizing pain. He shivered, his tongue dry, swollen, and feeling too big for his mouth. He had no idea how long he'd been forsaken in the dank cell. Days? He squinted to open his eyes and winced.

Twenty lashings with a cat-o'-nine-tails equated to one hundred eighty crisscrossing lines. Each one had split open his flesh. With the pain, warm trickles of blood needled his skin, prickling like dozens of stinging bees.

Something tapped the bottom of his foot. "I think he's still alive."

"Not for long, most likely," replied the other. The two cellmates lurked like ghosts waiting to escort him to Hades.

Reid sniffed, the stench making him gag. "Water."

"We drank your ration."

The other coughed—a hacking cough. "I drained some into your mouth first."

"How long have I been here?" Lord, his voice rasped.

"Five days. 'Tis a wonder you haven't bled out."

"Five?" Reid tried to remember. Yes, during his moments of lucidness someone had given him water. He wiped his hand across his forehead. At least Audrey would be in Scotland by now. The team most likely was just starting the crossing through the Highlands. Thank God she'd be safe there.

The other scooted nearer. "I reckon you'd be pushing up daisies by now if it weren't for me."

Reid ran his tongue over chapped lips. "Remind me of your kindness when we're out of this place." Blinking, he forced his eyes to focus on the man sitting in rags an arm's reach away. Where in God's name had Captain Fry deposited him? An earl should have a cell to himself or at least a cell with other noblemen. "Who are you?"

"William Potter, esquire." The man gestured to another. "And that there's Jamison Crowe."

"Have you heard what they're planning?"

"Aye, to keep us here until we rot."

"That cannot happen. I am innocent."

Potter snickered. "That makes three of us."

"When the queen hears of this outrage, she will strip Fry of his commission and he will live out his days in poverty."

"Have you not heard, gov?" asked Crowe. "No one ever leaves Durham Gaol. The best you can hope for is death, and if the captain doesn't think you've suffered enough, he'll make you pay with another pound of flesh."

Reid smirked, his eyes rolling to the back of his head. "I haven't another pound left."

* * *

At last the day came when Mr. MacRae announced they were ready. Though the chieftain treated Audrey like a featherbrained waif, she knew something of the plan because he'd asked her to forge the queen's signature on a missive. They'd taken a proclamation from her father's papers that had been signed by Queen Anne, and Audrey practiced a dozen times before she thought the forgery was good enough to pass a cursory inspection.

She'd read the missive, too. It requested that Captain Fry release the Earl of Seaforth into Major Hargrove's hands for transport to London. The major would be played by the butler, Gerald, because he was the least likely to be recognized and he spoke with the right inflection.

In the courtyard, the men were preparing the horses for their journey. Mr. MacRae had told Audrey she was only allowed a satchel, in which she packed a medicine bundle she'd prepared and a few necessities, though there was no room for a single gown. She didn't care. If she carried a gown, someone might find it. She regarded herself in the mirror and squared her shoulders. The dragoon's uniform she'd tailored for herself had been crafted with the most care of any of those she'd sewn, and she planned to wait until she was called to make an appearance.

Leaning closer to the mirror, she pressed her fingers along the mustache she'd made from clippings of her own hair. The gum adhesive smelled like pine and made her nose itch, but the mustache looked genuine. With a step back, she admired her handiwork, then pushed the tricorn hat she wore for riding low on her brow and turned sideways. With boots up to her knees and her hair braided and looped up so it appeared to be shoulder-length, she could pass for a man, especially if she remained mounted.

Satisfied with her costume, she moved to the window and pulled the draperies aside only far enough to peer through. Mr. MacRae waved his arms and pointed as if he were in command of an entire battalion of cavalry while Gerald stood motionless with his hands behind his back, looking very much like a butler in a major's uniform.

Audrey chewed her lip. This ruse had disaster written all over it. Though it was brilliant in a way, there were too many things that could go wrong.

"Miss Audrey," Mrs. Hobbs called from the corridor. "Are you ready?"

"Yes." She picked up her musket and slung it over her shoulder before opening the door.

The housemaid's jaw dropped. "What on earth?"

Audrey marched out so there was no chance Mrs. Hobbs would attempt to lock her within. "You can keep your comments to yourself. There's no chance I will hide on the outskirts of town whilst they attempt to rescue my guardian."

"Lord save us." The matron's voice resounded down the corridor, but Audrey didn't want to hear it. She sped her pace, steeling her nerves for the next battle.

And the next battle came all too quickly.

Once she stepped outside, the MacRae chieftain stopped beside his horse and gaped. "God on the cross, the female thinks she can take on an army of dragoons."

Twenty-six pairs of eyes shifted Audrey's way as the men burst with laughter.

Searching the men's faces for a sympathetic soul, she saw not a one. Even Graham was doubled over, holding his belly. Well, she'd been humiliated beyond belief when the dance master at Talcotts told her she should join the orchestra, and she doubted this instance was any worse than that. Besides, it was her duty to do anything she could to see her guardian rescued. With no time to dash away and hide, Audrey raised her chin. "I'm a good shot. Better than most men."

"You reckon so?" Mr. MacRae sauntered toward her, giving a deprecating once-over. "What happens when the time comes to affix bayonets?"

The laughter subsided.

Audrey stood her ground. "I thought you said this would be a peaceful exchange."

"That's the plan, but this mission is dangerous. Make no bones about it, if something were to go awry, we could have a nasty fight on our hands."

That's exactly what she'd guessed Mr. MacRae would say. "What about Gerald? He's seventy years old, you know." Before the chieftain could spew a rebuke, she sliced her hand through the air just like Reid would do. "I will stay to the rear, and if a fight ensues, I will help His Lordship slip away."

"Och, you have it all planned, do you?"

"She has a point, Dunn," said Graham, God bless him. "Not counting the butler, you only have four uniformed men. She could be useful if we need a fast escape."

The stubborn chieftain shook his head. "I don't like it."

"I look like a man and I'm going, regardless." She'd asked Jeffrey to saddle a younger mount with a man's saddle. They'd be riding hard for the Highlands, and it was highly likely that they'd have to change horses. Allegro would be much safer remaining in the stable at Coxhoe, where Jeffrey could care for him.

"Bloody, miserable bleating hell. Mount up and keep your mouth shut." Mr. MacRae shook his finger under her nose. "And by the saints, do not dismount whilst we're in the company of the government troops. If they catch a gander at your female arse in those breeches, we'll have anarchy on our hands."

Chapter Twenty-Five

*F*ortunately, there was an archway that led to the prison gates, which was a perfect place for Audrey to stop and remain in the shadows while holding the mount they'd brought for Reid. Three MacRae men disguised in government uniforms also blocked anyone from seeing her. Ahead, Gerald and Dunn had dismounted to demand an audience with Captain Fry.

Audrey craned her neck to watch when the captain came out to meet them.

Thank heavens, Gerald played the part of pompous major perfectly, waving the forged missive. "I have been commissioned by Her Highness, Queen Anne, to take possession of the prisoner Reid MacKenzie, the Earl of Seaforth, and escort him to London."

Fry scratched his chin and looked from Dunn to the others. Then he squinted and peered around the guardsmen, taking a gander at Audrey. "So soon? I only dispatched notice of his arrest a fortnight ago. Her Majesty must be very eager for his execution."

Gerald coughed. "Indeed." Audrey's heartbeat spiked, pulsing in her temples as the butler handed over the missive. "My orders, sir."

This is the moment of truth.

She held her breath as Captain Fry examined the seal. Seemingly satisfied, he ran his finger under it, opened the missive, and read. "Verification, Lieutenant," he said, passing the letter to the man on his right.

The lieutenant took his time studying the seal and then the signature Audrey had forged. Then he gave a nod and handed it back to Fry. "All looks to be in order, sir."

Keep breathing, Audrey reminded herself.

That proved not to be difficult as they were asked to wait outside the gates for ages while the soldiers fetched the earl. Gerald and Dunn stood at attention, looking very official. The spare mount decided he didn't care much for the gelding in front of him and bit him on the rump.

The gelding whinnied and reared. "Blast it, keep that nag under control," said Callum, the Highlander sitting the bitten mount.

"I'm trying," she hissed in a hushed whisper, tugging on the lead line, but Reid's horse skittered sideways. It was all she could do to hold on tight enough while simultaneously preventing the beast from dragging her out of the saddle. In fact, she would have fallen by now had she been using a sidesaddle.

With a clatter of hooves, Callum circled his mount and steered him far enough forward not to bother the stallion. Dunn marched toward them, giving her a dastardly look. "What the blazes is going on back here?" he snarled under his breath.

Audrey bit her tongue. If she tried to explain, someone might recognize her voice as female. She inclined her chin toward the naughty horse.

"I reckon Seaforth's stallion is growing impatient," said Callum.

"Jesus Christ," Dunn mumbled, tugging the lead line from her hand. "Bloody women." The word *women* was barely perceptible, but Audrey didn't miss it. The chieftain had been acting chapped ever since he saw her wearing a government uniform.

Nonetheless, she didn't care what he thought. Reid had been incarcerated on account of her. If Papa hadn't asked the earl to be her guardian, he would be at Brahan Castle enjoying his herds of sheep and cattle. Early on he might have been a bit pushy about insisting she find a husband, but he'd always acted with her interests in mind—had treated her kindly, too. Dunn MacRae, on the other hand, clearly couldn't give a fig about Audrey's welfare. He was about as refined as a wild boar, growling at her upon every opportunity.

Everyone's gaze snapped to the gate when it creaked open.

Mr. MacRae strode forward, leading Seaforth's horse.

Peering ahead, Audrey couldn't help her sharp gasp. Reid stepped out wearing nothing but his kilt and a pair of boots. She had to blink to confirm it was he. The poor man's hands were bound with manacles, and he stooped like he was eighty years of age. He was gaunter than he'd been merely a fortnight ago, and his face was drawn and dirty. He raised his hands above his eyes as if the sun, hidden by clouds, was painfully bright.

Dunn continued to move forward, but Captain Fry

looked to the tunnel scowling straight at Audrey. "What the devil?"

She covered her mouth with her hand. Blast it all, if only she could take back her gasp.

"The condition of this man is deplorable," Gerald said with scorn filling his voice, drawing attention from Audrey. "My Lord Seaforth is an earl. By my oath, he's not fit for travel. He'll perish of exposure before we arrive in London."

"No shirt," Reid grunted through clenched teeth, showing not a hint of recognition. He then turned his back to Gerald.

Audrey clapped her other hand over her mouth to stifle her cry. For pity's sake, they'd mangled his flesh into mincemeat. No wonder the poor man looked like death.

"Christ." Even Dunn winced.

Gerald thrust his finger at the captain. "I will be filing a report of this outrage."

"The earl's headed to the gallows, is he not?" Captain Fry slapped his gloves in hand. "I was fully within my rights as warden of this gaol to ensure order amongst the prisoners. I serve queen and country just as does every other officer of the crown."

Audrey suspected the captain had uttered such drivel many times in the past. She prayed this would be the last of his sedition. If Seaforth didn't file a complaint when this was over, she would.

"Mount up!" Dunn hollered, handing Reid the stallion's reins and shooting Gerald a look.

The butler puffed out his chest like a commanding officer and strode for his horse. "We ride, men!"

Though Reid's gaze shifted her way when he rode past, he kept his expression impassive. Audrey did her best to conceal both her relief and her horror. She patted the musket holstered to her saddle and reined her horse into the same formation they'd used when entering Durham.

The only problem?

She didn't expect to ride out of the tunnel to be met with the steely-eyed glare of Wagner Tupps.

* * *

Immediately dropping her gaze to her hands, Audrey dug in her heels, the reins slipping in her palms.

"Audrey?" Wagner shouted, reining his horse around and cantering up behind.

She leaned forward, demanding more speed.

Dunn drew his pistol and turned in his saddle, taking aim.

"Christ, it's Seaforth's mob of filthy Scots!" Wagner reined his horse beside her and reached for her arm.

"Shoot!" Audrey shouted as the horses thundered down the cobbled street.

Boom!

With a flash of gunpowder, the shot fired from Dunn's flintlock.

Wagner's horse whinnied and reared.

Thrown, the man shrieked, then thudded to the ground.

Without hesitation, Audrey slapped her reins harder until she rode in beside Reid.

The earl's face was hard and determined as he hunched over the stallion's withers and kicked his heels.

"Are you well enough to ride?" she shouted.

"No choice," he growled as musket fire erupted behind them.

Audrey stole a backward glance. Red-coated musketeers ran, lining the city's wall.

"Fire!" an order bellowed in the growing distance. A
brilliant flash of fire flickered through a crenel.

Boom!

A cannonball howled on the wind.

"Faster!" Audrey shouted.

"We're out of range," Dunn bellowed from the lead.

Now in the open, the little band gained speed as they
raced north toward Seaforth's waiting men.

As they crested a hill, Audrey turned around and
searched the city gates for riders. Thank God the redcoats
hadn't yet assembled their horses, but she had no doubt
they'd soon be making chase. If only they could stop to
tend Reid's wounds, but doing so would see them all arrested.

Graham and the remaining men rode out from a copse
of trees, joining them at a gallop. The earl's knuckles
were white as he gripped the reins, his face intently focused on the path ahead. Audrey urged her mount faster.
They'd been successful thus far, and she intended to do
everything in her power to ensure they continued to evade
Fry and his scheming dragoons.

About three miles from Durham, they slowed to a post-
ing trot, a gait the horses could sustain for hours. Every
time she glanced the earl's way, his face grew paler as
if each jarring step sent a shot of pain straight down his
spine.

Audrey prayed Dunn had a plan.

Chapter Twenty-Six

*I*t was well past the witching hour when they stopped the horses just outside the village of Jedburgh. Since fleeing Durham, they'd only rested the horses once. Fry had given Gerald the key to Reid's manacles, which they had removed immediately and buried well off the path in Kielder Forest. Hunched over his horse's neck and too weak to lift his head, Reid raised his eyebrows high enough to see the outline of Jedburgh Abbey against the moonlit sky.

"My mount will not make it another mile," said Gerald.

Since his rescue, Reid had formed a new respect for the old butler. The man had acted the part of major so flawlessly, even he had almost believed the ruse until he saw Dunn. Why the devil they had allowed Audrey to ride with them had him baffled, but he'd deal with that later. Presently, it was all he could do to keep his arse in the damned saddle. The cold night wind bit his skin, and his teeth had been chattering since dusk.

"I reckon we all need rest." Thank God Dunn said it. Reid could have dropped to his death a dozen times since they'd set out. His head throbbed like he'd been hit with an iron hammer, but that was nothing compared to the welts on his back still stinging with the venom of a hundred angry hornets.

Christ, he'd never been this close to death.

"We'll go to the croft to the west," he barked, the effort making his head spin. "Mr. Laidlaw has never turned us away."

"Aye, but we've never knocked on his door at three in the morning," said Dunn.

"Tell him we'll pay him double as long as he agrees not to reveal our whereabouts."

"I must tend to your wounds," Audrey said as they headed westward.

The gentle tenor of her voice startled him. He'd been aware of the lass's presence during the entire ride, though she'd kept mum for the most part. Nonetheless, her frequent glances of pity galled him. He didn't want her pity, and he damned well didn't want her to see him like this, no matter how soothing her ministrations might be. He was a warrior. An earl, for Christ's sake, a fact the captain had overlooked. Indeed, Fry's barbarism would cost him his commission and just might cost the man his life.

Reid forced himself to sit straighter, making stars dart through his vision. "I'll be right in a day or two. Mark me."

"You reckon?" Dunn snorted. "If you ask me, you look like the angel of death is hovering above your head."

"Shut it," Reid growled.

It took an age to ride the mile to the croft while Reid's flesh jarred with his mount's every step. They gathered outside the cottage, the steam from their noses wafting around their heads. After removing his red doublet, Dunn took care of waking Mr. Laidlaw. Once the man appeared in the doorway holding a candle, it wasn't long before he gaped at Reid. "Good God, m'lord. What happened to you?"

Reid tried not to grimace. "Met a cat-o'-nine-tails and lost."

"Red-coated villains no doubt?"

"The same," Dunn replied.

Mr. Laidlaw gave Audrey and the others wearing uniforms a quizzical once-over. "Why are you riding with bloody dragoons?"

"A ruse used for surprise," said Dunn. "We'll change into proper gear if you'll grant us use of your stable."

"Och, you'd best haste in there and stay. The bastards have been making a habit of riding past morning and night."

"My thanks," Reid said, his lips cracking when he tried to smile.

"Do you have any bandages we can use?" asked Audrey.

Reid shot her a frown.

"I brought a salve for abrasions," she whispered.

Didn't she realize how much it pained him to have her see him bent and broken? If only Dunn would have thought to send her ahead on a transport to Brahan Castle, Mrs. Hobbs and one of the guards could have escorted her northward and the lass would have been spared this hardship. Spared seeing him as a broken man.

Bless Mr. Laidlaw all the same. He gave Audrey three rolls of bandages, and then they retired to the stable. Reid managed not to cry out with pain as he climbed the ladder to the loft. But once his feet were flat on the floorboards, he took one look through the dim chamber and stumbled face-first into a pile of hay.

* * *

Audrey dashed to Reid's side. "Gerald, light a lamp straightaway. I need a pail of water and a cloth. And someone had best lend His Lordship their blanket. I've been listening to his teeth chatter since the sun set."

She placed her hand on the earl's shoulder, feeling his skin was much too warm. "Rest, my lord," she said for her own reassurance more than anything. "You've done nothing but see to my protection, 'tis now for me to see to yours." She knew he'd slipped into unconsciousness because he didn't move, didn't utter a word of discord. Throughout the journey, he'd done nothing but growl and bark in an attempt to prove his manhood, no doubt.

As soon as the lard lamp hanging from the rafters was lit, Graham hauled a pail of water from below. He kneeled beside her and handed her a folded piece of linen. "This is the drying cloth from my kit."

"Thank you." She took it and doused it in the water. Her stomach churned as she examined Reid's injuries. "'Tis such a mess, I cannot tell what is dried blood, what is skin or where the lacerations start and stop."

"I reckon he needs a good wash, and it is best you do it afore he wakes."

Her hands shook as she wrung out the cloth over Reid's back.

Graham grasped her wrist and steadied the trembling. "His Lordship needs you now. I heard what you said, and you are right. 'Tis time you see to his care."

Gulping down her revulsion, she nodded. For the first time since they'd met, Reid MacKenzie needed her and she would not fail him. She continued to use the cloth to saturate the earl's back with water as it ran down his sides in streaks of red. Once she'd emptied the pail, she sent Graham for more as she began the laborious process of wiping away the grime-encrusted blood, trying not to abrade the places where scabs had already started to form.

While Audrey worked, she recalled how the heiresses at Talcotts had complained when the matron insisted they study the healing arts. Why, Sarah Smithfield had turned up her nose and accused the poor instructor of witchery. The woman replied that understanding how to tend the sick was necessary for everyone, no matter their station in life. Now Audrey knew why and was glad she'd paid attention.

Reid didn't rouse once, though his breathing remained irregular with his shivers. After she was satisfied that she'd cleansed the wounds thoroughly, Audrey pulled the jar of salve from her satchel. She spread a thick, even coat over his back, careful to ensure the worst abrasions received a healthy portion. The tincture contained avens to help prevent the wounds from turning putrid, though from the pus she'd wiped away, some lacerations had already begun to fester.

She held up a bandage roll and bit her lip.

"Shall I try to rouse him?" asked Graham, who had faithfully remained by her side.

She returned the bandage to her satchel. "Let him sleep. I'll wrap him come morn." After draping the damp cloth over the earl's back, she pulled a blanket over him. "I wish we'd gone to Durham sooner."

"Ye reckon?" asked Dunn, coming up behind them.

"Captain Fry was already suspicious when we arrived as early as we did, carrying a missive from the queen. Any earlier and we never would have been successful."

Gerald cleared his throat like he was entering the parlor to make an announcement. "Any later, and His Lordship very well could have perished."

Audrey's stomach twisted into a knot. She would have been devastated if that blackguard had killed him. "Why would someone act so vilely, and on the word of a rat like Wagner Tupps?"

"Some people in Fry's line of work gain pleasure from releasing their ire on others," said Dunn.

"Bastard," Graham cursed. "Beg your pardon, Miss Kennet."

"No apology necessary." She brushed her hands on her breeches. "His Lordship cannot continue to run like this."

Gerald gave a solemn nod. "I agree."

"One more day of hard riding," said Dunn in a tone that indicated he wouldn't entertain an argument. "We're halfway to Edinburgh. Seaforth keeps a town house near the Grassmarket."

Audrey pursed her lips. "Will that not be the first place the government troops look?"

"Most likely, but I'm not planning to tarry. We'll use it as a base long enough for men to arrange transport."

"You mean to sail?"

"Aye. A sea galley will be faster than riding and will be easier for Seaforth to bear. After watching him suffer on the ride from Durham, I agree. He's not fit for anything aside from bed." Perhaps the chieftain had a softer heart than he led everyone to believe. At least he showed a modicum of concern for his friend.

Audrey shifted from her aching knees to her bum, sitting with her legs tucked to the side. "How long have you pair been friends?"

Dunn grinned. "My family have been the constables of Eilean Donan Castle for centuries. You mightn't ken, but Eilean Donan stands on MacKenzie lands, defended by MacRaes. My clan pays the earl fealty."

"And the castle? Do the MacKenzies lay claim to it?"

"If you ask me, 'tis a MacRae keep, though I intend to continue to preserve the good relations between our clans." Dunn shrugged and looked away. The question obviously bothered him. Perhaps that was why he always acted gruffly. He was a chieftain of an entire clan, yet servant to the MacKenzie. He turned back, his countenance stony again. "You'd best sleep; it will be daylight soon."

Audrey placed her palm on Reid's shoulder, the only place not raw and mangled. "I feel as though I must sit up with him."

"Och, he's nay going anywhere, and I do not want two worthless souls on my hands on the morrow. Rest your head. I'll wake you if he rouses." Now that sounded more like the domineering Highlander Dunn MacRae had proved himself to be.

Around them, most of the men had mustered up a bit of hay and were already sleeping. With a shrug, she nestled onto Reid's clump. She might doze for a few minutes, but there was no chance she would leave his side.

Chapter Twenty-Seven

*T*hey rode like a herd of fleeing deer the next day, and Reid didn't feel a lick better. If anything, he was worse. His head pounded and his back itched and stung like a blanket of iron nails had been fused to his skin. His face was afire, yet he couldn't stop shivering. Audrey had insisted on wrapping him in bandages before they rode. He didn't know what was worse, traveling with his flesh exposed to the elements and freezing half to death, or suffering the prickles that came with being enwrapped.

The intermittent rain through the day didn't help matters, either.

He clenched his teeth and endured in silence. Morning turned to afternoon, followed by dusk. Gerald checked his pocket watch when they rode past the gray stone walls of Craigmillar Castle and announced the time was ten o'clock.

Dunn took one of his men and cantered the remaining three miles into the city to ensure the town house was safe. A half hour later, Reid and the others met them on Candlemaker Row.

Dunn gave him a sober nod. "'Tis clear."

Reid returned the nod. Though he couldn't show it in the presence of Audrey and the men, the relief racing through his blood served as an elixir to help him travel the remaining paces to the town house. He'd lay his head upon a soft pillow within the hour.

Thank God.

Infused with renewed hope, he even thought his strength might be returning, until he dismounted in the stable yard at the rear of the close. His damned knees gave out as soon as he hopped to the ground. Had there not been a post within reaching distance, he would have planted his face in the dirt.

"Bloody oath, you look like shite." Dunn was never one to mince words, and he pulled Reid's arm over his shoulder. Audrey slipped under the other arm.

Reid's gut clenched. He didn't need help from a wisp of a lass. "I can manage," he said in a tone that was gruffer than he'd intended.

"Aye, and the horse you just fell off will strut down the alley and dance a reel." Dunn sank his thick fingers around Reid's waist, sending blinding pain shooting up his side.

His knees buckled again with his wince.

"Hurry," Audrey said, as if she planned to continue to provide a crutch.

Reid shot a look over his shoulder. "Dammit, Graham, you cannot expect a lady to bear my weight."

"Sorry, m'lord." The warrior released his horse's girth strap. "Saddles stay on?"

"They do," said Dunn. "I'm not taking any chances."

"Och aye?" Reid snorted while Graham exchanged places with the lass. "Not taking any risks aside from riding into Edinburgh, where the largest battalion of dragoons is but a quarter mile away."

Mr. Drummond, the town house butler, and his wife opened the rear door with a candelabra in hand. Fortunately, they had rooms ready as Reid expected. He only stayed in Edinburgh when he had business dealings there, but he employed a skeleton staff to keep the house during his absences. They were to expect his arrival at any time day or night, which was infrequent, regardless. His head swam as the men helped him up two flights of stairs.

"I need whisky," Reid bellowed.

"Gerald, please see to it His Lordship has whisky, and willow bark tea brought to his chamber," Audrey ordered from behind.

"Yes, miss."

"And I need a ewer of hot water for a sponge bath."

Damnation, she couldn't leave it at a dram of whisky.

Dunn sniggered.

"You can keep your opinions to yourself, you bullheaded Scot," Reid mumbled under his breath.

"I didn't say a word."

"Forget the bath," he growled over his shoulder. To be honest, the only thing Reid wanted was a damned bed. Relief flooded through him when Graham finally opened the door to his chamber. Together they headed for the bed as fast as Reid's legs would move.

"Set him in the chair first. By the hearth." Audrey strode inside like a whirlwind. Since when had she become so assertive? "Would you gentlemen please see to lighting the fire? And I need more light to change the earl's bandages and apply salve."

"I'll be fine," Reid groused. "I just need a bloody night's rest."

Audrey's fists snapped to her hips, blocking the path to the bed like a guard dog. "I beg to differ. I saw the state of your back, and it will take sennights, if not months, to heal. Must I warn that you are in grave danger of succumbing to fever. I've already lost my father. I'm not about to lose my guardian."

The men deposited Reid in a damned chair, his spine hitting the backrest before he could stop his momentum. Stars crossed his vision. "Bloody sheep's piss, that hurt!" His head swam as bile churned in his gut.

"How could you men be so careless?" Audrey chided as she gently pressed on his shoulder. "You must turn and sit sideways, my lord. That's the only way I'll be able to change the dressing without causing undue pain."

He gave her a look of exasperation that seemed to have no effect, because she tugged his shirt over his head without a lick of modesty. "I'll work as quickly as I can, and then you'll be free to rest, my lord."

He nodded, the cool air attacking his flesh, making him shiver again. Bless the lass, she was trying to see to his comfort, yet the only thing he wanted was to sleep.

As she promised, Audrey worked quickly, unraveling the bandage while the men set to lighting a fire as well as the candles.

Gerald came in and cleared his throat. A man always knew when the butler made an appearance by the sound. "A flagon of whisky and the willow bark tea, miss."

Reid held out his palm. "Put the flagon right here. Miss Audrey can drink the tea. I reckon she's suffering aches and pains after riding two days without repose."

"I'm fine. The tea should help cool your fever, something I am certain whisky cannot do."

Reid pulled the stopper and took a long swig. The fiery liquid burned on the way down, but as soon as the libation hit his empty stomach, his head whirred with a welcome hint of intoxication.

Gerald bowed, then turned to Audrey. "Mrs. Drummond advised there is a chamber across the corridor that you can use, miss."

"Thank you, but someone must sit up with His Lordship."

Reid took another drink—guzzled it this time. "I'm fine."

"I will determine that," said Audrey, stepping behind him and examining his back. "Oh dear, this looks awful. Did you bring the water?"

"Mrs. Drummond is bringing it directly."

No sooner had the words left Gerald's mouth than the housemaid pushed through the door, her husband following with a candelabra in hand. "My heavens, what happened?" the matron asked.

Reid raised the flagon. "Compliments of Her Majesty's Royal Dragoons."

"You cannot be serious?"

"'Twas a misunderstanding," said Dunn, standing from his place at the hearth and brushing off his hands. "I expect to have matters sorted out on the morrow."

Everyone in the chamber pursed their lips as if silencing themselves from speaking further or asking more questions. It was best if the Drummonds remained unaware of the reason for Reid's arrest. Besides, there were too many unanswered questions at the moment.

"'Tis good to hear you've been using your head,

MacRae." Reid doubted his friend had thought much past securing a transport for passage home. "My preference would be to remain here for a fortnight of respite afore sailing for Brahan."

The dark look that flashed across Dunn's face made the whisky in Reid's gut churn all the more. But he dismissed him with a flick of his wrist. In fact, he wanted everyone out. "Go on, the lot of you. The best thing for me now is a good night's sleep."

Ignoring him, Audrey fished inside her satchel. "I'll be but a moment. The rest of you are free to leave us, and thank you."

"I reckon you'd best not tarry, miss." Dunn grasped Audrey's elbow.

She snatched her arm away. "Not until I've seen to His Lordship's wounds."

He looked to Reid, then back to Audrey. "You'd best not grow too fond of your guardian."

"As I've said a number of times, I've already lost my father, and I do not intend to lose the earl. Not today, not ever."

Dunn pursed his lips and eyed Reid. "That's not what I meant."

"Go find your pallet," Reid said. "You're grousing for naught."

Throwing up his hands and mumbling something akin to clan duty, Dunn took his leave.

Letting out a sigh, Audrey dunked a cloth into the bowl of water left by Mrs. Drummond and lathered it with a bit of rosemary-scented soap. "I do believe the MacRae chieftain doesn't care much for me."

"He's just a curmudgeon. Pay no mind to him."

"He does care very much about you, however."

"He's a good man."

"I suppose he is, even through his rough exterior."

The effects of the whisky swam in Reid's head and he leaned into the warm cloth as Audrey smoothed it over his face. "Mm," he rumbled.

"I must clean away the grime and stench from the prison."

"Forgive me," he slurred. "I am not fit to be in a lady's company."

"Not to worry. I've been in your presence for two days. And now we're in a city, it would be abominable for an earl to be seen in such a disheveled state." She stepped around and examined his back. "Sssss. It looks inflamed."

"It feels bloody inflamed."

"I think it would be best to let it air overnight."

Reid took another drink. "I agree."

Careful not to cause further pain, she used quick flicks to cleanse him. "I'll need to apply more salve." He raised the flagon, but she stopped his hand, taking the whisky and replacing it with the cup of damned tea.

He made a sour face. "Willow bark is always bitter."

"Not any worse than whisky, I'd wager."

He reached for the flagon, and she shuffled away, just beyond his grasp. "Drink the tea down and I'll give it back."

"You bloody sound like my mother."

"She must have been a good woman."

Reid eyed the saucy lass. Must she have a comeback to his every jibe? "She was."

He took a sip of the bitter brew while Audrey scooped two fingers full of salve. "I'll make quick work of this, and then you'd best head for bed."

Reid winced and grunted as soon as her fingers touched his tender flesh.

"Forgive me," she apologized as she continued with the torture.

God, he hated weakness. He prided himself on staying fit and avoiding illness, and there he sat like an invalid, suffering the ministrations of a wee lass. A woman. His ward. But she was right about one thing: He needed to look like the Earl of Seaforth again. "Will you give me a shave, lass?" Since he was already seated in the chair, he might as well stay there while the whisky lasted.

Her hands stilled. "Now?"

"You've seen fit to give me a sponge bath," he said, his voice growing deeper. "And a bath wouldn't be complete without a shave. The kit's atop the bureau."

"Very well."

When she went to retrieve it, Reid leaned forward and snatched the flagon from the table.

Turning, her gaze traveled to his hands and she frowned. "You'll end up with a sore head if you keep swilling that."

"I already have a sore head." He took one more drink, but this time refrained from guzzling.

She made a lather in the soap bowl and used the brush to spread it over his whiskers. He sobered a bit when she flicked open the razor. "Have you used one of those before?" he asked.

"Yes. Papa taught me how."

He raised his chin. "Then do not forget the neck."

The scent of lavender filled his nostrils as she neared. Reid reached for a lock of hair that had slipped from her braid. He twirled it around his finger as she worked. Her hair was fine and soft, just like her body. Closing his eyes, he rubbed his thumb up and down the ringlet he'd made. Audrey stretched the skin on his cheek and shaved him with languid strokes, her hand firm but practiced. Just like everything she applied herself to, she proved skilled— except perhaps dancing, and Audrey wasn't near as bad on her toes as she'd let on.

With a sigh, he released the lock and moved his hand to her waist. "You're a fine woman."

She placed her finger on the tip of his nose and gently pushed it up, shaving above his lip. "Thank you."

"W-why have you not been spoken for?" His words were beginning to slur.

She smiled and doused the cloth in the bowl. Good Lord, she was bonny. "I suppose Papa had more important things to take care of before he started looking for a suitor. Just as you've told me a number of times."

When she faced him and wiped the soap from his face, Reid sunk his fingers into the arc of her waist. "I have?" He shook his head. "I mean, I do. But were you not home with your da during the summers? What about seasonal balls? Did he not escort you to London?"

She heaved a sigh and met his gaze with those hypnotic midnight-blue eyes. "I'm a dancing failure, if you do not recall."

He recalled very well. She'd enticed him so, he'd backed her against the wall to show her how a man and a woman...

Reid swayed in his chair. "You seem to have danced quite well in my arms."

She giggled. "I recollect that during our lesson in the assembly hall you swept me off my feet. And..." A sudden blush filled her cheeks as she looked away and set the cloth on the table.

He brushed his knuckle across her silken, rosy skin, leaned over, and looked her in the eye. "And what?"

Though he didn't need to ask what she was thinking, he enjoyed teasing her, enjoyed watching her bashfulness, especially because he knew when she shed her inhibitions, Audrey might just prove to be a wildcat in the bedchamber. While Reid's head might be swimming, his loins were stirring.

She shook her head.

"Tell me." He tugged her arm and pulled her onto his lap, ignoring the needling pain in his back.

"You kissed me," she whispered into his neck.

"I did." He leaned away so she'd have to face him. "And do you recall you kissed me back?"

"I . . ."

"Let me help you remember." Blast his aching back and blast his duty as guardian. The lass had a chance to retire, and chose to stay. The entire time he'd been locked up in the bowels of Durham Gaol, he'd thought of no one else but Audrey Kennet. The memory of twirling her across an empty ballroom, the memories of riding with her, listening to her music, breaking his fasts with her kept him sane during a fortnight of hell.

No, he didn't care about suitors or abeyances. He didn't care about the coal mine or villainous bastards like Wagner Tupps. Right now, he cared about the lass in his arms, he cared about kissing her. Jesus Christ, even through his pain, he couldn't ignore how her breeches caressed those tight buttocks, displayed those slender legs. And now, the cleft between her pillow-soft arse molded to his cock. Within a blink of an eye, he was harder than the candlestick on the hearth.

A moan rolled from her throat as he sealed his lips over hers and tasted sweet woman. Desire consumed him, body and soul.

Closing his eyes, Reid slid his fingers up to her breast, but too much cloth separated them.

"What?" he asked breathlessly.

"I bound them."

He shoved the red coat from her shoulders, untied her cravat, and tugged the shirt over her head.

Audrey crossed her arms over her chest, covering the linen that had been wrapped around and around. "We should stop."

He fingered the top of the cloth and grinned. "Aye? But I don't want to stop at the moment."

"I'd be mortified if you saw me bare."

He looked to his own chest. "I'm bare."

"That's different."

"I disagree." He untied the knot that secured her bindings. Nuzzling into her neck, he ran kisses down her skin as he pulled away the linen. "A wee peek is all I ask."

She shivered with her next exhale.

"I ken you like me, lass." His head swam but still he couldn't stop himself.

"I...I...I—"

He silenced her with a kiss while his palm filled with soft, warm, intoxicating breast. The wee pebble went instantly hard against his hand, and he swept his mouth downward to claim it. Dear God, her nipples were raspberry ripe, showing him exactly how much she craved his touch. He moaned as he took the right into his mouth and plied it with his tongue. Audrey gasped and arched her back while Reid's fingers trailed downward.

Her heavy breathing made him harder as he rocked his hips into her and found the front tie to her breeches. With a flick of his fingers, he opened them and slid his hand inside.

With her next gasping arch, her legs parted ever so slightly and Reid used the motion as an invitation to touch her most sacred treasure.

She gasped and tried to pull back, but he held her fast. "Let me inside," he growled.

"But—"

"Och, I'll not take your innocence. My role is to protect you." *To adore you.* He slid his finger into the moist folds. Holy hellfire, she was so wet, he could slip inside with ease. His cock pulsed. God, how he wanted to be inside her.

"Mm," she moaned, her eyes rolling back.

"That's it. Allow yourself to feel the passion that lies deep within your soul."

Her breathing sped. "I-I…"

He captured her mouth with a raw, unapologetic kiss, plundering her mouth as his finger slid inside her womanhood and swirled.

The tiny noises coming from Audrey's throat practically sent Reid over the edge. While he continued the kiss, his finger was relentless, probing her slick core and teasing the pearl just outside. Her breathing grew more impassioned, her hips moving in concert with his tenacious exploration.

And suddenly it happened.

A cry of elation caught in Audrey's throat as she pulsated around his finger.

Forcing himself to refrain from plunging inside her, Reid squeezed his eyes shut and buried his face in her neck. "We need to sleep, *mo ghràidh.*" He wasn't so inebriated to speak the endearment for *my love* in English. Regardless of his aching loins, a man on the run couldn't declare affection for anyone or anything.

* * *

Audrey's eyelids were heavy, yet she wanted this moment to last forever. How could she sleep? "You've been knocking on death's door for days. You must rest."

He brushed a wisp of hair from her face. "You cannot go without sleep, either."

She glanced away. "I will not leave you." Standing, she took his hand. "Come."

He grinned, following her to the bed. To think, a man in as much pain as Reid MacKenzie could grin at a time like this? He'd put his hands on her. He'd kissed her. He'd whispered Gaelic in her ear. She turned down the bed-clothes for him. "Now rest."

"And you?"

She glanced over her shoulder. "I'll bring the chair over."

"Nay." He sat on the bed and ran his hands down her arms. "Go lock the door. No one will ken if you're in my arms or sitting in a chair."

A wicked grin played on her lips. "You are a devilish earl, are you not?"

"Och, practical comes to mind."

She moved across the floor, feeling like she was float-ing. "Whatever your ruse, I like it."

He crawled onto the bed and lay on his side, opening his arm for her.

After locking the door, Audrey curled beside him, their bodies molding together like a matched set. "I feel safe with you. Content."

"And I would have you nowhere else," he whispered. "Now sleep."

Content in Reid's arms, she closed her eyes. How on

earth had he made her body feel so miraculously light and airy? Is that what the girls at Talcotts had meant when they said they had shattered? Did they even know what shattering was? Gracious, Audrey hadn't a clue, but there was no doubt that she'd shattered this night. Shattered and soared on the clouds.

She regarded the earl's handsome face over her shoulder. As soon as his head hit the pillow, he'd fallen asleep. The amber glow from the hearth cast shadows over his chiseled features, making him look like a statue.

What did this all mean? What did *mo ghràidh* mean? He'd uttered the endearment with such affection, yet he hadn't mentioned a word about the future. Though with all the trouble with the Government, it may have not been the right time to talk about what might come.

Regardless, Audrey knew he liked her, too. Every time she was alone with him, he flirted shamelessly. She hadn't been alone with many men, but she was certain the earl was more than a little enraptured. If only he would realize it himself.

Once he cleared his name, would Seaforth continue on his quest to marry her to the highest bidder?

No. I cannot believe he will.

Audrey closed her eyes and snuggled into his warmth. She wouldn't allow herself to think about the future. Not when so much uncharted territory lay on the horizon. They were running from government troops, for heaven's sake. Who knew what the morrow would bring? And why couldn't she just let things happen? All her life she'd worried about the morrow, about doing everything perfectly, and if she wasn't polished at something, she'd not do it at all, like dancing. Come to think of it, every time she ended up in Reid's arms it wasn't perfect, but it was amazing. How could being so imperfect be incredibly sublime?

No, she would not allow herself to think about the future this night. She would close her eyes and sleep cradled in the brawny arms that protected her. Even when knocking on death's door, the Earl of Seaforth could make her feel secure. And through his rugged exterior, he cared deeply for her on some raw level, on a level Audrey didn't yet understand. And tonight, he'd proved it beyond doubt.

With her next sigh, she drifted into blissful sleep.

But it only seemed like moments had passed when urgent pounding sounded at the door. "Seaforth. You must wake!" Dunn boomed from the corridor.

Chapter Twenty-Eight

*A*udrey jumped off the bed like someone jabbed her with a poker. Mortified, she dashed to the hearth and pulled her shirt over her head. "Reid? Are you awake?" she whispered as loudly as she dared.

A garble came from the bed while the pounding grew louder. "Dammit, man, the redcoats are here!" Dunn shouted through the timbers.

Quickly, Audrey pulled on her breeches and dashed to the door.

With a snarl, the chieftain shoved inside, holding a torch and glaring at Audrey as if she had committed a ghastly crime. "What the bloody hell took you so long?"

"I…" Mortified and unable to think up a decent response, she dipped her chin, whipped around, and raced to don her boots and coat.

"And why are you not in your chamber? Did you sit up with His Lordship all bloody night?"

What was she supposed to say? And why did Dunn's

voice sound so accusing? "Ah...I did." Regardless of the chieftain's query, what she did or didn't do last eve was none of his concern.

Reid sat up and swiped a hand down his face, the bedclothes dropping to his waist. "Ballocks."

The MacRae chieftain strode across the floor. "Jesu, you look like you've been mauled by a lion and left for dead."

"Feel like it, as well." Reid grunted as he swung his legs over the bed's edge. "Not to worry, I'm coming good." He shoved the heels of his hands against his temples.

Audrey hastened to button her doublet. "I knew drinking an entire flagon of whisky was not a good idea."

"Do not don that red coat!" shouted Dunn. "Drape a plaid over your shoulders for Christ's sake."

Groaning, Audrey discarded the doublet and grabbed a tartan from the foot of the bed. Then she hastily shoved her tricorn hat over her slept-on braid.

The earl pushed himself to his feet and hobbled toward the washstand. "I'll be fit as soon as I splash my face with a bit o' water." He reached out for the ewer, but it crashed to the floorboards and shattered as Reid stumbled backward.

Audrey dashed to help, but the earl gained his balance and batted her hands away.

"We haven't time for this. I cannot have an injured man and a woman slowing us down. We'll be captured for certain," Dunn continued with his tirade. "M'lord, 'tis best if you and the lass spirit out the escape tunnel, whilst I create a diversion with the men."

Audrey handed Reid his shirt. "You have an escape tunnel?"

"I'm not running." The earl swayed on his feet as he pulled the garment over his head. "I've done nothing wrong."

"Aye? Tell that to the lackwit who made a draught-board out of your back." Dunn beckoned with his fingers. "Now haste."

"Damnation, this is my fight, not yours, and most definitely not Miss Kennet's."

Holding the torch aloft, Dunn marched straight up to the earl and grabbed the collar of his shirt in his fist. "I love you like a brother, Seaforth, but it would be suicide to meet the redcoats in your condition. Now take the lass out the tunnel and be gone with ye afore the bastards bust down the door." Dunn hesitated for a moment while he tightened his grip. "Just remember your father's promise to Cromartie."

Audrey glanced up and met MacRae's steely-eyed gaze. Sometimes that man could speak in riddles, but this was no time to set him off by asking for clarification.

"Bloody hell, I ken my lot," Reid grumbled under his breath, his hair mussed like a wild man. While he finished dressing, Audrey hastily stuffed the salve and a cloth from the washstand inside her satchel.

"Come." Dunn raced down the passageway, the pair struggling to keep pace. Audrey because her legs were far shorter and Reid because he was at death's door.

"I'm in your debt, MacRae."

"'Tisn't the first time."

Reid's pace became more assured while they hurried down a narrow stairway. "I'll take the lass to Blair Atholl. The Marquis of Tullibardine owes me a favor."

"Good thinking. The men and I will create a diversion

out the back. Then we'll head for the wharf at Leith and arrange a transport to the Cromarty Firth."

"Stay out of trouble."

Dunn sniggered over his shoulder, the shadows of his face made eerie by the dancing torchlight. "That would be no fun at all." He handed Reid the torch and shoved a bookcase out from the wall, revealing a small door. "I'll meet you at Brahan Castle in a fortnight. Two at most. There's a gathering to attend and you're the master of ceremonies."

Reid opened the hatch and grasped Audrey's hand. "I'll be there. Mark me."

"What should we do with the butler?" asked Dunn.

"Give him coin for his return fare to Coxhoe," said Reid. "He can cover our backs there if need be. Bloody oath, the man's acting impressed me at the gaol."

Peering through the darkness and trying to be courageous, Audrey followed Reid inside the dank tunnel. "You didn't tell me you had a secret escape route." The tremor in her voice betrayed her fear as they proceeded further into the darkness, lit only by the torch's flicker. It was drafty with damp walls, a dirt floor, and a ceiling so low, Reid had to stoop.

"It never came up. I had my men tunnel to Greyfriars Kirk after Tullibardine was nearly caught when he tried to help Lady Magdalen when she was locked in the pillory in Grassmarket Square."

"I beg your pardon?"

"Long story," he growled. "Remind me to tell you about it when we're not running for our lives."

Thank heavens it wasn't long before they reached the tunnel's end. Reid found a key hidden in a crevice on the wall, and unfastened the heavy black padlock. Before opening the door, he doused the torch in a heap of dirt.

"It appears you planned well."

"A man never kens when he'll need to make a fast exit."

Audrey squinted when they stepped out into the sunlight, right behind a crypt. "A graveyard?"

"No place better to hide a secret passageway." Reid turned full circle. "No one about. Come, we'll hire a coach to take us to Queensferry."

Having never been to Edinburgh, Audrey had no choice but to follow. Reid needed a physician, not a coach. Lord only knew what kind of toll fleeing was taking on the man's body. It certainly was making her nervous. She was hungry and soreheaded and tired, and Seaforth must be feeling ten times worse.

But onward they continued. Now out in the open, Audrey's spine prickled with dread as she glanced over her shoulder every few steps, positive the redcoats would be chasing them at any moment.

But the earl knew right where to go. There were two black coaches waiting for fares at the end of the church's drive.

Reid hailed the first. "To Queensferry Wharf."

"Queensferry?" the driver asked incredulously. "That will be two guineas."

He motioned for Audrey to step inside. "Carry on then."

Realizing she was still dressed in men's clothing, she pursed her lips and climbed aboard without assistance.

The coach bumped and jerked over the cobblestones while she clutched her satchel with both hands, her gaze fixated out the window, scanning every nook and cranny for any sign of a redcoat. "You said we're going to a wharf?" she asked in a whisper.

"Aye, we'll take a skiff across the Forth and we'll ride from there."

"Will they have stables on the other side?"

"Scotland's a vast country, lass. We'll alight in the Kingdom of Fife, and aye, we ought to find a pair of garron ponies."

"Garron?"

"Stout Scottish-bred horses made for the Highlands. I'd take a garron any day before riding one of those English mounts. They might be faster but they cannot climb like Highland ponies."

"Then how far is it—?"

Reid sliced his hand through the air. "Keep mum. The journey will take an entire day at a healthy trot."

She craned her neck, the water coming into view. The Forth was grand indeed—the other side barely discernable. "A day? That's so far."

"I've ridden the distance many times." He leaned forward and rested his head on his hand. He was as white as bed linen, though Audrey knew better than to ask how he was feeling. What choice did they have? If they didn't escape from Edinburgh this instant, Reid would be captured and quite possibly tortured to death. She prayed the marquis could offer them protection. Then she resumed her lookout until they reached the wharf and alighted from the coach.

As soon as her feet touched ground, her heart nearly jumped right out of her chest. "Redcoats," she whispered while Reid dug in his sporran for two guineas.

Two dragoons stepped out of a large skiff with four oarsmen. They proceeded down the wharf straight toward them, sauntering like they were seeking out trouble. One frowned and eyed her as if he could tell she was a woman.

Reid stepped between them and pointed to the skiff. "Is that ferry returning to Fife soon?"

One of the oarsmen stood, making the boat bob. He held out his palm. "If you have the coin, we can head back straightaway."

Reid gave Audrey's elbow a tug and skirted past the soldiers.

Keeping her gaze downcast, she affected a swagger and stared at the deck timbers until they reached the skiff.

"What is your business up north?" asked one of the dragoons, following, blast him.

She pretended she didn't hear, nearly tripping into the bobbing boat. One of the oarsmen looked at her as if she were daft, but Audrey ignored him and acted as if she was in a hurry to gain a seat, quickly planting her bum on the first empty bench.

Reid shrugged at the redcoat like he hadn't a care. "Same as always. Visiting my brother in Dunfermline."

"Family business, aye?" The dragoon looked around His Lordship and eyed Audrey head to toe. "I advise you to put on some muscle, lad. Grow into those breeches, else you'll not be cut out for any vocation but the clergy."

Reid shot the man a scowl before climbing in and taking the seat beside her.

She held her breath when the meddler sauntered up to the boat and shoved his fists into his hips. "Why do you look familiar, sir?"

"Do you make this crossing often?" Reid asked.

Audrey wanted to scream at the dragoon and tell him

to leave them alone, but the man just scratched his chin. "No. But not to worry, it will come to me."

Reid held out a guinea to the oarsmen. "Cast off."

Audrey watched the oarsmen row the boat away from the wharf, praying they would make the crossing before the miserable dragoon's memory returned.

Chapter Twenty-Nine

*F*ortunately, the dragoon went on his way and they made the crossing without being identified. Once Reid had secured a pair of horses, they rode hard at a fast trot, but still, it was dusk before the white turrets of Blair Castle came into view, peeking above the trees.

During the entire journey, Reid had clenched his teeth and borne his misery, all the while worrying about meeting outlaws along the way. He might be about as useful as a bairn, but he'd die to save Audrey from the hands of a plunderer. A weight lifted from his shoulders when the vast Atholl estate opened from the forest of Scots pine and sycamore. Reid pulled himself together as they were ushered into the castle's dark-paneled hall, complete with rows of stag antlers.

"My God, Seaforth, what have you been up to this past year?" Aiden Murray, the Marquis of Tullibardine and son of the Duke of Atholl, received them with open arms.

"Bugger all," Reid said, forgetting present company. But he wasn't so crass to completely forget his manners. He bowed and gestured to Audrey. "Please allow me to introduce Miss Kennet, daughter of the late Nicholas Kennet."

"Och, when word came of his death, I wept. Such a loss for the kingdom." Tullibardine took her hand between his palms. "'Tis a pleasure to meet you, my dear. Your father was a good man."

Audrey smiled. "He was."

"Tell me, Seaforth, why are you both looking so bedraggled?"

Reid let out a long sigh, his back stinging like a dragon was breathing fire behind him. "'Tis a long story."

"Then let us retire to the drawing room and join Lady Magdalen for refreshment. She will enjoy this tale as well."

At once they were whisked above stairs where Tullibardine introduced his lovely wife to Audrey. Reid gave a brief explanation of their plight, mentioning a "bit of trouble" with the government troops while the couple listened intently.

He half expected Tullibardine to throw him out—or offer a bed for the night and then tell him to be on his way, but Lady Magdalen stood, crossed the floor, and grasped Audrey by the hands. "My dear lass, you must be exhausted from your ordeal. Please, allow me to offer you a bath and a fresh change of clothes."

Twisting her mouth, Audrey glanced to Reid. "But my Lord Seaforth needs respite far more than I."

"Go on, lass," Reid urged. "Allow Lady Magdalen to pamper you. I'll wager you're so weary, your knees are about to give out at any moment."

"You'll be all right, then?" she asked.

Reid gave her the most convincing smile he could muster. "Go on. I need to sample Tullibardine's latest batch of whisky."

"That he does," agreed the marquis.

Once the women took their leave, Aiden poured a dram of amber gold for them both. Leaning forward and resting his elbow on the armrest, Reid sipped gratefully. "No better cure for pain than a tot of aged Atholl whisky."

Aiden held up his cup in toast. "*Sláinte*." After taking a swig, the marquis rapped his fingers on the side table. "Good God, mate, you look like you've been through the wars and lost. Tell me, it doesn't take a seer to realize there's more afoot than the quick report you just delivered to my wife."

Reid could barely sit straight while he relayed the details of his incarceration and subsequent rescue. What worried him now was the damned nosey dragoon at the wharf in Queensferry. Once the man learned that Reid was on the run, he'd remember his face, no doubt.

"Did you tell anyone where you were heading?" asked Aiden.

"Nay."

"Good. I reckon that purchased you a day at least."

Reid arched his back against the stinging pain. "Unfortunately, I need a fortnight of respite."

Aiden stood and moved behind him. "Let me have a look at the damage."

"'Tisn't pretty." Reid pulled off his shirt.

Peeling away the bandage, a glimpse was all the marquis needed. "Jesus Christ. An officer did this?"

"Aye, Captain Bainbridge Fry."

"'Tis an outrage. A disgrace to the uniform." Aiden had been an officer in the Royal Navy before he'd met with a bit of trouble of his own and opted to resign his post. "Good God, you weren't wrong. But I reckon you need a month of rest at least. And I'll be lodging a formal complaint against Fry and the Durham Gaol."

"Not yet." Reid pulled his shirt back over his head. Allow me time to clear my name first."

"I'd prefer to act swiftly, but if you need time, I'll wait." Aiden resumed his seat. "In the interim, go to my hunting cottage for your convalescence. 'Tis hidden deep in Atholl lands. So remote, few ken it exists. You'll be safe there."

Reid considered. "But I have Miss Audrey to care for."

"Do not worry about the lass. Lady Maddie will enjoy having another woman about for a change. Besides, I owe you a favor, mate."

True, Reid had helped Tullibardine escape the redcoats when Lady Magdalen had been wrongfully accused in a plot to assassinate the queen.

He nodded, but then the room began to swim. Overcome with the sensation of falling forward, everything slipped into oblivion.

* * *

Feeling fresh for the first time in days, Audrey regarded the borrowed plaid kirtle in the looking glass. "It is ever so kind of you to lend me a gown."

"Consider it a gift." Lady Magdalen came up behind her, smiling. "Any friend of Seaforth is a friend of mine."

"He told me you had an unfortunate altercation with the queen."

"Och, do not remind me. Those were frightening days I'd rather forget."

"I'm happy your name was cleared. I couldn't imag—"

"Maddie, may I enter?" The marquis's voice rumbled through the timbers.

The marchioness looked toward the door. "Aye."

But the grim look on Tullibardine's face made Audrey's hackles stand on end. He stepped inside, his frown growing deeper. "Seaforth is out cold."

Audrey clapped her hand over her mouth. "Oh no, I shouldn't have left him. He's not well. I must tend him straightaway."

The marquis blocked the doorway and held up his hand. "My healer is tending him, but he cannot stay. If what he says is true, my guess is we'll have dragoons at Blair within two days."

"No," said the marchioness.

Tullibardine's gaze shifted between the two women. "I'm taking him to the hunting cottage at dawn."

Maddie collected her satchel from the table and clutched it to her midriff. "Then I'm going as well."

"Nay, lass." He shook his finger. "You'd best stay at Blair. The cottage isn't for young ladies. It's rough, and remote—removed from civilization it is."

"Heavens, Aiden." Lady Magdalen moved beside Audrey. "I stayed there with you."

"That was different."

"If I'm not there, who will watch over His Lordship whilst he's healing?"

"Ah…" The marquis's eyes shifted.

Audrey's spine straightened. "I'm going. And you'll not keep me from it. Reid MacKenzie is my guardian. I broke the law for him. As a matter of fact, the men who are looking for him are looking for me as well. If I remain here, I'm putting you and your family in as much danger as if the earl were here himself."

"But—"

"Good heavens, Aiden. Can you not see the lass is determined? Send ample supplies and she'll be able to tend Seaforth and see to it he doesn't die up there."

Audrey fixed her gaze on the marquis and raised her chin indignantly. "'Tis settled then."

"Bloody hell, a man hasn't a chance when faced with two women." Tullibardine beckoned her with his fingers. "Come on then. I'll take you to his chamber."

"Thank you," she said, following him down the passageway.

He arched an eyebrow at her. "Tell me, do ye ken out to cook?"

"I'm shamed to admit, no."

"Then you'd best have a word with Cook as well."

* * *

If only my damned head would stop pounding.

At the sound of rustling, Reid opened his eyes. He was lying on a bed in a small chamber with crude stone walls. Above, the rafter beams were exposed, supporting a thatched roof. Across the chamber, a maidservant had her back to him, bent over a hearth, stirring the contents of a blackened-iron kettle. The smell of broth wafted to his nose and he salivated, his stomach growling like he hadn't eaten in a sennight.

The lass hung her spoon on a nail and turned.

Dear Lord, Audrey was clad like a Scottish lass, complete with arisaid and kirtle.

She smiled. "You're awake."

Reid swiped a hand across his eyes. "Where are we?"

"At the marquis's hunting cottage. Do you not remember?"

"The cottage?" Through the fog, he recalled Tullibardine's offer. "How in God's name did we end up here?"

"His Lordship's men tossed you over a horse and hauled you up the mountain."

"They didn't." Good God, not a becoming sight for an earl.

"They did, else you might be returned to the hands of the redcoats. Word came the day after we arrived at Blair Castle that dragoons were in Dunkeld asking questions."

"Bloody hell, will they not give it a rest?" Reid squinted his eyes and regarded her, his head clearing a bit. "And why are you here? You're supposed to be staying at the castle with Lady Magdalen."

"I wasn't about to leave you in the care of some stranger, and I told the marquis so. Besides, I'm most likely as wanted as you are."

Wanted by Wagner Tupps was what she was.

"Are you thirsty?" she asked, picking up a cup of something awful, no doubt.

Reid tried to roll to his back and winced, quickly shifting again to his side. Damn, his wounds could have healed while he was abed. "I can eat an entire stag all by myself."

"That's a good sign." She sat on a wooden chair beside the bed. Something told Reid the lass had spent a great deal of time there.

Still, he wasn't happy. "What the devil was Tullibardine thinking to bring you all the way up to the Highlands and leave you alone?"

"It was my choice. And I'm not alone—you're here. Besides, he left us with enough supplies to last a winter, and a musket."

"We're not staying here long." He tried to sit up, but only managed to get as far as his elbow. "We must be on our way soon."

She shook her damned finger at his nose. "We're not leaving for a fortnight. I heard what Mr. MacRae said. We have time."

Reid licked his lips. "At least give me a healthy portion of meat. Your stew smells delicious."

"First broth. If you can keep that down, then we'll try a bit of bread. Then mayhap a bite of stew."

He groaned. "You're going to be the death of me."

"Truly? I'd say it's the other way around." She reached for a spoon and dipped it in the cup. "See if you can sip this. 'Tis near impossible to ladle broth into a man's mouth when he's sleeping on his side."

He pushed up a little and opened his mouth. The broth spread across his tongue and made him ravenous. When Audrey pulled the spoon away for another scoop, he leaned forward, following her hand. "More."

She smiled and offered him another, and another. Reid wanted to swipe the cup from her hands and drink it down, but his supporting arm was already trembling, damn it all.

"Your back is healing. Scabs have formed."

"It itches like the devil."

Chuckling, she set the spoon in the cup and sat back. "That's another good sign."

He licked his lips, staring at the cup forlornly. "Is there more?"

"I think you should rest for a bit before you have another cup."

Reid had enough. This invalid routine had to end. Now. He ground his teeth and shoved himself up. "God bless it!"

Gasping, Audrey clutched her fists to her chest. "I do not think 'tis a good idea to push yourself overmuch."

"Aye? Most likely, if it were up to you, I'd stay abed for another sennight so you can play at your bloody healing."

Hurt flashed through her eyes. "Not true. I am thinking only of your welfare."

"And that means helping me rise from this bed." He shook his head. "No, that means standing back whilst I rise under my own power."

"Very well." She stood and shoved the chair toward him. "Use this as a crutch, you ungrateful oaf."

That's right. He was an oaf, and it was about time she realized it. Grumbling, he pulled the damned chair in front of him and placed both hands on the back. With a hearty push, he took his weight onto his legs with ease. The only problem was his head spun like a top. He squeezed his eyes closed and shook his head. "Ballocks."

It took a deep inhale to steady the spinning. Then he shoved the chair aside and took a step. "You see? I am fit."

"Oh?" She crossed her arms. "Then why am I not impressed?"

He took another step and wobbled a little. In the blink of an eye, Audrey slipped under his arm. "Allow me to help."

"Curses, woman, can you not see I need no help?" He pulled his arm away and strode for the door in as straight a line as he could manage. Without looking back, he stepped outside and stumbled for the wood heap. Practically panting like he'd run a footrace, he balanced himself by resting his hand on the pile while he caught his breath. Dammit, he'd never been this weak in his bloody life, and now he'd gone and barked at Audrey.

Didn't she know not to cosset a man? Didn't she know he would need to rebuild his strength as soon as possible? And blast it all, she ought to know how much he hated weakness in himself.

He put a stick of wood on the chopping block and ground his teeth against the tremors while he picked up the ax. It was all he could do to raise the bloody thing above his head and swing it down. The damned ax head must have been blunt because it bounced off the wood like a mallet. Christ, the last time he'd missed a chop, he'd been a lad of nine.

But that didn't stop him. If anything, his failure infused him with strength. He widened his stance and hefted the ax above his head. Bellowing with his downward strike, he split the wood in half.

"That'll show you, ye bloody stick of miserable oak." Again he inhaled, the mountain air filling his lungs. He leaned on the ax handle and took in the surroundings. The cottage was whitewashed, encircled by a forest. The ground was soft with a carpet of moss underfoot, and beyond, a loch cut through steep mountainous slopes. On the windless day, the water looked like glass. Could he spend a season there? Aye, if he wasn't the leader of *the cause*. Every Jacobite clan in the Highlands was relying on him to help stop the Occasional Conformity Act and see to it James Francis Edward Stuart was the next successor to the throne as was his birthright.

Squaring his shoulders, Reid placed another stick of wood on the chopping block. This time, he split it on the first try, but the effort sapped him. He leaned the ax against the heap and rested his hands on his knees to catch his breath.

Then he looked to the cottage again. Audrey was still inside.

Damn.

He'd acted like an arse.

* * *

Audrey shoved her hands against her face to keep herself from crumbling into a blubbering heap. She didn't want to cry. No, she wouldn't let that dastard yell at her, storm out of the cottage, and turn her into a weeping dotard.

Though she might scream.

For pity's sake, ever since the earl's incarceration she'd thought of nothing but Reid MacKenzie. She'd stayed up all hours sewing dragoon uniforms for his rescue. And all the while, she'd endured audacious remarks from Mr. MacRae. She'd dressed like a man, put her own life in peril, broken the law, and had run from government troops, all to help that bombastic Scot outside now attempting to prove his masculinity to the blasted beasts of the forest.

Worse, there she stood in a rustic cottage in the midst of the wild Highlands of all places. Could she be any farther removed from her home? She was an English-bred lady, and rumors had abounded at Talcotts about the distrust Highlanders harbored for Sassenachs. What overbearing, arrogant Scot would want to marry an English woman anyway?

Though the Earl of Seaforth had no qualms when it came to fondling them.

Regardless of the opposing and confusing feelings he managed to stir up inside her, Audrey had applied herself to the task of tending to Reid's needs. It was overwhelming to be in the midst of nowhere with a fevered guardian, food galore, and no one but her to prepare it. Audrey had done her best to follow the few recipes the cook at Blair Castle had barked at her faster than she could write. Talcotts hadn't offered a course on cooking for well-to-do ladies. They fully expected their students to be catered for, to marry into wealthy families. After all, a Talcotts graduate was supposed to be a good catch for any man.

Except for me.

Feeling completely inadequate and worthless, she sat in the uncomfortable chair and looked at the hearth—far cruder than anything she'd experienced— with a rack of stag antlers hanging above it rather than the porcelain rose-painted plates in the drawing room at Coxhoe House. At no time in her life had Audrey been faced with such primitive conditions. Because she was so worried about Reid, she'd gone against every argument to stay at Blair Castle, where she'd be cosseted.

She didn't want to be cosseted. She wanted to be helpful. And she'd made do for an entire day, had thought the cottage quaint, if not rustic.

A little recognition for her efforts would be agreeable. Was that too much to ask?

Blast it all, there she sat in the middle of godforsaken

Scotland trying to be caring, and she'd been barked at like she was a worthless dog. An unbidden tear dribbled down her cheek. She swiped it away and sniffed. Heavens, she was tired. If only she had her harpsichord or her paints, she could cast aside her misery and focus on something productive—something at which she was proficient.

Clearly, she was a complete failure at caring for an injured man and preparing food.

The door swung open. Startled, Audrey nearly fell off her chair. Reid loomed in the doorway, his face dark and hard. He stared at her with fiery intensity in those deep green eyes. His beard had grown in again since she'd shaved him, and his dark stubble contrasted with the tawny tresses hanging over one eye, making him look wildly dangerous.

Gulping, Audrey hopped to her feet. Cool mountain air wafted into the cottage, sending a chill across her skin. She wrung her hands, meeting his predatory stare. She would apologize for nothing.

"I-I acted like a bloody lout." Reid dipped his chin, suddenly looking more like a scruffy puppy than a fierce warrior. "Please forgive me."

The Earl of Seaforth was apologizing...to her? Certainly he should apologize, but Audrey hadn't expected such an atonement to come from the likes of him.

Her mouth dropped open. "But you...and then..." Dear Lord, she should let it pass. Perhaps her emotions had run the gamut. "'Tis understandable. You're not well, and you're in pain."

"Nonetheless, I should not have groused at you."

The look on his face alone made her want to rush to his

side and proclaim her undying love. But such an outburst would be unforgivable. She must first make him realize that he cared for her. She knew he harbored affection for her, she just needed to do everything in her power to help him realize it.

She gestured to the bench at the table. "If you'll sit, I will serve you the plate of stew you wanted. I'd like to offer you more, but given the circumstances, stew, broth, and oats are the only things the Atholl cook taught me how to prepare." She cringed. *Not a good way to start making him realize his affection, Audrey.*

He chuckled. "You didn't learn to cook at that fancy school of yours?"

"Did you learn at university?" *Can I not stop myself?*

"Nay."

Again she gestured, this time pinching her lips closed so she wouldn't blurt out yet another flip remark. Reid's Adam's apple bobbed as he shut the door and staggered to the bench. As much as Audrey wanted to help, he'd been clear about not needing assistance. He made it, though he moved like a man who'd been flayed with a cat-o'-nine-tails—which he had been.

After dishing up two bowls of stew, Audrey sat opposite the big Highland earl. He looked oddly at home in this rustic cottage. Big, rugged, and rough around the edges after his ordeal.

"My thanks for the meal." Reid picked up his spoon and stirred the stew like he mightn't be as ravenous as he'd let on. "You said the redcoats had been asking questions in Dunkeld. Do you reckon they ken we stopped at Blair Castle?"

"The marquis said he doubted it since we traveled up through Perth."

"But anyone who might have seen us…"

"That's why the marquis brought us here. He said we'd be safe tucked away in the Highlands and it would allow you time to heal. He's used this place to hide himself, said we can stay as long as we need."

Reid took a bite. "Did he, now?"

"Yes, and he'll also let us know if there is any danger coming our way."

"Tullibardine is a good man. Makes the best whisky this side of the Highlands as well."

"I must agree—with the good man part anyway." Audrey sighed and picked up her spoon. "'Tis comfortable enough here. As long as you can put up with my cooking."

"Och, if this stew is any indication, your cooking is fine, but that is not what worries me, lass. Who kens we're here aside from His Lordship?"

Audrey chewed and swallowed. "Let's see…Lady Magdalen, of course, and two guards the marquis said he trusted with his life."

"That's good, but still I'm concerned about your reputation. You shouldn't be holed up in a hunting cottage with the likes of me, or any man."

Audrey looked down and stirred her stew. Of course the same concerns had crossed her mind, but she'd pushed them away. Besides, her father had entrusted Reid with her care. It was expected that she would remain by his side. And she wasn't about to let some stranger tend to Reid's healing while she hid in a grand castle and ate sugared dates. "Likes of you?" She shrugged her shoulder as if the topic were a trifle. "You're my guardian and an earl."

"An earl wanted for treason—until I clear my name."

She reached across and patted his hand. His fingers were warm to the touch, and their gazes met and held. "You mustn't worry, my lord. There isn't a soul within a hundred miles who knows who I am."

Chapter Thirty

There were two things wrong with hiding in the Highlands with a bonny English maid. The first was that Reid's responsibility to *the cause* didn't diminish. He needed to clear his name and unite every Jacobite peer and chieftain to repeal the Occasional Conformity Act and prepare to defend James's ascension to the throne. Secondly, now that he'd regained his senses, living, breathing, eating in a one-room cottage with his beautiful ward was about to kill him. The sooner they set out for Brahan, the better, lest he'd dig himself a hole from which no man could climb.

A ray of morning light streamed in through the window. Reid opened his eyes and groaned. Every morn for the past two days he'd awakened with a painful erection, and today was no different.

After gaining his senses, he'd insisted Audrey take the bed, and he lay on a pallet made snug by layers of sheep pelts. He glanced to where Audrey slept on her side. With her back to him, he admired the deep arc in her waist, curving up to a feminine hip. His cock throbbed and he ached to climb into the bed beside her and trace his hand along her curves. Hell, he wanted to do a great deal more than touch her, though brushing his fingers over silken skin would be a start.

Casting the bed furs aside, he snatched his plaid from the foot of his pallet, found a cake of soap, and tiptoed out the door. Once he reached the shore of the loch, he waded up to his thighs to where a rock protruded from the water, and set the soap atop.

Highland bred to his bones, Reid dived out into the depths and swam. The icy water stung his back, but after fighting through with powerful strokes, he found his pain soon ebbed. There was nothing better than a brisk swim in a loch to clear his mind and help him focus on more important things than his confounding lust. His wounds had healed a great deal in the past few days, and he'd soon be ready to head home. God knew he missed it, and so many things needed to be done.

He hadn't made it far when his strength was sapped. Damnation, he hated weakness. On one hand he needed to meet the Highland chiefs, but it would be folly to face Ewen Cameron or the Duke of Gordon when he felt weaker than a bairn. In the coming days he must apply himself to the task of regaining his strength, and that didn't mean swinging an ax a couple of times and calling it good. He needed to run, to spar, to swim, and to lift.

Audrey said they had time, but would a fortnight be enough? After treading water for a moment, he pushed himself to swim a bit farther.

The water soothed him, took the sting from his wounds away, and made him feel weightless. Before swimming back, he floated for a while and watched the puffs of clouds sail overhead. Midsummer was his favorite time of year. The harshness of winter was completely gone and the rains of spring were behind. True, in Scotland one could experience all four seasons in one day, even in summer, but the blue sky peppered by fluffy clouds promised sunshine.

After inhaling deeply, Reid started back to the shore. The return swim proved to be more enlivening, and he stopped by the rock to retrieve his soap. Again standing with the water lapping his thighs, he rubbed the bar across his chest and under his arms. The scent of lavender wove its tendrils through his nose, reminding him of Audrey, of the fragrance of her hair and how much he'd like to go inside and bury his face in those blonde tresses.

With a growl, he clenched his molars and worked the soap faster. A wee breeze made gooseflesh pebble on his skin as he slid the bar down and lathered his loins. Christ, his knees went weak at the slippery friction along his cock. Though he'd been without a woman for far too long, must his every other thought be consumed with lust?

He closed his eyes and saw a vision of Audrey, melting in his arms while his hand slid up between her thighs. Yearning made his fingers wrap around his shaft and stroke. If only she weren't his ward, he could bed the lass and have it be done with. Everyone knew forbidden fruit was the most enticing. And once tasted, it was finished. Forgotten. Once tasted, the insatiable appetite vanished.

With a growl he forced himself to release his grip. Then, cupping his hands, he scooped water over his head. Again and again, he splashed the soap away, reveling in the cold and the way it infused him with strength. He shook his head and a splay of droplets showered from his hair just as the sun peeked over the trees.

Invigorated, he took a step toward the shore and his plaid.

Movement near the cottage caught his eye. Reid's hand immediately moved to his hip, grasping at air rather than his sword's hilt.

But he needed no sword.

Audrey stood with her hand on the door, her lips forming an O. She looked as if she'd dashed outside, and stopped short when she'd seen him naked. Rather than hiding her eyes and slipping back into the cottage, she froze in place and stared. Aye, she stared like a starved woman gazing upon a feast.

Reid couldn't help his grin, fully aware his cock was hard and pointing directly at her. He liked to have her eyes on him. He liked the predatory glint in her gaze.

Before he realized what he was doing, his legs strode forward as he stooped to retrieve his plaid. But rather than wrap it around his waist, he kept walking while he swiped it across his face and over his chest.

Audrey's gaze languidly swept from his eyes, down his chest, and stopped at his cock.

Och aye, he grew harder. He gasped, too.

When he reached her, he stood very still as those stormy-blue eyes meandered back up until she met his gaze. Her breaths came with heavy gasps, her eyes nearly black. She wore only a shift with an arisaid clutched around her shoulders, her face flushed with desire and her lips parted. There could be no question as to what was on his mind, and by the way she raked her gaze over him, she felt the same.

"I want you, lass."

Giving a single nod, Audrey dropped the arisaid in silent permission.

Tossing the plaid over his shoulder, he lifted her into his arms and carried her into the cottage, consequences be damned.

* * *

Audrey hadn't been able to make her voice work, but when Reid swept her into his arms like she weighed a trifle, she forced herself not to swoon into him and think of his care. Worried that she might be hurting him, she touched her fingers to his cheek. "But your injuries."

"The devil with them," he growled as he strode to the bed. He carefully laid her atop the mattress and kneeled over her. Naked. Virile. Masculine. "Just don't dig your fingers into my back," he whispered as he nuzzled into her neck.

A cry caught in Audrey's throat. With a look this man could make her shudder from her head to her toes, could make her tingle all over, her breasts swell and her womb ache with longing. For days now she'd yearned for him to touch her, yearned for him to act upon the smoldering desire in those dark eyes. He'd held her in his arms once, denied himself to bring her pleasure.

And now he kneeled over her, the extent of his desire powerful and demanding. Seeing him naked made her crave his touch. Made her wanton. Made her thirst to reach the pinnacle of passion he'd taken her to before when they'd been locked in his chamber in Edinburgh. Her appetite for him grew unquenchable, and moreover, she craved to show him the same pleasure he'd bestowed upon her.

His kisses ran down the length of her neck, and a low chuckle rumbled from her throat, sultrier than she'd ever heard her voice before. She couldn't close her eyes. Reid was far too beautiful, and she wanted to take in every muscle and scar. She wanted to run her fingers down the ridges of his abdomen and through the tawny curls from which his manhood jutted.

He untied the bow of her shift, and his lips traveled to her breast, taking the tip into his mouth. He wasn't as gentle as before, but urgent and demanding. Audrey arched up with a sharp gasp as his tongue swirled around her sensitive flesh. He moaned, causing waves of delightful tremors with the rumble of his voice. In two tugs, he pulled her shift over her head. And suddenly not a stitch of clothing separated them.

With a gulp, she had to ask before she exploded with need. "May I place my hands on you?" she asked in a whisper.

He stilled his lips on her breast while a whistle of air caressed her taut nipple. Then the corner of his mouth turned up in a devilish grin as he met her gaze. "If you lay a single finger on me, I'll not be able to draw back when the heat grows too hot."

Her tongue tapped her lip. "'Tis not too hot already?"

"Nearly." He licked her nipple. "But I'm still in control."

And I want to be.

Wickedly, she touched the center of his chest with her finger. A gush of heat flooded between her legs at his shuddering reaction. Her eyes widened as she scraped her teeth over her bottom lip and watched him tense as she slowly traced her finger downward. As her finger continued on its torturously slow path, Reid's breathing labored, his eyes half closed as if he was trying to restrain himself from showering her with kisses...or something far more provocative.

Her fingers trembled as she brushed them over the tip of his manhood.

A feral growl erupted from the depths of Reid's throat, and he arched his back with a shudder.

Audrey stilled her hand. "Did I hurt you?"

"Nay." His voice came out hoarse.

She lightly brushed her fingers along his shaft. "Does it feel good?"

"Too good."

Another low chuckle rumbled through her throat. She'd finally discovered a way to give this man pleasure. Oh, yes, she needed to understand more of this side of him. "Good like when you touch me?"

"Better," he whispered and met her gaze with fierce intensity. "Wrap your fingers around me."

She did as he asked, surrounding him in her hand like handling warm steel. "Show me."

Covering her hand with his, he guided her, taught her how to slide up and back in a steady rhythm. His breathing came in gasps.

Audrey tensed. "Am I hurting you?"

"Not at all." Pulling away, he rocked back on his haunches and ran his hands along the curve of her waist. "But I cannot lose control."

"I like it when you do." She reached for him, but he caught her hand, his eyes growing darker still.

"I want to kiss you, lass."

She liked his idea. But he didn't kiss her lips. He slid down the bed a bit further and swirled his tongue in her navel. "And I want to make you come again and again."

"And make love with me?"

"Aye." He glanced up. "If you'll have me."

"I want you to." Since the day Reid pulled her from Wagner's galloping horse and cradled her in his arms, she knew how much she wanted this man. Now she must convince him to want her, too. If she declared her love too soon, he might stop.

He slid down a bit further and brushed her nether parts with the pad of his thumb. He'd touched her like that once before, and Audrey had oft thought of little else. She trembled with unabashed anticipation.

He placed a palm on her abdomen. "Trust me."

"I do."

But rather than use his fingers, he licked her. Crying out with a gasp, she rocked her hips. In no way could she stop, not while he stirred a ravenous fire within her and claimed her mind, body, and soul. His finger slid into her core, his tongue lapping faster, driving her to madness. Up and down Audrey rocked her hips until, cresting with a wave of euphoria, she arched her back. Her thighs shuddered as she found glorious release.

When at last she opened her eyes, he kneeled over her with a grin spread wide on his face. "You are so fine to me, lass."

She smoothed her hands over his beautiful chest. "There are no words." She glanced down to him, and a renewed spike of longing surged through her insides as she slid her hands to his shoulders. "There's more, is there not?"

"So much more." His teeth raked over his bottom lip as his damp hair shrouded one eye. "The first time can be painful."

Her tongue slipped to the corner of her mouth. Reid

was a large man, but he'd been so gentle with her, how could lovemaking hurt? "I want you. All of you."

"You have no idea how much your words make me feel like a man."

"You are a man. My man."

Crinkles formed at the corners of his eyes as he lowered himself over her. The head of his manhood brushed her core, still wet with longing. "I want it to be good for you."

She slid her hands down his arms, careful to avoid his back. "It will be."

Audrey held in her gasp as he slid inside. Yes, it stung, but she would not deny him. Ever so slowly, he pushed inside until he filled her wholly. Staring into each other's eyes, they froze for a moment, connected, joined and filled with love. Her passion rising, Audrey swirled her hips.

"Mm. If you keep doing that, I'll burst."

Wickedly grinning, she swirled faster. "Is that not what you want?"

"It is." He matched her, making deep thrusts.

Audrey's desire ramped up with the speeding of his breath. Who knew the effect she could have on this man, on this earl? He might have wanted to wed her to another, but now she knew, without a doubt, he was the only man for her. Holding on to his shoulders for dear life, together they rode the maelstrom of passion. Just after she shuddered and found paradise, Reid slipped out and spilled into the linens. "Och, *mo leannan*. I cherish every moment I can hold you in my arms."

* * *

Reid pulled the musket down from the mantel and ran his fingers along the barrel.

Audrey wiped her hands on her apron. "We never did go shooting together at Coxhoe. And this is a hunting cottage, after all."

He grinned. "I reckon we could use some fresh meat."

She licked her lips. "Venison on a spit?"

"Mm, my mouth is already watering."

"Shall we take the horses?"

"I thought we might hike up the crag and have a gander. Mayhap come across some tracks." He found a pouch of musket balls. "Would you be up for a climb?"

"I'd enjoy it."

Och, how he loved it when she smiled. The primitive cottage brightened, making him feel buoyant. Her wee grin made him feel as free as an ordinary man sailing a boat on the open sea. Reid slung the musket's strap over his shoulder and led her out the door.

Audrey looked up, the sunlight capturing flecks of silvery blue in her eyes—colors he'd never noticed before. "You wouldn't have been able to do that a few days ago."

He arched his brows at the musket. "You're right."

"Does it hurt?"

"Not overmuch." He wasn't about to admit that it did.

The climb up the crag was steeper than it had looked from the clearing, but Audrey kept pace, holding her skirts up to her ankles. It made his heart swell to be able to lend her a hand as they picked a path up the crag.

At the top, Reid tugged Audrey up beside him.

"Heavens," she said, her voice filled with awe. He loved how her expression filled with wonder, her cheeks rosy from exertion.

"Aye, my sentiments as well." The scene was almost as

breathtaking as the woman standing beside him. Below, the loch stretched lengthwise, almost like a still river cutting through a pair of majestic peaks, blanketed with grass and peppered with trees. For miles and miles, jagged mountains stretched to the clouds, each one daring them to pass over her treacherous cliffs.

"'Tis so vast. I never imagined." Audrey held fast to Reid's hand. "I thought we'd traveled so far from Blair Atholl, we'd nearly crossed the mountains."

"Och, we're still in the southern range."

"And your home is in the north?"

"Up past Inverness, aye."

Releasing his hand, she turned in a circle. "There are so many places for deer to hide."

"There are." A bit of scat caught Reid's eye and he crouched down to examine it. "This is fresh."

"They're close then." Shading her eyes, Audrey joined the hunt. "A print." She raced ahead. "And another."

Reid looked beyond her, but saw only trees. "Go on then, we've picked up the trail, there's naught to do but follow."

She glanced over her shoulder with a happy grin, then started down the hill, pointing. "This way."

Reid followed, enjoying watching her lift her skirts and lithely leap over rocks as she maneuvered around shrubs of heather and broom. Audrey reminded him of a meadow nymph, lovely, happy, and without a care. She ran ahead up the crag and, at the tree line, she circled her finger above her head and pointed.

Reid readied the musket and hastened after her. With his next blink, he saw it, too; a glimpse of tan fur moved through the foliage. A thrill darted through his blood as he lined up his sights and crept ahead.

The deer stopped and looked, her ears shifting forward. Her nose twitched.

As he planted his feet, Reid's finger closed on the steel trigger. He held his breath to ensure a steady aim and squeezed, the shot making the butt kick hard into his shoulder. His ears rang as he waved his hand and cleared away the smoke and smell of char. *Blast.* He'd missed. Branches cracked in the distance as their quarry escaped.

Behind him, Audrey shrieked.

Tumbling from above in a shower of rocks and debris, the lass came to a rolling stop under a bush of yellow gorse.

"Good God." Reid's heart flew to his throat as he lowered the muzzle and ran toward her.

"Ow." She tugged her arm away from a nasty thorn and rubbed.

"Are you hurt?"

She scooted away, the gorse catching her skirts as if it had teeth. "Mayhap a scratch here and there."

"Stay put," he said. The damned briar had her trapped. "Allow me to release your gown."

She bobbed her head in a nod, as if she was trying to keep tears at bay.

Dropping to his knees, he began the task of gently pulling the wool away from dozens of thorns. "My heart nearly stopped when I saw you falling."

She smiled and swiped at a scrape on her chin. "Sss."

Reid cringed. "You *are* hurt."

"No." She looked at the line of blood on her fingers. "Nothing that won't heal in a day or two."

He pulled her sleeve away from the last thorn, then smoothed his palm over her skirts. "And to think I believed you to be a delicate rose when we first met."

She chuckled. "Even roses have thorns, my lord."

He tweaked her cheek with the tips of his fingers. "Upon every passing day you surprise me with something new."

"And you as well." Audrey cupped his face, circling her fingers around his cheek. "Though I shaved you this morning, your stubble has grown anew." Then she scratched with her nails like she might do to a pet. "I like the roughness of it."

Reid lowered his gaze to her lips. A welcome pull of desire coiled deep inside.

She emitted a sultry chuckle. Moving her fingers behind his neck, she drew her lips to his.

A low growl rumbled from Reid's throat. He liked it when she took command. And being with Audrey in the wild with a cool breeze whipping her long, silken locks across his face heightened his need for her. She must have felt it, too, because her hand deftly slipped to the hem of his kilt.

He waggled his brows as he captured a tendril of her hair. "You have a hankering to charm the dragon beneath my sporran, do ye, lass?"

Her eyes flashed wide with mischief. "A dragon, is it now?"

Releasing her hair, he toyed with her skirts, inching them ever higher while she moved onto his lap. "But ye ken I like to explore, too."

He coaxed his hand between her thighs, and she parted her legs ever so subtly. "That sounds amusing. Possibly even more invigorating than the hunt."

"Och, far more." When at last his relentless fingers found her quim, she gasped, and Reid muted the sound with his mouth. He slid his finger inside her using her moisture to tease the pearl that could drive her to ecstasy. Audrey mewled like a cat as, beneath her bottom, he grew hard.

As she glanced downward, her breath caught. "It seems you were successful on your quest while my hands have become idle."

He chuckled. Aye, she could talk like that all day. Between them, he tugged his kilt up and exposed his shaft.

"Mercy." She slowly wrapped her fingers around him, making his balls clamp taut. "You're as big around as my wrist."

A pulse of pleasure gave him a shudder. "You ken what a man wants to hear, lass."

She ran her fingers up, then down. "Can it be done...um...here?"

He nodded. "Straddle me."

A sexy gasp caught in her throat as he grasped her by the waist and lifted as she shifted her legs, sliding her wet core along his cock.

He thrust his hips flush against her. "Do you want this?"

"Yes," she whispered breathlessly.

When her tongue slipped across her lips, Reid groaned, the erotic scent of her womanhood washing over him. A gust of wind tantalized his exposed skin, heightening his need. Reid claimed her mouth with ravenous swipes of his tongue. Brazenly, Audrey guided his cock inside her. She was so wet, he could come with a single thrust.

He clamped his fingers around her hips. "Look at me, Audrey."

Those deep blue eyes turned darker as they stared at

him. With his hands guiding her hips, he used languid strokes to control the rhythm. Her breathing sped as she rocked up and down, then arched her back and took him deeper. Reid's eyes did not leave her bonny face, but his lips parted while his breath came in short gasps. So erotic was their bond, he'd not last more than a few more strokes.

Throwing her head back, Audrey's short gasps of ecstasy came quickly. The pressure built. Reid forced the tempo faster. A cry caught in the back of her throat. Though he nearly burst in unison with her peak, he clenched his bum cheeks and held fast until her quivering subsided. Then, after two deep thrusts, he bared his teeth and forced himself to pull out, bellowing like a savage.

Collapsing against him, Audrey ran delightful kisses along his neck. "You've turned me into a wanton woman."

He chuckled. "And I've become a slave to your wiles."

She rested her head on his shoulder. "I wish we could stay here forever. It's as if we're the only two people in all the Highlands."

Reid ran his palm up her back and held her in a tight embrace. If only there were some way he could make her wishes come true. If only he could spill his seed inside her and claim Audrey as his own. But there was the matter of his father's promise. He'd ignored the situation long enough, and continuing to do so would serve no one. When he returned to Brahan, he would summon his uncle and attempt to negotiate an amicable resolution... as soon as he cleared his name.

Chapter Thirty-One

*A*s the days passed, Reid's injuries began to bother him less. Every day, to regain his strength, he swam, chopped wood, and practiced sparring against a post. Every night he cast his guilt aside and reveled in Audrey's arms as they made love into the wee hours. It was a time of healing and a time to build his strength, to redevelop the muscles that had slackened during his misery in prison. One day without exercise was noticeable. A fortnight combined with his injuries? It would take him twice as long to recover and rebuild. Perhaps three times.

When thoughts of the future came, he pushed them away, refused to think of anything but the now. Alone in the cottage in the midst of the Highlands, it was as if he and Audrey were the only two people in all of Christendom. There in the wood, *the cause*, clan and kin, and all the reasons why he couldn't have Audrey as his own faded into oblivion. For the first time in his adult life, he didn't allow himself to think about the outside world and all that was wrong with Britain. He didn't care about the Occasional Conformity Act. That James was being pig-headed about remaining faithful to the pope didn't matter. Not now. Even his uncle Cromartie and the pact between the two septs of MacKenzie clans didn't matter. There in the wood, they were removed from the political posturing that had incited wars on two continents. If only they could remain there forever. If only thoughts of his duty would continue to remain at bay.

Aye, Reid had nearly convinced himself he could hide with Audrey forever until the Marquis of Tullibardine rode into the clearing with his Highland army in his wake. A visit that shattered Reid's oasis of happiness.

Reid set aside the ax he'd been using to chop wood and shot a wary glance to the cottage, where Audrey was preparing their noon meal. "An army?" he asked. "What's afoot?"

The marquis inclined his chin northward. "Redcoats are headed to Brahan Castle."

"Ballocks. I kent I shouldn't have stayed here for so long. I hate hiding like a coward." Not that he'd tell Tullibardine how much he'd enjoyed the past fortnight of solace.

"Aye?" The marquis dismounted. "By your color and that heap of firewood, I'd say the respite has been what you needed to mend your angry arse."

"My arse was about the only thing on my backside that wasn't angry."

Tullibardine laughed. "Are you good to ride?"

"Bloody oath I am." His heart sank. He wanted to ride no more than he wanted to walk naked through an ice storm. But one's duty had a way of catching up to a man. He had naught but to stand and face it.

"My spies report the dragoons are taking the drovers' pass through the glens like they always do. The Sassenachs have no idea how to cross the Highlands."

"'Tis a good thing. That route will take them days longer—cuts miles west."

"It does. So if we leave now, we'll arrive at Brahan Castle before those bastards by a good two days."

"Give me a moment to gather my things."

As he strode for the cottage, all the reasons Reid had been fighting for *the cause* came flooding back. His care of his clan and the Highland chiefs. What the hell had he been thinking, spending lazy nights in Audrey's arms? He needed to avenge her father's death. He needed to settle his affairs with the Earl of Cromartie. And moreover, he needed to gather the Highland chieftains, insist on solidarity, and decide their next steps.

He stopped midstride. "The crossing is too treacherous for Miss Kennet."

Tullibardine nodded. "My man-at-arms will take her back to Blair. She'll be safe with Lady Magdalen until this is over."

"It may never be over." Reid's lips thinned as the lass stepped outside.

Her eyes filled with alarm as she looked to Reid. "What is it?"

"Government troops are marching on Brahan. I need you to go to Blair Castle and wait."

"Wait? Shouldn't I stay with you, my lord? I can be of assistance."

"I cannot allow you to put yourself in harm's way again."

"But—"

"No!" he bellowed forcefully while the hurt in her eyes

stabbed his heart like a saber. But Reid had been thinking of himself for too long now—had put off the inevitable. He knew more than anyone his life wasn't his own, no matter how much he cared for the lass. *The cause* had always been far more important than any one man. "You'll return to Blair with the guard. Now go inside and collect your things."

The look on her face smote him like taking the saber and twisting it. But she lifted her chin and turned on her heel, making no scene, just like a proper well-bred English rose.

Reid felt like a heel. Everything about their affair had been wrong. He'd gone against his own vow to stay away from his ward. He'd allowed himself to enjoy the comfort of a woman's arms while too many unsolved problems troubled Scotland. Too many people relied on him and his good favor with Queen Anne.

Worse, he had his duty to the MacKenzie clan. The damned alliance forged by his father still hung around his neck like an anvil. Until *and if* he reached a settlement with his uncle, Earl of Cromartie, he had no business wooing any woman. He had no business pursuing happiness and his own desires. His duty was to clear his name and see to it James Francis was named the next successor to the throne, lest Britain fall into the hands of a Hanover. In fact, Audrey needed to find a man who could spend his days showering her with affection, not a Highland earl who was forever fighting government tyranny—running from bloodthirsty dragoons. Her marriage had been his goal from the day they'd first met, and yet he'd lost his way.

Tullibardine gave him a quizzical look. "Do you need a moment with the lass?"

"I'll fetch my musket and sword and we'll be off."
Clenching his fists, he slipped inside to face Audrey.

She followed and stood with her back to the door. "I'm
as skilled a rider as anyone."

"You kent this day would come."

"You think I'm weak because I'm a woman."

"Your father entrusted me with your safety. You want
to take to the Highlands, running from the likes of Wagner Tupps—or, worse, Captain Fry?" Reid snatched his
sword from where he'd stowed it behind the door. "The
Marquis of Tullibardine is right. You cannot go with us.
Not this time. 'Tis too dangerous."

"What if you're killed? What then?"

No matter how much his heart told him to stay, told
him to make promises he could never keep, he refused to
obey. "I will not be killed."

"Do you think you're too tough to succumb to a musket ball?"

He grasped her shoulders firmly. "Audrey, you ken I
am a man with a great many responsibilities. Clan and
kin are relying on me. I'll not die, and you will go to
Blair Castle until I can make other arrangements for
your care."

"My care? And what, exactly, would that be?"

His lips thinned.

"What about us? W-what about all that we've shared?"

"I—" He reached around her and grabbed the latch.
"There are things I must set to rights—things which have
tied my hands from the outset." He turned and regarded
her over his shoulder. "You will always be in my heart,
lass, but I have no choice but to go."

His heart twisting into a knot, Reid pushed out the
door. Dammit, he hated seeing her hurt, but the lass

would be better off without him. Christ, he was the biggest arse in all of Britain. No, he couldn't risk ever seeing her again, because if he did, he'd never be able to let her go. When this was over, he'd write to the queen and make a plea for Audrey to marry a courtier. A good man who wasn't involved with wars and *the cause*, or a victim of an alliance forged by his father.

* * *

Through the entire journey down the mountains, Audrey didn't say a word. She wanted to be sick. She wanted to rein her horse north and follow Reid and the Atholl army. It wasn't that they were leaving her behind, but something written on Seaforth's face told her he thought their affair was over. The marquis had ridden into the camp, and suddenly the fairy tale they'd been living in the Highlands had come to an end.

But nothing was over as far as Audrey was concerned. It had only just begun. Reid believed he was in too much trouble to think of marriage? Why could he not realize what an asset she could be to him and his cause? Did it matter so much that she was English? He trusted her father enough to sail to France with him on a dangerous mission, and yet he didn't trust her.

So many times during their days at the cottage, she'd wanted to discuss their future, but she'd kept mum for fear of bursting their bubble of happiness. Instead of talking, she did everything in her power to show him that she would be the perfect wife for him. She'd kept the cottage clean, she'd cooked, she'd tended his wounds, which had been healing nicely. Worst of all, she'd lain with him. Not that their nights of passion weren't fantastically enjoyable, but no one needed to tell her what happened when a maid gave a man her virtue.

She was ruined.

Now the only other man who might have her was Wagner Tupps, and if that ended up being the case, Audrey would rather sail a sinking ship to the Americas than submit to that blackguard. She shuddered. Where was Mr. Tupps now? Was he riding with the regiment led by the awful captain? And where were the multitude of Highlanders who'd sworn fealty to the Jacobite cause? Reid spoke as if he owed them his life. Why did they not reciprocate? He was their leader, was he not?

By the time Audrey reached Blair Castle, she was angry and hurt and completely ready to take matters into her own hands. She'd do whatever was needed, from sailing to London to plead with the queen, to closing down the mine and recruiting the laborers to join her army. She was a wealthy heiress. Perhaps it was time to spend a bit of her coin.

Lady Tullibardine met Audrey with outstretched hands and a warm smile. "How was your journey?"

"I must say it was frustrating to be traveling in the wrong direction." She didn't care if this woman was a marchioness, Audrey wasn't about to sit idle and do nothing. She squared her shoulders, ready for rebuttal, but one didn't come.

"I take it you wanted to continue on with the Lord of Seaforth?"

"Of course I did. But His Lordship thinks I'm incompetent and completely useless."

The marchioness led her up the stairs. "I doubt that. Men can be blinded by their own importance, however."

"I'll say."

"But do you not think Seaforth was acting in your best interests—trying to keep you from danger?"

As they exited on the second floor, Audrey groaned. "But I've proved myself useful over and over again." She cringed. There had been the one instance when she'd been recognized by Mr. Tupps, in Durham—but experience was a great teacher, and that would never happen again.

"And you cannot bear to be separated from him for a minute."

"Exactly."

Her ladyship stopped with her hand grasping a doorknob. "That's because you're in love with him."

"I—" Audrey froze with her mouth open, quite certain she was blushing right down to her toes.

"You may as well admit it, my dear. We all succumb to our hearts sooner or later." Opening the door, Lady Magdalen gave her a knowing smile. "However, men oft and incorrectly think they're the only ones who can take matters into their own hands." She beckoned Audrey into the drawing room and gestured to a chair. "Now, as you most likely are aware, my husband supports *the cause*."

"I gathered."

"And my father is the Earl Marischal of Scotland."

"Oh?" It was common knowledge that the Marischal had spent time in the Tower accused of treason, and was only released because he insisted the men he'd taken to Edinburgh to meet James, Queen Anne's half brother, were a welcoming party and nothing more. Ultimately, the queen granted a pardon, most likely to avoid a civil war. Audrey still crossed her arms. "Then you know why the Earl of Seaforth was captured and beaten."

"I do."

"And you have something up your sleeve, my lady?"

"Please, call me Maddie. My closest friends do."

"Very well. But my insides are bursting with anticipation."

The marchioness let out a long sigh. "Truly, 'tis but an idea, though you should be aware that I spent a great deal of time in London when Reid MacKenzie was still a ward of Queen Anne."

"That's right, he was."

"Aye, his mother died of childbed fever, and his father passed when he was still a lad. Queen Anne had him brought to court as a ward of the crown because she feared Seaforth had Jacobite leanings, and also believed she could sway him to her side."

"But she didn't."

Maddie waggled her eyebrows. "Well, Reid led her to believe she had. If you haven't noticed, the Earl of Seaforth can win hearts with a wee grin."

Audrey nodded, wondering how many other women with whom he'd spent a fortnight in the midst of the wilderness.

"Of all the Scottish nobles, I'd say he's Anne's favorite. In her eyes, Seaforth can do no wrong."

"So are you saying we should appeal directly to the queen?"

"I am." Maddie held up a finger. "However, I mightn't be the one to do so. Though I was eventually cleared of all suspicion, Her Highness threw me out of court after a chandelier fell on her meeting table."

"You? Why did she believe you were responsible?"

"I was the queen's harpist, and a very unpleasant countess blamed me for the accident in front of her ministers and her ladies. As a matter of fact, if it weren't for the Earl of Seaforth, I could have very well been led to the gallows before my father had a chance to clear my name."

A hundred thoughts whirled through Audrey's mind. This woman was a fellow musician, and had experienced grave danger. They had far more in common that she'd ever imagined, but she couldn't yammer on about any of that now. Not when Reid was headed north to face certain battle. Besides, who knew if the queen would forgive him for taking up arms against government troops?

Audrey shook her head. "Then we should make an immediate appeal to the queen?"

"I—"

"M'lady." A valet stepped inside and bowed. "Pardon the intrusion, but a messenger has arrived. A royal messenger. Says he must speak to you immediately."

Lady Magdalen waved her hand through the air. "Send him in."

The valet looked to Audrey and twisted his mouth disapprovingly. "Now, m'lady?"

Snorting, Maddie's expression grew emphatic. "Miss Kennet is my trusted guest. Now send him in."

Audrey looked between servant and lady, all too aware that she was a foreigner in a land suspicious of English subjects.

"Unfortunately, Highlanders have always been wary of the English, and now even more so. Not to worry. Once they come to know you, they'll learn to be more trusting."

"My lady," he said in a Londoner's accent. "I have a missive from Her Majesty, Queen Anne, for the Earl of Seaforth."

Maddie's lips formed an O as if such news was a surprise. "Whyever would you bring it here?"

"The earl gave Her Highness an address in Coxhoe,

but the butler advised the earl is unreachable and the letter should be left with the Marquis of Tullibardine."

Audrey covered her mouth with her hand, forcing herself not to jump up and snatch the parchment from his fingertips. *God bless Gerald.*

"And you're aware His Lordship is not here," said Maddie.

"Indeed." He took a step nearer. "Do you know where I can find him?"

"Not precisely. However, you can leave the letter with me. My army will take word to him." She emphasized the word *army*.

The man shook his head. "But I must see this into the hands of the earl with haste. If the marquis were here, I could have entrusted the missive to him..."

Audrey scooted to the edge of her seat. "But—"

Lady Magdalen held up her palm, demanding silence. "You are an English messenger, are you not?" she asked with a very thick brogue.

"I am, my lady."

"I can assure you there is no chance in all of Christendom that you will find the Earl of Seaforth or the Marquis of Tullibardine unless they want to be found. You could very well spend months and months scouring the Highlands to no avail. You have no option but to entrust the letter into my care. After all, I am a marchioness, and a vassal of the queen."

Still on the edge of her seat, her hands tightly folded, her knuckles white, Audrey nodded in eager agreement.

The man chewed his bottom lip, as if considering. "Would you be willing to sign a writ stating that you take full responsibility for the delivery of such a document? 'Tis a *royal* missive, after all. Signed by the queen herself."

"Indeed I will. And I give you my word that it will reach His Lordship with haste."

Crossing her arms to allay the jittering of her insides, Audrey waited patiently while Maddie moved to the writing desk and took up parchment and quill. In minutes, the marchioness handed the messenger her pledge to deliver the letter to Reid, and the exchange was complete.

As soon as the man left the drawing room, Audrey hopped to her feet.

Maddie pulled a small knife from her sleeve. "Do you want to do the honors?"

Guilt coiled around her stomach and she swallowed against it. "'Tis from the queen?"

"You heard the messenger." Her ladyship turned the missive over and pointed. "It bears a royal seal."

Audrey took the letter and the knife with trembling fingers. No matter how much her conscience berated her, she must know what the letter contained. It was a matter of life and death, and if she saw something untoward, Reid would simply have to forgive her. Taking a steadying breath, she set it on the table and carefully ran the blade under the wax so as not to fracture the glob—just in case they needed to reseal it.

She read aloud.

My Lord Seaforth,

It was with great joy that I received your letter, until I read its contents. I should summon you to London forthwith and demand an explanation as to why you visited my half brother in France without advising me first. After consideration, I do, however, believe your motives were carried out in good faith. As you are aware, the succession concerns me greatly. But hear me, Seaforth, I have made it my life's mission to ensure there will never be another Catholic king on the throne of Britain. Popery has been extricated from the kingdom, and shall never return. It is with a sad and heavy heart that I learn Prince James obstinately refuses to convert to Protestantism as I am well aware the days of my reign are numbered.

I commend you in your efforts to plead with James to come to the true faith, but I also must caution you. The Occasional Conformity Act must pass. Parliament will not accept a monarch who only poses as a Protestant. The next ruler of Britain will accept our faith in mind, body, and soul and condemn popery with his every breath.

On the subject of your sea galley, the lord high admiral will conduct an investigation into your claim and issue appropriate discipline to the captain and officers of the Royal Buckingham *should it be warranted.*

Please carry this letter for presentation to any Government officers who may misunderstand the purpose of your peacekeeping visit to James, for you have my pardon and my blessing.

I require you to make supplication to me in person before undertaking any future visit to the prince.

Most sincerely and reverently,
Anne, by the Grace of God, Queen of Great Britain, France, and Ireland, Defender of the Faith

Maddie threw up her hands. "Good Lord, if only this

had arrived before the dragoons befell Coxhoe House, all Seaforth's misery would have been avoided."

Her heart thumping in her chest, Audrey shook the missive. "I must leave for Brahan Castle at once. I've already lost a day. Reid is in grave danger of being attacked, and he's received a pardon!"

"I suspect a formal pardon has already arrived at Durham Gaol as well."

"A lot of good that will do to keep the dragoons from killing him. They're already headed into the Highlands through the drovers' glens."

Maddie tapped her fingers to her lips. "There might be a faster way. As long as the winds are in our favor."

"Tell me."

"There's a wherry moored on the riverbank."

"A river flows up to the Highlands?"

"Of course not, silly. But the Garry flows into the Tay, which flows into the Firth of Tay and out to the North Sea."

"We can sail to Brahan Castle?"

"The wherry isn't sturdy enough to battle the sea, but once we reach Perth, we shouldn't have any difficulty finding a captain who'll ferry us north."

"A captain who will do the bidding of two women?"

Maddie winked and rubbed her fingers together as if she were rubbing a coin. "With the right incentive, your gender matters not, lass."

Chapter Thirty-Two

*T*he breeze caressed Reid's face as the outline of Brahan Castle came into view. Home was a welcome sight for weary eyes. Built by Reid's great-grandfather at the turn of the seventeenth century, Brahan was more like Queen Anne's Kensington Palace than like a medieval motte and bailey fortress. All the same, it was an enormous home that housed servants and an army of men, as well as served as seat of the Earls of Seaforth for a hundred years.

Rain spat from the sky, but if anything, the weather made his home look all the more inviting. Fires would be burning in the hearths and smells of Highland cooking would waft from the kitchens. For the first time in months Reid would sleep in his enormous four-poster bed.

Dunn rode out to meet them with Reid's deerhound, Cluny, bounding in his wake.

"What took you so bloody long?" As soon as Dunn reined his horse beside Reid, the big dog fell into step at his flank as if he'd never been away.

Reid shifted his gaze to his ally. "Och, so you haven't a care that I survived Fry's mauling, you ungrateful flap-dragon?"

"You look well enough to me, and a damned mite better than the last time I saw you." Dunn glanced back to the line of Argyll soldiers and gave a nod of welcome to the marquis. "Where's the lass?"

"At Blair Castle with Lady Tullibardine."

"Rid of her at last are you? Thank God."

Reid's hackles prickled on the back of his neck. "Miss Kennet is still my responsibility."

"Aye? And so is Mairi MacKenzie, if you've forgotten."

His jaw twitched at her name. God's teeth, he'd been home for all of two minutes and the first thing out of Dunn's mouth was to pester him about Mairi. His gut churned like a millstone. No one needed to remind him about the promise his father had made eighteen years past when the lass was a bairn in her mother's arms—a promise Reid needed to rescind in due course without causing a feud that might tear apart the MacKenzie dynasty. But that didn't allay the fact that the last person Reid wanted to think about at the moment was his distant cousin, or her overbearing father. Until his name was clear and he'd settled his quarrel with Captain Fry, he must keep relations copacetic with his uncle, the Earl of Cromartie.

Good Lord, Mairi was more like a sister than a wife. Aye, she was bonny enough, though he'd never harbored amorous feelings for her. As he'd thrown his efforts into the purpose of the Jacobite cause, he'd always hoped Mairi would find another, more suitable husband. Indeed at gatherings she always managed to turn heads, and now that she'd come of age, she might even have a secret suitor in the wings...*God willing*.

Reid shot Dunn a leer. "Leave it alone."

"You have to face it soon, 'cause I've summoned Cromartie."

The millstone in his gut ground a bit harder. "Why the bloody hell did you do that?"

"You didn't think the redcoats would leave you alone, did you, m'lord?"

"Nay, but I have enough men to face them." Reid raked his fingers through his hair. "Shite." What was worse, facing an army of dragoons, or facing his great-uncle and breaking the ridiculous betrothal the man had entered into with Reid's parents when he and Mairi were infants?

Dunn scowled as if he knew exactly what Reid was thinking. "Mayhap you can marry Miss Audrey off to Kennan Cameron. I've sent word to his da as well."

Reid's fist tightened around his reins. He loved Dunn MacRae like a brother, but the bastard could use a good fist to the snout about now. "What the hell for?"

"For the goddamned gathering. Jesus Saint Christopher Christ, Seaforth. Did that back lashing addle your mind?"

"Shut it." Reid pulled his horse to a stop outside the stables and checked his anger. "The redcoats are coming up the drovers' glens."

Dunn's expression suddenly grew sober. "How many?"

"A regiment of two hundred, if they don't pick up more along the way," said Aiden, finally joining in the conversation. It had been wise of the marquis to keep his mouth shut about Audrey—at least until Reid straightened the shambles crashing around his ears. "'Tis why the women-folk stayed behind."

"How much time?" Dunn asked.

Reid dismounted and handed his reins to the stable hand. "We reckon two days." Cluny rubbed up against his leg, demanding a scratch.

Dunn snapped his fingers before he hopped off his horse. "Blast our miserable luck."

Reid gave his dog's wiry coat a good scratch. "Don't tell me you haven't been preparing. Why the hell did I send you ahead—"

"Of course I've been bloody preparing." Dunn thrust his finger westward. "But half the Highland Jacobites will be here four days hence. Two days too bloody late."

"I'd as soon keep them out of it. The MacKenzie will face them." Reid ground his fist into his palm while the raw torture of being whipped and humiliated spread like wildfire through his chest. "Together with the Atholl and MacRae men, they'll be outnumbered and outmatched."

Tullibardine brushed the rain from his velvet doublet. Christ, he was the only man Reid knew who looked like a courtier even after he'd ridden a hundred miles. "Aye, and there's no chance in hell the queen would turn a blind eye to a cavalier captain riding against an earl, a marquis, and a clan chieftain."

Reid grinned. One way or another he'd exact his revenge. "Enough talk. We've a battle to plan."

* * *

For hours the sea galley fought through white-capped swells of the North Sea while rain stung Audrey's face. She and Maddie huddled together on a bench near the rudder. Soaked clean through, she clutched the arisaid tight under her chin in a futile attempt to stay warm. But no matter how firmly Audrey clenched her muscles, her teeth continued to chatter.

Captain Ferguson manned the rudder, holding on with both hands while the sail billowed erratically with wind. Throughout the entire journey, it would fill with air and assist the oarsmen to gain speed, but then an angry gust of wind would slam into the hull, rocking the galley so far to the side, Audrey had to cling to the bench to keep from being tossed overboard. The sail would flap like bed linens hung out to dry while the captain bellowed orders, fighting to steer the vessel back on course.

"If the storm grows worse, we'll have no choice but to sail ashore and wait it out," the man bellowed in a thick burr.

Audrey's stomach churned with the next enormous wave and she crouched, pressing her fists to her forehead. *Dear Lord, have mercy!*

She'd wrapped the missive in a pouch and secured it with oiled leather to ensure it stayed dry, but she couldn't let it fall into the sea. Before they'd set sail, she'd placed the parcel under her skirts and secured it in place around her waist with a leather thong.

To the north, a bolt of lightning lit up the sky.

Gasping, Maddie grasped Audrey's arm. "This is horrendous."

"But we cannot stop."

Three fingers of lightning streaked above, followed by a deafening boom. The galley tipped and swayed. In a blink, the rain came at them in sideways sheets.

"Portside oars, heave!" Releasing one hand from the rudder, Ferguson thrust his finger toward the sailor manning the boom. "We're rounding Kinnaird Head, tack west."

The surf grew increasingly angry. Waves crashed over the hull.

Changing course, the boat eddied and bobbed. Audrey squinted through rain pelting her face and filling her eyes. "We're headed for the rocks!"

"Nay, lassie, we're headed for the safety of the cove yonder," Captain Ferguson shouted above the roar of the sea.

Lightning flashed overhead so near, Audrey jolted and ducked.

Maddie grasped her arm and screamed. "Dear God. The mast's afire!"

"She's taking water," hollered an oarsman.

The captain pulled the rudder hard left, his face contorting with his effort. "Heave ho, straight for the shore."

"Rocks starboard!" shouted the navigator from the stern.

Audrey threw her arms around Maddie. The two women clung to each other as jagged rocks scraped the underside of the hull. Icy water washed over Audrey's feet.

"God, save us," Maddie prayed under her breath while shouts of doom came from the oarsmen.

"Hold the course!" the captain yelled. "We'll run aground afore she sinks. I'm no' about to lose my lady to the sea. Not this bloody day."

Audrey held tight and seethed through her teeth, "We cannot fail. Not only is Reid's life at risk, your husband is riding beside him."

The water rose to her knees.

"Can you swim?" asked Audrey.

"A bit, but we'll not be swimming for our lives this day." The marchioness pointed to the walls of a dark castle looming above the stony beach. "I have a plan."

The ship groaned and bumped, shrieking like a sea monster as it came to rest in the shallows. Rain continued to pummel them while the sailors carried the ladies to the shore.

The women and crew stood dumbly, watching their boat as if she'd suddenly repair herself so they could be under way.

"She'll be grounded for months, I'd wager," said Audrey, though no one even turned his head her way. She might as well have been talking to the sea.

Must she be thwarted at every turn?

"Captain Ferguson," called Maddie with an assured voice, as if she hadn't just been through a harrowing ordeal. "Please accompany Miss Kennet and me to Kinnaird Castle. We must have a word with Lord Saltoun forthwith."

Audrey leaned nearer her friend and pulled her aside so not to be overheard. "You know the master of this castle?"

"Through my father, aye."

"And he is loyal to *the cause*?"

Maddie grinned. "He was arrested with my da in 1708 when James tried to pay a visit to Edinburgh. My guess is he understands the meaning of Highland hospitality."

"Then let us pray we find him at home."

Chapter Thirty-Three

Do these mountains never end?" Though Wagner wore a well-oiled cloak, the rain had soaked him clear through to the bone. Driving wind drove the icy droplets and stung the exposed skin on the back of his neck.

But after a fortnight of misery, the goal was finally in sight. Their Highland tracker had led them to an encampment of government troops near Urquhart Castle. Before their guide prepared to leave, Wagner stopped the burly man who looked like a bloody heathen with his bare knees. He wore a dirk in his belt on one side and an old sword on the other. Between the two hung his leather purse in the Highland style. What was it with these savages and their emphasis on the need to protect their cocks? Did a one of them know how to fight fair?

He doubted it.

"How far to Dingwall?" Wagner asked, eyeing the purse. No doubt the tracker had just been paid by the way it bulged. If only he'd met the man in a dark alleyway

without two hundred soldiers milling about, he might re-
lieve him of his coin.

"What're you hunting up there?"

Wagner shrugged as if it were a trifle. "I'm told the
Earl of Seaforth makes the best whisky in the Highlands."

"Aye? 'Tis nay bad, but if you want the best, I'd ride
south to Glenlivet and sample the Duke of Gordon's still."

"I just may need to try them both." Wagner ran his fingers down the beard he'd been unable to groom for the
past fortnight. "But you didn't mention how far the ride is
from here."

"Nay. I didn't." The man smirked and pushed past,
mounting his horse. He rode away without a backward
glance.

Anger coiled around Wagner's gut. It hadn't been easy,
but he'd folded into the ranks like a mercenary and kept
his mouth shut for the most part. Coxhoe House should
be his. The mine should be his, and moreover the income
from the mine. Watford had promised he'd secure it. The
miserable solicitor had told him to stay patient while he
kept the estate in abeyance until the Earl of Seaforth was
forced into accepting Wagner's proposal for Audrey's
hand.

He snarled and flexed his freezing fingers. Nothing
would stop him from taking what was rightfully his. He
was the only surviving male heir, regardless of his whore
of a mother. He was the only man who could take charge
of the mine and his uncle's daughter.

"Tupps," said Captain Fry, coming up beside him. "I
would have thought you'd be overjoyed to have come
through the drovers' trail. My God, that passage never
gets any easier. It's miserable up here."

"And Seaforth. When will we meet up with him?"

"The lieutenant tells me his castle is a half-day ride from here."

"So why did we stop?"

"Because I'm in command of this regiment. And I'll decide how and when we engage." Fry gestured toward a ramshackle hovel with smoke curling up from the thatch. "Come, let's move out of the rain. You can buy me a drink. God knows I could use one."

* * *

The great hall at Brahan Castle hummed with the chatter of Highlanders seated at long tables. Every man knew a fight was coming. It was just a matter of when and where.

Though Brahan contained a separate dining hall for the noble family, Reid chose to eat with his men while Dunn and Tullibardine joined him.

Reid speared a lump of black pudding with his fork—a utensil he'd grown accustomed to using during his days at court. "Last eve spies reported Captain Fry's regiment rode into the encampment on Loch Ness."

Dunn reached for his cup of cider. "Right on cue, just as we predicted."

Tullibardine nodded. "Honestly, I thought we'd have another day or two. The bastard must want you with a vengeance, especially with all the rain we've been having."

"The storm's broke," Dunn said with his mouth full of food.

Reid looked between the two men. "I'm not surprised. Tupps wants nothing more than to sink his thieving fingers into the Kennet estate."

"Aye." Dunn washed his bite down with another swig

of cider. "And I reckon he'll ruin it and Miss Kennet within a year."

Reid slammed his fist on the table. "That parasite will not be touching the lass or Kennet lands! I'm still guardian, and I'll not allow it." He angrily tore off a piece of bread. "You're certain the lookouts are on full alert?"

"Bloody oath they are. Spoke to each one myself."

Tullibardine spread conserve on his bread. "The Atholl men are itching for a fight."

"As are the MacKenzie."

"And the MacRae."

A sentry marched through the big oak doors, heading straight for the high table. "M'lord, the Earl of Cromartie is on his way with reinforcements."

God's bones. Though Reid would have preferred it if his distant uncle and his men had stayed at home, he couldn't reveal his sentiments in front of his clansmen. "Good to hear. When—?"

Gilroy MacKenzie, the Earl of Cromartie, strode through the door before he could finish the question. "Feasting when there's a battle to be waged?" the braggart hollered across the hall.

Tullibardine nudged Dunn with his elbow. "What was that you said about your lookouts? With spies like that, the redcoats will be upon us afore we finish breaking our fast."

The MacRae chieftain gaped. "Beg your pardon, but Cromartie came from the west. The bloody dragoons will be coming from the south, m'lord...ye maggot."

"I love you, too, MacRae." At least the marquis had a sense of humor.

Reid shoved his chair back and offered his hand as the earl crossed the floor. "Thank you for coming."

The man grinned. "And miss a fight? I would have run through a burning forest to meet a mob of redcoats after the 1708 debacle. 'Tis about time we stirred things up a bit."

Reid offered the man a chair while his meal churned in his stomach. It would be a hell of a lot easier to avoid a confrontation altogether. If only Queen Anne had answered his missive, but there had been no reply waiting when they'd arrived at Brahan. "A battle could bring the attention of the crown. Attention we do not need."

"Och, are you going soft?" asked Cromartie. Then he raised his voice. "Come, Mairi. There's bountiful food."

The back of Reid's neck burned as his second cousin peeked into the room with an enormous grin. "Why the devil did you bring Her Ladyship to a fight? This is no place for womenfolk."

"Agreed," said Tullibardine. He'd been smart enough to leave his wife at Blair Castle, where she would be safe.

The older earl looked at Reid as if he'd grown two heads. "You don't intend to lure the bastards to Brahan?"

"Of course not. We'll set an ambush this side of the River Conon, but Mairi should have stayed at home," Reid clipped in a whisper before the lass reached the table.

"I reckon it's high time she paid a visit," Dunn mumbled from behind his damned cup.

Jesus Christ. Though Reid's mind was made up, this was no time to break an age-old alliance. Mairi bounced up to the table wearing a smile as if she were about to cross the threshold into wedded bliss.

Every man stood.

Reid's tongue felt too big for his mouth as he took her chilly fingers and politely kissed the back of her hand. "I'm surprised to see you, m'lady."

"Well, I'm no' overly surprised to see you, m'lord." She gave him a wee snort before shifting her gaze to Dunn and turning a shade of scarlet. "Though I wasn't expecting to see you here, sir."

Dunn bowed his head. "M'lady."

Reid introduced the Marquis of Tullibardine and they all sat. Mairi managed to position herself into the seat straight across from Reid, where she promptly leaned forward and stared at him. "What kind of trouble are you in, m'lord?"

He stopped a low growl threatening to rumble from his throat as he gave her a sober frown. "'Twas a misunderstanding with a warden in Durham, and I aim to settle it anon." He looked to her father. "I suggest you take Lady Mairi home, where she'll be safe."

"I'll protect her," said Dunn.

Reid cracked his knuckles under the table, wishing he could plant his fist in MacRae's mouth about now. And why the bloody hell was the chieftain staring at the lass as if he hadn't had a meal in a sennight? He nudged his friend with his elbow. "Nay. I need you with me."

"Mairi ought to be safe from harm if she stays above stairs," said Dunn as if he were in charge. "We'll see to it no one comes close."

Reid pushed his chair back. What choice did he have? His heart had been claimed by a lovely English rose and across from him sat the lass who, at five years younger, had been a thorn in his side at every clan gathering he could remember. Aye, Mairi had become a woman. And though she was now bonny and grinning at him, Reid couldn't push away the love he felt for Miss Audrey Kennet.

Love. He couldn't help but admit that he had fallen in love with his ward. Would he ever be able to clear his name and claim the woman who'd stolen his heart?

Chapter Thirty-Four

*L*ord Saltoun was an older man with a mop of gray hair and a beard that hung down to his chest. He'd no sooner opened the doors to them than he began shouting orders for hearths to be stoked with peat and food to be prepared. He not only appointed Audrey and Maddie with chambers above stairs, he offered his stable to Captain Ferguson and his crew.

Once Audrey explained their purpose, Lord Saltoun immediately rose to their assistance. "I've two eighteen-oar sea galleys moored in the cove." He gave Audrey a wink. "We'll set sail come first light."

She clasped her hands and bowed her head respectfully. "How can I ever thank you, my lord?"

"It's thanks enough to have a chance to face that mob of backbiting dragoons. They ride through the Highlands like God granted them dominion over our lands, and I'd relish any opportunity to feed them their own tripe." He looked to Maddie with a furrowed brow. "The only thing I do not understand is why I'm just hearing about this now, m'lady."

"Seaforth was in hiding," the marchioness explained. "He'd hoped things would cool down afore the redcoats marched against his lands, but that was not meant to be."

"But I have a missive that will settle the question of his guilt once and for all." Audrey clutched her satchel tight around her waist.

"You're kindhearted for a Sassenach."

After a fitful night's sleep, Maddie and Audrey continued on their journey with Lord Saltoun and his crew of Highland oarsmen. Audrey stood aft and watched the bow break through the swells, as they headed toward the confluence of land from north and south grown nearer. When they sailed into the Cromarty Firth, Lord Saltoun regarded her from his position at the rudder. "'Tis a good thing the tide's in. My wee boat is small enough to sail up the River Conon."

"Does that river cut through MacKenzie lands?" asked Maddie.

"Aye, m'lady. Look around you. His Lordship's influence stretches far and wide. Every man from here to Applecross pays fealty to the Earl of Seaforth."

Audrey had no idea how much land that encompassed, but she was awed. In the distance, it seemed like mountains stretched to infinity. "That would be a great many souls, would it not?"

"Aye, a great many."

Wringing her hands, she watched the scenery sail by. The oarsmen heaved and strained to pull the boat against the wind, though with the protection of the firth, the swells weren't as unforgiving as they had been the day prior in the open sea. As the time passed, Audrey's unease grew, especially when Saltoun announced they were entering the confluence of the River Conon. "How much longer?"

The man frowned. "Don't go wishing your life away, lass. We'll drop anchor soon enough."

"I only hope we arrive before the dragoons," said Maddie.

"Me as well." The words barely escaped Audrey's mouth when the unmistakable crack of a musket resounded on the wind…followed by another, then another. She met Maddie's startled gaze. As the boat rounded a bend in the river, the roar of a battle in full force raged. Along the bank, redcoats were running toward kilted Highlanders, with bayonets affixed and swords pointed forward.

"Oars up!" shouted Lord Saltoun. "Tack to shore and drop anchor. Ready your weapons. We'll be fighting redcoats afore this hour is done!"

"We're too late." Audrey shot Her Ladyship a panicked grimace.

Maddie pointed. "Aiden!"

Audrey sucked in a gasp as she saw Reid leading the cavalry straight for a line of foot soldiers wielding bayonets.

The marchioness covered her eyes. "I cannot watch."

Audrey couldn't turn away. Swinging his sword in an upward arc, Reid cut through the front line at a gallop, heading straight for the next line of formation. He sat his stallion like a Viking, his hair whipping on the wind as he bore down on his next opponent. Men fled as he easily broke through a line of pikemen. Reid never once stopped to look in his wake. Surging forward, he continued to strike.

Lord Saltoun's men climbed over the hull and raced into battle.

"Haste!" Audrey grabbed Maddie's elbow and dashed forward, climbing over rowing benches until they reached the bow.

Watching Reid cut down his next attacker, she suddenly couldn't breathe. "God, no! He's heading straight for Captain Fry."

Audrey's gut twisted as the two men meet on horseback. Their swords clanged, the echo making her teeth rattle. Her muscles twitched as if she were in the midst of their fight. Reid's horse was taller and his reach longer, but Fry attacked like an asp, thrusting and pulling away to avoid Reid's hacking strikes.

The two opponents were equally skilled, expertly maneuvering their horses as each fought with savage strength.

"Dear God!" Gulping, Audrey clapped a hand over her mouth.

"We can't just stand here helplessly," shouted Maddie.

Audrey glanced down. A musket and powder horn lay at her feet. She snatched them from the deck. "See if you can find musket balls." She pulled the cork with her teeth and charged the weapon with black powder.

Maddie straightened with a pouch in her hand, pulling out a lead ball. "Here."

"Thank you." She took it and dropped it down the barrel, ramming it with the rod as fast as she could. Taking aim, she willed her trembling fingers to still as she waited for a clear shot. With his reins in his teeth, Reid chased Captain Fry, launching himself at the fleeing blackguard. The two men tumbled to the ground in a flurry of fists and blades.

"Aiden!" Maddie cried, thrusting her finger toward her husband.

With no clear shot to help Reid, Audrey panned her sights to the marquis, now battling man-to-man, his sword clanging loudly against a beastly dragoon's cutlass. An attacker ran toward Tullibardine's back, bayonet aimed for a lethal strike. Audrey sucked in a deep breath and squeezed the trigger.

Click-boom!

The weapon fired with a forceful kick. Skittering backward, Maddie grabbed her arm and helped Audrey steady herself before falling over a rowing bench. She waved her hand to clear the smoke. The attacker was down.

Audrey snatched the powder horn and recharged the musket. "Hand me another ball."

Across the battlefield, the fighting grew fiercer. Fry was running away from Reid. Now would be her chance, blast it.

"Here."

Audrey stuffed in the tow followed by the ball and shoved it all down with the ramrod. Both Reid and Fry had lost their swords. Fighting like dogs, the captain got away and started to run. Reid made chase, took a running dive, and tackled Fry. They rolled on the ground, fists flying. The earl gained the advantage and threw a jab to the captain's jaw. A flash of steel whipped out from Fry's sleeve.

"Watch the knife!"

Reid evaded the blade as it sliced too close to his throat.

Groaning with frustration, Audrey headed for the ladder. "I need to be closer."

"No." Maddie caught her arm. "Stay on the boat. 'Tis too dangerous."

"You'd do what you could to save the marquis, would you not?"

Her ladyship released her grip and gave a nod. "Keep low and out of sight."

"I will." Audrey pushed the musket into Maddie's hands. "Keep the barrel pointed up and hand it to me once I'm over the side."

The hem of Audrey's gown got soaked as she waded through the knee-deep water to the gravelly shore. Crouching under the willows, she held the musket at the ready as she hastened toward the fighting. Men grunted and screamed, the stench of blood thick on the air.

Fight well, my love. I'm coming.

A branch cracked behind her. With a gasp, her back stiffened. An arm slung around her throat while the musket was torn from her grasp. Her shoulders crashed into the wall of a man's chest.

"If I didn't know better, I'd think you were fighting for those filthy Scots," Wagner Tupps growled in her ear, his voice as menacing as the keenly honed dagger he leveled at the pulsing vein in Audrey's neck.

When she opened her mouth to scream, the thug stuffed a dirty rag inside, gagging her as he dragged her into the shadows of the forest.

Chapter Thirty-Five

*R*eid's muscles burned like the glowing heat from iron scorched by a smithy's bellows. Captain Fry fought as dirty as he'd wielded his cat-o'-nine-tails. Upon Reid's every jab, the man came back with a crippling punch to the kidneys or a strike to the jaw. He'd drawn a blade from his sleeve and another from his stocking. Every time Reid disarmed him, Fry came again with a fiendish attack.

But Reid was bigger and stronger, and the time he'd spent at the cottage rebuilding his strength kept him alive.

As the fight persisted, Fry tired. He resorted to vicious jabs to the newly healed scars on Reid's back. But pain had long since been overcome. With Fry's next strike, Reid seized the man's wrist and bent it downward until the captain dropped to his knees, cringing in pain. As the captain crumbled, Reid drove his knee into the man's face while he twisted Fry's arm harder.

"Mercy!"

"Did you take mercy on me?" Reid demanded as he landed another knee in the man's snout. "How many innocent men have you savagely whipped?"

"I will ruin you!" Blood streaming from his mouth, the captain struggled to wrench away from Reid's grasp. "I was doing my duty. I am an officer of the queen." Fry raised his hand and grasped Reid's knee, trying to jerk Reid off balance. But hours of training and honing his strength paid off. Reid's knee broke through Fry's defense, connecting with the man's chin. The captain's head snapped back, and he dropped to the ground in an unconscious heap.

Barking, Cluny bounded straight for them and pounced on Fry's chest, sinking his fangs around the man's throat.

"You're a bit late, old fella."

Cluny growled and held fast, the dog's eyes wild.

"Good lad. Hold him there until they lock him in irons and ship him to Inverness for trial." Reid wiped his hands on his kilt, taking in the scene. The fighting had stopped, and his men were mustering the redcoats who were still able to stand into the center of the lea and binding their wrists.

"Och, 'twas a bloody good feud. One I'm glad I didn't miss," said an old man with bowed legs and blood spattered across his face.

Reid shook his head as recognition set in. "William Fraser, Lord Saltoun?" Grinning, he shook the man's hand. "What the bleeding hell brought you down from your dunghill?"

"It seems your Sassenach lassie was attempting to deliver a missive to you from the queen in hopes to avoid a battle. Though I daresay she's a wee bit late."

"Audrey? What the—?" Reid shot his gaze downriver. Good Lord, the Marchioness of Tullibardine was sprinting toward them.

"Maddie!" The marquis hastened in beside her. "What the devil are you doing here?"

Her Ladyship clapped a hand to her chest as she sucked in consecutive breaths, looking straight at Reid. "A-a man has taken Miss Kennet!"

He clenched his fists and looked beyond Her Ladyship. "Bloody Tupps," he growled and sprang into action.

The varlet had a hold on Audrey's arm while he dragged her from the forest, straight for the galley. Reid ran for his horse, leaped aboard, and gathered his reins. Slamming his heels, he demanded a gallop, heading straight for the boat. *I'll kill you, ye bastard!*

Horses pummeled the ground behind him, but Reid didn't spare a backward glance. Tupps shoved Audrey over the hull and into the boat, and climbed after her. The feisty lass whipped around and attacked, pounding her fists on his chest.

Tupps snapped his hand back and slapped her face. Stumbling, the lass disappeared below the edge of the hull. His gut roiling with bile, Reid leaned forward and demanded more speed from his stallion. As they reached the galley, he launched himself from his saddle into the boat. Crouching, he regarded his quarry. "You've caused enough trouble for one lifetime, ye illegitimate cur."

Tupps whipped around and drew a knife. "Did you not take enough lashings from Fry?"

Reid's eyes narrowed. "The captain's cat-o'-nine-tails is retired for good."

Wagner sliced his knife through the air, making it hiss. "I'll have to finish what he left undone."

With one hand, Reid moved Audrey behind him as he drew his dirk with the other. "In your dreams, little man." Tupps pattered behind the rowing bench, making a show of flailing his dagger. Seaforth wasn't impressed. "Are you planning to use that thing, or are you dancing a jig?"

Baring his teeth, the man roared and lunged forward. "The Kennet lands are mine!"

Reid pushed the knife away to protect Audrey, smashing his shin into a rowing bench. He grimaced in pain but kept hold of Tupps's knife-wielding hand. With a twist toward the thumb, he forced the weapon to drop to the timbers.

Tupps swung around, landing a jab to the jaw. "I want the girl," he grunted.

Rage shot through Reid's blood, but he managed to maintain his grasp. "You'll never touch her." He jabbed for Tupps's flank with his dirk, but his opponent pivoted aside.

Audrey shrieked as the bastard landed another punch, hitting the side of Reid's head. As he winced, the slippery eel twisted from Reid's grip.

Wagner lunged for his knife, wrapping his spindly fingers around the hilt. Springing from the timbers, he drove his blade straight for Reid's heart.

With a sharp inhale, Reid rolled aside, the blade skimming past his arm. After the long fight with Captain Fry, his endurance had reached the ragged edge, and now his back was prone to his assailant. Reid hastened to his feet. A loud crack thudded. Ready for anything he whipped around, dirk at the ready.

Tupps lay flat on his face, a pool of blood spreading beneath him.

Audrey squeaked in a high-pitched gasp. She stood over Tupps's body while an oar dropped from her trembling hands. "He—he—he fell on the knife. I didn't mean to k-k-kill him."

In the blink of an eye, Reid climbed over a bench and pulled her into his arms, shielding her face from the gruesome sight. God, she was a warrior princess, tough as the Highlands. But he knew the remorse that came with taking a life. He held her close to his chest and touched his lips to her ear. "It's all right, lass. You did what needed to be done. You are the bravest woman I have ever met."

She trembled like a leaf in the wind. "He was going to stab you."

"Aye, and you stopped him."

"I did."

He kissed her forehead. "My God, you are astonishing."

She coughed out a nervous laugh. "Do you mean that?"

"Did you not just save my life?"

When she gave a nod, Reid inclined her chin upward and skimmed his lips across her mouth. In that moment, the only two people in all of Christendom who existed stood wrapped in an embrace in the belly of a boat. It didn't matter who saw. It didn't matter what had come before or what would come after. Reid claimed Audrey's lips and kissed her with the deep love filling his heart. He closed his eyes and plied her mouth with more emotion than he'd ever experienced in his life. He ran his fingers through her hair and held tight, never wanting to be separated from her again.

Dear God, he loved this woman.

"Beg your pardon, Seaforth," Cromartie's voice brayed from the shore. "It seems you've forgotten you're promised to another."

Chapter Thirty-Six

One moment Audrey was kissing Reid and melting in his arms, and in the next, her blood ran cold as realization sunk in. No wonder he'd never spoken of the future.

Reid was promised?

Her stomach convulsed. Pushing away, she had to cover her mouth to keep down her breakfast. "Is...is this true?"

His features grew dark as he reached for her. "I can explain."

She snatched her arm away. Everything spun. "Explain what, exactly?" Audrey's fingers trembled as she dug in the oiled leather pouch and pulled out the missive from the queen. With a surge of rage, she threw it at him. "You've received a pardon, though I daresay you don't deserve one." How could she have fallen for his charm?

He had deceived her in every way.

Reid shoved the parcel in his doublet with an angry

glare as if it were her fault he was promised to another. "Audrey, you don't understand."

"No?" She stamped her foot. "What more is there to understand? It seems quite simple." She searched the shore for Lord Saltoun. Not seeing him, she announced to the gathering crowd, "I'm ready to sail back to England now." Her head swam as if she were underwater. Then she made the mistake of glancing down only to meet with the gruesome image of Wagner's ghastly face turned to the side, his eyes frozen in a wide stare as if he realized his folly before he fell on the knife. Unable to stop herself, she dropped to her knees and wretched. Over and over her stomach heaved. Her throat burned while she crouched, willing herself to regain control.

"There, lass. Let it go. You'll feel a great deal better once the sickness has passed." Reid placed his hand on her back, only making her tense all the more.

"Go. Away," she managed between gasps.

"Nay. You're coming with me." He handed her a kerchief, but before she wiped her mouth, the brute wrapped his arms around her, hefting her over his shoulder. "We shall gather at Brahan and celebrate our victory this day," he bellowed like a proud plunderer. "Lord Saltoun, I expect to see you and your men there as well."

"Aye, m'lord. I wouldn't miss a gathering for all the gold in the queen's coffers," said the traitor. Blast it, Audrey needed him to sail away with her this instant.

The man who'd announced that Reid was promised blocked the earl's descent from the gangway. "I demand to know who this woman is!"

"My ward." Reid brushed past. "And we need to talk."

"Aye, we most certainly do."

Seaforth set Audrey in the saddle and mounted behind

her without another word. The ride to the castle was miserable while the earl held her captive between his arms, leading the army of Highlanders with an edge to his jaw. Audrey could feel his anger, but he had no right to be irate. She was the injured party. No wonder Seaforth had tried so hard to find her a husband. Even when their mutual fondness became clear, he still insisted that she marry another.

And now I know why.

Neither one of them spoke. The backbiter maintained his glaring countenance, looking straight ahead and cantering the horse through the gate and straight for the castle entry. Brahan looked like a palace, with a grand staircase leading to ornately carved doors. Ivy grew up the stone walls, extending four stories. Countless chimneys spouted smoke that swirled overhead like a greeting from the devil.

Reining his steed to a stop, Seaforth quickly dismounted. Before Audrey could slip to the ground, he pulled her into his arms like he was carrying a child. "I've matters to settle afore I can speak with you properly," he growled, his harsh gaze slipping to her face.

"You're speaking as if this is all my fault."

"'Tisn't."

A woman with wild red hair burst through the doorway, her eyes round as coins. "Reid! Have you been victorious?" The girl's gaze shifted to Audrey and suddenly grew hateful. "And who might this be?"

"Go tend to your father, Mairi. Tell him to meet me in my solar forthwith."

"But—"

"Do it, I say," he snapped at the girl as if she were but a servant.

Audrey gave his chest a thump. "Do you treat every-one with such a bad temper when you've acted like a buffoon?"

His humorless glare shifted to Audrey's face as a low growl rumbled from his throat, but he said nothing. He kept mum as he bounded up three flights of stairs with Audrey in his arms as if she weighed a trifle. Then he took long strides through the passageway until he kicked open a door.

"I want you to stay put," he said as he set her on her feet in a bedchamber bedecked in yellow—a color far too happy for Audrey's present state of mind.

She whirled to face him. "I do not want to stay here for another moment. You've wanted to be rid of me since the outset, and now I understand why."

"You understand nothing. I've never loved anyone with as much resolute passion as I love you." He strode to the door and grasped the handle. "I'll return anon." Then he slipped out and shut the door behind him. The sound of metal scraped, followed by a click.

Audrey ran forward and pulled down on the latch. But blast his evil temper, he'd locked her within. "Reid MacKenzie! Release me from this chamber at once!"

Tremors spread through her limbs as she collapsed to the floor. She'd just killed a man, and in the blink of an eye, she'd discovered the only man she'd ever loved had deceived her. He'd taken advantage of her. He'd ruined her. And now he'd declared his love without sealing it with a promise of marriage.

"Dear Lord, what have I done?"

* * *

Reid strode away from the chamber with his fists clenched. Damnation, Audrey was supposed to stay at Blair Castle and wait for him. Now Cromartie would be calling for blood and Audrey might never forgive him, a fact that cut deeper than any of the lashings he'd endured. Worse, if the look on her face was any indication, she'd sooner run a dagger through his heart than forgive him.

Things would be so much easier if he weren't a god-damned earl. He had so much more to consider than his own desires. Clan and kin relied on him. *The cause* relied on him. Hell, even the queen expected him to make this alliance with Cromartie's daughter.

I cannot.

Christ, he'd put off the idea marriage for ages, telling himself he wasn't ready—that he'd never be ready. But now Mairi had come of age, and he had naught but to release her to be courted as she deserved.

The truth?

He hadn't been ready for marriage because his heart hadn't found the right woman. And now that he had, he was about to crush his only chance at happiness. Audrey would most likely never speak to him again. She'd go back to Coxhoe House and run the mine. The lass certainly was capable. He'd make sure the estate was released from abeyance. He'd testify to her ability to manage her affairs herself. If she refused him, he'd release her, allow her to live her own life. He owed her that much and far more.

Reid opened the door to his solar and met with Cromartie's scowl. "Jesus Christ, Seaforth. What the hell are you on about?"

"I'm her guardian." Moving to the sideboard, Reid poured two drams of whisky.

"It appears you've exploited your responsibility."

After putting the flagon in front of Cromartie, Reid gave the man his drink and took his seat at the head of the table. "I'm ashamed to admit I have."

"The Sassenach looks to be of marriageable age. Have you tried to find her a husband?"

"Aye."

"Is something wrong with the lass? Has she no dowry?"

"She's an heiress. Her estate is worth as much as mine."

"Then there should be no problem."

Reid threw back his whisky, then wiped his mouth with the back of his hand. "Except there is." The words came out with bold surety as he met Cromartie's gaze. "You see, I'm in love with her."

"Jesus, Seaforth. You are honor bound by an oath. Do you have any idea what breaking the betrothal I agreed to with your father will do to our alliance?" The earl pounded his fist on the table. "You dare risk a feud? Your lands, your kin over a Sassenach lass?"

There hadn't been enough time to think this through. He'd been on the brink of death, and everything had seemed so easy at the cottage. Christ, he could have stayed there loving Audrey for the rest of his days. Aye, he was an earl with a great many responsibilities, but Reid was a man first. At court he'd watched many noblemen marry for family alliances. They all were miserable. They all took mistresses.

He poured himself another dram and offered Cromartie the flagon. "You haven't answered me," the man pushed.

"Ye ken I want no part of a feud between our clans."

Cromartie scowled. "Nor do I, and I intend to make a good match with my daughter's hand."

"Aye, Mairi will be a stalwart lady of a keep. A good wife."

"Now you're making some sense, lad."

"But she's not for me." As the truth slipped through his lips, immense weight lifted from Reid's shoulders.

Cromartie shoved his chair back and stood, leaning his knuckles on the table. "Good God, you do not mean to break the betrothal?"

Reid thrust his finger at the earl's chair. "Sit and hear me out."

Grumbling, the earl slowly sank down. "This better be good, else I'm marching off your lands with my army, and the next time you'll see me will be across the line on a battlefield. I'll take your kin, I'll take your cattle, your sheep. I'll bleed you dry until you are ruined."

With a steady hand, Reid filled the man's cup. "There are a hundred unwed gentlemen in the Highlands who would jump at a chance to wed your daughter."

"Only to sink their fingers into her dowry."

"Think on this..." Somewhere between his first and second dram, Reid had come up with a bargain. "To compensate you for your hardship, I offer fifty head of cattle and two thousand pounds."

Cromartie scratched his chin. "You think me daft, offering so little?"

A flicker of hope made Reid's heart stutter. He'd started the negotiation low enough to allow him room to maneuver, but high enough to let the earl know he was serious. "Four thousand pounds." He offered the same amount as Mairi's dowry, and they both knew it.

"Och, you think I'm so easily bought?"

"What do you need? I mean it. I desire to avoid a feud."

The earl's lips curled. "You won the prize with your stallion at the Inverness show. How many foals has he sired?"

Reid's shoulders tensed. Christ, he'd give Cromartie just about anything before he'd part with his prized stallion. He turned the cup between his fingers. "A colt thus far, and three broodmares are set to foal within the month."

"I want him."

"I'll give you the colt."

Cromartie sipped his whisky, taking his time to mull over Reid's offer. "The colt and my pick of the foals."

"Done." Reid stood and offered his hand before the earl could change his mind.

Following suit, Cromartie sealed the bargain with a firm handshake. "But let it be known I am still disquieted by your decision."

"I understand, though I hope our clans will continue to be allies as we fight for *the cause*. For no one clan can stand alone, and it will take all of us to challenge the succession when that day finally comes."

Chapter Thirty-Seven

*R*eid strode across his chamber floor and opened the top bureau drawer. He stared at the wooden box that he hadn't opened since his father gave it to him ten years ago. He'd always looked at that box as if it would burn his fingers, but now he plucked it from its resting place and opened it. Inside a sapphire ring shone as if it were brand new. The piece was set in yellow gold and had been his mother's.

Today he hoped he hadn't acted so poorly that Audrey would reject him. He slipped the ring into his doublet pocket, then headed for a door he'd never used. At one time his father had frequented the door to visit his mother in her bedchamber. And now Reid prayed it would become useful once again.

He slid a skeleton key into the lock and with a click, he opened it. Audrey pushed up from where she lay on the bed and quickly stood, facing him. Her lovely eyes were swollen and red, much like they'd been the first time he saw the lass. But today his heart squeezed as he gazed upon the stunningly beautiful English rose who had stolen his heart.

She looked beyond him. "You come to me from another door. Is this the house of mazes, a house fraught with deception?"

Reid gulped. He knew winning her wasn't going to be easy, but he had to jump in with both feet. He inclined his head toward the portal he had just passed through. "It leads to my bedchamber."

"Oh? So now you believe me to be so promiscuous that you put me in a chamber with an adjoining door to yours? Who in the castle knows of this door? Will everyone be laughing at me and saying, 'Oh, that's Audrey, the earl's courtesan'?"

Reid raked his fingers through his hair. "Bless it, you ken I would never put you in such a compromising position."

"But isn't that what you've just done?" She thrust her finger toward the door. "You admitted that is your bedchamber and you have locked me within the only chamber that adjoins yours."

God's teeth, this was not how Reid wanted this conversation to proceed. Time to change course. "First of all, I must apologize to you for putting you under lock and key, but I didn't know any other way to keep you from running whilst I set things to rights."

She crossed her arms and gave him a heated glare while her lips thinned.

Reid took a step toward her, spreading his palms wide. "I beg for your mercy, miss."

Thrusting her hand forward, Audrey bade him to stop. "Do not take another step, my lord. I can no longer trust you."

Her words cut Reid to the quick. "Please allow me to explain."

She shook her head. "You lied to me."

Lord, how deeply her words wounded. "Aye, I admit I haven't been entirely forthright, but nothing I have ever said or have ever done has been out of malice. I have tried to act with your best interests in mind. And now I need make amends."

"The time for that has passed, and you must now take me home. My father never should have trusted you. *I* never should have trusted you. For the love of God, Reid, I could be with your child and ruined for life."

"Jesu." He again combed his fingers through his hair. Nothing was proceeding as he'd planned. And now she could be with child? He couldn't turn away from her even if she refused him, hated him with every fiber of her body for the rest of her days. Taking a deep breath, he gestured to a chair near the hearth. "I bid you sit, m'lady."

Audrey shook her head.

"Please sit, Miss Audrey." He thrust his finger toward the chair a bit more forcefully this time. If he had to pick her up and tie her down, he'd do so, but it would be a hell of a lot easier if she would cooperate on this one thing.

Thankfully, Audrey pursed her lips, moved to the chair, and sat. Of course she had to cross her arms and her ankles and stare at him as if she had a dagger up her sleeve and was waiting for her chance to use it. For all Reid knew that's exactly what she was planning.

His stomach tightened as he moved and stood in front of her. She wasn't making it easy, but he refused to give up. Ancient Celtic MacKenzie blood coursed through his veins. A descendant of Gilleoin of the Aird, he was a warrior and a leader of men. He would persevere regardless.

He dropped to one knee and reached for her hands, but Audrey kept her arms folded, not giving an inch.

Reid lowered his hands to his sides and looked her square in the eye. "When I was a lad of five, my father agreed to an alliance between a lesser MacKenzie clan and agreed to a betrothal with Gilroy MacKenzie, who has since become the Earl of Cromartie. I have been promised to a distant cousin most of my life."

She shot him a heated glare. "You should have told me you were promised before you seduced me."

"You're right. I should have disclosed my lot to you. But I was too afraid I might lose you."

"And now your fears have been realized."

Gulping, Reid could no longer keep his hands to himself. He placed his fingers on her shoulders and grasped her firmly. "Please hear me through before you close your heart to me."

Her gaze dipped to her folded hands while she gave a single nod.

"All those miserable hours I spent searching for a husband for you, the more reluctant I grew to let you go. And soon I realized you'd completely won my heart. I never should have forced you to look for a husband because you're perfect the way you are. Moreover, from the very outset I knew there was only one husband for you, and now I realize it must be your choice if you are to accept him."

A tear slipped from her eye.

"I have loved you since the first time I heard you play the harpsichord. I have loved you since you introduced me to Lady Ne'er-Do-Well. I have adored you since you attended Baron Barnard's ball in your scandalous red dress. At every turn, you have shown your brilliance, your caring, your tenacity, and I have loved you more deeply with each passing day."

"I risked my life for you," she whispered.

"You did. You risked more for me than I would ever expect from any other, man or woman. You are brave and tenacious, and I am wholly in your service, madam."

Audrey wrung her hands, her cheeks now glistening with tears.

Reid didn't hesitate to seize the opportunity to grasp her fingers between his palms. "You are the most selfless, most giving and kind woman I have ever met, and I cannot go through life without you."

"But—"

"Audrey Kennett, I would be cut to the quick if you refuse my proposal of marriage. For though I am unworthy of your love, please know that I will love you with my entire being for the rest of my days."

She finally slid her gaze up to meet his eyes. "But what about the redheaded MacKenzie daughter of Cromartie?"

"My oath, I am daft. Did I not say when I entered that I had rescinded the betrothal?"

She smiled through her tears. "I think that tidbit of information may have escaped me."

"Och, *mo ghràidh*. Now that I have met you, how could I ever look upon another woman?"

"You truly love me?"

"I love you more than anything. More than my home, more than the air I breathe. I would lay down my life for you, *mo ghràidh*, and I will live the rest of my days proving my love." He reached inside his pocket and pulled out the ring. "Please honor me by agreeing to be my wife."

A gasp caught in the back of her throat as she touched her fingers to her lips. "You are aware, everything I did was for you. I've known I wanted you since you rescued me from Tupps. And since the day we danced alone in the ballroom, I've known you loved me, too. I just needed to find a way to make you realize we were meant to be wed."

He grinned. God bless her, she could forgive. "Sometimes a MacKenzie can be a bit thickheaded, but once we've made up our minds, we're difficult to sway."

"Yes, in so very many ways."

He slid the ring onto her finger. "Then will you do me the honor of marrying this rugged Highlander?"

She nodded in rapid succession. "I will."

Standing, he pulled her into his arms and twirled her across the floor. Her laughter rang out like angel's bells, the happiest sound he'd ever heard. Gently placing her on his feet, he kissed her, lovingly and tenderly. "You've made me the happiest man in all of Christendom."

Her face shone like an angel, casting a glow around her. "I was so angry and now I cannot believe the joy bubbling throughout my insides. I feel as though I could burst."

He cupped her face between his hands. "What you said about being with child...could it be true?"

Her brow creased with worry lines. "Honestly, I'm not sure. So many things have happened, I fear I have lost track."

"Then we must wed straightaway to avoid a scandal."

"I would marry you this instant if I could."

"Two days hence all the clans will arrive for the gathering. Let us wed in the chapel before the feast, and then we can announce our nuptials to all."

"A quiet wedding?"

"Does that meet with your approval?"

"Oh yes, I don't know what I'd do if I had to walk down the aisle with hundreds of people staring."

"You would look beautiful, and everyone would adore you."

"There's only one person I want to adore me."

He pulled her into his arms and savored the warmth of her body as it molded to his in a perfect match.

* * *

Audrey's head swam. How could she go from the depths of melancholy to the height of elation in the course of an hour? Too many things had happened for her to think beyond the man in her arms.

He smoothed the rough pads of his fingers along her jaw while long lashes shuttered his eyes. Heat spiked deep and low as his lips neared. Capturing her mouth, a low moan rumbled from his chest. Accepting him, he stroked her tongue languidly.

Sweet kisses caressed her neck.

Closing her eyes, Audrey rubbed against him, the intensity of her need growing. "There are so many people below stairs," she said breathlessly.

"What about them?" he growled.

"Are they not waiting for you?"

"Let them wait." He gathered her in his arms and grinned like a devilish rogue. "I aim to prove my love so there's no question in your mind of how much I adore you."

He set her down beside the bed and took his time, first slowly unlacing the front of her kirtle and sending it to the floorboards around her ankles. Then he bade her to turn and unlaced every eyelet of her stays. As she stood in her shift, his hands slipped around and cupped her breasts while he rubbed himself against her buttocks. "Do you want me?"

The insides of her thighs quivered. "Yes."

Slowly, he drew up her shift and stroked a finger over her sensitive flesh.

Sighing, she rested her head against his chest. "Yes, yes, yes."

His kilt dropped to the floorboards around their feet, followed by his shirt.

Audrey started to turn, but he held her shoulders. "Stay."

As she nodded, he drew her shift over her head. "Spread your legs for me, lass."

His heart pounded against her back as he circled a finger around the tip of her breast, while he slipped himself where she craved him most.

"Mm," Audrey whimpered.

"I want to make love to you all afternoon."

She chuckled and faced him, scooting onto the bed. "Over and over again?"

"Aye." He climbed over her.

Stretching her arms around him, Audrey made love to her Highland earl. The first time fast as if they were running a footrace, fanning flames until they reached the pinnacle of passion. The second time, they entwined their bodies in a slow burn of exploration, taking them to new heights of desire.

Completely satisfied, they lay in each other's arms, comforted in a cocoon of intimacy meant only for them.

Chapter Thirty-Eight

*I*t was a blessing to have Lady Magdalen at Brahan to help Audrey prepare. For two days all she'd done was float on air with her head so benumbed, it felt full of wool. Audrey Kennet was to be married without a long courtship or a long engagement. And she couldn't be happier.

Since his capture she had been so intent on helping Reid to clear his name, Audrey hadn't allowed herself to think much about the future. Things had been incredibly dire, and planning a wedding had been the furthest thing from her mind. But now she would be wed this day. And by the grace of God, she would marry the one man who had captured her heart.

Though there hadn't been much time, they'd found chests filled with exquisite gowns left by Reid's mother. Audrey chose a silk of silvery blue, and after a few alterations by the local tailor, the gown fit as if it had been made for her. To finish off perfection, they added a train of ivory lace to the back including a matching veil.

Audrey held on to the bedpost while the chambermaid finished lacing her gown. The marchioness stood back, supervising with a critical eye. "You are ever so bonny, the earl is a fortunate man, he is." Her ladyship dismissed the servant with a flick of her fingers. "Please leave us."

Barely able to take in a deep breath, Audrey moved to the looking glass and regarded her reflection. There she stood, Talcotts greatest wallflower in full bloom. But she'd no longer be hiding against the wall. She would be a countess, sitting beside her husband in the center of the hall for all to see, and she'd never been so filled with happiness in her life. Perhaps she wasn't shy after all. She'd just needed a brawny Highlander to draw out the courage hidden deep in her soul.

Maddie ducked into the garderobe and came out with a posy. "Aiden and I went for a wee stroll this morn and picked these fresh."

"Bluebells?" Audrey accepted the bouquet, adorned with ribbons of lace and satin. "They're perfect."

Maddie stepped back and clasped her hands. "I must say the flowers complement your gown ideally. And they bring out the color of your eyes."

Audrey skimmed her teeth over her lip. "Do you think so?"

"I ken it."

"I am infinitely grateful to have you here."

A knock came at the door. "Are you and Miss Kennet ready, lady wife?"

Audrey looked to her friend excitedly and smiled. "By the end of this day I shan't be referred to thus again."

"Nay, and you must become accustomed with the servants calling you 'my lady.'"

Audrey drew a hand over her heart. "Oh, my. I hadn't thought of that."

"Och aye, you will be the Countess of Seaforth before this day's end."

Lord Tullibardine cleared his throat from the passageway.

"We're coming, my dearest," said Maddie, taking Audrey by the elbow and ushering her out the door.

The chapel was at the rear of the castle on the second floor, but if it weren't for the marquis, Audrey would have been lost in the maze. But now they stood outside closed doors while a gentle hum of voices carried through the timbers.

When the steward opened the double doors, Audrey's stomach flitted with a frenzy of butterflies. The guests stood and turned her way. She knew a few, Dunn, Lord Saltoun, and even the Earl of Cromartie was in attendance, though he was the only person not smiling. The chapel was filled with clan chieftains and their ladies who had arrived the night before, and who were all dressed in Highland finery. But the finest-looking man in the entire hall was standing in front of the altar.

Reid MacKenzie, the Earl of Seaforth, regarded her with a wide grin, his eyes shining as if they were filled with candlelight.

Lord Tullibardine offered his elbow. "Are you ready, miss?"

"Indeed I am."

Audrey didn't remember much about walking down the aisle on the marquis's arm. But she would never forget taking the hands of the man she loved and gazing up at his handsome face while the priest chanted the Catholic ceremony—Papa would have been ever so proud. Though the father could have recited the twenty-third psalm, for all Audrey knew. She was standing before God beside the man she loved, and no words could express the love she had in her heart or the extent of her promise to cherish him for the rest of her days.

Chapter Thirty-Nine

*R*eid almost regretted having a Highland gathering on the day of his wedding. He wanted his bride to himself. Even an earl was entitled to be selfish on a day like today. And when Audrey appeared at the rear of the chapel looking more radiant than a queen, so many emotions coursed through him—to protect her, to succor her, to provide for her, and most of all, to love her.

He stood before God and declared his undying love, making a promise to the woman of his dreams to honor his vows until he took his dying breath. He would love her, cherish her, and place her at the pinnacle of his life forever.

Now they sat side by side at the high table as Lord and Lady Seaforth, presiding over the feast. Reid's chest swelled. Every man in the hall looked to him with admiration. He'd not only married the bonniest lass in Britain, not a soul doubted her bravery or her loyalty to *the cause*. They'd all heard the tale of how she'd joined in the fight against the government troops and had struck the blow that had made Wagner Tupps fall on his knife and meet the devil.

Making the introductions was like reading from a scroll of the most influential men in the Highlands: the Duke of Gordon and his wife, Lady Akira. Of course, Audrey knew Lord and Lady Tullibardine. The Baronet and Baroness of Sleat; Ewen Cameron, the chieftain of Clan Cameron; Hugh and Charlotte MacIain, survivors of Glencoe; and the list went on.

When at last the steward finished announcing the guests, Reid stood and raised his glass. "Welcome, my esteemed guests. I hope you've enjoyed your day of rest, for on the morrow there shall be tests of skill and brawn as we hold the games to determine the strongest, the fastest, and the most accurate with a musket. *Sláinte*, my friends!"

"*Sláinte!*" everyone bellowed in unison, including Lady Audrey.

The Marquis of Tullibardine stood, tapping his spoon to his glass. "Allow me to make a toast to the honorable couple." He grinned and waggled his eyebrows. "It seems my wee cottage in the Atholl Forest has a certain charm with young lovers."

Under the table, Reid grasped his wife's hand and squeezed, whispering, "I'd have to agree with him there."

Tullibardine gave a regal bow. "May I take some credit upon this joyful occasion?"

"You may."

"The lass never would have arrived on the River Conon if it weren't for my wee boat," added Lord Saltoun.

Audrey squeezed Reid's hand in return. "Very true."

The marquis frowned at the Fraser baron; clearly he

wasn't yet ready to give up the floor. Clearing his throat, he raised his glass higher. "I wish you the bounty of the earth, the favor of our Lord. May sunshine brighten your home, may your crops yield abundant fare, and may your children be healthy young bairns to bring you pride and unabashed happiness."

Raising his glass, Reid grinned at the faces across the table. "*Sláinte!*" he repeated as the hall erupted with cheers.

In the entryway, Dunn caught his eye, waving his thumb over his shoulder. Reid gave a nod and held up his palms. "Friends, I have a gift for my bride."

Beside him, Audrey gasped. "My lord?"

After giving Dunn a nod, he grasped her hands and pulled her to her feet. "I want Brahan Castle to be as much your home as Coxhoe House."

"I am quite certain—" Stopping mid-sentence, Audrey's mouth dropped open as she drew her fingers over her lips.

"I did not forget, lass," he whispered in her ear.

Happiness danced in her eyes as she regarded him. "May I?"

"If you didn't, I'd be crestfallen." He gestured to the harpsichord Dunn and the men wheeled inside.

Audrey gave him a shy cringe. "'Tis not presumptuous of me to play amongst so many?"

"This is Scotland," said the Duke of Gordon. "Highlanders appreciate fine talent."

Reid took her hand and escorted her to the new instrument he'd sent Dunn to fetch from Inverness the day before. Audrey ran her fingers over the inlaid wood lovingly. He lifted the top and propped it up. "I haven't any scores of music for you as of yet."

She took a seat on the stool with a smile. "Not to worry. Most of it is in my head."

"Then do me proud, wife." Reid stood back while Audrey began Pachelbel's canon in D, a melody he knew she could play in her sleep—for at Coxhoe House he often awoke to that very tune. As the notes resounded from the harpsichord, the hall fell completely silent. All eyes focused on Audrey. An aura of mastery captured their hearts as she lovingly struck the keys.

When she finished, the final chord made a shiver course up his spine as it gradually faded. His wife shifted her gaze to Reid while the silence continued. The corner of her mouth turned down as if she thought her performance might have been anything other than magnificent.

With his next breath the hall erupted in thundering applause.

Reid offered his hand. "My lady."

"Did you like it?"

He walked her in a circle, egging on the crowd for more. "'Like' doesn't even come close to describing how much I enjoyed watching you play."

She curtsied before they started back for the dais. "'Tis such a relief. Now I can play with the orchestra whilst the others are dancing."

Reid squeezed her hand and stopped. "Nay. I want to dance with my wife."

A look of panic crossed her face. "But you said I wouldn't have to dance again if I was mortified and averse."

"That was after three lessons, and you've only had one." He knit his brows as Cluny slid between them and shoved his enormous head under her palm.

She gave him a pat. "You wouldn't make me dance, would you, big fellow?"

Reid pointed to the hearth. "Back to your rug, you oversize hound." The dog dipped his tail between his legs and obeyed.

Audrey's mouth twisted. "I think Cluny would enjoy dancing more than I."

He took her hands. "Let us make a truce. I bought you the harpsichord, and you will dance with me at gatherings."

"Can I wear a shocking red gown?"

"You can wear anything you please as long as you are on *my* arm."

"Very well then, but you'd better wrap some lamb's wool around your toes."

"I'm certain that won't be necessary."

With that, the piper and the fiddler took their places. Audrey might object to minuets, but Reid had no doubt she'd take well to lively Highland reels. Much like a country dance, Highland dances were pleasurable and raucous with lots of clapping.

And when he led her to the line, she didn't disappoint. Laughing, she danced like Lady Ne'er-Do-Well. All the while she swung on Reid's arm, though he doubted the lass missed a single step.

Epilogue

Six months later

*I*t was late winter when Audrey awoke beside her husband at Coxhoe House. Snow shrouded the bedchamber window, and she pulled the coverlet up over her shoulders. Beside her, Reid slumbered, facing her on his side. She could never grow tired of watching him, be it in slumber or awake. He was bold and brawny and ever so handsome, and moreover, he was hers.

She grinned as she rolled over and spooned her body into his. Reid emitted a wee moan, surrounding her with his arm as if he wasn't yet ready to wake.

They had decided to winter at Coxhoe House where the season wasn't as harsh. That also gave Reid an opportunity to meet with Mr. Poole, who had been promoted to governor of the mine. The man had proved honest and hardworking, and ran the business with a good mind for enterprise.

They'd received word from the magistrate in Inverness that Bainbridge Fry had been found guilty of excessive treachery. He was stripped of his rank and shipped to the Americas to serve time in a prison farm. Audrey accepted his punishment, though she felt it a bit lenient. Reid's back would always bear the signs of that man's savagery.

Behind her, Reid nuzzled into her hair and hummed. "I like waking up beside you, lady wife. You always smell like a garden of lavender."

Giggling, she took his hand and held it against her growing belly. "Your son is restless this day."

"Aye?" He held very still.

A thump kicked her womb.

Reid gasped. "Was that he?"

"Yes." She smiled, overcome with the wonder of the child growing inside her.

"He's a fighter, that one."

Audrey nestled against him. "It could be a girl."

"Aye." His kisses fluttered along the arc of her neck. "Be it lad or lass, we shall love the bairn. For it will be half you and half me, and shall be the beginning of our legacy."

Author's Note

Thank you for joining me for *The Highland Guardian*. This story was formed around William MacKenzie, 5th Earl of Seaforth, and his wife, Mary Kennet, who was the only child and heiress of Nicholas Kennet, a prominent businessman from Coxhoe. Though the story of their meeting and romance is fictional, I found the architecture research for this book amazing. The manor Coxhoe Hall was once considered one of the finest houses in County Durham. It came into the possession of the Kennet family through marriage in the seventeenth century and was set high on a south-facing hillside adjacent to the site of Coxhoe medieval village. A tree-lined avenue led to the manor, and it was surrounded by grounds with terraces, and a walled garden. Interestingly, poet Elizabeth Barrett Browning was born there in 1806. The Earl of Seaforth and his countess did use Coxhoe as their winter estate. The manor fell into disrepair in the twentieth century and was demolished in 1956.

In the year 1611, Brahan Castle was built by Colin

MacKenzie, 1st Earl of Seaforth. Clan MacKenzie were notable Jacobites. The Siege of Brahan took place in November 1715, where William (Reid) MacKenzie was forced to forfeit the estate. The castle was later sold back to William's family, where it changed hands many times. In the early 1950s the castle fell into disrepair and was demolished.

On *Wikipedia*, under *William MacKenzie, 5th Earl of Seaforth*, there is a lovely portrait of Mary (Audrey) Kennet, who bore him three sons. So much of her character can be interpreted in her picture. A true English rose, she appears to be both petite and courageous, and I hope her character shines through in this book.

When Akira Ayres finds a wounded Scot
on the battlefield, she will do anything to
save his life. As the redcoats close in on
them, the fearless lass heals the
Highlander's body—and steals his heart…

Keep reading for an excerpt from

THE HIGHLAND DUKE

And don't miss Dunn MacRae's story in

THE HIGHLAND CHIEFTAIN

Coming in Summer 2018.

Chapter One

Hoord Moor, Scotland. 21 August 1703.

*T*he dead Highland soldier stared vacantly at the thick, low-hanging clouds. Akira clutched her basket tight to her stomach. Concealed in the tall moorland grass, this man needed no healing. Now only the minister could offer help to redeem the hapless warrior's soul.

Death on the battlefield bore none of the heroics she'd heard from fireside tales. Death on the battlefield was cold and lonely, dismal like the mist muffling the shrill calls of the buzzards.

And for naught.

Gulping back her nausea, Akira turned away. A breeze rustled through the eerily tranquil lea as if putting to rest the violence that had occurred not more than an hour ago. She scanned the stark meadow, searching for men who might have need of a healer's attention. She cared not whether they were Government dragoons or clansmen from Highland regiments. Anyone suffering from battle wounds this day needed tending, regardless of politics.

A deep moan came from the forest beyond the tree line not ten paces away. She jolted, jostling the remedies in her basket. "Is s-someone there?"

When no answer came, she glanced over her shoulder. Her companions had moved on—women from the village of Dunkeld who had helped tend the wounded before red-coated soldiers marshaled the men into the back of a wagon. Where they would go from there, Akira hadn't asked, but she hoped they wouldn't be thrown in a prison pit, at least not before their wounds were healed.

The moan came again and, with it, a chilly gust that made her hackles stand on end.

Cautiously, Akira tiptoed into the trees, peering through the foliage to ensure she wasn't walking into a trap. A telltale path of blood skimmed over the ground, leading to two black boots beneath a clump of broom. Had the man dragged himself all the way from the battlefield to hide?

"Are you injured?" she asked warily, her perspiring palms slipping on the basket's handle. Could she trust he wouldn't leap up and attack?

"My leg," said a strained voice.

There was no disguising the pain in his tone. "Goodness gracious," she whispered, dropping to her knees in the thick moss and pulling away the branches and debris that covered his body.

Vivid hazel eyes stared up at her from beneath a layer of dirt. Wild as the Highlands and filled with agony, his gaze penetrated her defenses like a dagger. She'd never seen eyes that expressive—that intense. They made her so...so unnerved.

"What happened?" she asked.

He shuttered those eyes with a wince. "Shot."

Akira's gaze darted to his kilt, hitched up and exposing a well-muscled thigh covered with blood.

"You a healer?" he asked, his Adam's apple bobbing.

"Aye." She peered closer. Puckered skin. A round hole. "A musket ball?"

His trembling fingers slid to the puncture wound. "'Tis still in there. It needs to come out."

Care of musket wounds far exceeded her skill. "I-I'll fetch the physician."

Opening his eyes, the man clasped her arm in a powerful grip. The pressure of his huge hand hurt. Gasping, she tugged away, but his fingers clamped harder, and those eyes grew more determined.

"No," he said in an intense whisper. "You do it."

She shook her head. "Sir, I cannot."

He released her arm, then pulled a knife from his sleeve. "Use my wee dagger." The blade glistened, honed sharp and shiny clean against his mud-encrusted doublet.

She shied away from the weapon. "But you could die."

The mere thought of performing surgery after the loss of her last patient made her stomach turn over. And it had been Dr. Kennedy who'd carved out the musket ball in that unfortunate patient's knee, though she'd tended the lad through his painful decline and eventual death. Regardless of the physician's role, the man's passing had taken a toll on her resolve.

"Do it, I say." For a man on the brink of death, he spewed the command like a high-ranking officer. "I cannot risk being found. Do you understand?"

Licking her lips, she stared at the wound, then pressed her fingers against it. He was right; the ball needed to come out now, and if he refused to let her find a physician, Akira was the only healer in Dunkeld skilled enough to help him.

He hissed in pain.

"Apologies." She snapped her hand away. "I was feeling for the musket ball."

"Whisky."

She glanced to her basket. "I've only herbs and tinctures."

"In my sporran."

The leather pouch rested askew, held in place by a belt around his hips. Merciful mercy, it covered his unmentionables. Moreover, he was armed like an outlaw, with a dirk sheathed on one side of his belt, a flintlock pistol on the other, and a gargantuan sword slung in its scabbard beside him. Who knew what other deadly weapons this imposing Highlander hid on his person?

His shaking fingers fumbled with the thong that cinched the sporran closed.

She licked her lips. "You expect me to reach inside?" Goodness, her voice sounded shrill.

"Och," he groaned, his hands dropping. "Give a wounded du—ah—scrapper a bit o' help, would you now?"

Akira scraped her teeth over her bottom lip. The Highlander did need something to ease his pain. Praying she wouldn't be seen and accused of stealing, she braced herself, shoved her hand inside the hideous thing, and wrapped her fingers around a flask. She blinked twice as she pulled it out and held it up. *Silver?* Gracious, a flask like that could pay for Akira and her family to eat for a year or more.

She pulled the stopper and he raised his head, running his tongue across chapped lips. "Give me a good tot, lass."

His fingers trembled while he guided the flask in her hands, drank a healthy swig, and coughed.

"I'm ready," he said, his jaw muscles flexing as he bared his teeth—straight, white, contrasting with the dark stubble and dirt on his face. Dear Lord, such a man could pass for the devil.

The faster she worked, the less he'd suffer. With a featherlight touch, she swirled her fingers over the puncture and located the hard lump not far beneath the skin. Thank heavens the musket ball had stopped in his flesh and hadn't shattered the bone.

Though she'd never removed a musket ball before, she had removed an arrow. Steeling her nerves, she gripped the knife and willed her hand to steady. "Prepare yourself, sir." But still she hesitated.

He grasped her wrist and squeezed, staring into her eyes with determination and focus. "You can do this, lass."

Setting her jaw, she gave him a sharp nod. Then she returned her gaze to the wound, quickly slid the knife through the musket hole with one hand, and pushed against the ball with the other. The Highlander's entire body quaked. But no sound other than a strained grunt passed his lips.

Blood gushed from the wound and soaked Akira's fingers. Gritting her teeth, she applied more pressure, pushing the knife until she hit lead.

I cannot fail. I will not let him die.

She gritted her teeth and forced another flesh-carving twist of her wrist. The ball popped out. Blood flooded from the wound like an open spigot.

The man jerked, his leg thumping. Akira dove for her basket and grabbed a cloth. Wadding it tight, she held the Highlander's leg down with her elbows while she shoved the compress against the puncture with all her might. Looking up, she stared at his eyes until he focused on her. "Hold on," she said. "The worst is over."

Though he never cried out, the Highlander panted, sweat streaming from his brow. Not blinking, he stared at her like a yellow-eyed wildcat. "Horse."

Akira pushed the cloth harder, the muscles in his thigh solid as steel. "The soldiers took all the horses."

"Damnation!" he swore through clenched teeth, his breathing still ragged. Then his stare intensified. "I will...purchase...yours."

The man could die with his next breath, yet he still issued orders as if in charge of an entire battalion of cavalry. His tone demanded she respond with instant agreement, but she could not.

"I can barely afford to feed my siblings. I have no horse. Not even a donkey—not that I'd let you have it if I did." There. She wasn't about to allow this Highlander to lord it over her as if he were the Marquis of Atholl.

His eyes rolled to the back of his head. "Buy one."

"I told you—"

"There is...coin...My sporran."

Akira glanced at the man's sporran again. She'd have to sink her fingers deeper this time. Though she might be poor, she was certainly no harlot. Fishing in there was as nerve-racking as carving a musket ball out of the man's thigh. With a grimace, she tried shifting his belt aside a wee bit. *Curses*—the sporran shifted not an inch.

And he was still bleeding like a stuck pig. "Even if

I did purchase you a horse, you couldn't ride. I'd wager you'd travel no more than a mile afore you fell off and succumbed to your wound." Still holding the cloth in place, Akira reached for her basket. "Let me wrap this tight and I'll call the soldiers. They're helping the wounded into a cart."

"Absolutely not!" His eyes flashed wide as he gripped her wrist. The man's intense stare, combined with the hard line of his jaw, wasn't the look of a pleading man—it was the look of a man who would not be disobeyed. "Atholl's men must not know I'm here."

She gave him her most exasperated expression while she wrapped the bandage around his thigh. Asserting her authority as a healer, Akira squared her shoulders. She was in charge, not he. "You ken they can help you."

"The Government troops? They're murderers." He winced. "They'd slit my throat for certain."

Since the battle's end, she hadn't seen anyone slit a throat...but then she hadn't asked where the soldiers were taking the injured. She'd just assumed to the monastery to be tended by the monks. But the pure intensity of this man's cold stare told her to do as he said. Beyond that, she believed him.

The hairs on her nape stood on end as she twisted the bandage like a tourniquet and tied it while questions needled her mind. If this man was as important as he seemed, why had he been left alone? "Who are you?"

"Merely...merely a Highlander who needs to haste back to his lands"—he drew in a stuttering breath—"a-afore the ill-breeding curs burn me out."

She narrowed her gaze. *A man of property?* Akira wasn't daft—especially when her mother's larder was bare. "I'll fetch you a horse if you pay me a shilling."

"Done," he said, as if such coin meant nothing. "Make haste and tell no one I'm here."

Gulping, she glanced down to the sporran. She'd been in there once before. Besides, the Highlander was in no shape to do anything untoward. If it wasn't for the need to care for her mother and three sisters, she'd call over the dragoons and let them see to this man's need for a mount. But for a shilling? Ma would be so happy.

Akira's fingers trembled.

Taking a deep breath, she reached inside the sporran. Her hand stuck in the neck, forcing her to twist her wrist to push deeper. Something hard flexed against her fingers. She froze. *Holy hexes*, she was shoving against the rock-hard wall of his inner thigh. She had no choice but to look down.

Dear Lord, please do not let anyone venture past us now.

With her hand completely buried in the man's sporran, she looked like an alehouse harlot toying with his...unmentionables.

"Are ye having trouble, lass?" The man's deep burr lulled with a hint of mischief, practically stopping her heart.

"No." With a blink, she wrapped her fingers around a number of coins and forcefully drew her hand free.

Akira's tongue went dry. Three silver shillings and two ten-shilling pieces filled her palm. She'd never seen so much coin in her life. No, she should not feel badly about asking for payment. After dropping one shilling in her pocket and returning all but one of the other coins, she held up a ten-shilling piece. *This ought to be enough.*

Standing, she hesitated. "What is your name, sir?"

A deep crease formed between his brows. "'Tis no concern of yours."

He didn't trust her—not that she trusted him, either. The only man she'd ever trusted was Uncle Bruno. "I won't reveal it." She crossed herself. "I swear on my grandfather's grave."

His lips thinned. "You can call me Geordie. And you, miss?"

Geordie is no given name I've ever heard. Odd.

She curtsied. "You may call me Akira." Blast, she wasn't going to say "Akie." Only her sisters referred to her thus. And "Ayres" would make him suspicious for certain. Her family might be descendants of Gypsy stock, but they'd given up their heathen practices generations ago. If Mr. Geordie wanted to hide his identity, she certainly would hide hers.

* * *

After the healer left, George Gordon closed his eyes and prayed the woman had enough sense to keep her mouth shut. After Queen Anne had rejected the Scottish Parliament's proposed Act of Security, the entire country was in an uproar—and ready to strike against the Government at last. Yes, he'd agreed to stand by his cousin and challenge the Government troops. The queen's Act of Settlement was nothing but a sham, created to subvert the succession of the rightful Stuart line behind the guise of Protestantism.

Thank God he hadn't worn anything to reveal his true identity. He'd even kept to the rear beside his cousin William. After he was thrown from his horse, the skirmish had raged on and the clansmen had charged ahead across the moorland, leaving Geordie for dead.

Once he'd dragged himself into the brush, he must have lost consciousness until that wisp of a healer found him. He thanked the stars it had been she and not a redcoat. His lands would be forfeit if Queen Anne discovered he'd ridden against the English crown.

James Stuart may be exiled, but he is the only king to whom I will pay fealty. I would take ten musket balls to the thigh if it assured his coronation.

Geordie's leg throbbed—ached like someone had stabbed him with a firebrand. But through the pain, he must have dozed again, because it seemed that Akira returned in the blink of an eye.

He eyed her sternly, as he would a servant—an inexplicably bonny servant. "Did the stable master ask questions?" he demanded, forcing himself to sit up. God's teeth, everything spun. The sharp pain made his gut churn.

"Pardon?" she replied in a tone mirroring his own. Never in his life had he seen such a haughty expression come from a commoner. "'Tis a bit difficult to conceal a horse beneath my arisaid. Besides, I didn't *steal* the beast." She thrust a fist against her hip. "He asked where I came up with that kind of coin."

Gordon licked his lips with an arid tongue. "How did you reply?"

Akira's fist slid down to her side—a more respectful stance for a wee maid. "I told him I'd received handsome payment from His Lordship for tending his cousin."

"His Lordship?"

"The Marquis of Atholl, of course."

Smart lass. "Do you ken the marquis?" *Bloody hell*, he hoped not.

"If you call paying him fealty knowing him, then aye. So does everyone around these parts. He's lord of these lands."

And he supports the Government troops, the bastard.

Geordie needed to mount that damned horse and ride like hellfire. If anyone recognized him, he'd be shipped to the Tower of London, where they'd make a public mockery of his execution.

He leaned forward to stand. *Jesus Christ!* Stars darted through his vision. Stifling his urge to bellow, he gritted his teeth.

The lass caught his arm. "Allow me to help."

His insides clamped taut. Must she look at him with such innocent allure?

He gave a curt nod, hating to accept any help but knowing it was necessary. "My thanks."

Clenching his teeth, he slid his good foot beneath him. Akira tugged his arm while he pushed up with the other.

"Christ Almighty!" he bellowed from the depths of his gut before he had time to choke it back.

She slung his arm over her shoulder. *A lot of good that did. The lass might make a useful crutch for a lad of twelve.* "If they didn't ken you were here before, they do now."

"Ballocks!" he cursed, trying not to fall on top of the woman. Then he looked at the damned nag. "No saddle?"

She held out a few copper farthings. "There wasn't enough."

"Damnation."

The urchin narrowed her eyes at him. "I'll not be cursed at like a doormat whilst I'm merely trying to help you."

Geordie grumbled under his breath and removed his arm from her shoulder. He took quick note of the surroundings. They needed more cover for certain. He pointed deeper into the wood. "Lead the beast to the fallen tree, yonder."

She didn't budge. "Oh my," she said with a gasp. "Your leg is bleeding something awful."

He swayed on his feet. Good God, he couldn't lose his wits. Not until he had ridden to safety. "Can you stanch it?"

"Give me your belt."

He slid his hands to his buckle, when a twig snapped behind them.

"Who goes there?" demanded a stern voice.

Akira's eyes popped wide.

The beat of Geordie's heart spiked. With a wave of strength, he grabbed the lassie's waist and threw her atop the horse. Taking charge of the reins, he urged the beast into a run, steering it beside the fallen tree. Agonizing pain stabbed his thigh, but the pressing need to escape gave him herculean energy.

Haste.

In two leaps he landed astride the gelding, right behind the lass. Slapping the reins, he kicked his heels into the horse's barrel as he pointed the beast down a narrow path. Stabbing torture in his thigh punished his every move.

Musket fire cracked from behind.

Geordie leaned forward, demanding more speed. He pressed lips to Akira's ear. "Hold on, lass, for hell has just made chase."

About the
Author

Amy Jarecki is a descendant of an ancient Lowland clan and adores Scotland. Though she now resides in southwest Utah, she received her MBA from Heriot-Watt University in Edinburgh. Winning multiple writing awards, she found her niche in the genre of Scottish historical romance. Amy writes steamy edge-of-your-seat action-adventures with rugged men and fascinating women who weave their paths through the brutal eras of centuries past. Amy loves hearing from her readers and can be contacted through her website at AmyJarecki.com.

RENEGADE COWBOY
By Sara Richardson

In the *New York Times* bestselling tradition of Jennifer Ryan and Maisey Yates comes the latest in Sara Richardson's Rocky Mountain Riders series. Cassidy Greer and Levi Cortez have a history together—and a sizzling attraction that's too hot to ignore. When Levi rides back into town, he knows Cass doesn't want to get roped into a relationship with a cowboy. So he's offered her a no-strings fling. But can he convince himself that one night is enough?

THE HIGHLAND GUARDIAN
By Amy Jarecki

Captain Reid MacKenzie has vowed to watch over his dying friend's daughter. But Reid's new ward is no wee lass. She's a ravishing, fully grown woman, and it's all he can do to remember his duty and not seduce her...Miss Audrey Kennet is stunned by the news of her father's death, and then outraged when the kilted brute who delivers the news insists she must now marry. But Audrey soon realizes the brave, brawny Scot is the only man she wants—though loving him means risking her lands, her freedom, and even her life.

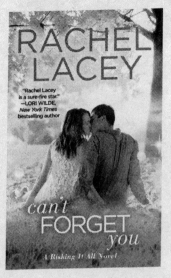

BACK HOME AT FIREFLY LAKE
By Jen Gilroy

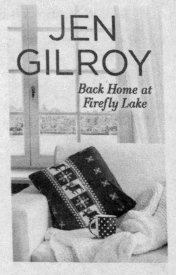

JEN GILROY

Back Home at Firefly Lake

Fans of RaeAnne Thayne, Debbie Mason, and Susan Wiggs will love the latest from Jen Gilroy. Firefly Lake is just a pit stop for single mom Cat McGuire. That is, until sparks fly with her longtime crush—who also happens to be her daughter's hockey coach—Luc Simard. When Luc starts to fall hard, can he convince Cat to stay?

FALL IN LOVE WITH FOREVER ROMANCE

SIMPLY IRRESISTIBLE
By Jill Shalvis

Now featuring ten bonus recipes never available before in print! Don't miss this new edition of *Simply Irresistible*, the first book in *New York Times* bestselling author Jill Shalvis's beloved Lucky Harbor series!

NOTORIOUS PLEASURES
By Elizabeth Hoyt

Rediscover the Maiden Lane Series by *New York Times* bestselling author Elizabeth Hoyt in this beautiful reissue with an all-new cover! Lady Hero Batten wants for nothing, until she meets her fiancé's notorious brother. Griffin Remmington is a mysterious rogue, whose

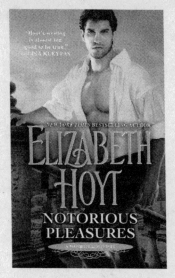

interests belong to the worst sorts of debauchery. Hero and Griffin are constantly at odds, so when sparks fly, can these two imperfect people find a perfect true love?